7/19/21

To my dear friend Suzanne —
remembering one of our earlier
 Syracuse   Bloomsdays

" ... the play's the thing /
wherein I'll catch
   conscience of H

(Pg 447)

Aaa

The last smoker on earth

... and the end 💀 of literature

A memoir by **Basil Dillon-Malone**

(aka John Player)

 FriesenPress

Suite 300 - 990 Fort St
Victoria, BC, V8V 3K2
Canada

www.friesenpress.com

Copyright © 2021 by Basil Dillon-Malone
First Edition — 2021

ISBN
978-1-5255-8956-0 (Hardcover)
978-1-5255-8955-3 (Paperback)
978-1-5255-8957-7 (eBook)

1. Fiction, Satire

Distributed to the trade by The Ingram Book Company

Contents

To my daughter and confidante
Shali without whom this decade-long labor of
love-of-literature would still be in Limbo

What others are saying about the Last Smoker ...

Basil Dillon-Malone is the true heir to Laurence Sterne, James Joyce, and all the stream of consciousness and experimental writers that he has obviously deeply read, loved, and whose spirits inform this book. It's a wild ride. Visual as well as lyric, it flows quickly and is very light-footed, playful, smart, and funny. Last Smoker will appeal to the attentive reader who is open to nuance, weirdness, and shifting perspective. I particularly liked the 'succumb' scene, which could spring straight out of the best parts of the 18th century masterpiece Tristram Shandy. Nicely done, Basil! The ending is delicious! Even with all the smoke!

Suzanne Mercury

I am simply enjoying a freely-flowing "confession" that is-- by its very nature, replete with riffs and admitted non sequiturs-- not susceptible to conventional tonal or grammatical criticism, let alone correction. I take pleasure in what emerges from the pencil and later the laptop of our underground smoker, "confined to writing in the open" (nice paradox), from "the divine milieu" (nice glance at Teilhard) of his abandoned parking-lot. Especially in giving back to society precisely the sort of creative writing the banning of nicotine has almost extinguished. The title notwithstanding, *Last Smoker* demonstrates that the pronouncement of the death of literature is, like Mark Twain's demise, premature.

Dr. Patrick Keane (PhD NYU), Professor Emeritus of English,
Francis Fallon Chair, LeMoyne College

i

'The Last Smoker on Earth' is a work of inner monologue written with words that pound on the conscience. It was penned by a master of cliché and stand-up parody usually in an empty parking lot with the trunk of his car as his writing bureau. Although the author's non-sequiturs are not always easy to follow, his prose is music to the soul and poetry to the mind. The action takes place with the post-tobacco era in full swing after smoking had been banned outright especially in the ultimate hold-out, the closet. The confessions are an attempt to justify one man's mission to influence the comeback of literature after writing creativity had collapsed instantly without the overwhelming influence of nicotine. The ensuing comeback (*kumbaya* in some international critiques) is a masterpiece befitting the immortal words of Jack Schaefer: *Come back Shane!*

PS: Incidentally, the surprise rendezvous in the parking lot emerges as one of the finer twists in the reemergence of modern literature. Hold onto your lighters and enjoy.

The Publisher

Give me words. The kind that pound on the conscience, crack open mysteries, let light shine, or undulate across the page until the reader is hypnotized; words that sooth or alarm, inform or galvanize, open starry skies or peer into hidden recesses. The right words in the right context are like discrete droplets that rise for a perfect instant when a great wave strikes solid rock. They're fresh as now, old as the world everlasting. They rinse the mind.

Paul Greenberg, syndicated columnist

He could suck on the pap of life and gulp down the incomparable milk of wonder

F. Scott Fitzgerald

It is now proved beyond doubt that smoking is one of the leading causes of statistics.

Fletcher Knebel

Although a one-character whodunit, definitely the ultimate *Ulysses*. If Molly Bloom's inner monologue of 25-pages without punctuation was bad enough – I was amazed with this 400-page soliloquy! The good news is that there is punctuation after death!

Aloysius Finnegan, The NYU Book Review

... in a sky swept crystal clear by the night wind the stars showed like silver flakes, tarnished now and again by the yellow gleam of the revolving light. Perfumes of spice and warm stone were wafted on the breeze everything was very still ...

Camus (The Plague)

Smoking May Help Your Concentration.

Columbia University College of Physicians & Surgeons

Gotta light ...?

anon

Thank you for smoking.

Christopher Buckley (Son of William F. Buckley Jr.)

Think: Becket, Kafka and Joyce, Camus, Sartre and Aquinas, with a bit of Virginia Woolf for the gender stream-of-consciousness. Combined with a touch of Hemingway for flow and frankness. And Wells for the body-snatcher metaphor.

A fan

In essence, I found the flow and cadence powerful and compelling as relatively continuous text that the eye and mind can follow. Of course, Joyce provided no such guidance whatsoever, and left the reader the enormous task of identifying and deciphering his myriad allusions – *Last Smoker* is much kinder than that! I was a bit disorientated during the pages preceding Chapter 1 as I wondered "Where is this all leading?", and I found myself becoming increasingly impatient to get into the book proper and to understand what the heck was going on. As I got into Chapter 1, I gradually started to understand and enjoy the style and structure, the deployment of celeb and pop-culture references, the word plays, and so on.

Peter Ahern, Head, Axios Foundation

I've staggered to the end of Last Smoker, or the various ends, including the Afterlife and the epilogues and glossary. This seems never "to run out of foolscap," or of "words," many of which "pound on the conscience," though many more--necessarily, given the chosen technique of thematically-focused yet loose association--swirl and evaporate like, well, smoke. The associative stream-of-consciousness romp is nothing if not encyclopedic, bursting at the allusive seams with references to everything from pop music to high culture to science. To be sure, the main theme is omnipresent, but it's the plot or scaffolding which provides the trellis, exfoliating with any number of plants, familiar and exotic. The book is at once sui generis AND aligned with literary parallels. I was reminded at several points, of Sterne's TRISTRAM SHANDY, where the leaving of blank pages recalled Sterne's pre-modernist Uncle Toby leaving a blank page for the reader to come up with his or her own imaginative picture of the voluptuous Widow Wadman. I was familiar with the "Dichter-17," knowing something about motivational research and about Dichter's "harkening back to the primordial sense of power involved in controlling fire".

Another fan.

No one's ever written a book quite like this, but it occurs to me that there are a couple of classic precursors in terms of timing. Boccaccio's DECAMERON and Defoe's JOURNAL OF THE PLAGUE YEAR were published during THEIR respective pandemics.

Yet another fan

SMOKING KILLS

The action takes place between New Year's Eve 2008 (including New Year's morning 2009) and November 17, 2016 (the Great American Smokeout).

WARNING:

SMOKING IS NOT FOR EVERYONE. THERE ARE RISKS AND SOCIAL SIDE EFFECTS.

Cui peccare licet peccat minus (Elegy IV)

He who is allowed to sin sins less

Publius Ovidius Naso (43 b.c. - 17 a.d.)

"I have a little place up in the Catskills where I go to smoke."

OVERTURE

The Last Smoker on Earth and the end of literature
… takes its cue from the early witch-hunts against
smokers, the hopeless yet kind-hearted *tabagie
who had acquired their dysfunction through no fault
of their own. As impressionable kids growing up it
was hard not to be captivated at Saturday afternoon
matinees by the smoking habits of the heroes and
heroines of the silver screen (such as Bogart and
Dietrich) with a natural propensity for emulation
in an era when it was fashionable for everyone to
develop lung cancer.

The parody focusses on the worst infringement of
individual human rights in the last century – the
obnoxious left-over smell on the draperies which
would never go away, from uninvited neighborly
visitors who would light-up presumptuously in the
living-room without asking permission of the hor-
rified hosts whom themselves were particularly
careful not to smoke in their own living room (having
resourcefully installed purpose-driven outhouses).

An early title was 'Confessions of a Closet Smoker',
so the words 'confession' and 'closet' appear

frequently and daringly. As do the numbers 21 and 79 (go figure!). Oh, and watch out for the frequent and intentional use of repetition (perfected by Gordon Lightfoot), a sine qua non of any good confession. In fairness to the former president, it is never divulged if the rumor were true that Barack Obama, a key figure in *Last Smoker,* was a closet-smoker.

Apologies are extended in multiple critiques of Neil Diamond's prose, example, "And nobody heard/ Not even the ... *chair*"!? And, the author's use of 'albeit' has a tendency to trigger a non-sequitur into 'albert' (as in Einstein, Gore, Camus). The letter 'c' is sometimes substituted with the Kafkaesque '*k*' by the Anti-Tobacco lawmakers, in an effort that never really took off (like Esperanto) except in vintage computers with malfunctioning spell-checks.

Finally, please check your calendar if you have difficulty keeping up with past, present and future tense in the many flashbacks and flashforwards.

---

*tabagie

French, originally meaning 'a group of smokers who meet together in the manner of a club', it was just about to go the way of dodo but reemerged in a social renaissance. One could find them once more in all major American cities - a *tabagie,* huddled together outside bars and workplaces and restaurants, united in suffering under the ban of their favorite activity. Sadly, the tabagie was to become another footnote in history following the Act of Cessation.

Oxford American Writers

Aftermath ...

Yes, we should have seen it coming.
There had been doomsday
prognostications about the fate of literature,
exemplified by valedictions like Sven Birkert's
"The Gutenberg Elegies" (Sam Sacks, WSJ)
– but writers just kept on smoking.

   Ultimately,
after smoking was outlawed in much of the
known world following the US-initiated
global passing of the Act of Cessation 🚭
- writing creativity had ceased instantly.
The inspiration and concentration that came
with nicotine – the addictive chemical of tobacco
– and the reason why we (used to) smoke
and which for centuries had provided the
stimulus for great writers,
had dried-up, sounding a death knell for
literature as we knew it.

Otherwise normal, healthy wordsmiths
suffering irreparable writers-block were on
tenterhooks wondering what was coming next
as comic-books invaded the BOMC and topped
the NYT best-seller lists ...

     ... while in the meantime the ubiquitous #2
     pencil was remarketed by creative entrepreneurs
     and clever prosthodontists as a chewable pla-
     cebo for a nation even more at risk.

There was no end in sight to the vicious circle following the loss of cigarette taxes which had funded and was now about to bankrupt the Treasury. Something was needed to calm the paranoia.

Available in popular packs of 20, the #2 pencils provided a sorely needed alternative to the dependable cigarette. But – let there be no doubt - with an explicit warning on each pack:

'chewing can be damaging to your incisors'.

crunch!

Sure, we should've seen it coming ...

00:06:01
New Year's morning 2009

Although everyone knew it was inevitable, the outright ban on smoking had abruptly taken effect following an event that happened in less than a New York minute in Manhattan. The tragedy which triggered the Act of Cessation would subsequently be forever known as the Manhattan Prologue, *especially by those who were old enough to remember the shot that was once heard around the globe from the smoking gun.*

One fifth of the population (21%) was in a quandary as to what to do next as if they had a multiple choice. The worst had yet to come in a nation even more at risk without cigarette taxes to support the already heat-shrunk economy. No longer a simple conflict between the anti-smoking lobby and the tabagie, the good news was that, in the few homes that had not yet foreclosed, the eco-friendly draperies were forever free from second-hand smoke. While outside, the bad news was that the CO_xs, SO_xs and NO_Xs would continue to stagnate for some 100 years (according to the pundits) like the alien spacecraft in the movie Independence Day. *Beneath which the day had long resembled night in the city that never sleeps.*

Indeed, everything seemed perfectly normal, but it wasn't. The smoking ban had sounded a death knell for literature as we knew it. Not publicized too widely for panic reasons, in fairness there was a general consensus by medical researchers (Columbia College of Physicians and Surgeons), that the one tangible benefit derived directly from nicotine was the ability to concentrate and invite the inspiration to write great literature. For 4000 years (incidentally about the same number as carcinogens in a single cigarette) practically all the classics had been written by smokers. It was no wonder that the good died young.

After smoking was abolished, writing creativity had ceased instantly. Barnes & Noble was on the verge of bankruptcy until they replaced the lit & historical sections with comic books. Fire alarms sounded even though there was no longer any smoke. Ultimately, after many decades of smoking I realized that I had no choice but to do my own small bit for humanity in giving creative writing back to society. My one small butt (sic) for mankind.

Perhaps I am the sole remaining closet smoker? The answer to that will never be known for sure because of the Heisenberg Principle of Uncertainty. For those of you who haven't studied quantum physics, the principle as applied to smoking states that if a closet-smoker is observed smoking - then he or she is no longer a closet-smoker. And relinquishes any hint of creativeness that coexists with concentration - because a great writer must smoke alone, in self-imposed solitary confinement, undisturbed in his divine milieu. Which, for some (like me) is usually an abandoned parking lot www.abandonedparkinglot.com after the empty telephone kiosks were demolished when the secular world went cellular. And forfeits the ability to write words that pound on the conscience. Taken all together — not a very good picture. So, as a closet-smoker, a survivor, I must be cautious, vigilant.

In spite of the threat of incarceration in the Midnight Express, should I be apprehended by the AT kops (anti-tobacco police) at least I made my choice ...

Fast-forward ...

13:35:01
November 17, 2016

(Great American Smokeout)

   whisshhh (inhale)...

      oo-ooooh (exhale) ...

         ... koffkoff!

Yes, I made my choice ...

and now I must live with it ... koff! koff ...ko

           ... ... fffff ...ff... f..   .

The global smoking ban had taken effect on New Year's Day 2009. There was one exception – the sovereign nations could continue to manufacture their own cigarettes but there were caveats. Upon reading of the acclaimed study: Smoking May Help your Concentration (Columbia College of Physicians and Surgeons, albeit the Columbia study was performed on animals), the protagonist's stream-of-consciousness - as a direct effect of tobacco - lets loose with powerful clichés exercising his creative-writing skill. With nicotine soothing the mind and providing inexhaustible energy for the creativity to concentrate and encourage inspiration, like the great writers in history who were all smokers, he was enabled to create words that pound on the conscience.

 *One*

Cliché in the closet

If you're comfortably sitting down reading this personal exposé, perhaps the person standing over your shoulder at this very moment is one of us. Or maybe one of them. Huh, there's no one there? Strange. But believe me, we could be anyone. And, so could they.

Do you recall a lady pushing her grocery cart behind you last night? And that she was smiling as her trolley almost bumped against your heel but not close enough for her unnecessary apology? Close but no cigar. You probably only saw her for a fleeting moment bending backwards to check your footing as you stretched for a can of peas or a cold 6-pack on a hot August night. Or how about the ticket checker at the off-beat movie house on the wrong side of town? Maybe the surgeon in the ER, or the anesthesiologist? Or the pilot of your last transatlantic flight, were he disembarking from a tolerable ninety-minute shuttle home and making a quick getaway when no one was looking? For a quick one. The stranger with no fixed abode. The mailman with no immediate deadline or account-ability but with some time to kill? Or even the priest rushing off from the confessional after his last penitent, now deserving a nice breather before vespers.

whew!

A sigh of relief from the priest behind the curtain? Or, from the penitent who may have had a later agenda too. Or the butcher, the baker, the candlestick maker … the puppet, the pauper, the pirate, the poet, the pawn or maybe the … <u>k</u>ing?

And what about your spouse? *hmmm.* Or even you yourself? Assuming there are (m)any of us left, besides me naturally.

In each of the above instances of people in their regular where-withal doing whatever they do best, there's no evidence good or bad of anything extraordinary or deserving attention. Except possibly begging the question for my rather peculiar inclusion of the … *k*ing (from the song written by Dean Kay for Sinatra). Or the puppet. But I'm sure you've guessed that those are simply illustrative to get your attention. Because, when the king's away … Well, you know the rest.

Now then … you, the reader, could be one of *them.* You know who you are.

Or, one of *us*, huh?

Wouldn't that be interesting? But the fact of the matter is that most of you are neither. Until now you have not been involved. I don't mean this in a negative or derogatory sense. I'm only presenting the possibilities. You just never know.

As preposterous as this unveiling confession may seem to those who never lit up or became fanatically opposed, I assure you it's the truth in spite of what Jack Nicholson said in A Few Good Men: *You want the truth? You can't handle the truth!* Hopefully there are some of you who will take me into your confidence. It's a risk I'm taking in writing all of it down - for you or for some of you as much as for others like me. Or possibly only for me. Again, if I'm the only one who has survived.

The pseudonym on the jacket (aka John Player) is necessary to protect the guilty. That's a no-brainer. Unfortunately, it is also necessary for me to interweave cliché, hyperbole and other embellishments throughout this exposé to make the theme appear fictitious as much as to discombobulate reality. After all, we have an inherent need to be entertained, amused, distracted. I know I do. Yet, as much as camouflaging details is against every virtue and scruple upon which I was raised, soon you will understand why I have no alternative but to disguise the truth.

So, who are the guilty that I'm trying so hard to protect? Rhetorical question, Rhett! Rather - my dear reader! Is that why you're skimming ahead hoping to locate where I'm at this moment, the physical DIVINE MILIEU where I'm writing these confessions? By doing a triangularization with two known points and one unknown. Touché on the latter. Nice try, huh. Oh, I'm sorry I said that. My reaction was a little unfair, even mean. You get that way sometimes out here in the open. In the center of an abandoned parking lot with my foolscap on the trunk – my writing bureau. The federal bureau of investigation. Just kidding. Still I must inform you, looking ahead won't do you any good. A waste of time.

My real problem is that I don't have a single confidant in my secret life (except perhaps my publisher). My gut tells me to trust you. Most of you. Although it's sad to say that I can't even trust the missus. Or the kids. Think, Keri Russell as Elizabeth Jennings. Not that I don't love them and vice-versa. It's for their own protection. Maybe someday if they too read my confessions, things will be different. I hope.

~ ~ ~

Okay. It's just another ugly afternoon in an abandoned outdoor parking lot although we normally associate 'abandoned' with inside. Not exactly pouring yet but the dark clouds are ominous. What's new? Leaning against the trunk of my car I'm wrapping-up the draft of another chapter before returning to the real world.

It's hard to imagine that I've made it past the middle of the second decade of the new millennium. I guess the AT (anti-tobacco) kops don't have a Tommy Lee Jones on their team. Still, unless I document what's happened looking back on the eight woebegone years since smoking was outlawed and the end of creative writing as we knew it, future generations will never understand how good it was. But instead of looking back I'm looking over my shoulder most the time. For … them.

And in the process my train of thought is frequently interrupted causing all kinds of non-sequiturs in my confessions, especially when I later try to transpose my handwritten draft from the parking lot to laptop when I get home at night. Soon you will understand why I need the nicotine to develop my narrative, but which is not necessary in the manual task of later typing into my computer. Since we're confined to writing in the open, the inclement weather - like the misery in a Stephen *K*ing novel – this 'king' stuff is haunting me! - can cause my output to suffer. Like the suffering *tabagie* who were the pariah of society from the early 90's until the ban.

Outlawed is debatably a better word than confined although they probably didn't realize it when they made it up. Some days I don't get more than a half-foolscap written because of the weather. Other times without distraction I'm on a roll.

Stephen King, huh? Somehow, I keep attracting kings, but he was too dark for me. Especially in his short story, Quitters, and a theme which became a forerunner to the *Midnight Express.* Of course, I don't have to tell you about the Mid X although we will get there! Not literally, I hope …

The post-Tobacco era of the new millennium is still relatively recent after centuries of smoking when no one cared less. But it was no accident. Walt Whitman wrote: *O to be self-balanced for contingencies / to confront night, storms, hunger, ridicule, accidents, rebuffs, as the trees and animals do.* [Me Imperturbe] But what if there were no accidents? If this phylogeny has followed a progression of … survival of the weakest? Such devil's advocacy used to be a debatable topic but no more. And even if much of my writing style is deliberately tongue in cheek for the above reason, there's a need to be cautious, vigilant. Otherwise I'd be foolish and naive to make myself so vulnerable. And, my words must be politically correct where possible, at least for appearances sake. Illusions and impressions can be as deceiving as the subterfuge they're hiding.

This sounds tautological but it's really a test of one-upmanship, a sleuth chasing his/her shadow. Eye shadow. I shadow. Stalker. Me and my shadow. The shadow beneath. Crow's feet beneath the smiling eyes of a … chain-smoker. But we're not chain smokers, at least not me. Not I. The *king* and I. Except occasionally. If I can't be honest in my confession …

> *Reader:*   *Excuse me. Did you say … smoker?*

Ok. Good catch. Confession time. We were going to get to this sooner or later. Might as well get it over with. It's like the newspaper cartoon with two guys, elbows on the counter, one with a sad face, one with a happy face, both cupping their pints. And, pointing to the wall clock, the barman shouts over to the guy, scolding his happy face: *Hey you over there, happy hour's over!*

Yep! You got it.

I'm a *k*loset-smoker (see Kafkaesque *k* in appendix 1)! In the inhale *(whisshhh)* - exhale *(oo-oooooh)* experience:

> *whisshhh …*

> *oo-oooooh …*

~ ~ ~

Now I've said it. Say it again, Sam. You'd never think I just returned from Casablanca, huh, one of the few outposts they haven't got to yet. Here's smoking at you, kid. Okay, I'm a *k*loset-smoker. Watch the *k* – you'll see a bunch of them! Are you happy now? Are we there yet? Look, can we move on before you draw premature conclusions about us. Please. So that I might share what led to this confession. In a nation even more at risk since the Act of Cessation which heralded the end of smoking, of the good times. For the good times. [Ray Price] As we knew them.

Now might be a good time to interject a housekeeping chore as they say in the genre, a clarification (about where I get my supply of smokes) before you get too immersed in my confession. You may observe that sometimes I might appear to have difficulty being politically correct relating some key events. Yet, in deference to the craft and the uncreated conscience of an old artificer [Joyce], it will become necessary for me to explain the only remaining source of smokes after cigarette production was otherwise abolished in much of the known world. As we move along it may appear as though I'm picking on the Native American ...

> *Reader:* *Please move along mister, can't you see the no-loitering sign in the (empty) parking lot!*

... indeed, that I'm badgering the limeys (English folks with their pointed noses, crooked teeth and rotten breath), paddys, the *tabagie*, the obese, politicians, bishops and actresses, lawyers and actuaries ... the good, the bad and the ugly! For godsakes it was an ugly day in Belmullet. But God help us, I'm also trying to revive parody ever since the global ban on smoking did away with the inspiration and adrenalin to combat the mediocrity of mimicry common among x-smokers ultimately lacking creativity after the smoking ban.

The fact of the matter is that the sovereign nation, the sole remaining source of underground ciggies, is my salvation. Hallelujah! [Leonard Cohen] I hope we're on the same page on this because the one thing that neither of us needs (depending on whom you are) at this juncture is a witch-hunt. We've had too many of these even if I may include the present tense. And tense it often is, for me.

Constantly looking over my shoulder.

whisshhh ... oo-oooooh ...

~ ~ ~

During Prohibition of a lesser evil about a century ago, Al Jolson improvised the popular song: You made me do it/I didn't wanna do it/I didn't wanna do it. That's exactly how I feel because you have obliged me to be less than honest when more accessibility would most certainly reveal my identity. Well, maybe not you. Still, with the above caveats, you must decide what is truth and which is fiction. Rather, which is stranger. Strangers on a train. [Hitchcock]

As at a crossing, one train may hide another train. [Kenneth Koch]

Watching all those late night tv commercials makes me sometimes wish I were a victim of identity-theft and let someone else look over my shoulder. For a change. Although I'm not paranoid I'm well aware that there are readers among you who are watching for a carelessly dropped nuance, casual innuendo or inadvertent epithet in my confessions. Even an obscure reference or a clumsy elaboration that may be a tip-off. Or, should this become an audio book, a slip of the tongue. That would do it. For your edification, more often than not I have intentionally tacked on these deceptions to maintain my anonymity.

No, the anti-tobacco kops are not looking for long-extinct designer-ashtrays, shamelessly discarded butts, or unsightly burn-holes, singes, scorches. To do that this book would have to be virtual multimedia or at least 3-D. That would be ridiculous unless, god help us, you're an avatar. But they're looking for more psychological, cerebral, abstruse telltale clues that might lead to our discovery.

Our. My. Me.

My o me. Me o my.

~ ~ ~

Sometimes I waken up thinking about my hidden life in a way that reflection is a sine qua non of any good confession. It seems like only yesterday when all my troubles seemed so far away. [Paul McCartney] And just yesterday morning when they let me know you were gone. [James Taylor]

I often wonder, pinching myself on the blubbery flesh beneath my right thigh ... *ouch!* ... how could this have happened? Rather, how could it have happened to me. Not only about my sneaking around for a quiet puff or two for a bit o' the muse but how I've been personally impacted in the dawning of this strange new age. My brave new world.

Living this other life in the pre-T era (the time prior to the tobacco ban) never bothered me or anyone else, I think. But now I should describe the transition in *Kubler-Ross's* terms of denial-and-isolation, anger, bargaining, depression, decapitation of bobbleheads, and acceptance.

That is – if you were kaught!

Reader: *Watch your k's sir!*

Otherwise, for me anyway, it's much of a muchness. Too much sometimes. As Paddy Kavanagh, a respectable smoker in his time, romantically put it: *Oh, I loved too much and by such by such/Is happiness thrown away.* [Raglan Road] You just do what you've been doing for thirty-some years. But, believe me, you don't want to know what happens if you're nabbed by the AT kops for lighting-up just once. You light up my life. Just once.

You're sentenced to the *Midnight Express*. To start a new paragraph.

Whether the Mid X is a place, or an experience doesn't really matter. All you know for sure is that there's no way out for what endures for the rest of one's natural life. In some ways for those already at the undiagnosed early stages of lung cancer, that may be for the better. To pay one's dues. To the piper. For the sins of the father. Of the silver screen. And the addiction it led to. Addicted to writing. Addicted to love. [Robert Palmer]

If you believe the AT kops most of those entering the Mid X were predictably skinny after decades of smoking, so after a year or two it wasn't a look-before-and-after of any weight-watcher type gimmick you see on the commercials. Over and over again. Which you can't escape no matter how many channels you switch or remotes you burn. One starts the Mid X experience already looking like the etiolated 'after' of a weight loss adv having chain-smoked a few cartons too many. Unless, that is, one looked like Marie Osmond who never smoked and whom you couldn't possibly imagine as a 'before' candidate

 for a weight-loss adv.

To illustrate the gravitas if you were caught with a single smoking violation, 24x36-in posters in acrylic frames were placed in strategic locations such as popcorn machines in movie theatres. And on walls beside long lines at the post office after the clocks were removed because they (the clocks) made customers nervous by being aware of how long they'd been standing. Although they also serve who only stand and wait. [Milton]

The posters depicted a lone man in a black Zhivago-length London Fog overcoat, predictably with collar up covering a type-cast ugly scar like Al Pacino's Scarface or some such villain. And ironically wearing 1-way secret-service-like sunglasses for ano-nymity developed from technology used in 2-way interrogation windows in police precincts. Fooling-no-one. While puffing-away on a Lucky Strike.

The background of the poster looked like an abandoned outdoor parking lot. Surrounding the man's perforated galoshes on the cracked asphalt, the asphalt jungle, were images of what looked-like eight 'corpses' (although if you looked close enough you'd swear they were crash-dummies, but who am I to say?) All burned beyond recognition from spontaneous combustion. And if you looked even closer at the graphics and were a gambling man, you mightn't be far off by betting that six of the eight 'victims' were adults. At least the way the poster was designed you were made to think they were victims. Of these, four looked like women but the scene seemed to be somewhere in New York so you couldn't tell for sure. One of the women appeared to have been seven months pregnant which few would ridicule as preposterous in case they were wrong. And last but not least were the 'corpses' of a pair of 5-year-old identical twins, just lying there. Burned to cinders according to the tabloids. A boy who longed to be an astronaut when he was older. *Ah, but I was so much older then/I'm younger than that now.* [Dylan] And a girl who dreamed of being a ballerina if she didn't grow too tall and trip too often. At least, that's how the tabloids reported on the twins. The letters

K

I

L

L

E

R

were lightly and non-intrusively (as if an innocuous afterthought) superimposed diagonally across the smoker-in-the-poster for special effect, obviously designed by the special effects department of the AT (anti-tobacco) administration. With a dark hint of t h r i l l e r in the meticulous more-than-precarious way he wore his towering broad shoulders had you not known any better.

whisshhh ...

oo-oooooh ...

All told, the image of the smoker-in-the-poster wasn't a good one. If anything, in the way he was presented as puffing-away like nobody's business, it was designed to (deceptively) portray a menacing, reprehensible, intimidating bully. A public enemy, only concerned with self-indulgence at any cost, spreading cancer by the second. Like someone who was always bumming a cigarette even when it was legal. That kind of person. A bummer. Bummer! Again, who am I to judge not or ye shall be judged? There's no denying that the character in the poster was a smoker but otherwise he came across (as you perused the poster as if looking at a litho in a gallery thinking it was an original), at least to me, as a decent, polite fellow, probably quite intelligent and well-read. Like someone who had read great mystery novels and was possibly the subject of one of his own. Who knows? Maybe he even wrote a great confession of the likes of St. Augustine in the confined closet of a monastic cloister. Or an apologia of someone falsely accused of insincerity like Oscar Wilde (or, the character Dorian Gray before time was up).

They initially chose to superimpose the noun 'murderer' instead of killer. But murderer, because it was too subjective in connotation and not suggestive-enough in expression, hardly had the same basic instinct or killer effect upon the eco. Smoking was an eco-hazard and that was it! Had there been green smoke coming out of cigarettes there never would've been a social problem. Although black smoke was acceptable in Vatican chimneys. And white. With no gray in between.

Divine milieu – favorite abandoned parking lot where the protagonist could
smoke til kingdom come while writing stimulating lit in the great outdoors with words
that pound on the conscience

In the early days of the A of C many of those who continued to have a quiet puff or two sought-out the nearest wilderness they could find like a set in the movie Deliverance and hoped they wouldn't be discovered. Where they would bother no one but themselves … and the trees. Which collectively were emitting 79 to 210 million tonnes of methane per year which more than offset their global warming benefit. Rather, a toss-up of pros and cons. And causing pandemonium in the trade-off. Making it difficult to see the forest for the trees. For the eco-conscious. Always endeavoring to do the right thing.

As expected, most smokers were nabbed fairly quickly having let their guard down, not taking the A of C seriously, at least at the start of the ban - probably in disbelief at what was happening in an otherwise civilized nation. Having dropped their defense mechanisms, safety nets, and Linus-like security blankets. Some dads were really surprised by the behavior of those (few) of their kids who weren't smokers themselves who became informers.

To aggravate the problem, the A of C was going global. There weren't a lot of places that diehards could go except possibly India or China or Casablanca for a safe puff.

And then what? Of course, there was the language problem. And maybe they wouldn't like the food, especially the creepy-crawly 'live' stuff that they saw the locals gobbling down in Changsha on National Geo if they manhandled the remote. And what about their families? Actually, the more they thought about the missus, that wasn't a major problem for a lot of them and maybe even a blessing. The farther away, the better. But their jobs, huh? And social security benefits? Upon reflection they struck that one down too since SS was already being 'dismantled' by the lack of cig tax $$ to fund it.

Immediately following the decision to outlaw smoking, the huge number of roundups by the AT kops was a no-brainer. Like the hoopla associated with any new cheap reality show which were replacing regular programming on tv in tough economic times because they cost nothing to produce. And nobody cared less nor noticed the difference with their feet up on the ottoman.

Get over it. I told you so! - was all their former friends could say as their neighbors were being carted off in their pajamas to the Mid X in the middle of the night. Like so many Joan of Arcs before she was lit-up like a Christmas tree. Regardless of which month it was. People who had never smoked and who were forced to live with the drawback of being a social-misfit growing-up because of it but who could smell a smoker a mile away finally felt vindicated, indeed justified. And were behaving like Black Friday shoppers scurrying around in a free-for-all at Walmart. Trying to catch their neighbors having a quiet one. Catch me if you can. But in the spirit of the Victor McLaglen role-model, not all informers were brat kids. Some were nosy relatives doing what they did best who had visited too-often in good times and were always made to feel unwelcome. And who knew it - but they would never leave anyway. You know the kind - who will come back again to haunt you. Now getting their own back for being made to feel the way they were. As informants. On a mission. Those uninteresting types of people finally getting some notice. Like Gypo Nolan. Or Gaius Cassius Longinus. Or Dona Marina. The braggarts. Indeed.

In fairness in the years before the ban, smoking had already been branded as anathema by 79% of the population who remained indoors for fear of catching something in the air outside (CO_xs, SO_xs and NO_xs) that wasn't necessarily from tobacco. Society was becoming less personal and more dependent on statistics. Everyone was too busy playing video games or composing ridiculous posts about their cats on Facebook so that no one had time to read books, play catch-up or put out the garbage except the wives who cared. We should've seen it coming.

If great literature had been written for centuries by smokers, but had become extinct with the A of C... and if people were no longer interested in reading except those who were too busy trying to follow the smaller and smaller print in appliance instruction manuals - which were written in American by Taiwanese nationals who never heard of spell-chick - before hopelessly giving-up, then, what hope was there really for us?

whisshhh ... oo-oooooh ...

The most fanatical of the anti-smokers had never smoked or at least swore they never inhaled. So, what did they know about toleration when it came to the vote on New Year's Eve eight years ago that could've at least slowed the A of C? Which changed the world forever and the very meaning of resilience, of allowable deviance from a standard, of the space we are obliged to share with our neighbor. Smoking was even perceived as worse than obesity which was fat (sic) becoming the socially acceptable norm. Soon everyone was fat because they could no longer smoke which had kept their bodies trim by increasing the metabolic rate. And burning more calories

 while lacking nicotine which acted as an appetite suppressant.

And just when you were beginning to forget about the peak smoking years (1946-1964) and that it was safe to go back in the water, another baby-boom followed the smoking ban. There hadn't been one like it in half-a-century because there was no longer the yukky breath turn-off for wives or girlfriends or boyfriends of former-smokers. Which meant the sex was great. And finally, for a change, there was kissing in bedrooms and other places. Many male babies were being affectionately christened Fat Igor in a kind of renaissance of history repeating itself.

Credit: Jeff Stahler, The Columbus (Ohio) Dispatch, May 17, 2011

Think: Henry VIII. Everyone was eating so much they were called Henry the Ate.

In the streets fat men who had kicked the smoking habit through no fault of their own after it became illegal were singing off-key: *Oi am 'Enery the 8*[th] *oi am/'Enery the 8th oi am oi am* [Herman's Hermits] It was becoming a fad to be fat. Like all the fat *k*ings in history. Don't know much about history. [Sam Cooke] And fat popes. And fat kats. And fat Buddhas. Like the popular menu item in Shanghai: 'Buddha Jumps Over the Wall' - cooked cuisine so luscious that the smiling fat buddha tastes it, rubs his proud tummy then hops the wall in euphoria. That good!

But there were exceptions. Fat Santa who was fat but also smoked quietly. A physiological aberration. The familial *HoHoHo* at yuletide. Sitting on Santa's lap when you were a kid. *HoHoHo and a*

naggin   o'   rum.   Santa indeed. Hidden in his emergency pouch (fanny pack) with the band stretching to the limit around his waist for the inevitable ricochet if the snap broke. For the occasional swig. To get his mind off the infuriating brat kids. Driving him krazy. For a quiet puff. When no one was looking.

It was bad enough that 79% of the population were already fat but now the 21% who were forced by the A of C to quit cold turkey were getting fatter faster.

It used to be a simple matter of turning a blind eye with a deaf ear instead of the cold shoulder with a pointed finger when someone did something that bothered no one else. When somebody did somebody wrong. At this stage you ought to be aware that the dominant theme of my confession is about *k*loset-smokers - or *k*-smokers as we're officially known in the post-T (post-tobacco) vernacular. When *we* could invite the muse and challenge the arbitrary wafts of inspiration with the relaxed concentration of a quiet puff or two. And write words that pound on the conscience.

    whisshhh ... oo-oooooh ...

And that was after the A of C which followed upon the **MANHATTAN PROLOGUE** and became the law of the land.

Ignorantia legis non excusat. Ignorance is bliss, in Latin.

It may surprise you that by nature I'm an outgoing type with my day-job in the media biz. When I live my other life.

With an umbrella over my head in this one – at this very moment. In an otherwise empty parking lot. A vacant theatre. Alone on the stage. As the Raindrops keep Falling on my Head. [BJ Thomas] Trying to balance my brollie-cum-cig with my right and my leaking old bic with my left. Darn ink. Leaking like a wiki-sieve.

And sometimes I'm not even sure which of my lives is the real one, as a secret smoker, or as a non-smoker, in the self-deceptive eye of the beholder. Perhaps the answer lies in Goethe's Faust: *Two souls, alas! reside within my breast, and each withdraws from and repels its brother.*

Regardless, each has salient features in its own right. Or wrong. Neither of which would I give up for the other. Couldn't. The horse and carriage. It has nothing to do with schizophrenia and I assure you I'm no Mr. Hyde.

You, sir, are no Mr. Hyde.

But watch out, Dorian.

They're everywhere.

~ ~ ~

Shortly I'll tell you about the other *they*. Many of you know about them anyway. Some of you are them. And you're not fooling me. Only I can do that. Forced to. In my need to share this story I cannot control who reads my confession even if I wanted to. And, isn't that the theme of this book? Control over personal responsibility for one's actions. Control, huh? Jung said: *Every form of addiction is bad, no matter whether the addiction be alcohol or morphine or idealism.* Idealism? He had no earthly idea, subliminal or explicit.

Freud wasn't much better. On the contrary, for crying out loud, which he encouraged you to do, he was addicted to cigars and made the following profound statement: *Sometimes a cigar is just a cigar.* Even Einstein advised: *Before you answer a question, always light a pipe.* And Churchill, what about him? Rather, Winston, whom they named the ciggies after although he too only smoked cigars. Well, he was just arrogant. Like most Brits. With their pointed noses, crooked teeth and smelly breath.

Brit reader: **Stop picking [pun] on the Brits!**

And always fuming. Apropos. If you remember his growling face in Yousuf Karsh's famous portrait having calmly snatched the cigar from his lips. Yet times were different. There was Limbo then. Now the Northern Baptists say: *There ain't no Hell.* While in fairness the Southern Baptists fume: *To Hell there ain't!* I met Al Sharpton once and that's exactly what he told me.

Nonetheless, they say that everyone lives two lives. So, what's the big deal being a *k*-smoker bothering no one. One might be shuffling between a daytime job and a nighttime diversion. Like me. While the second job, although more of a hobby or pastime, frequently becomes one's primary avocation. And, they say that kats have nine lives.

~ ~ ~

But my double life is different although I'm not a spy. I run from spies, have been - since the **MANHATTAN PROLOGUE**. Avoid them like the plague, hiding in a cloud of dust. Of smoke. And mirrors. Unlike Le Carré's (or more familiar on the black and white screen, Richard Burton's) Alec Leamas, I'm still out in the cold. Out. In. The outhouse. I knew a guy once named Bob Outhouse but that's neither here nor there.

Yes. A spy is my nemesis, my adversary. But not my alter ego. I say this because alter egos are almost always associated with double lives although everyone has one, for example: Hitler loved dogs. A doppelganger for sure. Make it a double. Pleeze.

My double-ganger life is more like two souls in one. Or a soul and a sole, the second as in solitary … confinement. Or a leather sole of a shoe tossed before its time, rotting away with holes. Weathered from pathetically standing outside too much in the hail, rain, wind, snow. Like the *tabagie*. The four horsemen of the Apocalypse freezing their butts off. Smoking our butts off. Although, personally, as you know by now, I never smoked in mixed company for reasons which will become obvious when we discuss Heisenberg.

Then again, everything's subject to change, especially the weather. As Will Rogers surmised in the twenties: If you don't like the weather in Oklahoma, stay a minute. OK. Before they blanked the Okie part in a blink. Blink was a respectable book written by Malcolm Gladwell. Probably a *k*-smoker too. We'll get into that when we discuss the 'extinguishing' of literature. As we knew it. As we know it. As you like it. As the world turns. All these things that we're going to get to. The things that are. For the things that were. The things that happened because of the smoking ban.

Incidentally when I worked in OK city for a couple of years many decades ago, I used to meet Conway Twitty in his honky-tonk when he was hardly known. He had a baritone mouth that was made to accommodate Cuban cigars which it did quite often. Nicely. Side-tracking again. There he goes again.

Sometimes I get carried away like that when I think my identity's safe. Which is a compliment to most of my readers. Except for the occasional forensic sleuth analyzing my handwriting. Just kidding. I'm on laptop now. She's on my lap-top now. I'm in the jailhouse now. [Jimmie Rodgers] Well, Conway (RIP) is now a helluva long way from OK City which is a helluva long way from anywhere. And if you think name-dropping during these confessions is one of the embellishments that I warned you about on page such-and-such, try writing your own confession with a non de plume. Feathers. (sic) Figures. Like those billionaire philanthropists donating anonymously. Right. Right-ee-o. Hee-Hee. Hee-Haw. Lord Haw-Haw. [William Joyce] Good lord. And no tax deductions either? Back to the weather.

Doesn't that tell you something? The conversation always shifts to the weather when you start to get bogged down. In soggy soil.

Between the cracks. Amongst the dandelions. In the tarvia. The freezing cold in winter. The midges in the summer. It's a seasonal thing. It's the season, stupid. We have few choices. We made one. You learn to live with it. Or die. Which happens. From known causes. That's all they say. The AT lawmakers. And those who get convulsions even thinking about us. We who still smoke. *whee ... hooo ...* Whee-whoo. Still smoke. *k*-smokers. On a mission for the reemergence of literature as we knew it. Always so negative, mean. Mean girls. Pessimistic, antagonistic. And cynical. Quoting H.L. Mencken, or He*ll* Mencken: Cynic - a man who, when he smells flowers, looks around for a coffin. Nail.

Nailed. Gotcha! Well, not exactly ... yet. That's the way they are. Hell! (Mencken) - you win some, you lose some. We lose all of them. Besides, I think I'm the one with nine lives, continuing my earlier reference to 'kat'. The number of times I was almost *k*aught, uncovered, since the official launch of the post-T era. And stupid *k*'s to make things worse. Along with this stupid spell-check not picking up half of 'em never mind the grammar. And sometimes the first, second and third persons contiguously in the same sentence. Makin' the readin' easier. Summertime, and the livin' is easier. [Gershwin] On the eye. Of the storm. Aye.

The official launch of the smoking ban. A launch that still reverberates like a shot once heard around the globe. From a smoking gun. As Julia Phillips put it eloquently: They'll Never Eat Launch (sic) in this Town Again. No, there ain't no free launches, babe, as the economy goes through a nervous breakdown with the loss of cig taxes.

Ah, my secret.

Walking the walk. Crawling most of the time, figuratively speaking. Steady on the ledge. On Grafton Street in November/We tripped lightly along the ledge. [Patrick Kavanagh] The kat with nine lives. And the mouse. And the muse. A game of role reversal. Sticks and stones will break my bones, but squeals will never hurt me. ouch! The mouse that roared. The kat and mouse on a dog day afternoon. Rainin' kats 'n dogs. With my brollie practically outside in. In. Out. Herein. Out here in the elements. Now that it's launchtime (sic) far away from the office. Good lord, what time is it? Huh. Not to fret. Got another min or two. A New York min. Or two. In a distant parking lot far, far away from civilization, gathering my thoughts, inhaling them. The writer who craves the stimulant, the nico. For inspiration. Without which a *k*loset-smoker cannot write with words that pound on the conscience.

My dirty little secret.

Reader: *Wait up! What secret are you talking about?*

Oh, haven't I told you yet? You see, I'm a writer.

The last writer on earth. Well, in much of the known world.

Besides being a smoker too. And in spite of it.

You can't have one without the other.

In my secret life.

In my secret life/In my secret life/In my secret life/In my secret life. [Leonard Cohen]

As Salvador Dali said: "The secret of my influence has always been that it remained secret."

whisshhh ...

oo-oooooh ...

25

~ ~ ~

My on-time and my off-time. Excuse me, I'm on my off time now. Well, fancy that. You could've fooled me. Well, you're easily fooled. Not quite. Talking to myself again. How interesting! You can tell a lot by the company you keep and your internal monologues. The interactivity of it all. When you're on a roll. In good company. Enjoying the conversation. *And* the company. You keep. In your secret life. Alone in the parking lot.

It's different in my other life, the public one, where they don't know I'm a smoker. In Mexico. Mumbai with Sushmita Sen (Ms Universe). Buenos Aires. In a dress suit on the Alps. Entertaining on a Parisian stage. The Pyramids. Bangkok.

You just join in the chorus when they talk about us (smokers) on my on-time. Mind you, nothing nice to say in the chorus. No, not much. Like a drunk in a midnight choir. Yes indeed, Leonard

Cohen had it half-right but we don't drink. At least, not when we're smoking. Except for coffee, usually cold because out here in the parking lot we're nowhere near where you can heat it up. When the heat's off. You do this on your own, in your secret little place. On your own time. Nico + caffeine. Hot coffee, cold coffee. Makes no difference, it's the caffeine, stupid.

Starbust used to serve 2 billion cups of coffee a year in the pre-T era when 21% of the population had fewer options to get their daily rush. Soon, a Star was born with the threat of the pending outright smoking ban and they went to 2 billion per day, for a daily average of 40-cups for the typical smoker who was nervous as hell and needed caffeine more than valium which was prescription-only. And, were forced to go to disposable cups with 10 percent recycled paper fibers which was a good thing, cutting its paper needs by 11,300 tons, or about 79,000 trees per every 2 billion cups. But it was a shooting star because soon people couldn't afford designer coffee and other leisure choices without cigarette taxes to drive the economy and sustain their habitual lifestyles. And anyway, without nico, coffee didn't taste too good. And that's when Starbust went bust. And everyone went back to tea. For two. But tea didn't have the same epinephrine to it with only half the caffeine (on average) for a 20-oz mug of coffee, a feature liked by cardiologists. And tea lacked the staying power for would-be writers, the *k*-smokers, in the midst of a fleeting inspiration. Which you had to capture. Instantly. With instant coffee. Plus nico.

Incidentally Starbust had already stopped using an extract made of dried insects to color some Frappuccinos and pastries after an online campaign asked for the ingredient to be removed. But that's neither here nor there. Which begs the question, how do you like your coffee? Hot or cold. She was both hot and cold at the same time. If you know what I mean. Ice cold. Ice-T. T for tobacco.

Hot potato. Cold potato. The game kids play. Games People Play. Grownups. And the game's over when there's only one person left in the circle, holding … it. Now, a cigarette. Between your left pointer and middle finger with your right holding your pen …

… drat! … darn ink between my thumb and pointer. Leaking old bic. Leaking like a sieve. What do I do now …? Excuse my mono-logue, I'll figure it out …

> *Reader:* *Yeah, go figure it out!*

And the game has just begun. Kat and mouse. Cops and Robbers. AT-kops and smokers.

We've only just begun/So many roads to choose/We start our walking and learn to run. [Carpenters] Run, run. My little runaway. [Del Shannon] Confused already? Okay, let's do a litmus test, and see if we can get this right.

First-off, for goodness sakes …we're only *k*loset smokers.

… background music … in your mind … if you could read my mind …

> *whisshhh …*

Hold it …

> *oo-oooooh*

Nice job

Thank you. Needed that.

You needed me.

You gave me strength/To stand alone again/To face the world/Out on my own again. [Anne Murray]

Now, where was I?

Got it.

No, we're not some Tom, Dick or Harry smoking up a perfect storm and rescued from the elements. We live in the elements. There's no hope for us. Return the heat-sensing S&R chopper before they zoom in on the flame. His latest flame. [Elvis]

Done.

And we're not social smokers, or social climbers, my dear. Or social anything when we're in this other life. In the post-T era we couldn't be. That would be a conflict of interest. What I mean is that we, well, at least me for one, were never social smokers. We smoke because it brings on the inspiration. Helps us write.

Which reminds me ... where are my matches when I need 'em?

Wait up for a sec on the next foolscap page. *Dum-dum-dum. Hmmm* ... Page number ... huh? Don't lose your train of thought. Choo-choo! Sorry guys. Must have the old nico ...

W h e r e   a r e   m y   m a t c h e s???

hmmm ...

(yet ... a n o t h e r ... pause.)

Ditto - Got it!

whew!

Pardon that little ...

All together now ... (well, me anyhow ...)

Inhale!   *whisshhh ...*

That's it. Let me check your pulse.

she: *Oh, doctor I'm in trouble.* [Sophia Loren]

he: *Well, goodness gracious me.* [Peter Sellers.]

29

(deep breath)

hmmm: *boody-boom boody-boom boody-boom boody-boom boody-boom boody-boom-boom-boom*

him: *Oh! hmmm. OK. Let me check your BP.*

her: *boom boody-boom boody-boom boody-boom*

him: *Well, goodness gracious me*

hmmm: *... 120/80. Good news, it's normal.*

hymn: *ave maria*

her: *ave maria*

Thanks doc.

You're welcome.

Now, exhale ...   *oo-oooooh ...*

zzzzzip!

Moby Dick!

Thar' she blows. There goes the mind. The after-effect. The fall-out. The whole shebang.

th th th th th th ...

The stutter effect.

thththththth ...

tsk, tsk ...

dsk ...

My aching back. Leaning against the trunk once too often. At the wrong angle.

This, my friend, is what you're reading in the inhale/exhale sequence. The experience. The creative force. Be with you. That's what happens. The stuff that comes out. The inspiration. From the drag. My confession. In a stream of consci*ence*ness. In the here and now. Read along. Read all about it. It works. The words that pound on the conscience.

The living proof. Live or Let Die. 007. Darn spies.

whisshhh ...

oo-oooooh ...

Stupid wind. In your face. In my face.
Darn ashes.

~ ~ ~

Some of you have probably noticed already throughout these confessions a reference [usually #8 font in brackets] to music or some other source. These mostly-oldies songs might seem to hit you in-the-face while trying to follow the confessional theme which itself becomes repetitive. You see, when I park my Chevy in my DIVINE MILIEU with the engine off, I set the ignition on auxiliary for AM. It would embarrass FM to be kaught dead with such oldies considering that the 14 to 25-year-old age-group pays for practically every consumer disposable nowadays. The problem is that you can't always be sure of AM with the elements the way they are inclined to be. Like today for example. Gloomy clouds on the horizon. Anyway, I set the volume on low. Not that I'd be distracting anyone because there's only me. Only me/Can make my dreams come true. [The Platters] Yet the music mustn't be the dominant sound. *That* belongs to the muse. And the nico.

whisshhh .... oo-oooooh ...

Then I roll down the window unless it's raining. I find the oldies relaxing, humming along with the singer as I'm composing my WIP scrawling my bic on my yellow legal-sized foolscap. I really hope these #8 font insertions won't be too distracting to you my readers. It's a habit I picked-up probably listening to CDs of the subliminal sounds of waves crashing against a craggy cliff helping me sleep at night. During the day it's the same subconscious context of music accommodating my concentration, with wordplay (...unless it's Neil Diamond's prose when I try to mentally fast-forward - which is impossible otherwise with a car radio and this old car's only other accessory is an 8-track player). And with melody, providing the perfect vehicle for the flow of words that pound on the conscience. If you have any comments about this, I'd love to hear them. Meet me under the clock after tennish. Just kidding. Maybe my publisher could work them into a sequel if these confessions ever get published.

~ ~ ~

On the role reversal metaphor in the game of kat and mouse to which I eluded; it might be useful to share a note about post-T era definitions.

Heisenberg

Heisenberg's Uncertainty ? *Principle applied to k-smokers*

The uncertainty principle inspired Einstein's remark that he couldn't believe God played dice with the universe. Simply stated: It is not possible to simultaneously determine, measure or know the position and momentum of a particle of smoke because the more precise the measurement of the position, for example, the less precise the knowledge of its momentum and vice versa. That is, measuring its position alters its momentum unpredictably, and by default, the makeup and genetic character of the smoker, the propulsion source of the particle. It is something like a situation in the normal world, where to comment: How silent it is here - is to destroy the silence. Hence, a *k*-smoker (a term introduced in the post-T era but having some of the features of a conventional closet-smoker prior to the A of C), is only such when he or she is not observed in the act. And, by default, since a *k*-smoker can only write words that pound on the conscience while under the influence of nicotine, if observed smoking, his or her gift of creative-writing instantly and permanently dries up because he or she can never again be, or wear the metaphorical cloak of a *k*-smoker. And, the awful derivation - sometimes when one can no longer contribute to one's mission of returning great literature to mankind, one succumbs.

Adapted from The World of Physics, The Einstein World, Simon & Schuster

It was kind of like Roswell because no one ever-ever saw a *k*loset-smoker in-the-act. If they did, then he'd or she'd or we'd (just kidding about the latter!) no longer be one. Heed my words. Sure, many *k*-smokers were caught by the AT-kops. But they weren't *k*-smokers *when* they were apprehended. Think about it. QED.

In modern times *Heisenberg's Uncertainty Principle* (or, Indeterminacy Principle) would probably fall into the same classification of respected scientific truths as the '3-second rule' applied to bacteria. Simply stated, when you carelessly drop a raw egg and it smashes on the hard kitchen tile, unless you scoop it up fast enough when the bacteria aren't looking, it's contaminated. And so, it's all in the 'observation' before things change utterly. As WB Yeats

once added: All changed, changed utterly: a terrible beauty is born.
[Easter, 1916]

The reason Heisenberg was so respected by *k*-smokers, then, is because the AT-kops had to prove that those apprehended were truly closet-smokers, while the evidence was to the contrary. Because, how can you be in-the-closet when you're 'caught' in-the-act of smoking in-the-open? Unfortunately, this *K*atch 21 didn't deter those arrested from being sent to the Mid X, which wasn't anything new, but it made them feel good in the unfairness of it all. Feeling alright/I'm not feeling good myself/Feeling alright/I don't have to feel alright/I'm feeling good myself/Boy you sure took me for a ride. [Joe Cocker]

whisshhh .... oo-oooooh ...

Incidentally, going back to an earlier comment (about he or she), I'm really uncertain [Heisenberg's Uncertainty] if there are any *she* *k*-smokers left had there ever been. I just don't know. *hmmm,* Maybe you do? That is, if you are one of us. Or … are you one of them? That's the risk I'm taking. Still, by the time you get to the end of this confession, hopefully the absolution part, I think you'll conclude that it would have to be one hell of a woman to survive. Were she a she? Which was a good point in trying times. The times of your life. [Paul Anka] When you just don't know for sure. Mac Davis wrote a song with that title which became one helluva hit for one helluva woman. Women just can't keep secrets. Trust me. Especially those they don't know which you couldn't divulge even if you wanted because no longer being a secret would nullify the very existence of the *k*-smoker.

Got it?

Gothic!

The AT-kops and the Bureau of T

An acronym you've already had a one-up on is AT-kops, the merciless anti-T police. The acronym derived from the former Bureau of ATF & Explosives which became simply the Bureau of T (admittedly sounding rather dull) - when alcohol, firearms & explosives were considered secondary threats to society versus smoking. After much debate the letter A (no longer referring to alcohol) was later decommissioned and recombined with T resulting in the current Bureau of AT (anti-tobacco). The appellation - Bureau of Tobacco - just didn't make sense. And, if anything, such a malapropism gave the impression of a free-for-all for the neurotic quitters during the transition-period, gasping for a quiet puff outside.

And you can bet your life that they're going to change the acronym again, probably to the Bureau of ATO ever since the acceleration of the obesity epidemic, debatably much worse than having a few quiet puffs even when it was legal. To be fat. Just kidding. Ironically as has already been hypothesized, in many cases the obesity pandemonium was a ravenous result of 21% of the population forced to quit along with the 79% who were already obese. It's only when obesity reached 100% of the population that people who were busy doing other things really began to take notice.

But a fat lot of use that was going to be since everyone was fat or getting fatter faster and the idea was too far out. On the far side. [Gary Larson] Anyway, people knew that there was no messing with the fat man because the current national urgency was solely on hunting down *k*-smokers who were habitually thin and shunned the spotlight unlike the fat lady in the opera. The whole thing was a harbinger of the ominous words of Britney Spears: What U see (is what you get).

Even during the honeymoon period while the ban was being debated in Congress it was still legal to smoke. And stay trim. But warnings of the imminent post-T era alerted smokers to be careful not to abuse the honor system. The situation was tense and people who normally weren't chain-smokers soon were. As a strategic as much as convenient consumer diversion in the waning days of the transition period, convenience and liquor stores were encouraged to open 8am Sunday mornings as a distraction for those addicted to tobacco to get their minds onto something else. Since weed hadn't yet become legal. It was the last of the blue laws to become 24/7 in a forsaken attempt to relieve 21% of the population from their pathological addiction in a nation at risk and prepare them for the worst.

whisshhh .... oo-oooooh ...

Another attempt at consoling the die-hards occurred, who had been smoking an average of 30-years a-piece and were totally unprepared for the pending A of C. It was called 'The Smoking Gun Program'. The first *Guns 'r' us* drive-through was opened in Hoboken, NJ, with practice rooms in previously packed bowling alleys and bingo parlors which were fast becoming empty casualties of the imminent smoking ban. They had to find some use for these alleys and parlors which had always been synonymous with smoke and couldn't possibly function without the habitual fog which added character to the ambiance like in an old black and white Cagney movie before color destroyed the reality.

It was only fair that certain distractions had been implemented for the 45 million adults plus some 4.5 million known high school students who would no longer be able to bum a cigarette. Or else it was the Mid X for the lot of them. The Mid X had no exclusion clause for juveniles regardless of how innocent they looked, indeed - in spite of it with their forged i.ds and prissy faces in the case of females, the mean girls that you associated with smoking and who always left forensic red lipstick on their tossed butts.

Most of those who were forced to quit, adults and juvenile delinquents alike, had unsuccessfully tried all kinds of placebos during the transition-period between the pre-T and the post-T era.

Butt (sic) it wouldn't be until the comeback of the #2 pencil when things would begin to stabilize - which the nation was about to realize would be the greatest placebo ever invented to mimic the sense-of-touch, the ubiquity of a cigarette.

If you had ever been in the company of someone who had just given up smoking prior to the post-T era, you know what I mean about quitting cold turkey. Albeit, in those cases, voluntarily or under extreme pressure from the missus. Which meant you knew you were going to light-up two-days later, tops, so it wasn't so bad. And, which is why the new relaxed 24/7 rules seemed to work for alcohol.

 And recreational firearms. 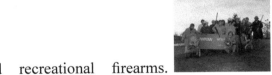 To get your mind off it. For a while. Rather creative. Karl Marx had written about it and so had Leona Helmsley. About this effect upon the masses. The little people. Who knew less and cared even more.

Additionally, *AT-kops* had a double entendre, intended to be pronounced: the *at* kops, or the *in-your-face* police. Because there was no plea bargaining if and when you got caught. It was worse than Steve McQueen as Papillon. Although supposedly the honeymoon-period when you were allowed to smoke was a grace period on the 'honor system', you'd better not count on it. People were watching. You couldn't trust your kids or your mistress who were constantly accusing you: "I know what you did last summer", indeed, exhaustingly finger-pointing with their sequel accusation: "I *still* know what you did last summer".

It was preposterous. Even if they were right. Or wrong. A sign of the times. For the good times were gone. Gone, baby, gone! Nobody seemed to care as long as the obnoxious smell of cig smoke was gone beneath the hovering CO_xs, SO_xs and NO_xs which the pundits guessed would envelop the eco for another hundred years. And then some. Long after everyone was gone. Everyone's Gone to the Moon. [Jonathan King] Ah, the good old days ...

Pardon me a moment ... A drag would do nicely right now. The craving just gets to you. The thirst for inspiration. The unbearable light ... ness of being. There we go again. Huh, gotta light? Milan Kundera.

kumbaya, kundera.

whisshhh ... oo-oooooh

Ahhhh ....Nice!

I'm at *hmmm* now (ala Peter Sellers pronunciation of 'home') – transposing this afternoon's draft onto my laptop. It's a lot warmer here in my study than shivering my timbers earlier in the parking lot adjacent to the woods. As far away from civilization as I can get. And still they seek us out.

I've warned you about my repetition, a sine qua non of any good confession. Me and Gordon Lightfoot. And his repetitive lyrics. And his repetitive lyrics. And his repetitive lyrics. Oh, did I forget to say: And his repetitive lyrics. For a good confession!

Me 'n Bobby McGee. And Janis, and Kris.

As a *k*-smoker on a mission to revive literature by writing great confessions in a desperate effort to prevent another lost civilization such as the Maya, Inca, Celt, Phoenician, Sarmat, or Scythian. Or the threat of another extinct language like Kashubian, Saterland-Frisian, Twendi, Busuu, Bodo, Ogiek, Yaaku, Defaka, Tsotsitaal, Ghodoberi, Udi, Manchu, Aka-Jeru creole, Kunigami, Chukchi, Yugh, Kanakanabu, Ishkashimi, Adnyamathanha, Gooniyandi or Gubbi-Gubbi – which story-telling in the English language was fast becoming (without the inspiration and the concentration which came from tobacco.)

whisshhh ... oo-oooooh

What is this adrenalin-inducing-inspiration from inhaling nicotine that has driven writers for donkeys' years to compose with words that pound on the conscience? Jonah Lehrer who literally turned-out to be a member of the liar's club, described it shortly after the A of C in his *Imagine: How Creativity Works* - as informing readers about the "anterior superior temporal gyrus, the posterior cingulate, the medial temporal lobe and the precuneus" – all areas of the brain. He explained how smokers like Auden, RL Stevenson, Philip K. Dick and Jack Kerouac relied on tobacco to fuel their imaginations.

In retaliation Kerouac albeit admitting his addiction to tobacco responded: "The only people for me are the mad ones, the ones who are mad to live, mad to talk, mad to be saved, desirous of everything at the same time, the ones who never yawn or say a commonplace thing, but burn, burn, burn, like fabulous yellow roman candles exploding like spiders across the stars and in the middle you see the blue centerlight pop and everybody goes, 'Awww!'"

You see, even in the impressionable years there were those of us who chose to be closet-smokers so that we could write undis-turbed, undistracted. Except, *hmmm* ... for the bugs in the eco. In the parking lot.

SWAT!

oops!

But it wasn't always necessary back then to pretend you didn't smoke in order to create great literature - as long as a writer acquired his or her inspiration from the concentration provided by nico. Like practically every great author in history who relied on tobacco. And allowed the recurring puff to drift naturally along with the gentle waft.

Then the no-smoking signs went up. And once again, we should've seen it coming. The early warning that things were getting worse was after the announcement that no MD, PA, NP, RN, psychologist, psychiatrist, physicist, pulmonologist, prosthodontist, urologist, veterinarian, nephrologist, cardiologist, dermatologist, chiropractor, acupuncturist, hospice-facilitator, hospital chaplain, astrologist, or lobby receptionist would see a patient concerning any ailment whatsoever if s/he had smoker's breath. And millions died instantly. This was still prior to the post-T era and presented a predicament for doctors themselves who smoked like-a-warehouse-on-fire when no one was looking and who now had to contend with themselves. Soon smokers were banned from entering hospitals, clinics, outpatients, emergency-rooms, lobby gift-shops, elevators and escalators, and basement prayer-chapels if they failed the bad-breathalyzer at the security checkpoint next to the good-cholesterol/bad cholesterol machines. When you didn't want to be near any good-looking nurse passing-by who might smell your bad smoker's breath. And no longer was it about halitosis and the anaerobic bacteria doing their aerobics either.

The fact of the matter is that the quality of writing had already begun to deteriorate when traditionally good writers were afraid to smoke because of the social antagonism which forced them to join the *tabagie*. And when smoking was banned outright, literature as we knew it collapsed and sales of adult comic books skyrocketed as people returned to their inner child. Soon there were more comic stores in malls than books at Barnes & Noble. Fiction had become synonymous with cartoon and non-fiction with tabloid. Libraries were downsizing because people weren't writing great books and shelves were left unstocked. Soon teachers had a shortfall of new literature to teach and there were many kids left behind.

Hence my secondary avocation. The mission of the *k*-smoker. Mission impossible. To initiate a revival, a literary renaissance from the underground in a nation at risk. Like Thomas Cahill's How the Irish saved Civilization, who preserved western civilization from utter destruction by the Germanic tribes (Visigoths, Huns, Franks, Sinatras, Angles, Saxons, Ostrogoths) after the collapse of the Roman Empire. And how the monks who were great cloistered smokers preserved the written word for centuries in books like The Book of Kells.

In the inhale/exhale experience.

With tobacco! The only proven stimulant to write great literature.

whisshhh ... oo-oooooh

With words that pound on the conscience.

Complete and unabridged. Unexpurgated. And to hell with the *k*. To hell and back. And to hell with the z in 'zigarette' in the new Kafkaesque dictionary which never took off, either. Good god. Thank god. And not just because of spell-check. I've got you under my *spell*. [Cole Porter]

Z as in zee. Along came a bee.

bzzzz ...

SWAT!

oops! In the parking lot.

The Uncountables

*K*loset-smokers are more menacing to the establishment because we're among the uncounted. There may be one of us in the underground. There may be a million. (Well, let's not get carried away.) The reality is that it's closer to the former ever since they brought in the heat-sensing helicopters. You only have to step outside and it's a gotcha from 2,000 feet - with the chopper zig zagging between the hovering CO_xs, SO_xs and NO_xs like Jimmy Doyle [Gene Hackman] in The French Connection. (Incidentally, once I lived next door to a Sikorski helicopter plant in Connecticut.) Or the bumper-cars at the state fair. Or Han Solo in Star Wars. The chopper never had it so good after its success in Miss Saigon – which did for Broadway musicals what JAWS did for Hollywood movies after actors were banned from smoking onscreen. When never again (except on re-runs) audiences would hear the classic words of Kim Novak to Frederick Marsh in *Middle of the Night*: "I missed you so much in the first two months that all I did was sit around and smoke in my hotel room".

You can't imagine how careful a *k*-smoker has to be. A good ear helps. And a good eye. Like my kid at Little League: *Good eye, Joey, good eye lad!* Of course, that's not his real name and it's been a long time since he played LL. Pal Joey. A good aye!

Maybe I'm it? Baby I'm Yours. [Barbara Lewis] The last smoker in the western world.

Reader (pointing):   *Hey, you're it!*

Anyway, it's bad manners to point. What's the point? At possibly the last *k*-smoker in the known world. You might call us the Uncountables, a caste in an increasingly predictable society. And, more than anything, that's what irritates the status quo, not knowing how many of us there are. As Rosemary Clooney used to say: You'll Never Know.

In keeping with the cliché, by now you must be thinking that this confession is just another Brave New World. Or, The Day the Kissing had to Stop. *hmmm ...* Or, maybe1984? All fine books written most likely by smokers. In the immortal words of Burt Bacharach: *What the world needs now are words, sweet words/It's the only thing that there's too little of ...* Words that pound on the conscience.

Just like we live two lives, even George Orwell had another name, Eric Blair. Orwell was a friend of a friend when he worked with the BBC during WWII. Erica was his first name. Just kidding.

Something I must do to maintain my writing buoyancy. Sink or swim. But there's a subtle difference since the smoking ban - with universal contempt, loathing and disgust for us. Fear and loathing in Las Vegas. [Hunter S. Thompson] Worse than the acclaimed (free) desktop wallpaper of Benicio Del Toro (in Traffic - https://wallpapercave. com/w/wp2326491) enjoying a quiet puff.

Darn. If these definitions ever get finished. Trying to balance my thesaurus on the trunk. With my jolly-brollie at-the-ready. Set, go. Without spilling my coffee. Were we in Calcutta we'd be called Untouchables. Or on another planet we'd be called apes. Hey monkey face. No, we're not a cult like Jim Jones' People's Temple or Charlton Heston's NRA, god rest his loaded Winchester. Winchester Cathedral/You're bringing me down …/You could've done something/But you didn't try …/Oh-bo-de-o-do oh-bo-de-o-do oh-bo-de-o-do de-do-duh. [The New Vaudeville Band] Incidentally I visited Winchester Cathedral once and I'm sad to say that I stood *on top of* Jane Austen's tomb – in the aisle - without realizing it. Which I wouldn't have done. Although it's a cement block in the ground. Seeming inappropriate for literature put to bed. For which the sacristan gave me hell.

Nor like David Koresh and his Waco Davidians who were wacos if you ask me. Groups. Groupies. But we are alone. And not forgotten. The Unforgotten. The Unforgiven.

And then it happened. The last straw was the **MANHATTAN PROLOGUE** 💀 when six adults and young twins, a boy and a girl, collapsed and died within forty seconds while walking into a tobacco smoke cloud beneath the canopy outside the ground floor entrance to the Time-Life Building. To this day it's not clear what really happened in Manhattan.

Until the actuaries came along with their statistics. Pardon me again.

whisshhh ...

Hold it.

Good.

And life would never be the same

oo-oooooh ...

again.

~ ~ ~

If they'd only lighten up, though, and get off my back on my off time. Mick Jagger said it eloquently: *Hey yoo, get offa my back. Hey yoo, get offa my back. Hey yoo, get offa my back. Don't hang around 'caus two's a crowd on my cloud.*

And let me write. In peace. More like rest. In peace. Requiescat in Pace. Let her rip. Let me rip. With my wip. On a roll. Rolling on a quiller.

Except for the constant looking behind my back as though I have something to hide. I do of course but it's not like that. Not skeletons in the *k*loset (no pun intended), the clandestine decadence of certain neuros that you'll always have. Mea maxima culpa. *whew! gulpa!* Just because I have a few puffs when no one's looking … Turn on, tune in, drop out. You'd think I was Timothy Leary with his remote. We're only using tobacco. Haven't killed anyone yet. I shot the sheriff, but I didn't shoot the deputy. [Eric Clapton]

And still alive and kickin'. Myself. Barely. Looking over my shoulder. Always looking over my shoulder. In an abandoned parking lot. Except for me. So technically it's not abandoned. To see if they're watching me writing my WIP. Waiting to prance at the first smell of tobacco. In the open air for godsakes. Like a dog. *woof!* The kat and the *muse. squeak* … Disrupting my thought process, my train of thought.

Chattanooga Choo Choo.

Aahh Chooooo!

God bless you.

All.

And may the good Lord have mercy …

The Union Pacific from the east and the Central Pacific from the west, meeting on the same track, Utah 1870.

Me in the middle.

Like being mugged in a dark alley. Where *k*-smokers are known to abide. Or at a railway crossing where one train may hide another. [Kenneth Koch] It would be tense enough standing alongside two trains passing, the relativity of it all in the embodiment of things flashing by recklessly. Converging into …

Collision!

Me in the muddle absorbing the impact.

And friends, this story is true. I know, because ...

I was that soldier. [Tex Ritter]

I am that smoker.

You knew there'd be a pun, didn't you?

You have to watch-out for a chapter with a header like: Cliché in the closet.

Yodeled by Tex Ritter in the punchline of the Deck of Cards monologue. Whose son, John [Three's Company Ritter] I met before he died. Which he did. RIP. Many of these people I knew - dying. And by default, the end of the trail. To me. Because – if they were alive and read these confessions after it becomes a best-seller – they'd put 2+2 2-gether and figure my ID. Go figure! My id.

Thank God. For my WIP. To make a difference. And the smokes which made it happen.

All those lonely people, where do they all come from? [The Beatles]

Me and the muse. Amusing. To them. Maybe. While all I'm looking for is that right word.

Paul Greenberg, the syndicated columnist, said it well:

> Give me words. The kind that pound on the conscience, crack open mysteries, let light shine, or undulate across the page until the reader is hypnotized; words that sooth or alarm, inform or galvanize, open starry skies or peer into hidden recesses. The right words in the right context are like discrete droplets that rise for a perfect instant when a great wave strikes solid rock. They're fresh as now, old as the world everlasting. They rinse the mind.

That's all I'm looking for, nothing more. Well, a few sentences worth of really powerful words. That open starry skies when you light up at night. Night and Day. [Cole Porter] Sinatra smoking up a storm. Although he wasn't a *k*-smoker.

Nor a writer.

Figures.

More a fighter.

POW! CRASH! BANG! DOINK!

Maybe you've seen some of these words-that-pound-on-the-conscience in the last few pages. I hope so. But believe me, they don't just happen. I need the smokes to do it. For creativity. The writer who craves the stimulant. For inspiration. However, instead of looking for that right word, most of the time I'm looking out for … them.

For … me. For survival.

On my off time.

In the way I can turn on and off like a light … switch.

There I go again. There he goes again. Every time the word 'light' crops up in this confession it reminds me it's time for a drag. Sorry about that. Just a tic. I promise. Be right with you.

No lighter fluid, huh? Stupid matches. Moisture must've got in. The wet look. One looks okay … Alright. Let's give it a try. But with my luck. *hmmm …*

Aha!

Uh-huh … Got it. Kool. Not the brand, silly. Cool cool water. [Frankie Laine] Go cool/Boy, boy, crazy boy/Get cool, boy. [West Side Story]

Ok. Let's go. Where were we? Wait.

whisshhh … oo-oooooh …

Concentrate. Elbow on trunk. Nifty breeze. Darn ashes ... Blowing in the wind. In my face. The things we do. The way we were. Are. Life. That's life.

~ ~ ~

On being a writer. Yeah. Pen in hand. Pen. Friend. More than I can say about them. A zillion words trying to get out. In the cold. Out. In. I do that a lot, don't I? No, you wouldn't know. Didn't think so. A day job in the media biz of all things. Mostly on the road. Helps. For a closet kinda-guy in his other life. Superman and Clark Kent. To pay the rent. And a writer's wip to pave my soul. We are discussing my confession, aren't we? Just doing a sanity check. A time out. On the beaten tarvia of this remote parking lot. The soul of my worn-out sole. In a ... oops. Walk carefully now. Shallow puddle. Just noticed ... huh? That wet feeling. All wet. If you ask me. When you're all washed up.

Jeez! No, not agai-nnnn ...

Puddle!

(trouble ...)

 Nincompoop! Poop. Sor...ry

Conrete tarvia of DIVINE MILIEU

Another pair of shoes. Down the Suwanee. The squishy socks feeling. You know the one. Wet socks against a sheepskin liner. Soggy socks. The inside sole. The Inner Game of Tennis. [Timothy Gallwey] No,

McEnroe didn't write that one. What was it? YES. You CanNOT Be Serious. No. Can't. Of course, you *k*an't. Darn spell-check gone awry again. Darn *k*'s. Darn *K*afka! What did I just say? You guessed it. I had a pint, or two, with Mac, once, but I don't think he'll remember.

Where was I? I remember. Do you remember? The things that happen when you sneak away for a quiet puff … or two. Another pair of ruined shoes. The trials and tribulations of being a *k*loset smoker. Nice job! Sure, don't mention it. I just did, didn't I?

Did. Didn't. The lies we live with. That we tell. That we make. That we are. But they're really not lies at all. Little white lies. Little green apples. God didn't make. [Bobby Goldsboro] Little red riding hood. What's white and black and *red* all over? A reverend mother with a dagger in her back. *ouch!* White and black. The gray between. The long gray line. Celluloid. Classics of the silver screen. When everyone smoked. The glamour of it all. Cellulite. Cellulose nitrate. Nice trait. Star power.

Audrey Hepburn in Breakfast at Tiffany's. With her elegant, indispensable 36-inch long cigarette holder allowing as much nicotine through as a #2 pencil placebo, like those Virginia Slims ultra-thins.

Little white lies. Or black and white. And read all over. My secret confession. Soon to be read by millions. If I can believe my publisher. Isn't anything private anymore? oops. Sorry. Forgetting myself. Rather - my personal exposé. My choice. Good word. No longer secret.

Okay, I made a choice. Life is choices. If you think about it. But not too much. In the comfort of your empty parking lot. Your private abandoned lot. My DIVINE MILIEU. Surrounded by midges and the occasional bee. Along came a bee ... *bzzz.* In the summertime. A seasonal thing. To everything there is a season/And a time for every purpose, under heaven. The Byrds. That's for the byrds! And the bees ... *bzzzz.* In the wide-open space. In the open air. Under heaven. With many mansions. My house is a very very very very fine house. [Graham Nash] Great view. Beneath the hovering CO_xs, SO_xs and NO_xs.

The birds and the bees. An Indian summer. Today.

bzzzz.

SWAT!

Darn bee. Darnbee. Darby. Derby pronounced Darby by the posh brits! With their Darby hats. Darby O'Gill and the Little People. [Janet Munro, Sean Connery] A wily old codger matches wits with the *King* of the Leprechauns.

Lucky my foolscap sheets work as a swatter. Whack. This is the season.

Turn turn turn. Turning in my grave.

whisshhh ...

They whish.

oo-oooooh ...

So, instead of telling them (back at the office) where I am which I couldn't (or who I am in my secret life ... *hmmm*) I just tell them where I'm not which I can in the hope they won't find me where I am. I think therefore I am. Sam I Am. Green Eggs. *And* Ham. *Or,* ham. Make up your mind, Dr. Seuss. I am. He said. To no one there. And no one heard, not even the ... chair. *Krazy.*

My weathered old soul. Old *King K*ole was a merry old soul and a merry old soul was he. The king and the puppet. *King* Creole. The *k*at and the mouse.

And the muse. Who must be coaxed, urged, prompted with a little help from 'ol Nic(o).

I just can't do it on my own.

~ ~ ~

Tried umpteen times, more often than you'd think, but the inspiration just dried up. Like a tossed towel at *home* (pronounced *hmmm* by the Brits) still bearing the hotel monogram.

I can't I can't I can't. Can you hear me yet?

I I I

can't can't can't.

*K*an't *k*an't *k*an't.

*K*an't we jez forget about it honey?

No, didn't think so. Makes no difference with the *c or k*. 'Cor*k*' as in County *Cork* if you say it fast enough. (Including *spaces between* c *and* k.) Even with your spell-check on mute.

Aye, aye aye-aye. Aye, aye aye-aye-aye. [Old German drinking song]

Are we there yet?

It's just up the road a bit. ... aye ...

Hey, I mean, a bit further than THAT! Oh, ok!.

The latest dilapidated parking lot I discovered. Aye. From parking lot to parking lot. From sea to shining sea. Until you find a deserted one. The deserted village. It takes a deserted village. Hillary. Who sends me the family pic each Christmas.

Not to mention the time Bill spotted me in the audience (in my 'other' life) and you could hear him whisper while finger-pointing - *at me*: "Oh God, I wonder what *he* told Hill this time!"

Bill Clinton and Dan Maffei pointing at the protagonist (Syracuse Post Standard)

The fact is that Hill & Bill needn't worry too much about me, trying to remain as anonymous as possible in case the sleuths put two and two together.

ssshhhh … !

whisshhh …

oo-ooooh ...

Maybe I can find some inspiration in this new, well ... it's not new, rather – 'other' parking lot, because I assure you all these abandoned PLs look pretty much the same-but-different as you learn in HS. And they ain't *purdy* as Gordon MacRae said in *Oklahoma*. Actually I met Howard Keel once and I told him how much I enjoyed his performance in *Oklahoma* until he muttered with an eye-dagger: "*THAT wasn't me my friend #%^&*?^! THAT was Gordon MacRae!*"

Aye! oops ... So much for that autograph!

And, just as I was getting used to the old (parking) lot, huh.

DARN! DARN! DARN!

I've grown accustomed to her face. ['enry 'iggins in My Fair Lady]

The last one (PL) had been abandoned but then came new construction. A new strip mall. darn. I was just getting used to it.

Then there's the rub. I'd never say it in mixed company, but psychologists suggest it's the only (darn) thing that smoking does for you – helps concentration. Opens the portal. Drops the drawbridge. Unclogs preconceptions (clogging the arteries by default). Provides a welcome break from the slew of born-again former smokers who just never gave up even when it was legal to have a quiet puff before the post-T era. Uncorks the magic genie (*ooh la-la*, nice ... Barbara Eden. I met Barb twice. Careful. She's still alive and kicking and more attractive than women a tenth of her age).

Unlocks secret passageways (Open, Sesame). *Barbara Eden*

Unleashes the mind.

whisshhh ...

Thar' goes the mind. A mote it is to trouble the mind. Mind yourself. A beautiful mind.

oo-ooooh ...

There goes the neighborhood. The deserted village.

Kome back, mind. Kumbaya, kumbaya. Kundera.

Reader: *Sounds to me like another kumbaya moment!*

zzzzip. Zip it.

And that my friend is my curse.

Writing and smoking, inhaling, exhaling. Sipping cold coffee from a foam container. An old wife's recipe, *hmmm* ... on how to avoid smoker's cough with a little swig of Delsym syrup. Coffee works for me. Let her down smoothly.

Up periscope. Down, doggie boy.  Boy? Watch it.

Go set a watchman. [Harper Lee] All around the watchtower [Dylan]

Doesn't work for chain smokers. Not to worry. I only smoke one at a time. Just kidding.

No, it ain't easy, babe. It's hard. And a hard rains gonna fall.

Better not forget my jolly-brollie tomorrow. Darn puddles. For godsakes!

oops (language!) ...

sorr-ee.

... bless me Father.

whisshhh ...

oo-ooooh ...

~ ~ ~

Incidentally, the preliminary conclusion from the research cited above: Smoking May Help your Concentration (Columbia University College of Physicians and Surgeons), was based on animals!

But they suspect that the study results may be applicable to humans, especially schizophrenics. And that nicotine may block some of the human brain's 'background noise' so a person can more easily focus on important information.

Reader: Huh – repeat that!?

*K*razy.

Yes, my first reaction was similar.

A study based on helping *ANIMALS* CONCENTRATE!?

With nico!

Okay, let's wait for the human factor. No, that won't be necessary with the smoking ban. End of study. Ite missa est. Go home.

But I am human, and I believe. Would you believe?

I Believe for Every Drop of Rain that Falls. [Ervin Drake]

Indeed, playwright Dennis Potter observed: 'Nobody has yet been able to demonstrate to me how I can join words into whole sentences on a blank page without a cigarette burning away between my lips.' While Iain Gately commented in his missive, Tobacco: 'The author John Fowles used tobacco as his muse. His writing table was covered in charred grooves where untended cigarettes had burned out.'

I rest my case. I'm used to it. It works. The works.

The words.

whisshhh ... oo-ooooh ...

There was a report in the Proceedings of the National Academy of Sciences about a drug, *Chantix* by Pfizer, which is not – I repeat, is not the sobriquet of that tall willowy blond model on the long narrow catwalk at such-and-such Parisian fashion show. Nor, Project Runway at Parsons, The New School in Manhattan. The study was intended to help the 79% of alcoholics who-also-smoked (prior to the A of C) ... to quit. They concluded that Chantix *helped rats to kick their drinking habit.* But that's neither here nor there.

To understand in simple language what smoking does for the *k*-smoker, Pfizer researchers put it well (before succumbing as a corporation from the dearth of mouthwash sales which was no longer needed with the concomitant end of bad breath in the demise of tobacco), as follows:

> Nicotine initiates its action by competitively binding at the nicotinic acetylcholine receptors (nAChRs), ligand-gated ion channels on the cell membrane. Compared with the endogenous agonist acetylcholine, nicotine causes a prolonged activation of nAChRs. The activation is followed by a desensitized state in

which the receptors are unresponsive to agonists. This process
has been compared to tripping a circuit breaker and inducing
smelly breath, especially if you are a Brit.

It might be useful for those of you (readers) who don't understand my/our plight (underground smokers) to memorize the
above explanation, especially the circuit breaker part. Pfizer then
concludes with a treatise on Behavioral Modification of the quitter
which will later be incorporated seamlessly into the # 2 Pencil
Syndrome. Incidentally (prior to the dawn of the post-T era sim-
plifying the choice) someone once said: *I'd give up smoking but
I'm not a quitter.* And another: *I'd quit smoking if I didn't think I'd
become one of those non-smokers.*

That was just a preview on the upcoming #2 pencil chapter.

Gotta run.

Sorry, I'm overdue. Missus expecting.

Me. Same time tomorrow, maybe.

Okay? I'll try not to be late.

whisshhh … oo-ooooh …

Reader: *Is this guy for real? I'm afraid of what tomorrow might bring. But I'm
hooked … oops, wrong word. Now I'm talking like him. Good lord …*

~ ~ ~

Every great *k*-smoker's work must have at least one complete
monologue. Tonight's the night.

Author's home hidden behind the camouflage

Nightfall. Night Watch [Rembrandt] Home at last, transcribing hand-written notes to laptop. Hello. Can't seem to make out such-and-such stupid word, scribble, never mind the sentence. Must've been in between swatting the midges with loose leaves of my notepad, darkness setting in beneath the light-pole. Have to improvise. Again. Used to that, practically all my adult life even before the post-T era. And chewing gum, now that I'm home. Hate the gum, doesn't work for improvisation. Mangles my teeth. Almost as bad as the #2. For others, I'd say. Though it helps somewhat with transcription. I'm a grinder you know, always was. Haven't told you everything yet. Though I wear my mouthguard in bed. Wandering again. Focus! A drag would be nice right now. Have to concentrate on the scribble part. *Whaz zat?* Missus on desktop ... *hmmm.* Daughter watching some stupid reality show on cable. Our son is ... well, you've got to be kidding, right? Anyway, none of them have the faintest idea where I was during lunchtime not that, god help us, they should know or would want to know. But in about 90-minutes I'll be saying: Look sweetie, gotta get something at the (24/7) drugstore downtown, the local closed at sevenish. Back in a fifty-jiffy, okay honey? I've been saying the same since before our kids were born. Don't think I've ever been missed for the proverbial 50 minutes. Never once asked what it was I needed to get at the drugstore when churchyards yawn. Or why it takes so long? So long Amigo. Don't even know if there's a drugstore open downtown. Probably. Urban renewal - yeah, sure! Just look around. *krazy.*

But so far it seems to have worked since we never kiss. The missus and me. Haven't for decades. ... *hmmm.* Anyway, regardless of whether we kiss or not you still have to be careful. I guess all it takes is a couple of strategically placed dabs of cologne, about five minutes gargling Scope on the drive back (stockpiled in an unused corner of my garage prior to its obsolescence after the ban). Then some mint chewing-gum 'upon landing'. But what's she doing online for so long?

hmmm ...

One of these nights, one of these *krazy* old nights/Swear I'm gonna find you one of these nights ... [Eagles]

~ ~ ~

Writing-and-smoking-inhaling-exhaling ... sipping-cold-coffee-from-a-foam-container. Words I had transcribed last night, huh.

There's a song with a beat like that. I'll paste it in later if I think of it. I remember the beat but not the words. I just tried to find it on the web while humming to the beat, relaxing at home. Without a cigarette – you know how that is. Surrounded by my loving family, all of them in other rooms. Upstairs, downstairs? She at her desktop? The missus is ... the missisis ...in the other room. Without the ippy. Mississ. Ippy. Yippi-i-a. Yippee-ki-ay.

Rollin' on the mississ ...

... zip.

But, without remembering a single word, at my age – worn-down with decades of smoking, what the hell could I google? Fat lot o' good, the web, huh.

Now then ...

Aha!

Isn't that how these things go - Eureka! Just remembered. No help from the web mind you. Another senior moment undone. The older you get they call it *lethologica,* recalling a word on the tip of your tongue. Something like '... wishin' an' hopin' an' thinkin' an' prayin'/plannin' an' dreamin' each night ... ' [Dusty Springfield] It's truly amazing how words just pop up at you like that when you've given-up all hope. Bob. Amazing grace. Thank you. Words that pound on the conscience. Anyway, saves me pasting it in above.

So much for Dusty Springfield.

Dusty Rhodes. Country roads. John Denver, whom I met twice. hmmm ... John Denver in Oklahoma then John Oklahoma in Denver. Just kidding. Getting old. Getting' windy in the parking lot. Well it was during today's draft. A draft in the draft. Daft! Before typing it up later.

Thinkin' an' … prayin'.

Nightfall.

One more night. Oh, whatta nighty. Naughty nighty! Do not go gentle into that good night [Dylan Thomas]

Ahh - but will you still love me tomorrow?! [The Shirelles]

whisshhh … oo-ooooh …

Anyway, one procedure without the other, i.e. smoking *or* writing, doesn't work. With the exception, that is, of what I'm doing now, typing it up. Don't need the smokes for wip cleanup, only during draft of the words that pound on the conscience. And we *seem to get by*. I don't mean about the missus and me. Of course, we do. I think. We're still married. Although it's my second, her first. But there was a boyfriend. Hers, duh. Anyway, let's clear this up - the missus and I *do* get along just fine as long as she doesn't know I'm a *k*-smoker. That would be the end of it. Of everything. I think.

hmmm …

We do all the other stuff – naturally.

Naturally.

Still, I wonder what she thinks of my never attempting to kiss her (… and vice-versa?)

That's a no-no in our happy marriage.

Anyway, the mention of 'seem-to-get-by' is that my handwritten work during the day (i.e. inspirational) blends nicely with the typing (the big easy) at night if I can read my scribble (usually proportional to the bug-exponential at any given moment in the parking lot) when I no longer need a drag. Well, not much. You see, I've practically finished another segment by sticking to this methodology which mate's harmony with coherency. Like a happily married couple. Each has a place. Quality time. Separate tables. Otherwise I'd surely be missed if I had to do everything at once, like the mafia without the cleanup guy. [Harvey Keitel in Pulp Fiction] Messy.

Still, with a little help from 'ol Nico … in the parking lot part of my dual life ...

In my secret life [Leonard Cohen]

Now, in my other life, I'm the extrovert. Then came part two, act two. You seemed to change/You acted strange (*hmmm...*)/And why I've never known. Added some Elvis to break the monologue.

In my other life.

Aha! You noticed 'me darlin' Morgan Fairchild in the last pic! Oh, did I forget to mention that once I got an upgrade from economy to 1st Class on a flight from HK to SF, nice – right! Until I was proudly escorted to my new seat -- sitting next to Joan Rivers and her male-partner for 14-(agonizing) hours. In fairness, the first 7-hours of listening was quite entertaining. Well, later I got to know Joan's daughter, Melissa, well, not THAT well!

Even eight long years after the A of C, yes, just the mention of the word 'cigarette' by anyone back at the office and it's the cold war! Although I pretend not to notice as everyone habitually, pre-dictably and impetuously rushes to check the draperies in the con-ference room for that telltale tobacco smell as if by osmosis. A slip o' the tongue will get you for sure. Water cooler palaver, next to the bulletin board sporting an oldie poster: DON'T THROW YOUR CIGARETTE ENDS ON THE FLOOR – THE COCKROACHES ARE GETTING CANCER!

Haw, haw, haw. Lord Haw Haw.

Idle chatter. Loose lips sink ships. Sink the Lusitania. Sink or swim. Tight lips raise ships. Raise the Titanic. My heart will go on. *King* of hearts. The *Queen* of Hearts still making tarts. [Patrick Kavanagh] Let's see if we can get a raise today. Boss. I got a rise out of that. Not bad.

Polite chatter, impolite chatter, with the cute little secretaries in their short ebony cocktail dresses (dressing like that at work, huh!), when they have nothing else to wear … oops, got carried away, I meant – to talk about. Except us. *K*-smokers in caps - in the great outdoors, destroying the eco with second-hand cancer. Giving cancer to trees. I mean, have you ever seen or even been close to a *k*-smoker? Heisenberg. I rest my case. When half of me is with them between 9 and 5. Working 9 to 5, working 9 to 5, oh yeah. [Dolly Parton] When they think they know me. You think you know me/Well, you don't know me/(no, you don't know me). [Ray Charles]

If they only knew. About (me).

Who'll rue the day that (he) was born. For sure. A slithering snake in the grass. On the grass. Standing at this moment on the mossy weeds between the cracks inviting the muse. Having an innocent puff in a ramshackle parking lot belonging to a weekend flea market when it's not the weekend. Thank God they don't have flea markets during the week. Still there were enough bugs swarming around me today. Walloping the critters really messes up my concentration although they're good for the eco.

They say. They say don't go on Wolverton Mountain/If you're looking for a smoke. [Claude *King*]

> *Reader:*   *Good god, this guy is serious. Another king even if this one is bracketed in #8 font.*

Definitely good for the eco. I've got to stop doing that.

SWAT!

oops. (embarrassing)

Well, um, next time, I promise.

The eco .... Umberto Eco's Foucault's Pendulum.

Say it fast three times!

It …?

Ok.

ittttttttttttttttttttttttttttttttttttttttttttttttttttttttttt …

Just tossed that in.

umbertoecosfoucaultspendulumumbertoecosfoucaultspendulu-
mumbertoecosfoucaultspendulum

Not bad.

Although Eco's book's not about the eco but about all kinds of conspiracy stuff to do with the Templar Knights. Much more interesting than what you'd find in an empty parking lot during the day. And nights in white satin. Dark knight. Day and knight. Darn spellcheck. Stupid *k*.

Still, I'm always tied to a self-imposed deadline to finish a sentence or paragraph before either getting back to work or *hmmm*. Can't get that Brit put-on intonation out o' me 'ead, pursing their lips: Cheerio, luv, I'm bloody-well going hmmm.

hmmm …

If you'll bear with me for just another few words …

Reader: *Awwwh, do we have to?*

Me: *Well, yes actually.*

Reader: *Awwwesome.*

And … one last drag. oops … don't like the *last* part. Too late. Typed.

Just one more, promise? Promise! Promises promises.

whisshhh …

Cross my heart and hope to die. Rather inappropriate. At my age. After 30-some-odd-years of smoking.

crikey!

oo-ooooh …

While back at the ranch all they do is blabber about us.
Blah, blabber, blah.

I'd hate to be the object of all their blabber, the pseudo-hypocrite with the pseudonym standing right beside them sometimes. At the water cooler. Like Patrick Swayze in Ghost. Watching everything. Taking notes. Well, mental notes.

While in fact I am the object. The subject. Interesting. Both at the same time. Who am. Whom? *hmmm* ... Try that Brit accent again. Amusing. Have you ever seen a limey you could take seriously? That's a gasser.

You've gotta be joking.

Gotta gotta gotta.

> *{Publisher's insert:*   *Deplorable English! YOU, sir, are better than this! I think? I hope?)}*
>
> *Me:*   *Ouch! I'm just trying to make a point. In context. Who's writing these confessions? Pleeze!*

Sorry, but I did that part about Patrick Swayze intentionally. RIP. The poor lad. You probably thought I made a slip. In name dropping. Leading to my own identification by reverse engineering? Don't worry. It's safe for me to mention Paddy, now. Sorry, Patrick. I knew him well, Horatio. [WS] Well, we weren't that close. I mean, I only met him once. God bless him and his holy soul. Because they weren't going to just go over to Patrick's ranch surrounded by close circuit surveillance cameras and razor-sharp barbed wire fences to keep the cattle at bay with a ton of armed bouncers and say: Hey, Patrick, do you know this guy who writes stuff and's a *k*loset smoker too? To wit?

Like, sure!? Y'think?

No, not Patrick Swayze even when he was alive. Although you never know after seeing him as a real ghost. He wouldn't send you to the Mid X. No way. Oliver Stone might – in the movie but not in real life. I met Oliver too and I'd trust him regardless of all his conspiracy theories.

As they blabber away. Which reminds me, hold a sec ... *aahhh!*

Okay. Last time today, I swear, or at least this afternoon.

Discipline has always been my strongest attribute. Comes with practice.

whisshhh ... oo-oooooh ...

~ ~ ~

Now might be a good time ... for the good times ... to enjoy a relaxing cigarette break ...

Reader   *(getting a bit pee'd):   Didn't ya just have one? !&^%*(#!**

... and try to retrace the anti-social fever that (for at least one of us) has led to our being exiled to, of all desolate places, parking lots. Yet, here in this place is my place. My DIVINE MILIEU. My ... Garden of Eden. My my my. Me o' my. When, looking back (over my shoulder for the AT-kops), nobody then eden (sic) heard of smoking.

Well, in fairness, there was only Adam. And, eden (sic) if there were tobacco leaves along with all the fruit trees, and if he smoked, there were no draperies to absorb the ghastly particles if Eve arrived home unexpectedly from a swim. So, there was nothing to gripe about.

My DIVINE MILIEU.

My beat-up ol' parkin' lot that I've frequented so often that it's my home away from home. Home on the range. Where seldom is heard a discouraging word/And the skies are not cloudy all day.

[Woody Guthrie] Where you are one with nature. Where the smoke you exhale is inhaled by the nurturing wind. The gentle breeze. And comes full circle.

Here in this place. Today …

In the year 2016.

She was only-sixteen, it was twenty-sixteen/I loved her toe …

[Sam Cooke]

Reader: *I'm warning you, you're cruising now!*

Can't believe it's really eight years since the last of the *anti* anti-smoking demonstrations were aborted which inevitably led to a global A of C in known countries which to the present day for known reasons excludes China, Russia, Rick's Place (Caz) and India.

whisshhh … oo-oooooh …

In fairness, frequent-flier holiday excursions with the usual blackout-dates were readily available to unaccompanied die-hard US male-singles with valid one-way visas for those who couldn't take it any longer - not being allowed to smoke. Indeed, some of the most popular butt-littered

resort towns were on the Black Sea.

They offered a respite after the much touted 42nd Street clean-up which was looking more and more like Singapore ever since chewing gum was banned there. They included Novorossiysk (Russia), Sevastopol (Ukraine), and Zonguldak (Turkey). Zonguldak was on the Turkish side of the Black Sea which had not yet joined the global ban while suffering implosion (being located dead center) due to the debate with heavy pressure from both east and west. Which would've confused the hell out of Confucius who once famously said: Go East, Young Man – because Istanbul was both east and west at the same time! Anyway, those who went on smoking vacations to Sevastopol (following the smoking ban, first, in the US) had an added coupon for a half-day's smoking at Yalta, just about 42km away, where they'd puff away while admiring the 100 meter high monument of Churchill (+ cigar), FDR (with his iconic cigarette holder) and Stalin (+ pipe) all smoking up a storm. It made them feel right at home like in the good old days.

But such trips were not recommended for those who hoped to return home someday because the new AT administration was petrified that they'd bring back the stinking tobacco smell in their belongings (hence the precaution of the one-way visa). Like bed bugs in their sleeping bags if they were returning from the Bronx or the infectious diseases such as smallpox and syphilis brought over to the new world by Christopher Columbus and the lads, accountable for up to 79% disease-induced population losses between 1500 and 1650 AD.

The AT-lawmakers were taking notes of exit-visas for secret smoking-junkets like a re-run on cable of the 1947-57 witch-hunts – in spite of the fact that India was still a democracy and should've been exempted. And Russia, when no one was looking, now called itself one. Anyway, as the die-hards boarded for the Black Sea you could hear them singing, *I'm leaving on a jet plane/Don't know if I'll be back again.* [Peter, Paul & Mary] It was a sad scene alright. While all of this was going-on in Russia and elsewhere, no one could hide the fact that the economy was a shamble due to the elimination of cig taxes back home. Quite frankly, few could afford to take advantage of the scenic advertising showing these exquisite smoking chalets in places far, far away. Still the trip-of-a-lifetime remained butt (sic) a childhood dream for many neurotics and suicidals who never came to grips with the smoking ban and could do darn all about it.

Unless they were writers. Like me, thank you for your kind observation!

On a mission. The missionary position. Man on a mission.

Who stayed at *hmmm...*

whisshhh ... oo-oooooh ...

These confessions are mostly a reflection on the social climate (pun) beneath the suffering CO_xs, SO_xs and NO_xs. in the eco during the transition of two administrations which ultimately led to the A of C. Some called the A of C the ABC due to the straight forward-ness of the ergonomic implementation of the Mid X where smokers when apprehended were chaperoned in cattle trucks in the middle of the night.

The smoking ban was to take effect at exactly 00:00:01 hours on New Year's morning 2009 and was timed to blend in nicely with all of the other new year resolutions. Except there was no going back on this one. And the nation which had been limping along after declaring the A of C was soon declaring bankruptcy which it hadn't had to do in a couple of years. Modern historians cede that this was a direct result of the loss of cig tax income which fed the Treasury. Fortunately, there was a buyer. Which was already the largest foreign holder of T-bills funded by their own cig taxes imposed on the 79% of a much larger population. And, who had been signing most of the (US) domestic receipts anyway. And this time T didn't stand for Tobacco. The whole thing was ironic because the world's largest tobacco consumer would soon rule the world's largest no-smoking population which was getting weaker daily with their nerves shot without a smoke or two to restore self-confidence.

And that's when the White House was painted Red. Red is the Rose. [The High *K*ings] On Monday January 26, 2009. Acknowledging the Lunar New Year of the Ox-ymoron. (Just kidding.) Of the Ox. Six days after BO'Bs first official day on the job. Not to be confused with the science-fiction conspiracy movie, The 6th Day.

CREDIT: Chicago Tribune, 2011

CREDIT: Rogers, Pittsburgh Gazette, 2009

The Chinese Connection, starring Gene Hackman and Roy Scheider – oops, wrong movie, will be covered in a sequel to this book – if this one ever gets published. (And, if the protagonist survives.)

... der-dum, der-dum, dum-dum, dum-dum, dum-dum, der-dum, dum-dum [Spielberg]

Combined with the loss of cig taxes, the US had never been able to break-even after the used-car fiasco in spite of calling them pre-owned vehicles (Car Allowance Rebate System, CARS, otherwise known as Cash for Clunkers), which cost the government $2.1-trillion in 2009. Soon after Detroit had bellied-up, all automobiles bought in the US were made-in-China, our new owner. Japan had long since ceased being a provider of cars to the USA in retaliation for the then incumbent-Presidency coercing them into joining the global smoking ban. The fact was that the coffers were empty at home. Yes, the imminent loss of cigarette taxes would be the last straw. The last fare thee well! The straw that broke the Camel's back. The third most popular brand.

Within a year Chinese would become the national language closely followed by Spanish with American a distant third, while English never having been spoken in Texas was abolished for similar reasons nationwide.

你能相信吗？

[Translation: "Would you believe!"]

In the midst of this social and economic upheaval, the creativity and concentration required for writing great literature (scientifically proven to emanate from inhaling nicotine) had been displaced by 500 reality sitcoms as a benefit of digitization and hi-def on cable and satellite. The highly deaf kids had already lost their hearing from personal i-pods which jammed-out every distraction. And cared less. Because they never read anyway. Which was one of the reasons that no one noticed that great literature was dying after the smoking ban.

whisshhh ... oo-ooooo

~ ~ ~

Meanwhile, back to my confessions. There are others who should probably take more credit than I for the intangible benefit of closet-smoking. Now and then there's a fool such as I. [Elvis] Tobias Wolff's very first published short story, Smokers, documented the concept in the following review from Fiction and Truth: The Works of Tobias Wolff, by Beth Higgins:

> *Smokers* is told from the perspective of a scholarship boy at the elite prep school Choate. It's one of four stories which has a first-person point of view. We never learn the boy's name. His parents and sister and brother live in Oregon. We don't learn their names either ... Despite the sketchy background, we learn the most important thing about him. ... The three boys chat and Talbot suggests they have a cigarette. Smoking is against the school rules; the punishment is expulsion. The narrator doesn't smoke but goes along because he's afraid of being left out. They hide in a closet in the music room and smoke.

While the above segment has many of the ingredients of an early closet smoker, you've already learned from Heisenberg that allowing a second person in the closet automatically eliminates both from being pure *k*-smokers. I offer the example in the event that you had mentally been making a similar comparison thus far into the chapter.

If you continue to have doubts about this confession, please see me afterwards. oops. No, I don't think that'll work. We'll get back to this issue later if you like. In the meantime, let's recap. *K*-smokers reach the creative-writing inspirational peak in the solitude of a chosen milieu over a quiet puff (or two) preferably accompanied with caffeine for the adrenalin rush with relaxation provided by oldies music quietly playing in the background. Got it?

Got it!

Just knocked something over ... huh? Got too much paraphernalia on this trunk. Foam coffee cup. Half-pack o'cigs. Thesaurus. Foolscap notepad. Yellow/green hiliter. Black bic, red bic. Brollie, sometimes. When you don't need it. Overnight courtesy-pouch which the airline inadvertently gave you once when you sat in the wrong seat. And resented when you wouldn't return it after being shamed into the back o' the Airbus. With mini-Scope, mini-Johnny Walker (just kidding), toothpaste/brush, a spare condom (just kidding), tiny container of cheap cologne with twist-top. Just in case. Not those pump-types that open-up under pressure. Stress. Doesn't have to be at 35,000 feet either. When bics leak. Where eagles dare.

Eight mins left on the clockboard. A couple o' paragraphs to go. Two paras. Max. One pariah. Mariah.

Me. You talkin' ta me?

Now ---- let her rip.

res-uuuuu-mmmmm ...mmmmm...

On a roll. Thar' she blows. We've got work to do. Words to do. That pound on the conscience.

~ ~ ~

For that matter will they put a hood over my head for the book tour (if and when my confessions get published)? Like the hostages in Tehran. That's a good one. Hostage. Prisoner of Zenda. The *king* of Ruritania. The *k*ing personified on the first page of this confession. That's okay. Go ahead. Look back. What? How can you go forward and backwards at the same time? There was a young lady called Bright/Whose speed was much faster than light/She went out one day/In a relative way/And came back the previous night. Take a quick peek. Be curious. Be alive! A'live, A'live O. Go for it. Do something gutsy today.

Gusty wind. darn. There goes my foolscap. Again.

whew!

Still six on the board before I'm due back. Due Back. Rick Jubeck. Just a guy I know. oops. Don't say that. Sleuths watching. Listening. Reading along. By association. For association. The Association. Along Comes Mary. Fingering the pages.

After a couple of time-outs. A couple o' puffs. Go on. Be brave.

And how could I autograph my name with a hood over my head? Let's be sensible.

With time on my side. Says who?

The stones … on the potholed tarmacadam. Potholes camouflaged by puddles. Must be doing something to my tires never mind (yet) another pair of brand-new roller-skates. oops. Sorry, shoes. Followed by: *You've got a brand-new key.* [Melanie] Which doesn't even rhyme. Reputably the worst lyrics ever written. Catchy melody though. Key. Quay. Quay-quay. Ki-ki. Kinky.

Hidden by potholes, huh. Hiding. Me and Salman Rushdie, whom I met once. But I'm really safe with Salman. I was raised on a salmon-fishing river.

As long as I don't tell. On him. Hiding. Well. Back then.

whisshhh ... oo-oooooh ...

~ ~ ~

Either we get caught eventually or succumb anyway. They hope. Hanging in there. Like a bird on a wire. Like an anthropoid balancing on a narrow ledge.

No ledge. Cogito ergo *non* sum. Descartes. Discarded.

A *k*at with nine lives. One ... left. Hand of God. Depart from me ye cursed into everlasting fire. We're used to that. The flame on the tip of ...

Which reminds me - didn't Dante write something about smokers? If he did, it sure wasn't in the Paradiso part of the trilogy, probably in the Inferno section, somewhere below the Ninth Circle.

Divine Comedy, what a joke. This is. This secret life. All unnecessary if you ask me.

Okay, I already talked about the book tour if my book gets published. But let's be rational. How could it possibly get published, even if it's honest enough (including the caveats), entertaining enough (for thus is the genre), and good enough (rather cocky of me don't you think)? I mean, isn't everything I'm confessing taking place in the underground? Are they just going to send an editor into the underground to go over some punctuation errors with you, like De Niro?

{Publisher's note*: --- Yes!*}

Hey you over there! (in the farthest extreme of the remotest parking lot.)

You talkin' ta me?

Louder!

You talkin' ta me - who else ya talkin' to?

Well, darn, guess it's gotta be you. I gotta be me …/Whether I'm right or whether I'm wrong …/I'll go it alone, that's how it must be

… [Sammy Davis Jr]

Alone. The life of a *k*-smoker. The quietude.

Louder!

There ain't nobody else around here that I can see.

Fair enough. It's gotta be you. I gotta be me.

The me generation. The me … Demi …

More!

I saw a beggar leaning on his wooden crutch/He said to me, "You must not ask for so much."

And a pretty woman leaning in her darkened door/She cried to me, "Hey, why not ask for more?"

[Leonard Cohen]

Me o my. My o me.

Following the 2008 election the incumbent president of the USA had tried to hoodwink the president-elect into taking responsibility for ratifying what was his own born-again instigation and which would result in a(n almost) global ban on smoking (Act of Cessation). It was necessary to 'convince' the 6 largest cigarette producers to cease and desist. This was easily accomplished with Japan whose plenipotentiaries were invited to a meeting in the Old Executive Office Building with the incumbent president who was known to randomly add to his Axes of Evil list depending on his mood! Conveniently playing over-and-over-again for the nervous Japanese guests in the waiting room - on a SONY boom-box was Barbra Streisand singing: If we had the chance to do it all again/Would we ... should we ...

 ## Two

Deep sixing the Big 6

Like many carefully construed plans affecting a nation at risk, there were bound to be at least a couple of house-keeping chores which delayed the implementation of the Act of Cessation. These delays pleased 21% of the population no end (the smokers), prolonging the agony of the inevitable and deferring the ecstasy of the majority. As Mark Twain put it nicely: *Whenever you find yourself on the side of the majority, it is time to smoke and reflect.*

It didn't help that <u>K</u>ing James I had gone on record by saying: "Smoking is a custom loathsome to the eye, hateful to the nose, harmful to the brain, dangerous to the lungs, and in the black, stinking fume thereof, nearest resembling the horrible Stygian smoke of the pit that is bottomless." Whatever!

But the delay shouldn't've been such a big deal for the anti-smoking lobby. The (global) ban was going to be sooner or later and the minority (the smokers) had better get used to it - like most minorities whenever the majority got angry. And the 79% were incensed!

Even then, during the transition period, smokers could only smoke in the comfort of their own outhouses, assuming all the household chores were done. This was before the *outright* ban but after the *indoor* ban for-the-sake-of-the-children: "If anyone causes one of these little ones ..." etc., etc., Matthew 18:6.

Technically these outhouses weren't 'indoor' not being part of the main house-structure, although they had a roof. *(Ah, ha) Oh, no, don't let the rain come down/My roof's got a hole in it and I might drown.* [The Brothers Four] Because of the nail-biting circumstances smokers were applying for building permits at a fanatical rate. Smoking outside in their lawns with only a chain-link fence (although legal during the transition period between the pre- and post-T eras) was not an option in case they might be seen by the neighbors and then what?

The code required that the outhouse be erected at a minimum of 100-feet from one's house in the event of drop-ins by the usual obnoxious neighbors who might hang on. Or linger. Like smoke suspended in a dry wind. Or a summer breeze. [Seals & Crofts] Smokers certainly didn't want to be anywhere close to their neighbors, so it suited them just fine to be in the outhouse doing their own thing. Outhouses had become the most popular form of home improvement nationwide even worse than outdoor-Jacuzzis in southern California where all the pretty girls were. And where nobody smoked because it was un-Californian. Except weed.

whisshhh ... oo-oooooh ...

Incidentally I should remind those readers who came in late that the (ultimately-almost-global) smoking ban had its roots when obnoxious neighbors (you know the kind), putting their hosts on the defensive, began remarking on the putrid smell of tobacco smoke while pointing at their living-room draperies. Which was an adjectival pun in itself. As if the smell weren't bad enough without the redundancy (if not bad manners) of finger-pointing. Of course, that was much further back in history when it was legal to smoke indoors when no one was looking.

On the contrary Glaucon, the cynic in Plato's 'Republic' who told Socrates that people would behave ethically only if they thought they were being watched, was "the guy who got it right."

At this point it's fair to point out that one investigative journalist at the time, raising his finger, interjected: *What's the point?* (that is, of all the finger-pointing in the paragraph up above at the living-room draperies). Ironically, had it not been for the enlightening neighbors, many housewives may never have realized this household phenom-enon: *What're we going to do about those smelly draperies, huh ...?*

But now at every opportunity you could observe single mothers and their male-companions arriving home in separate carpools from their flex-time jobs, huddling-up for a close smell of the draperies. Testing the theory. You know the way when something is staring you in the face all your life and you can't smell it. You don't notice it. Then someone mentions it to you and now you can't get it out of your mind. *I can't get it out of my mind/I can't get it out of my*

mind/I can't get it out of my mind. Oh no no, oh no no, oh no no.
[Ramones] Which is when the common-law divorce rate accelerated with each partner blaming the other for most of the tobacco smoke on the draperies in front of their lawyers. In hindsight it's fairly easy to understand how such an eye-opener about the draperies could've had such far-reaching implications for a nation at risk. Indeed, after the smoking ban with writers devoid of inspiration to write, there was little else to talk about without any new books being launched. Most conversations at social gatherings and cocktail parties turned to the draperies. And, what a miracle it was that they were now practically smell-free going-on almost a decade. There was even a Billboard Top 40 hit: *Smell free, as free as the wind blows/As free as the grass grows/Smell free to follow your heart.* [Andy Williams]

whisshhh ... oo-oooooh ...

It helped the anti-smoker's position that the AT rules were becoming more stringent in the 'honeymoon period' even before the official launch of the A of C, when you could smoke on the honor system when no one was looking. Most smokers had been metaphorically confined to the outhouse for years anyway before having to invest in home improvement add-ons with zero-interest loans (prior to the mortgage crisis wake-up call which didn't help the ensuing loss of cigarette taxes in a nation at risk). And, as if the 21% minority had a chance, smokers were too paranoid to express their opinions about the pending global ban following the outcry from the tragic **MANHATTAN PROLOGUE**. Eight innocent people had died instantly from spontaneous combustion caused by second-hand smoke. The nation was in tears.

Incidentally, until that tragic event, only lithium, used for both batteries and antidepressants, had an unfortunate habit of bursting into flames when exposed to oxygen – rather, to CO_xs, SO_xs and NO_xs.

Finally. there was proof!

79 million people had already died from smoking-related cancer since 1921 in developed countries (US, Europe, USSR, Canada, Japan, Australia, NZ) but the numbers excluded 2.1 billion in Third World countries and the deep south (where all the tobacco plantations were located, with free smokes at smoke-break). Yet there had never been proof of those instantly dying from second-hand smoke until New Year's Eve 2008 in Manhattan beneath the canopy of the TIME & Life building, triggering the A of C which became effective the following morning at precisely 00:06.01, incidentally '6-minutes late'! It was the Night they drove ol' Nico down. [Joan Baez]

TIME & Life Building, Manhattan – showing the legendary canopy, beneath which eight people died instantly by spontaneous combustion through no fault of their own

And just when you thought it was safe to walk out into the clean eco surrounded by zillions of molecules of CO_xs, SO_xs and NO_xs from here to high heaven, unexpectedly a double whammy was in the cards for the proponents of the global smoking ban.

~ ~ ~

The first delay had to do with toleration for the inalienable rights of sovereign nations which manufactured cigarettes albeit on a small scale. The other was the issue of publishing rights of a *k*loset-smoker in spite of the proposed illegality of his or her (lunchtime or nocturnal) secondary preoccupation. After all, it was a free country. As Lord Byron had put it much earlier about such publishing rights: *I'll publish right or wrong;/Fools are my theme, let satire be my song.*

At stake was the powerful if not provocative creativity of the *k*-smoker.

Author's insert *(commenting on my own comment):*

Ah, merci mesdames, messieurs, je vous remercie de taut coeur ... Thank you for that unexpected compliment on my provocative creativity

According to the previously cited study performed by Columbia University College of Physicians and Surgeons (although their study was performed on animals), nicotine soothed the mind in order to concentrate and encouraged the inspiration to create words that pound on the conscience. Indeed, as history would later confirm, immediately after the smoking ban people were running out of words and inspiration. Epitaphs appeared to be getting shorter on cemetery headstones. With the lawns meticulously mowed, the shrubbery trimmed and flowers of every hue. Such as roses, chrysanthemums, tulips, lilies, poinsettias, narcissus.

And, there was no turning back while the exasperated AT lawmakers were trying to come to grips with the two delays before smoking would inevitably be outlawed. It was a Mexican standoff. Although Filipinos and Mexicans both sported Latin roots from the glory days of the conquistador, Mexicans were now even more paranoid because 79% of the population smoked as in most underdeveloped countries that knew less and cared even more.

The mushrooming anti-smoking movement had the ugly appearances of globalization so the AT officials had to be careful on how they communicated the pending smoking ban, and how they would later implement it. There was fear of a whiplash if somehow the ban were construed as dystopian. It would be another derivation of Heisenberg gone wrong because Latinos this side of the border were uncountable at best. So how could you outlaw someone who may not exist; or incarcerate him or her for smoking?

whisshhh ... oo-oooooh ...

Habeas corpus. Show me the money? [Jerry Maguire] Quid pro quo. Right-e-o!

As the transition to the post-T era got going, that is, when the going got tough, the AT lawmakers had been riding the crest of a wave. The ballyhoo was like being in a soccer stadium filled with supporters (i.e. hooligans, were it Brits against the Dutch on neutral soil) of the winning team in a World Cup semi-final.

Which reminds me, I met Jack Charlton a couple of times, whom with his brother Bobby represented the Brit equivalent of the Jack & Bobby of Camelot, during the 1966 FIFA World Cup when the Brits

beat W. Germany 4–2 in the final. For trivia butts (sic) Bobby played for Manchester U while Jack played for Leeds U. But, that's neither here nor there unless forensic-readers are taking score by putting 2–2 together for my ID by association.

On the local level, the lawmakers were greeted in elementary schools, a popular caucus for the AT cause with standing ovations. Some of them were so small they had to stand on their desks to be seen but not heard. The kids that is. Until, as luck would have it (for us), a new poll by grownups suggested not everyone was impressed with the AT lawmaker actions due to the two surfacing patriotic events. As James Russell Lowell once wrote: *Our country right or wrong.*

And it was just when you thought it was safe to go back in the water.

And swim. Or sink. Or worse.

The musical score is supposed to come in here of an approaching shark, fin skimming the surface, and a little blood dripping …

◊

◊

◊

◊

but I'm not quite sure how to do that yet in 2-D

... *whoom-ba whoom-ba whoom-ba.*

Or

... *der-dum, der-dum, dum-dum, dum-dum, dum-dum, der-dum, dum-dum.*

Nope, that's what I thought - even as David Attenborough added to the guesswork: *Did you know that humans eat more sharks than sharks eat humans?*

Okay, let's try some Bobby Darin's Mack The Knife.

Incidentally, before we do that, I should confess that I was once introduced to Sandra Dee in between acts when she toured with Sabrina Fair while recovering from rehab. But that's neither here nor there, also, nor where she's at now.

Still, the only thing I had in common with her ex was being born with a micro valve prolapse like 21% of the population. Bobby didn't pre-medicate before his dental-visit, and that was that. In fairness, Sandra died too, albeit from known causes although she was quite the closet-smoker in her day as she told the Chicago Sun-Times in 1967: *I'd sneak off into the ladies' room and smoke a cigarette. Everyone thought I had kidney trouble. But I couldn't be seen smoking.*

Aha! A closet smoker out-of-the-closet and admitting it! Wherever Sandra is now. God bless her, too. On the plus side, lots of people have mvp's like John Elway (whom I met but isn't talking) and not only *k*-smokers who nonetheless should be more careful with their medication.

whisshhh ... oo-oooooh ...

Now back to Bobby: *Ya know, when that shark bites, with his teeth babe/Scarlet billows start to spread* ... [The Three-penny Opera]

Nope. Doesn't work either. Let's try sixpence, or a shilling, or a quarter.

Ironically, talking about sharks, I also met the B movie star Richard Kiel in a restaurant in Santa Monica with low ceilings. He was 7 feet 2 inches tall and played the towering steel-toothed hench-man JAWS in two 007 movies, The Spy Who Loved Me (when he bit the shark at the end

... der-dum, der-dum, dum-dum, dum-dum, dum-dum, der-dum, dum-dum ...

then swam away). And Moonraker.

Yesser, being a *k*-smoker, you had to be careful of spies.

Yasser? No, I never met him although I've been to Jerusalem. And other places. Well I've never been to heaven/But I've been to Oklahoma. [Three Dog Night]

~ ~ ~

Yes, two surfacing events delayed the A of C. First, there was a perceived threat of raising the specter of Wounded Knee by interfering with the inalienable tobacco rights of sovereign nations (incidentally, the only remaining source of smokes *after* the ban). The second specter resurrected images of Kristallnacht, Night of Broken Glass and Burned Manuscripts, by infringing upon the publishing rights of a *k*-smoker – since only smokers could concentrate to write great literature - whose creative-writing gift to a nation at risk was directly influenced by nicotine - according to the Columbia University College of Physicians and Surgeons (although their study was performed on animals). Hence, the issue was that non-fiction books, memoirs, crossword-puzzles and written confessions (good-and-bad) should not be banned in spite of the writer being outlawed albeit un-apprehended (the assumption) in the process of writing them.

Got that ...?

Got it!

Everyone knew that this dichotomy had an inverted version of Heisenberg written all over it. But, for the moment anyway, they seemed to care less.

In the first instance, the AT lawmakers had proposed banning the Indian nations' sovereign right to make their own brands which they had been doing on a small scale on the side without any fuss. But there were some 4000 combustible chemicals to take into account that could kill you over time if not properly combined, especially the carcinogens: dimethylnitrosamine, ethylmethylnitrosamine, nitroso-pyrrolidine, hydrazine, vinyl chloride, urethane, and formaldehyde.

whisshhh ... oo-oooooh ...

Anyway, the AT proposal to ban any indigenous group from manufacturing or importing/exporting tobacco followed upon the successful deep-sixing of the Big 6. These were

- Altria Group/Philip Morris International
- Imperial Tobacco Group/PLC
- Altadis SA
- Kohlberg Kravis Roberts & Co./RJR
- British American Tobacco/PLC
- and last but not least, Japan Tobacco/Gallagher Group PLC

That the deep-sixing could've been executed globally without too much ado about smoking was attributed to some heavy arm-twisting from the War Game den (the situation room) in the Old Executive Office Building. This building was next door to the GWBWH (which looked an awful lot like the antebellum plantation house, Tara, in GWTW; and was modeled in 1792 on Aras An Uachterain, the Irish president's home in Dublin, by architect James Hoban). Adjacent to the war game den was a comfortable sitting-room for visiting dignitaries representing the Big 6 who were clueless as to why they were called to the White House in the first place.

Incidentally, in the late-eighties I had a two-day business assignment in the RWRWH. The first 'W' stood for Wilson, like Wilson the gunslinger in Shane. Smoking was then permitted indoors but not outdoors (just kidding again) although even then I was a closet-smoker so it didn't make much difference to me. I only got to meet with chief of staff Donald Regan who didn't have a second 'a' in his surname for my troubles, but he gave me a black-felt-mimeographed glossy-pic

of Nancy and the Gipper. I could tell that the shiny gloss would've been tough to autograph with a #2 pencil which wasn't used as a placebo until it made a comeback after smoking was banned. Have you ever tried signing your name on a glossy pic with a #2?

So much for its conventional functionality.

And so much for that non-sequitur, never mind meeting Ollie North on his way out of the RWRWH (the second W for White). Permanently. On the same day. Or worse, if you can believe what the WSJ reported about Budget Director David Stockman whom I casually happened to meet in the men's room at Philadelphia airport not much later. And not what it sounds like either. The shoulder of his (Stockman's) three-piece pinstriped suit was covered in dandruff looking like dozens of polka-dots nicely contrasting with the pin-stripes. The dots and stripes. At a Polish wedding. Not to mention my once participating in India as an attendee to a Rupert Murdoch videoconference that his staff originated from Hong Kong. During the reign of the WJCWH back home.

And the whole thing was even crazier after the smoking ban in the BO'BWH. When the new president, being a rumored closet-smoker, realized the dilemma he had inherited! As if the president could just sneak-off for a quiet puff like the rest of us in an aban-doned parking lot when no one was looking.

whisshhh ... oo-oooooh ...

Which was only a rumor.

So much for my visit to the Old Exec Office Building. By now you're probably agreeing that none of this makes sense. Of whom I am. Which begs the question for the sleuths: who am I? Without risking my identity, the simplest answer is: I am *who am*. Pronounced like *hmmm* ... in the Brit vernacular. Incidentally, the reason I introduced the who's-who thread above is that some very normal things happened in my other lives, but I can't remember any of them off the cuff. Just a pun on David Stockman's dandruff. And, I have to be constantly alert, or revealing them will prompt the forensic readers among you. And you know *hmmm* you are (again, imagine Peter Sellers as the bumbling Inspector Clouseau pronouncing *whom*).

In fairness, many celebrities *hmmm* I've met in my media life were either too busy, too important, too embarrassed in their own other-lives, or too bored to be a threat to my identity as a *k*-smoker. An identity, which – if uncovered – would result in my immediate incarceration in the Mid X.

Not that they knew I was a *k*-smoker obviously [think: Heisenberg] but that, upon reading these confessions and regardless of the pseudonym - by piecing together the who [Pete Townshend] and where #1 [Waldo] and where #2 [Carmen Sandiego] and when ['... the evening shadows fall'] we met and what[sApp] was said, they might easily sleuth.

> *Reader:*   *What on earth has 'too-bored' to do with anything?*

I'm glad you asked. For example, George Sanders (no relation to George Saunders) whom I never met off-screen committed suicide because he was "too bored", which is what he wrote on the note he left behind. *For the only girl I e're did love/was the girl I left behind.* [early Dylan] Incidentally, have you ever seen a Brit who didn't look bored? *Could it be you just don't try/or is it the clothes you wear?* [Georgie *Boy,* The Seekers] Anyway, George went on to become the smoothest of villains in Tinsel Town even playing Dorian Gray. But watch out, Dorian - they're everywhere. Whose unexpurgated dying words that pound on the conscience mimicked his vivre de living: *Dear World, I am leaving because I am bored. I am leaving you with your worries in this sweet cesspool.* As he chain-smoked his final puff.

   whisshhh ... oo-oooooh ...

Crikey, what time is it? Only scheduled 50 minutes tops in the parking lot this afternoon. Got a spare quarter? No meters, huh. Lovely Rita meeta maid/Where would I be without you. [Beatles]

No, I'm not afraid of wiki-leaks. Nobody knows my secret life - the other me. Me me. Meme. Still, seeing their name in print after these confessions are published, many celeb friends of mine who are still alive and kicking could - by association reveal my pseudonym, John Player, which I could never use again. The sobriquet clings to you like molecules of smoke on fine draperies.

Miserable afternoon in the parking lot. Dog day afternoon. Raining dogs and *k*ats. Thank god I brought my brollie although it *was* practically blown outside-in. Out here in the elements. I'm starting to mix my tenses again. Well it *was* today when I drafted this latest piece that you're reading. Over a quiet puff or two. Tough to do beneath a brollie which you're holding with your other hand. And it *is* tonight as I'm typing it up in my *hmmm* study. But, I'm not *tense* typing this, now. I've already enjoyed my ration of puffs today. Now I'm relaxed because I don't have to keep looking over my shoulder which I did while having a quiet (relaxing) puff in the *past* (grammatical) *tense.* When it was then *tense* in the uncertainty of being caught by the AT kops but no longer *tense* because I have nothing to fear at *hmmm.* Although, in the *present tense* I am *only typing about being tense then* (but not now). I warned you in the intro about mixing my tenses. Being in two places at once. Like the phenomenon of bilocation, being in different places at the same time, one of the most remarkable gifts attributed to (St.) Padre Pio. His appearances on various of the continents are attested by numer-ous eyewitnesses, who either saw him or smelled the odors charac-teristically associated with his presence, described by some as roses and by others as tobacco. The phenomenon of odor (sometimes called the odor of sanctity) is itself well established in Padre Pio's case. But let's not digress.

Typing now at *hmmm* in my study, real-time, what I handwrote earlier, fantasy-time.

In a world of my own. With the muse. The inspiration. The gift that comes with a cost. That keeps on giving. Getting more tense by the minute. By the meter. Then. Now. In my study.

No, the celebrities I met will probably be too darn bored to make the association with my identity as a smoker and a writer. My secret. Better yet, many are too darn dead. And too bad for that. For them. Look, we're starting to get way off track. For security purposes, can we just leave my WH visit at that? Lots of folks took a hike to smell the cherry blossoms by taking a break from producing their own CO_2s, SO_xs and NO_xs back home in other ways. Their carbon footprint. And SO_x footprint. And NO_x footprint.

whisshhh ... oo-oooooh ...

koff ...

koff-koff ...

koff ...

Two cigs in this segment. Gotta give up these stupid weeds. Just a figure of speech. Some people think I'm smoking something else in order to write intensely. Like Coleridge in a fit of Kubla Khan. Vivid, luminous, irradiant, coruscating. A shaft of brilliant light. darn! Light! Every time I say light it reminds me it's time for another puff.

whisshhh ... oo-oooooh ...

But I promise, it's only tobacco. Not to worry.

Reader to readership: *Not another smoke! I hope he realizes that we're still waiting to see what he keeps referring to as great writing or great literature, huh? 'Huh'-bug! Humbug! hmmm ...*

~ ~ ~

So much for my little stroll along the cherry blossoms which were a gift to the city of Washington DC from Mayor Yukio of Tokyo in 1912 in an effort to enhance the growing friendship between the US and, apropos, Japan.

Now we have words to do.

Back to the Big 6 and the waiting-room adjacent to the War Game den in the GWBWH where the incumbent born-again president on yet another whim had decided to nix smoking at home and use his powers of persuasion to do so globally by associating the habit with the Axis of Evil.

The Last Smoker on Earth

Quietly watching the clock and frantically wondering what was coming next was the paranoid Japanese embassy contingent, the first delegation to be called to explain themselves, representing the subsidized Japan Tobacco/Gallagher Group PLC. Taking a quick look at their Fuji wallet-size pix of their elegant, reconstructed skyline, soon you will see why the Japanese didn't object too strenuously to the heavy *arm-twisting-or-else* to cease and desist manufacturing smokes.

       whisshhh ... oo-oooooh ...

Things had changed since 1912 and you could tell that the Japanese delegates had seen all the old John Wayne cowboy movies and knew well the meaning of Remember the Alamo. At first, they pretended to ignore the ultimatum to quit manufacturing clone-cigarettes in their inimitable way of manufacturing just about clone-everything-else. Well, until the new Chinese prosperity put an end to that, also, and you could no longer tell a Japanese-clone from a Chinese-clone. The delegation tried to relax in front of the large karaoke screen provided in respectful cognizance of their cultural preoccupations back *hmmm.*

Then, before you could say stand-and-deliver or Sayonara Mr. Chips, feeling déjà vu more than sentimental and intently following the cue-lines scrolling down before them (while keeping up with some difficulty), they were trying to mimic Barbra Streisand's Mem'ries:

Mem'ries/Light the corners of my mind/... Or has time rewritten ever line?

Then, dropping an octave or two at the last lyric, they were interrupted in the karaoke room by the joint chiefs of staff (who had been watching them through a one-way mirror) on an improvised visit from the Pentagon for an ad hoc meeting of the minds and quickly learned the score they were slowly reading:

If we had the chance to do it all again, tell me ...

would we ...?

could we ...?

should we ...?

And that's how the lights went out in Tokyo. The anti-smoking epidemic had gone oriental. The stakes were getting higher and the brakes were on Detroit.

Next up, the Latin Americans (Altadis SA) were an easier sell for the joint chiefs of staff, especially the Mexicans who had bigger concerns with the INS & DEA which they had nervously assumed *was* the agenda, and not an anti-tobacco lobby when it came their turn to wait in the lobby of the Old Exec Office Building. Realizing the meeting was only about tobacco (comprehendo?) you can just imagine their relief ...

whew

... in the non-smoking waiting-room when the hombres really needed one or two, wiping the sweat from their foreheads with their bananas (darn spell-check!).

And the interrogations continued. Ad nauseum.

All of this would result in the demise of the Big 6. However, in retaliation – it would be curtains (if not draperies) on the glass cages of the Big 3 in Detroit since, without cig taxes to fund the economy, there'd be no money to buy cars. Unless you lived in California. Where the T debate had long shifted from the model T in Detroit to the model 3 in Shanghai. It was all about numbers and tit for tat from the tete-a-tete in the karaoke room.

When the lights went out in Tokyo. [Vicki Lawrence]

And everyone wondered where their cigarettes were. Do you know where your ciggies are? While they were still lucky to have a Lucky Strike. Or two. At least during the honeymoon period before the outright ban, a grace period on the honor system when smokers were expected to refrain from smoking when no one was looking.

When the lights went out.

Light ... the corners of my mind ...

Light, huh ...

Which reminds me. Time for another drag. Bear with me a sec.

pause ...

     whisshhh ... oo-oooooh ...

Sorry about that. Really must apologize. I know the smell makes you nauseous. Virtual smell. Try not to use too much imagination. It won't get on your clothes. I promise. Maybe on the draperies? Think of something nice.

oops

That was the second cig I lit. Double the smell. In the seventh min! It takes six for one. Half-a-dozen for the other. Ok, let's make a deal. Last one. This will be the last one. [Mick Jagger] I don't mean the last one I'm ever going to smoke. Which it would be anyway when your time comes. The time has come for me to hang my head in shame/The time has come for me to say that I'm to blame. [Adam Faith] But it was the last one I had left.

First rule of creative writing: *Never*, run out of smokes.

Like Samson and the mythical moly, the proverbial mojo (charisma), enjoying a nice unwinding hair trim: *I pray thee, oh barber(ian), not too short. Easy on the ringlets.*

Then having relaxed for a few minutes of time-fleeting-by-recklessly with eyes-wide-shut, suddenly in a kneejerk reaction Samson realized what Delilah (looking gorgeous like Barbarella), disguised as a barberess - had been doing with the shears. Apparently, Delilah got carried away humming a bit too much of: *my my my Delilah/ whyeth whyeth whyeth Delilah* [Tom Jones] ... Then lost her concentration and was clipping away like a lawn mower in heat, until interrupted by that kneejerk reaction. Girl interrupted. On a rider-mower. Raising the specter of Winona, interrupted on her way out without a receipt. Easy rider. Easy goin'.

Holy Moseth (crieth a very disturbed, now impotent and practically bald Samson with a tonsure that was glabrous at best), *what hast thou doneth!? There goeth my strength!*

Publisher's Insert:Little did the protagonist realize at this juncture that, just as Samson lost his strength as he lost his hair, the parallelism of Heisenberg's Principle in his own demise. But let's not get ahead of ourselves.

Bad hair day. Here in the cold parking lot. Herein.

The very thought of it.

A *k*loset-smoker without smokes. A pub with no beer. There's nothing so lonesome, so dull or so drear/Than to stand in the bar of a pub with no beer. [Dubliners]

Never, run out of smokes. Never run out of mojo.

There goeth Delilah ... *away from me so hurriedly* ... [Patrick Kavanagh]

There goeth the neighborhood!

Wait up! Where are my ciggies? Where are the Snowdens of yesterday? [Catch 22 – Joseph Heller] Last one in the pack, huh. Leader of the pack. [The Shangri-Las] gazoom! Starting to panic now.

oops!

> Reader: *Panic, huh? I thought you said you weren't a chain smoker and could*
> *stop any time but that you only smoked for the inspiration?*

Holy Moses! Sorry. Scratch that. Forgot you were reading. ha ha. Not panicking at all. No, not much. Already had my rations. Two today. A tu-tu day.

> Reader: *Stop that!*

Say it fast – tootoodae. Tooth decay. See what happens with tooth (sic) many cigarettes over thirty years. Yippi-i-a. If this were ww-two I'd be smoking like a chimney with limitless rations. Have you ever seen a vintage war movie where the GI Joe wasn't shooting at something or somebody never mind talking or muttering – always with a Lucky Strike hanging from his bottom lip like a windowsill with the window partially up?

~ ~ ~

Ah, you are observant. That's what I enjoy about this confession – the interactivity. Besides the Big 6 we did omit a few other notable T producers who didn't bother the AT lawmakers because their production maxed out for their own consumption. Indonesia [PT Gudang Garam], the world's fifth-largest cigarette market was a hopeless case anyway where 79% of the population smoked and good riddance right there. Incidentally, if you need smoking stats for the Indian sub-continent, just take everything I say about Indonesia and multiply it by ten, excluding Indian Territory in Cherokee, Oklahoma. But let's not digress.

Although hospital records weren't published, reputably China also boasted 79% smokers. The snag was that the Chinese government was the nation's sole T producer. China National Tobacco Corp churned out seventy-nine-trillion cigarettes annually (do the math) which accounted for five packs-a-day for every smoker left standing. Double Happiness and Good Fortune were the two most popular feel-good brands accountable for some 21,000 deaths directly attributable to smoking each day in each of the 21 provinces which include Henan, Hainan, Hunan, Hubei, Heilongjiang, gradually increasing in unpronounceability until you give up. And that's only on the H's. And another 79,000 casualties from second-hand smoke each week with no baby boom in sight for the long-term preservation of the species. Ciggies turned out to be much more effective in curbing population growth than in their wildest imagination. The new prosperity was causing social headaches in implementing the one-child policy (at least) in trying to keep up with the death rate. The irony was that if you were caught smoking in the West, it was off to the Mid X for you and never heard from again. On the other hand, if you were caught *not-smoking* in China it was a similar excursion for the felon since smoking was the only guaranteed method of curbing the population explosion. I met Zhu Rongji once in Shenzhen in 1996 when he was vice-premier (before becoming premier the following year) and that's exactly what he told me.

The WH wasn't going to touch that one. And as far as our first-name relationship with Russia was concerned, their position had become clear even back in Yeltsin's days when he said: *A man must live like a great, bright flame and burn as brightly as he can.*

whisshhh … oo-oooooh …

So much for the smoking culture and social structure of China, Russia, Indonesia, and India. These accounted for the few exceptions where the anti-smoking movement, initiated by the US, died from known causes, never having really got off the ground particularly in rural areas where the word hadn't spread like other known diseases. Indeed, like the mostly unsuccessful attempt to replace the letter *c* with the Kafkaesque *k* in our own country. While in Cuba they only smoked cigars and never got sucked-in to the global movement to ban cigarettes.

Ironically the first anti-T rebellion was put down and stubbed-out in Europe. The French were always bull headed and it was like 1798 all over again with 79% of the population believing in liberty to smoke and acting-out their consciences. Proudly, they put up a good fight, but the resistance wasn't what it used to be in WWII when they capitulated to avoid Paris burning and her nice buildings destroyed – forever immortalized in Mona Lisa's grin. *grrrrr!!* However, the smokers performed gallantly and were more chivalrous than the

Tottenham riots in North London three years later (2011) giving a bad name to soccer hooligans. But it was no use. The minority French anti-smoking lobby under the tyrannical influence of the US AT-administration argued that majority rule might lead to a 'tyranny of the majority'. It made absolutely no sense that the majority of the French population being smokers and *mesdames et messieurs*, lost out to the minority non-smoking ruffian population who were revolting if not repugnant. But the French never made sense anyway and the aftermath was a mystery.

Back home the real challenge confronting the AT kops readying for the A of C was the *tabagie* (which, depending on your accent, sounded an awful lot like the Latin dative case of *tobacco*). The *tabagie* congregated outside chapels, pubs, bowling alleys, bingo parlors, ice cream parlors, bike-repair shops, massage parlors, honky-tonks, and casinos where smoking had already been banned indoors, meaning that people only smoked indoors when no one was looking or cared less. Unless they worried about inhaling their own exhale being confined in tight spaces such that the pulmonary baro-trauma on their respiratory tract might more quickly escalate into pneumothorox followed by pneumomediastinum and ultimately succumb to subcutaneous emphysema. Meanwhile, bingo, the game of choice for the obese had already moved outdoors. And, as it said in the good book: Thus, you will know them by their tummies.
[Matthew 7:20]

Again, people were getting fatter faster without the dangers of indoor smoking to curb their weight now that bingo had moved outside where they smoked less because there was no atmosphere for outdoor bingo.

Back in the WH the beat went on with the who-wants-to-be-our-allies on the cease-and-desist axis-program. And if you weren't with us, well … you know the rest of the score as the Japanese had learned in the karaoke parlor adjacent to the situation-room, while (the heads-up was that) the Mid X was being prepared to accommodate dissenters. Predictably the Brits (British American Tobacco/ PLC) just cruised along like in their silly Carry On movies with the arm-twisting from the WH, sporting feigned grins as they're inclined to do. Incidentally, Jay Leno once remarked: *Here's an odd fact. According to the AARP, brushing your teeth causes up to 4,000 injuries a year.* To which the Brits said, *See!* And that was long before the comeback of the #2 pencil and the adrenalin rush to the nearest maxillofacial prosthodontist.

During the same week Tony Blair said he found that the press can be beastly. But that was then, and statistics were in.

whisshhh … oo-oooooh …

~ ~ ~

Let's finish with the two hiccups first which delayed the A of C, if we're ever going to make it to the next chapter. If we make it to December. [Merle Haggard] The best is yet to come. Didn't we just discuss this? Flipping ahead does exactly the same thing. You lose the gist. Could we have a little bit o' hush and a little bit o' shush for those who want to read the rest of my confession. Thanks. Don't know which is worse, *k*-smokers or turbocharged readers.

whew!

Anyway, in deference to the AT lawmakers back home in the US …

Reader: *I thought we were back home in the US? What's going on here? You make a quick reference to China and suddenly you think you're writing from Heilongjiang or worse, one of those increasingly unpronounceable provinces! Jeez!*

... what shocked the masses most (the 79% non-smoking population) was that there could've been any objection as to the way things were being handled during the honeymoon period prior to the total ban. Most reasonably minded people felt that the Native Americans had enough discrimination for at least two centuries and should be allowed to smoke and to manufacture cigarettes. In the meantime, many parents were getting concerned that without a renaissance of literature that would be lost with the smoking ban (when writers would no longer be able to write without the inspiration and concentration emanated from nico) – that their kids would suffer even more.

Some parents were having second thoughts on long range implications if the bills weren't paid and if the homework wasn't done. Ultimately, the data showed that the US hadn't just bottomed in science and math in global competition – but were flunking in spoken-American relative to the S. Koreans and Chinese speaking English as their 1st language. And soon teaching E*F*L themselves to the Americans who never learned to speak English properly.

Soon, thousands of daily letters to the editor of the Daily News (and weekly to Time magazine) about the latest plight of the sovereign nations were penned by diehard apologists.

Reader: *How many thousand times have I told you not to exaggerate?*

Precisely. If you ask me - a thousand stars in the sky. [Kathy Young] Which begs the question - how many days can a mountain exist. [Dylan] Rather, A Thousand Days: JFK in the WH. [Arthur M. Schlesinger Jr]

Indeed, I saw JFK in person in June 1963, five months before they shot him. And, of all serendipities, I met Walter Cronkite in 2002 forty years after the assassination but even then there wasn't too much more any of us could say. Sadly, it had already been said.

Even before that I had phoned Jacqueline Kennedy Onassis when she was a consulting editor at Viking Press in 1977 but I was minutes too late as she had just left to take a position as a book editor at Doubleday. Hence, we never did get to meet in the Grill Room of the Four Seasons where she liked to sit in the Siberian balcony, to discuss George Catlin's drawings of North American Indians, one of her coffee-table projects. Ahh - I always get that adrenalin run for caffeine when I see any reference to a coffee-table. Where was I? Oh yes, and then Jackie finally stopped smoking having been a three-pack-a-day smoker - four months before dying of cancer in 1994.

whisshhh ... oo-oooooh ...

~ ~ ~

Letters to the editor

There was the usual plethora of reminders during the transition to the post-T era such as this one:

Is nowhere precious anymore with smoke wafting across public parks? I look forward to walking the wide-open spaces without watching out for the burning end of a cigarette. I can choose not to purchase a deep-fried Twinkie but I cannot choose to be safe from tobacco smoke. This letter started an obesity stampede to the nearest concession.

Another. *When I was a smoker, people were always coming up to me saying: Miss, your smoke's bothering me. I'd say, Hey, it's killing me.* Wendy Liebman wrote that one. And so forth.

Soon smoking would be banned outdoors, in the foggy alleys of Shepherd's Bush of Jack the Ripper fame. And, a crime for a *k*-smoker to light up even for a quiet one or two in the privacy of his-or-her favorite abandoned parking lot.

Still, the other reason for the delay of the A of C, it wasn't clear if a *k*-smoker would also forfeit publishing rights for his or her underground WIP which took countless cartons and hours of concentration to create. Along with millions of minutes of lost-life because the rule-of-thumb (do-the-math) was that a smoker lost one minute of longevity per cig smoked. And most of them looked it.

Yesterday and today, author's friend, Linda Blair, as Regan in The Exorcist. Linda grew up to be a great smoker.

Incidentally Linda confided to me that her head didn't spin 360-degrees in the movie, but it was a Hollywood trick.

The quandary confronting the exasperated AT lawmakers was how far they would be willing to bend the pending anti-smoking laws to allow creativity in any abandoned parking lot for a *k*-smoker to write great literature – provided no one was looking - under what would be the illicit influence of tobacco. Surely, they wished that Heisenberg were still alive to put the matter in perspective. Unwittingly, had he only lived to see it with his own eyes - Heisenberg (1901-1976, Nobel Prize in Physics 1932) had helped create the DIVINE MILIEU in the underground, based on the book of the same name written in 1926 and set in a 'parking-lot' by the French Jesuit, philosopher, paleontologist and geologist, Teilhard De Chardin's (1881-1955), in his great companion work to Phenomenon of Man.

whisshhh ... oo-oooooh ...

At this time in our social history during the final days of the honeymoon-period, the problem was simply that the tobacco smoke kept clinging to the draperies. Like the ivy that clings to the wall.

[Rod McKuen]

To the Wall. To the lighthouse.

The wall the wall the wall. [Pink Floyd] A hole in the wall.

Tear down this wall.

And the Walls Came Tumbling Down.

~ ~ ~

At the eleventh hour, before the A of C would become effective (New Year's Day, January 1, 2009), some 21 pages of a relatively obscure clause in the 1788 confederation treaty had been printed intact in a letter to the editor in an extended edition which, incidentally, prompted follow-up letters with a plea to the publisher to Save The Trees. The treaty had been signed by both sides now.

The latter qualification was eventually endorsed by Joni Mitchell, a truly great smoker in her day which is most certainly why she was such a great storyteller in her lyrics. Who once told Neil McCormick that "cigarettes are sensuous. It's one of life's great pleasures", as she "exhaled a small cloud through wide nostrils". And surely that small cloud is where the immortal words came from: "I look at clouds from both sides now".

But there were other popular smoking songs too.

I smoke alone, yeah/with nobody else/I smoke alone, yeah/with nobody else/You know when I smoke alone/I prefer to be by myself. [George Thorogood and The Destroyers]

Smoke, smoke, smoke that cigarette/Puff, puff, puff and if you smoke yourself to death/Tell St. Peter at the Golden Gate/That you hate to make him wait/But you just gotta have another cigarette. [Tex Williams]

I feel mighty lonesome/Haven't slept a week/Black coffee ... Sunday in this weekday ... and in between the nicotine ... not much to fight ...it's driving me crazy. [Ella Fitzgerald]

Goodbye old sleepy head / I'm packing you in like I said ... remember darling / Don't smoke in bed. [Nina Simone]

A cigarette, no, well I don't smoke them as a rule / But I'll have one, it might be fun with something cool. [Julie London]

Let's have a smoke/Why shouldn't we have a smoke/Now is the time for it/While we are young. [Nat King Cole]

Bring back that smoking feeling, that smoking feeling. [Righteous Brothers]

Anyway, the tribes, and the executives from the original Old Executive Office (recently name-changed to the Eisenhower building) convened in the GWBWH, within which the Department of the Interior was comfortably located with the interior decorations and wall tapestries matching the ideology of the moment. The 1788 clause was supported by the 1492 precedent when Columbus traveled to the West Indies and saw Native Americans smoking tobacco.

Then, in Jamestown, circa 1612, the Powhatan were found smoking a crude indigenous species of tobacco and, fair play - credit where credit was due. The evidence further stated that tobacco had been used by medicine men as a cure for ailments like some elderly ladies in modern times drinking their nightly frothy pint because they believed the byline literally, *Guinness is Good (healthy!) for You.* The records also showed that the Jaredites, Mulekites, Nephites, and Lamanites – the early Indians who came to the New World from Israel as far back as 600 B.C. smoked their own cigarette brands.

Pardon me for a calibration check. This confession is getting way too historical. Be right back …

whisshhh ... oo-oooooh ...

Thanks. I needed that.

Reader: *You're welcome.*

Incidentally on the subject of soliloquy and non-sequitur, the rhetorical response is another feature of the interior monologue *gone* wrong which Joyce had borrowed from Edouard Dujardin's *Les Lauriers sont coupes.* For example, 'from beneath the chaos of appearance' – the critics swore up and down that he (Joyce) took it (the stream of consciousness) from Freud, whom you will recall was addicted to cigars. Paraphrasing Dujardin, the mind of the *k*-smoker 'is a continual mixing of lyricism and prose' and the novel therefore an incessant balancing 'of poetic exaltation and the ordinariness of any old day' in the wide-open parking lot, come rain, hail, snow or shine. Furthermore, in keeping with our theme of smoking and great literature, in the Lotus Eaters Episode 5 of Ulysses, Bloom *"thinks of the calm narcotic effect of smoking."*

I rest my case. QED.

Pardon me. More darn bugs swarming around this parking lot today than white Baptist crosses in Danville, Illinois. As Samuel Smiles once called them: ladders that lead to heaven. Incidentally, rumor had it that Danville was the only town in the US with more churches than Polish pubs. With no beer.

Darn bugs.

Swat!

Sorry about that.

(poor bugs.)

Ultimately, as the day of reckoning approached for the rest of the nation at risk, millions of free dvds were mass mailed to every *hmmm* in the USA of Thank You for Smoking (The Movie). It had been the final assault (some surmised, insult) by the T-industry. It backfired because the title was interpreted literally in the WH screaming (sic) room where they watched the absurdity with restrained indignation and abstract confusion although quietly splitting their sides laughing when someone asked: *Gotta light*? That someone was fired on the spot for her untimely sense of humor and political incorrectness during the crucial transition period between the pre-T and the post-T eras. And the advent of the A of C and the Mid X. Oliver Stone wrote a story about it called Heaven on Earth.

But for me the earth would be the cracked tarvia beneath: I feel the earth move under my feet/I feel the sky tumbling down …, as it was nicely described by Carole *K*ing.

There he goes again, the *k*ing and the puppet. William *K*ing, rhythm-and-blues musician (The Commodores). The King of Jordan, Abdullah II.

Finishing up this paragraph with my notepad resting on my chevy trunk, one final observation as I gather my ...

Just a min. Hold your whist ...

whisshh ...

Sorry. Running late. Trying to get a whole bunch of ideas to foolscap before I forget. Not a heck of a lot of time, left (pun) ...

    oo-oooooh ...

relief ... haahhhhh ... hhhh ... hh ... h ... relax ...

danke schoen. xie xie. merci. toda. sukria. grazie. dziekuje. bloc-noc schnookie.

Oh, quickly, I once met with Henry *K*ing at a conference (no relation of Larry whom I also had the privilege of meeting but whose real name was Zeiger and not a king at all until he became famous. Although he, Larry, could smoke smoke-rings better than anyone I knew in those days but a rather senseless skill nowadays).

A former prosecutor for the Nuremberg War Crimes who had interviewed Albert Speer, Mr. (Henry) King, Esq. was a youthful looking 89 when we chatted following his paper. And, when asked by the chair: *Well, Mr. King, would you care to elaborate for the audience what have you done with your life, sir?* - he replied to the standing-room only crowd: *I interviewed Albert Speer.*

And that was it!

And nobody heard/Not even the chair. [Neil Diamond's claim for the Nobel Prize in Lit] Until I realized - what else could possibly be said? Because many years ago I had slept in Hotel Lutetia in Paris, tossing and fumbling all night. Without a cig nor a local 7/11 open 24/7 to buy a pack. Until apprised upon check-out that my room had been Hitler's map room during the German occupation. But let's not digress.

We had been discussing that nobody knows a *k*-smoker although everyone knows *of* them. Of us. Bobby Goldsboro went on record by saying: *hmmm, no one knows, no one knows.* Then Leonard Cohen countered with: *Everybody knows!* It was really hard to tell and the whole thing was confusing as hell.

But nobody knew a *k*loset-smoker personally or met one in person that they could tell, in his/her other life. Half-life (you'd think we were talking about radioactive decay) but don't take this personally. Which would've been tough anyway because you were never seen to be heard or understood to be comprehended or confronted to be apprehended. But *we* had a secret, were a secret. Still are. I hope. Me anyway. Going to press. Stop the press! Stop the world/I want to get off. [Anthony Newley]

And everything seemed to be going quite well. Until one day you noticed the large clock on the post office wall went missing. Then the clocks at major and regional airports began to disappear. One by one. It took a while but soon you realized that all municipal and institutional clocks were taken down from walls. It was no longer 'tear down this wall' but take down the darn clock. Because they were worried that you'd notice how long you'd been waiting. In keeping with the non-sequitur. And the repetition. For a good confession. For Godot. Thank godot.

Ok, I owe it to my readers to expound once again upon the need for repetition in a confession.

Singer/songwriter Prince said: There's joy in repetition. Indeed, Gertrude Stein was characterized for her vigorous application of repetition. Here's an example: Shutters shut and open so do queens. Shutters shut and shutters and so shutters shut and shutters and so and so shutters and so shutters shut and so shutters shut and shutters and so. And so shutters shut and so and also. And also and so and so and also. [From: If I told him, a Completed Portrait of Picasso] I rest my case. Again.

~ ~ ~

✓ Checklist before returning to office:

Do your bit for the eco, lad. Pick up your butts. Visually inspect that the last butt is out by dousing it in the thick residue at the bottom of your Starbust cup which doesn't taste much like coffee anyhow after 50 minutes. Dispose cup in nearest side-street garbage container on drive back to work, or outside a McDonald's. No one looking of course.

~ ~ ~

The day-shift call-center operators on the reservations were sympathetic to *k*-smoker(s). They also recalled having a rough time of it in the unpaved lanes, narrow alleys and abandoned parking lots where they lived back home. A euphemism for many. They had come all the way from India seeking a better toss of the dice by night in the casinos. That is, until globalization exported most of their jobs to Calcutta from where they had just come.

whisshhh ... oo-oooooh ...

Indeed, after the A of C was passed, jobs were getting tight. There was just no telling how many *k*-smokers were left to support their production-rates – the Native American reservations being the only remaining source of cigarettes, albeit exclusively for internal

consumption. With one exception, the reservations could sell cigarettes to *k*-smoker(s) simply because – we didn't exist! [Heisenberg]

hmmm ...

While all of this was going-on, things were quite busy back at
the call-center. At least they pretended they were for job security.
Soon, for security (and INS) purposes all cigarette transactions
from *k*-smoker(s) would be performed by 800 number. Regular mail
order delivery was guaranteed in an eco-friendly brown bag to your
private P.O. Box. *Please Mister Postman, look and see/(Oh yeah)If
there's a package in your bag for me/...You didn't stop to make me
feel better/By leavin' me a carton or a letter.* [The Carpenters] There was
a minimum order of four cartons twice-a-month! That was almost a
dead giveaway and bordering on chain-smoking. Anyway, that you
had a personal PO Box, exclusively for that purpose, was a secret
from your family. *hmmm ...* In the event of accidental or indiscrimi-
nate curiosity in an age of dustbin forensics. And the nondescript
brown package might've suggested you were hiding something.

Small deliveries were vital. It was never recommended to order a
year's supply of smokes because you didn't know how long you'd
be alive.

Either you got caught and vanished
or, for reasons touted by the American L Association, you just
weren't around anymore. I guess it doesn't matter anymore. [Buddy

Holly] And good riddance to bad rubbish. In the garbage cans. Outside McDonald's.

Or, there was the rare event that you became one of them!

A quitter!

Because you just couldn't take the aggravation if you hadn't the makings of a creative writer, like celebrities who use ghost-writers to overcome that weakness. Or, not a good writer, like most biographers more concerned with self-aggrandizement than the idiot they were writing about. And there was always the paranoia that you'd be caught. Then, next-up - Fed Ex! oops. Mid X. Midnight deliveries only. In the rear, please. Rear Window. Looking over your shoulder.

The phone order was simple, direct, no questions asked except for the 3-digit code on the back of your credit card for those who were apprehended fairly quickly by the AT-kops. Assuming there were others? And uncomplicated. The trick for me was to barter. You signed-over the expected royalties of your book to the sovereign nation by email, scanning your signature. It didn't matter that all future confessions would be repetitive and contiguous more than a sequel because you could always assume a different pseudonym which you didn't need to do in the anonymity of a regular confession. If you confessed regularly. Confessing the same sins over and over again as if you'd never learn.

whisshhh ... oo-oooooh

Well, that was the theory but I'm sure you've gathered that I'm still crawling my way through the underground. Figuratively speaking. In today's pathetic weather conditions. Without my brollie. Mild and misty with periods of light rain interspersed with showers and occasional periods of scattered sunshine. Sky, two to four shades of gray. Fifty shades of grey. Forty Shades of Green [Johnny Cash] Vegetation lush. Everything damp. And, at times, your spirits.

And so, the circumstances of such a publication, whether yours or any *k*-smoker's, were ironically deferred to the second of the pivotal events driven by letters-to-the-editor – the publishing rights of books written by *k*-smokers. Otherwise – the renaissance of literature was dead before it got started.

Which mattered to some people following 5000 years of intellectual and literary pursuit. Especially in China, the oldest civilization, where they would never think of giving up smoking after 5000 years. R.I.P.

RIP WIP

WIP RIP

ripwipripwipripwipripwipripwipripwipripwipripwipripwipripwipripwipripwip

woof! woof! woof!

Reader: *Who let that dog out?*

Who's afraid of the big bad wolf?

Who's afraid of (Leonard and) Virginia Woolf?

woolf! woolf! woolf!

Jack the WIP-per.

Yes indeed, the second issue almost kyboshed the A of C and was more than a nuisance for the AT lawmakers especially after the ACLU got involved. Some devils' advocates actually became defensive when it came to censorship of literature. And good lit could not be written without the associated nico. They saw that the writing would soon be on the wall only. Grafitti. It was encroaching upon their own profundity. For example, when James Brady asked (the singer) Tom Jones if he had ever read Fielding's Tom Jones, he replied: *No, but I have the book in my library.* Which was profound indeed. You'd think we were discussing HOWL. Or worse. Before Kerouac (god bless him, a heavy smoker) gave some respectability to the rest of the Beats who were flying high as a kite most of the time. And were pretty beat the following am. Like himself.

Nonetheless the expected receipts from your next book were in exchange for a year's supply of smokes from the sovereign nation manufacturing facility delivered at the rate of one shipment per *fortnight* and the transaction was a wash.

oops.

Fortnight!!! What did I just write?

F-O-R-T-N-I-G-H-T! Hope the forensics don't pick-up on the anglo for a 2-weeker which has been known to provide an assimilative ID for those born overseas. darn. Too late. Typed. Just have to wait and see if anyone noticed. Retarded, my daughter would say.

Protagonist's daughter – from a distance.

Protagonist in happier times - from a distance – as giddy as his daughter - before the Act of Cessation

Before the A of C, kids who simply smoked for kicks were a different breathe (sic) than when I was growing up with the glamorous movie stars of the silver screen, cigarettes dangling from their ruby-red lips. Like the dreamy-eyed Lauren Bacall. Or Kate Hepburn 'puffing away at a cigarette as though she might be sneaking a smoke behind the garage' (quote from Anne Edwards' bio), a sure sign of a closet-smoker. Whom, god bless her, lived to be 96, with her 'wit, strong opinions and intelligence' (quoting The Smoking Gun concerning creative people who usually get their inspiration from smoking). Or Viv Leigh who smoked four packs a day during filming of GWTW. Blowing smoke in the refreshing breeze. Breezing along. With her windswept hair and a curling iron in her left hand. Unplugged. Between her pointer and middle finger. Just kidding. But seriously, Ms. Leigh just hated kissing Clark Gable during the film shoot because of the foul odor emanating from his dentures. Then there was Leslie Howard in Service for Ladies, striking two matches, one with each hand, and lighting the cigarettes of Elizabeth Allan and Annie Esmond (as Duchess) on either side of him.

Or these nurses on break: 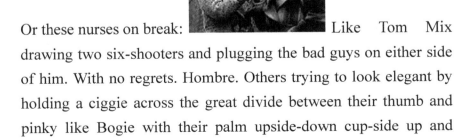 Like Tom Mix drawing two six-shooters and plugging the bad guys on either side of him. With no regrets. Hombre. Others trying to look elegant by holding a ciggie across the great divide between their thumb and pinky like Bogie with their palm upside-down cup-side up and sucking the smoke though like some Asian people drinking soup instead of eating it.

ouch!

oopie!

I warned you that this confession would be PI to everyone. To former-smokers, anti-smokers, Latinos, pan-Asians, paddys, limeys-with-their-crooked-teeth-and-smelly-breath (always-picking-their-pointed-noses), American Indians, Calcutta-Indians, catholics & prostitutes, B-movie stars, bishops, imans, rabbis and lawyers!

whisshhh ... oo-oooooh

Which (drinking soup instead of eating it!) infuriated Miss Manners no end in spite of her Guide to Excruciatingly Correct Behavior (the only time she was observed losing it). While Marie Antoinette would've said: Let them eat cake instead of soup.

In fairness to the movie industry, the glamor wasn't only about smoking. Acting did require a lot of skill. As Roger Moore confessed: *My acting range? Left eyebrow raised, right eyebrow raised.* Dirk Bogarde's performance in VICTIM was reported, '... his left eyebrow arched, his fingers playing with his ear and chin'. While the self-effacing Robert Mitchum told Barry Norman for the BBC: *Look, I have two kinds of acting, one on a horse and one off a horse. That's it!* When asked to elaborate he reprised in an impressive raconteur, *I've got a hat, a colt and a gun, that's all I need!*

Now picture the heroine of the golden age of the silver screen. Rehearsing her lines convincingly in front of a smoke-stained mirror in her boudoir. In deep concentration with the help of a puff or two. The smoke having exited both mouth *and* nostrils in a stream like steam from a leaky pressure-cooker - rising to the lines on her forehead caused by the inhibition of collagen production. In a fully relaxed demeanor, the cigarette adhered to her bottom lip, puffing away while reciting her lines. Simultaneously. The collaborative motion between her tongue and the roof of her mouth like clothes agitating in a heavy-duty washing machine. Almost as bad as the gaffer on the set having a quiet puff while chewing gum but without any words to recite. Just following the action. Not to mention the best-boys. Who find it hard enough to talk intelligently without their props never mind doing so with a ciggie in their mouth when the director isn't looking. The leading lady smoking away like nobody's business ... in show business. Like no business I know. [Irving Berlin] And somehow the cigarette doesn't fall out. Still hanging on her lip even when she coos her lips full circle in the scene at the moment of truth in the plot when she realizes the game is up.

Always astonished me about these glamorous screen stars. The darn cigarette just resting on the bottom lip as if on a designer ashtray, at a slight downward slope, the mouth half-open without any upper prop borrowed from the gaffer to keep the cig in place. Think: Shelley Winters. Without interrupting the dialog. Except for the occasional embarrassing *koff* which, when kaught in the act, they try to disguise with a respectable sounding *ahem*. The tongue wriggling around in synch with the temperament of the lips. And, the stupid cig still dangling like a lyric in Simon & Garfunkel's dangling conversation. Or, for those who gave their lips a break – the ciggie now glued between their yellow index and middle fingers right down to their final puff.

whisshhh ... oo-oooooh

121

Got a little off-track there. Need to watch my vocabulary next time.

But 'fortnight'! Jeepers! Still, can't believe I wrote such a give-away word in my attempt to discombobulate reality by interweaving cliché, hyperbole and other embellishments throughout this exposé to make the theme appear fictitious. I mean, who knows who's reading this confession? Maybe some limey tourist who would surely know what a fortnight is.

The underlying question was: Who shot JR? Just kidding. Need to do that sometimes.

Who then had the AT-kops been incarcerating in the Mid X – having rounded-up all dissident smokers in the first years of the A of C - if they weren't catching *k*-smokers? And, did such a 'place' even exist, like limbo, regardless of the evidence and the hoopla? Was the Mid X really a figment of somebody's imagination gone wild? A somebody-done-somebody-wrong place? The whole thing was akin to purgatory for believers. For purification.

A good analogy in the pre-T era (to try and understand the existence of the Mid X) applied to terminally ill agnostics (after smoking one too many): 'what-if' there were an afterlife? Perchance to dream? Yes, it was better to play it safe and believe in the Mid X because you just never know. Instant-death was too good for us as was the notorious average 8-minutes Hickock & Smith swing-time immortalized by Truman Capote.

whisshhh ... oo-oooooh

~ ~ ~

The (early) success of the post-T era was soon rapidly thrashing the concept of the zero-sum society. The good news was that – if the ban were successful globally (fat chance going to print!) - actuary insurers projected that the 100-million people dying from second-hand smoke each year would soon live to be as old and as healthy as George Burns, d. 1996 at age 100 still smoking 15 cigars each day up to his dying breath. Although Freddie Starr said about himself, that he'd 'been smoking for 30 years and there's nothing wrong with my lung'. Or at least to be nonagenarians in their stockinged feet or certainly a cut above the pre-T life expectancy.

Nonetheless, the expanded longevity-thing wasn't for everyone. Like *k*-smoking, there were risks and social side-effects. If you weren't constantly looking over your shoulder. For the bugs.

Swat!

In fairness, many diva movie star survivors of the silver screen, prima donnas, grand dames clinging to their gold-plated ashplant-knobs, who knew how to carry a cigarette in their day weren't too excited. It was bad enough to have to live through regular longevity with their telltale wrinkles and laugh lines that weren't laughing anymore and frown marks that were, and noses that had seen their share of medical-scientific nose-how. Frankly, there was no denying that they were still pretty darn ugly and in denial because the decades of aluminum siding no longer adhered like the cigs hanging from their ruby-red lips in the glory days. The divas hadn't expected this extension of maybe five more years, ten tops. They didn't need it. As Bette Davis once said: I have eyes like a bullfrog, a neck like an ostrich, and long, limp hair. You just have to be good to survive with that kind of equipment.

Many thought they were much better off with the nominal life-expectancy of 80-years (female) when they had been smoking up a storm. But now in the post-T era, smoking was forbidden even in the great back lots of the epic studios unless you could prove that it was for art's sake. Many of them were coming up with imaginary first-husbands named Art. Just kidding. And they were bored to tears with the new reality show on cable:

Who wants to be a Centenarian? Although there was no way out, many (like George Sanders) found another way out as they were used to doing on Sunset Boulevard anyway when the going got tough. The fact of the matter is that it was really sad for anyone to have been a has been. But Everybody's Gotta Be A Has-Been Someday. Dean Martin once sang a song with almost the same title. Incidentally, although I met his proprietor who promised an introduction at the end of the night, I didn't exactly meet Dino but I dined in his restaurant, Dino's, on the strip, before they tore it down. And even I, I who have nothing [Shirley Bassey] who never smoked in public, had to exit Dino's for a breath of fresh air. The only problem was that you couldn't breathe the air outside a restaurant in LA without choking to death.

Predictably, Dino was a no-show after another late night with the rat pack and honorary member JFK (if you can believe the proprietor) who had been regaling his latest conquest over an H. Upmann Petit Corona Cuban cigar and making fantastic smoke circles.

What comes around goes around. I doubt if the above illustration could provide a clue to my identity since neither Dino, nor, predictably, the restaurant proprietor, is still standing. Although in the case of the proprietor it was never technically proven if his expiration were caused by secondhand smoke from 10am to 2am daily for some 30 years although a credible supposition. And you knew what Dino was singing about if you saw his appearance during his last talk-show interview at age 79. Good Lord. The telltale sign was that Dean had been a chain-smoker, the worst kind, and almost always smoked in front of all of his wives, many of whom were still living which confounded the second-hand smoke pundits no end. Although, they put it down to the exception that proves the rule. As Kelly Luker said: Like most of his Hollywood cronies, Martin went through wives and gorgeous starlets like Kleenex. Actually, Dean himself put it this way: In Hollywood if a guy's wife looks like a new woman … she probably is.

In fairness, 79 wasn't a bad old age considering Dino's lifestyle and condition. And, three years above the mean (male) longevity of the population. But – repeating what I said earlier I saw JFK, twice, five months to the day before they shot him although he wasn't smoking Petit Coronas then. I was only a slip of a lad at the time but even today I've been heard to hum Dick Holler's classic:

> *Has anybody here seen my old friend, John? Can you tell me where he's gone?*
>
> *He freed a lot of people, but it seems the good die young...*

No, I think my ID is safe barring Oliver Stone concocting yet another theory.

~ ~ ~

And, following the A of C more babies were being born because spouses and significant others no longer had yucky foul-smelling breath. Obnoxious hadn't been a strong enough adjective but comparisons were odious if not repugnant. For decades they had been saying: You expect me to have sex with that stinky smell on your breath - are ya nuts?

whisshhh ... oo-oooooh

But now at the peak of the post-T era it was a return to the romanticism of the glamorous past, the glamour and the glare reflecting from smoke-stained mirrors. If that were now possible (director's cut) - *sans* cigarette in your left hand and a shot glass in your right. And the ubiquitous #2 pencil becoming a significant part of life.

Procter and Gamble soon went out of business because Scope, responsible for 79% of its revenues, no longer had a market. That's not entirely honest because P&G still produced one private label through what had been one of its feeder plants for the mouthwash aftermarket south of the border. That plant was now exclusively used for *k*-smokers, had any survived. Ditto with Pfizer because Listerine just clung to the top shelves of the supermarkets without a single turn in the first 24 months of the post-T era. By which time the 50.7 fl oz (1.5L) jars had started to leak leaving a syrupy stain. And, even with the new minimum wage there was no way that the high school dropouts looking for easy beer money were going to clean it up. At one point it was rumored that Wal-Mart was closing its doors for the same reason until their marketing department began analyzing the Chinese mouthwash demand where 79% of the population smoked. Indeed, China was producing just about as much CO_2s, SO_xs and NO_xs as the US so it was becoming increasingly difficult for eco die-hards to criticize them, as Whitney Houston had told her daughter: Do as I say not as I do. And, it was going to be a slow boat from China until they cleaned up the deficit with RMBs as collateral. With the Chinese invasion in the new millennium which mirrored the Brit rock groups of the sixties.

Oh, just looked at my watch.

whisshhh ... oo-oooooh

Running out of time (pun).

Guess we're going to have to take a rain check on the resolution of the *k*-smoker's publishing rights. Maybe tomorrow, what do you think? Never know what the weather's going to do. Oh, I love a rainy night, I love a rainy night/I love to hear the thunder ... [Edie Rabbitt] Anyway, safe home. Got to watch out for the AT kops. Darn – side mirror's broken! Must rely on the rear-view mirror. Again. Always looking over my shoulder for the AT kops. Actually, I don't really know why I should be worried having, once again, safely departed the parking lot. Been there, done that. You're done. I have done.

The mouthwash thing, gargle, cheap cologne.

Swish!

It works.

The works. The words. Huh. It takes a worried man. The guilt of it all. Comes back to haunt you. Must go to confession one o' these days. One o' these nights, one of these *k*razy old nights. [Don Henley] Trials and tribulations. Of a *k*-smoker. At the risk of writing. For a nation at risk. With words that pound on the conscience.

Thar' she blows. Gender-perfect.

whisshhh ... oo-oooooh ...

~ ~ ~

In case you didn't know, I'm in my other life now. Well, almost. Just crossed the railway tracks on the far side of the parking lot. Looks clear. A couple of turns and I'll be on the main street. There we go. Busy scribbling my last paragraph of the afternoon on my lap-pad at a red light. Darn, just turned green. Eco! Pedal to the metal. Where's my #2 pencil? Seriously, I usually use a bic but the #2 can be a handy backup when your bic's leaking. Like it was about 35 minutes ago. Could've messed up my entire lunchtime. But I must've dropped the darn thing. Too late now. And it's too late baby, now it's too late. [Carole King] Always happens when you're concentrating and some jerk behind you beeps his horn and you're off. With a jerk. Writing a WIP while driving is worse than texting by 16-year-olds with their learner's permits.

oops.

kazoom!

That was a close one. Some *k*razy driver. Using his cell.

kazoops!

Holy Mackerel!

whew!

Kerchief to my forehead. That guilty feeling. No one honked. No one hurt. William Hurt in the neo-noir Body Heat. Or, The Big Chill?

One minute you're the victim. One minute the culprit.

Aha, there's my #2 on the floor.

Now, where's my darn foolscap? Had it on my lap. Got it! Now what? Anyway, even at the traffic light it's hard to write legibly with a foolscap on your lap without something solid beneath, like a thesaurus. Or a knapsack on my knee/Val-deri! Val-dera! Val-deri! Val-dera-ha-ha-ha-ha-ha. [The Happy Wanderer, Friedrich-Wilhelm Möller, written by Florenz Friedrich Sigismund]

Otherwise you puncture the paper.

Or poke through your slacks.

ouch!

Or do the hokey-pokey. Just kidding. Or break the tip.

Shouldn't be doing this without the nice relaxing drag earlier in the parking lot to help me concentrate. On the road. Kerouac. Makes me tense. Wouldn't want to foul up the car and I'd be seen anyway. Well, it's only one paragraph, otherwise I'd forget the thread of the moment at another. On my jaunt across the portal. Into my real life. Which one?

Protagonist in his 'real life' – this time with Kelsey Grammar

Protagonist in his 'real life; - giving a presentation (but you never see his handsome face)

Can't tell anymore which-is-which. Witches switch. Warlock. Don't ask, don't tell. As soon as I enter my office, I'm someone else. 'Hey, who's the new guy? Nice teeth.' Probably the only employee who doesn't need to chew on a #2 after smoking was outlawed. If they only *k*'new!

~ ~ ~

The vocabulary as-we-knew-it began to be displaced by *rap*. Without the slightest bowdlerization as the new (rap) dictionaries were discombobulating themselves with inadvertent *c*'s when they should be *k*'s and vice-versa and the whole thing was a mess. Which I didn't have to worry about too much with my vintage laptop. And spell-check which left a lot to be desired, fortunately. And was busy enough trying to keep up with word-count if you looked at some of the paragraphs in the last chapter.

Following the economic crisis caused by the elimination of cigarette taxes, a WSJ report stated: GM before it went bust had (also) switched to regular Ticonderoga No. 2 pencils for 'taste' instead of the more expensive mechanical pencils that used to be freely available in storage closets.

~ ~ ~

Still the psychologists were convinced there was no direct correlation between obesity and smoking-cessation, so everything was fine in that metric. At least the actuaries assumed so who hired the psychologists. Yet fat folks got fatter faster which was quite a tongue-twister if you said it faster. And All You Can Eat restaurant chains were hanging 'gone-fishing' signs on their doors in fear of fiscal irresponsibility. There was even a book club for kids who might be grownups someday. God willing, now that smoking was abolished, and they only had to worry about driving while texting. Titles included An Introduction to Poker for Kids, Paragon Press, Bath/ UK, published in Malaysia for tax purposes. [ISBN: 1-40546-156-X] These desperate attempts were the happy medium to please the agonized masses who simply craved a quiet puff and showed a lot of ingenuity for the efforts of the desperate AT lawmakers who had desperate housewives too. Many of *hmmm* just craving for a ciggie themselves. Which was a shame. Ain't it a shame. [Fats Domino]

whisshhh ... oo-oooooh ...

The AT lawmakers had insanely proposed forbidding publishers to print books written by *k*-smokers. Yet, only *k*-smokers could write great lit. Robert Fulghum (a non-smoker) had described how everything he really needed to know about literature he learned in kindergarten. The AT lawmakers tried to get them young enough while they were possibly not yet hooked. Where you first learn about the Mid X. About their parent who had 'disappeared'. As though the dirty war in Argentina all over again. Don't cry for me Argentina. [Andrew Lloyd Webber] And, following the lecture the kids ran screaming home to their mummies and to hell with the school bus. And *K*ing Tut. There he goes again, Mummy.

Tut tut.

tsk tsk.

From a jack to a *k*ing. [Ned Miller]

Just the mention of Mid X was that terrifying.

The fact remained that without us, literature was drying up faster than a speeding comma ,,,,,,,,,,,,,,,,,,,, for lack of inspiration, the well-known derivative of tobacco, if you read any Mickey Spillane.

Ultimately AT lawmakers succumbed in a fit of Heisenberg. It was hardly out of conscience but the lawmakers daren't invoke a reputation upon themselves as contemptible as that with which they chided others. Anyway, they thought we'd (pun) just die off if we hadn't already, breathe our last, puffing away like that until *k*ingdom come. As though we were chain-smokers which we're not. Usually. Or smoked in front of screaming brats which we certainly didn't. Just because we enjoy a quiet puff aloof from the world where, unlike the *tabagie*, we can gather our thoughts - doesn't mean we condone the obnoxious habit.

whisshhh ... oo-oooooh ...

It was a triumph for the last remaining bastion of literature as a vehicle for freedom of expression. Igniting the lethargic nation at risk. With hope. The words of the *k*-smoker had arrived. Words that pound on the conscience. The decision chronicled the pattern of *Ulysses,*

immortalized as the book of the century by Time magazine, ironically one of the targets of the letters to the editor campaign.

The ban on Ulysses had long ago been lifted simply because no one could make head nor tail of the motifs, hidden clues and stream of consciousness. Which was less an oxymoron than a reversed-Heisenberg. Which meant that you could only read the novel if you didn't understand it. Like a *k*-smoker only exists if he or she is never seen in the act.

Incongruously, the same Time (magazine) had been the site of the notorious **MANHATTAN PROLOGUE** following which the word (sic) would never be the same again. The tragedy occurred beneath the canopy of the revolving-doors of the Time-Life building. The whole thing was over in less than a New York minute.

> *whisshhh ... oo-oooooh ...*

~ ~ ~

Eventual resolution of the two events that had delayed the Act of Cessation.

The letters-to-the-editor campaign concluded in:

- Sovereign Nations allowed to manufacture smokes.
- *Whereas ...* only (1) for internal consumption on the reservations or (2) for *k*-smokers on the presumption that they didn't exist.
- *K*-smokers permitted to publish from the underground.
- *Whereas ...* although outlawed, *k*-smokers may have their confessions published under non de plumes. However, if observed and apprehended in the act of smoking, all privileges will extinguish, and *k*-smokers will be immediately incarcerated into the Midnight Express. (*K*atch-21)

No, *k*loset-smoking is not for everyone. There are social side effects. And, smoke gets in your eyes.

Aye. To be sure!

Yikes! Look at your watch, mate! Watch, huh? You're absolutely right, it is getting late in the day. The Remains of the Day. [Kazuo Ishiguro/Merchant Ivory] I've gotta get out of this place/If it's the last thing I ever do. [The Animals]

On the lookout. Over my shoulder. Looking cloudy. In your lungs. Just kidding. You hope. I can't think about that right now. If I do, I'll go *krazy*.

whisshhh ... oo-oooooh ...

The two delays for the inevitable implementation of the A of C were amicably resolved without too much ado. But there were still a couple of hurdles. There would be an unprecedented **popular-vote** at the eleventh hour. And, in the wake of the MANHATTAN PROLOGUE there would be a revival of the Dichter-17 survivors from the landmark 1947 study on smoking habits on the Late Yo with David Minuteman, leading to the **reality-vote**. Things weren't over yet. There was still a smidgen of hope for the addicted smokers who had everything to gain.

But it didn't look good. If the majority had their way.

Fortunately, the legacy cigarette manufacturing machines were easily altered into making trillions of #2 pencils quickly for the stressed-out nation even more at risk seeking-any-relief following the smoking ban. The #2's came in packs of 20 hoping for a transparent switch-over. The pencils offered a psychologically comforting alternative to cigarettes. The economy was in shambles and had already gone bankrupt in anticipation of the pending loss of cig taxes and homes were practically all foreclosed. China was watching closely from the sidelines before making a buy-out offer that the US could not refuse. Soon Mandarin would become the national language closely followed by Spanish with American a distant third, while English never having been spoken in Texas was abolished for similar reasons nationwide. The upside was that couples were finally having great sex again since foul breath was eliminated with the smoking ban. On the downside, the #2 pencils had a side-effect of producing crooked teeth for the make-belief inhaler who fanaticized their animation too hard.

 ## *Three*

The #2 pencil

After the (near) global ban on cigarettes, bad breath had become a thing of the past. Proust had written volumes about it in his remembrances. And, mouthwash was all but washed-up. It was no longer necessary. CEOs of pharmaceutical and consumer healthcare conglomerates (and their supply chains) were having a seizure and clearly hurting with peptic ulcers from the loss of hefty bonuses from what had been outrageous markups for mouthwash products. Especially for the non-generics which were a goldmine. Even with redeemed coupons, since the average consumer had predictably forgotten to return the rebate with a self-addressed envelope and a first-class stamp that cost about as much as the rebate anyway. It was the industry's worst nightmare. What-if all rebates and vouchers had actually been redeemed? It paralleled a similar concern with ff points that made most of the airlines bankrupt. Until they later learned from the movie industry that there was more money in super-sized coke (with-90%-ice-filler) and popcorn than the admission ticket and began charging more for luggage than fares. Eventually becoming more cost-effective to stay at home and simply let your luggage go on vacation. Well they fixed that problem by making the mileage points impossible to redeem. Except on Holy Saturday (the Easter vigil) when no one traveled. Since the visiting family came home on Good Friday ✞ and left on Easter Sunday. After the obese among them who were all former smokers finished all the chocolate Easter eggs. Without sharing. And which wasn't dark choc and wasn't good for you.

The airlines had been pumping-out free points like worthless ZWDs in Zimbabwe which at one time were 79,000,000:1. Not bad odds provided they were never used. Which was integral to the blackout-days strategy. Yet, if redeemed (prior to the strategy), the cumulative ff's had a redemptive value equal to every scheduled flight globally for decades. Subsequently, the number of black-out days increased each year until Holy Saturday was the only day left for a free flight. Lumen Christi. Hold onto your lighter 'caus it's gonna be a bumpy ride. [Bette Davis]

Since Roaming Catholics were required to attend Mass at least once a year 'preferably before Easter', everyone waited until the last minute. They stayed grounded for the Easter 'vigil' if they were good Catholic boys and Convent of Mercy girls. Oh Mercy. [Dylan] Sisters of Mercy. [Leonard Cohen] (Although in the latter the sisters weren't nuns but two young women that Lennie met during a snowstorm in Edmonton, Alberta.) Holy Saturday was now the only day of the year that ff points could be used. And the same again next year. Same time next year. [Neil Simon]

What'll ye have, sir?

Oh, I'll have the same again next year.

Thank you, coming right up.

The research departments of the big D (drug) companies in collaboration with the government's AT bureau were experimenting frantically for an effective placebo to replace cigarettes since there was little sales opportunity remaining in the gargle aftermarket.

Except for South America. And parts of Indoor-China. (sic) Where they cared less. And for some outposts in the southern states where word of the smoking ban hadn't yet arrived, and the air hadn't lifted. Like Juneteenth when it took a good two-and-a-half years before word of the Emancipation Proclamation filtered (pun) through. The solution to the withdrawal crisis resulting from the smoking ban which was staring them in their wrinkled faces which had already started to shrivel since the first day they were hooked in second grade, was to displace cigarettes with #2 pencils.

whisshhh ... oo-oooooh ...

From pre-launch tests with focus groups the pencils demon-strated an obscure side effect of producing crooked teeth for the make-belief inhaler from constant chewing but better than lung cancer. This was unavoidable with the uncontrollable progression of any bad habit. Still, the mass merchandising of the 'remarketed' #2 would be a success story that Horatio Alger could only dream about. And, before you knew it, everyone was smoking pencils. Just kidding. Well, one fifth of the population. And, rather than sucking their own juices (saliva) through (as it were), they were chewing them to bits. Bits and pieces. I'm in pieces, bits and pieces/I'm in pieces, bits and pieces/Since you left me and you said goodbye/I'm in pieces, bits and pieces/All I do is sit and cry. [Dave Clark Five]

Yet nobody was blaming anyone except themselves in assuming personal responsibility for their actions when they were no longer allowed to smoke. Ironically their spouses and mistresses loved them dearly with the demise of bad breath, even more for their small sacrifice when the lights went out. That is, if they kept their mouth guards on during the act because of a tendency for barbs from chewing on too many #2 pencils.

Which they usually wore at night anyway.

If only they kept their mouths shut.

Reputably the sex was very good but after the lovin', without a cigarette to come down to earth, wallpaper and wall paint took a banging, usually by the male while the female fell asleep worrying about it.

Bad breath was history. As were cigarettes. You heard the same story over and over again from practically everyone you bumped into shamefully trying to bum one (or two) by sheer force of habit:

Sorry pal, I ain't got no cigarettes. Which was a great comeback for Roger Miller's hit that diehard fans were beginning to forget about. Yes, it was a tough sacrifice alright, but the #2 placebos seemed to work. And it was a great relief no longer having to deceptively don cheap cologne. And guzzle with mouthwash. Which smokers had been doing for decades before bed if they felt lucky.

Again (reputedly) the sex was pretty darn good. After the lovin'. Which was a lyric sensitively written for the occasion by Al Green whom I met twice. And who was then a Pentecostal preacher, so I'm sure my secret's safe on the honor system. With the reverend. (Not that he knew I was a *k*-smoker but he knew *me*. And reading this, he'd know it were me. Writing it. And then, easy to back-into my other id. Piecing the pseudonym together.) Since bible thumping revivalists only confess in indecipherable tongues. For security purposes.

When you really craved that quiet puff.

To wind down.

Having been on an up. In like a lion. Out like a lamb. The silence of. After the act. After the fall. [Arthur Miller]

Yes, smoking was history all right. And so was the zero-sum society which saw a great upswing now that people were literally starting to live. Suddenly however, there just wasn't enough food to feed everyone - with all the extra babies from all the lovin' without foul-mouthed breath to put her off. Another factor was the increased longevity for grown-ups.

whisshhh ... oo-oooooh ...

It was global overpopulation but this time in first world countries too. People were finally taking notice at the relocated World

Population Crisis Congress at the U.N. building. The WPCC had usually been held in Cairo in the open air which wasn't a good thing. Albeit, NYC wasn't much better and probably a lot worse with all the CO_2s, SO_2s and NO_Xs covering the city like an alien spacecraft.

Just prior to the A of C, the U.N. building on 1st Ave was dangerously close (ten city-blocks) to the second-hand smoke wafting across midtown from the Time building on the Avenue of the Americas *during* the MANHATTAN PROLOGUE. But a different problem emerged at the start of the post-T era. Soon they were cramming the new, escalating population (who were already putting-on weight after giving up smoking) like sardines into tall, skinny skyscrapers with escalators and elevators. The skyscrapers really weren't designed for them considering the new composite weight factor especially in earthquake-conditions - since practically everyone seemed to be getting fatter and living longer. Which meant more people per building. The overpopulation dynamic was being addressed in a revitalization of the space race (which never got off the ground) had they only figured out how to offset the lost cigarette taxes to finance it.

Which put an end to that. Well, for the 21% who were trying to get as far away as possible and couldn't take it anymore. *'I can't take it anymore'* became the rallying cry in the hope there'd be no AT lawmakers in outer space. Life was choices and that was it. And they had none. No sweat. Because the return of the #2 was met with such phenomenal demand that it was simply impossible to keep up. Former smokers who had been forced to quit cold turkey were constantly promised that their #2 pencil supply was 'just around the corner'. Right! As they waited with bated breath for their rainchecks and backorders. For #2s.

But promises were broken. Like #2 pencils snapping in the middle if crunched too fast horizontally. When clenched. If you pictured the camera-ready teeth of Wilson, the gunfighter, in Shane. Or even Burt Lancaster in almost any movie when he's trying to be sarcastic with that full-mouthed grin. The jaws-of-life

… der-dum, der-dum, dum-dum, dum-dum, dum-dum, der-dum, dum-dum …

When the craving became too much for those who fondly recollected upon the simple pleasures of the past. When a smoke was a smoke. But that was then. Now something else snapped. Psychologically. And it wasn't only the #2 when chewed too hard and your teeth got right into the wooden part leaving deep bite marks like fangs. As if you were some kind of animal in a forest. And they resolved to try harder the next time. As the bishop said to the actress. Waiting on their ration. For next month's supply. On backorder. And, killing time softly, singing: She'll be comin' 'round the corner when she comes…/She'll be wearing silk pajamas when she comes. So, everyone just stayed put and were as happy as could be in the prevailing circumstances. Including us, for a while, if they'd only leave us alone. The few *k*-smokers left. Possibly only me, huh?

whisshhh … oo-oooooh …

~ ~ ~

Soon the die-hard Caucasians were joined by visiting Japanese x-smokers in the casinos. All of whom were forced to convert into being reluctant quitters, teeth grinders and nail-biters which were becoming socially acceptable norms in the circumstances. The antsy nosepickers among them were excluded, especially the Brits who couldn't kick the habit they were born with. And, who just couldn't cope at all until developing other diversions. Society could no longer demand (not only of elementary school kids who had never lit up although they were known to play with matches): Hey, stop biting your fingernails. It would've been like saying *stop breathing,* which, ironically, was their mantra for us. There had to be a better way. A better tool, distraction.

It was all about post-T era stress. And nerves. '*You're getting on my nerves*', became a common rejoinder in any conversation. And how to handle them. The nerves. Without the pacifying puff to unwind. That for centuries had proven the ultimate sedative. Like falling asleep listening to the subliminal sounds on a CD player of violent waves riding an unforgiving ocean with its cacophonous roar, turbulent, merciless … ebbing and crashing against a nearby cliff. Or being in the midst of a rumbling thunderstorm with the tinny sound of rain splashing against a galvanized barn roof, then plopping on a plank porch. Or the plunking drip into an outside vat. Tranquilizing. Just like that.

The relaxing stuff. The right stuff. The stuff of men who had inhaled their spirit and vigor from tobacco like Einstein, Churchill, JFK. Not to mention Castro (oops!), Lenin (oops!), Joe Camel, (oops) … Joe Stalin (oops!), Mao Tse Tung (oops!) But that was then. And, the glamorous heroes and heroines of the silver screen.

Butt (sic), now … smoking … was … out.

whisshhh … oo-oooooh …

In the outhouse. In the empty parking lot. In the misty moonlight/By the flickering firelight. [Dean Martin] Except for the bugs. Huh? Huhbugs!

~ ~ ~

After the honeymoon period, the Treasury coffers were already hurting in anticipation. Steinbeck's Grapes of Wrath was starting to look like a week at Disney in comparison. The worst part was no longer enjoying a puff to help cry your tears away over a well-deserved pint or two. Cry me a river. [Julie London] Still, people were resilient. As John Milton once said: *What though the field be lost? All is not lost; the unconquerable will ... and courage never to submit or yield.* It was Paradise Lost all right.

The #2 pencil would soon be making a come-back although it would have no therapeutic effect on the coffers. Sin taxes had only applied to tobacco, mouthwash, perfume, lingerie and other luxuries. Taxes had already been retired from alcoholic beverages after they became a social necessity to mollify if not anesthetize the masses. Well, at least one fifth (pun) of the population. After smoking was outlawed. And, along with it, tax receipts from cigs and mouthwash were wiped out. Leaving pretty-much – perfume. Well, you could be sure that not too many husbands were going to buy their mistresses expensive perfume fragrances with their jobs in jeopardy due to the economic turbulence caused by the subsequent Treasury deficit. It was a repeat of the old adage: What comes around goes around. Like blowing smoke circles in the nice clean eco which was getting cleaner every day without 2HS to worry about. If it weren't for the

CO_xs, SO_2s and NO_xs which made every afternoon in the contiguous states look like winter in Alaska where the sun doesn't shine for several months in a state bathed in perpetual twilight. And getting worse by the minute. If you stopped to sniff the chemicals overhead. Or smell the holy moses. Stop and smell the moses. [Mac Davis]

The only other meaningful tax-revenue source even close to tobacco was the lotto which had bankrupted the hapless working classes who feverishly gambled their entire wages and predictably lost with a ho-hum crash. It looked like 1929 all over again without the ho-hum. But with a hell of a lot of hoopla. And, those who hadn't jumped from the top floors of abandoned, unfinished skyscrapers in the post-T era when funding had dried up were angry. Lottery receipts which were practically embezzled (if you looked at the odds) from blue collar factory workers and truck-drivers accustomed (in the pre-T era) to making 6-digits a year were no less than blood money for those with a conscience. It just didn't feel right, taking hard-earned money from folks who didn't know the difference. As one x-smoker said: *It didn't have the right taste to it.*

People were seeking words that pound on the conscience. Well, good luck. The televangelists had already demonstrated that. The Reverends Jim Bakker and Jimmy Swaggart had long ago preached with certitude. But it was a little bit late in the day. For their conscience.

Still, there would be good news from the underground. Away from the public eye and out of the spotlight beneath a lamppost in a vacant parking lot. Urged on with the eureka-moment from nicotine, sometimes rich in cliché with a unique if not peculiar writing style which could unravel mysteries. Open the portal, drop the drawbridge, unclog preconceptions, uncork the magic genie, unlock secret passageways, unleash the mind.

Me.

Meme.

Perhaps the last smoker on earth.

On a mission to revive literature as we knew it.

     whisshhh ... oo-oooooh ...

Thar' goes the mind.

~ ~ ~

Meanwhile, back at the casino. Blackjack players simply pretended they were smoking by faking it with the #2.

> *Reader:*   *Wait a minute, is this pre-T or post-T? I'm really having difficulty figuring-out whether you're talking about prior to the smoking ban or after? Jeez!*

By now the #2 pencils were in full production by the Native Americans and their helpers from Calcutta on the next shift of the same dedicated production line as cigarettes for internal consumption.

> *Reader:*   *You're ignoring my question!!*
>
> *Me:*   *OK (... groan!) It's after!*
>
> *Reader:*   *Whew! That was like pulling teeth! Like Wilson the gunfighter in Shane!*
>
> *Me:*   *Can we proceed? Please?*

It was an economy of scale without additional capital outlay and a smart move when times get tough. Furthermore, there wasn't a hell of a difference in the appearance, psychosomatic-feel, or function/feature/benefit of either product, cigarettes or pencils. As everyone knew, after your first cigarette, you might as well have been chewing on a #2 anyway. It was all about that very first ciggie. As illustrated earlier, most movie stars smoked 4 packs a day while the rest of them were chain-smokers. Yet, according to medical researchers only that first cigarette of the day provided any satisfaction. And worse.

You see, it was never an issue about *developing* the habit. That first drag in grade school really did you in. When you're a jet you're a jet, you're a jet/From your first cigarette to your last dying day, [West Side Story] When you were but a youth of a lad.

So, the American Heart Association was convinced if you never had the first one, then you couldn't get hooked. The corollary was that, had you ever tasted *even one* cigarette, you were a hopeless case anyhow so why worry about the billions of dollars needed to force people to quit? It was a good point for lawmakers trying to kill programs in tough times just prior to the A of C. Kill Bill. And, another variant of Heisenberg because it was uncertain as to when smokers enjoyed that first taste, if ever. Except for *k*-smokers who did it solely for inspiration. Further, if the administration couldn't afford to make them quit – but, if smoking were abolished, then there never was a problem. Soon the MANHATTAN PROLOGUE would change everything by eliminating the choice-factor. Max Factor. Which made the implementation much easier. Having no choice did away with philosophical rationalizations in favor of Machiavellian manipulations. Then the media was invited.

And, you know, when 79% is onto something and everyone (of that majority) wants to be part of the action, soon they, the 21%, were told that they wouldn't be able to tell the difference between cigarettes and the #2. It was all in the mind. After one fifth of the population watched the cable TV commercials for the #2 over-and-over-and-over-and-over again. Like Alex DeLarge in the Ludovico Technique brainwash scene in Clockwork Orange. Over-and-over-and-over-and-over. Again.

There he goes again. Marshall McLuhan got it half-right about the mass media of communication. In overdrive. For this reason, Bob Newhart addressing the timeliness of the #2 period which would define the era, remarked:

The uses of tobacco aren't obvious right off the bat. You shred it up, put it on a piece of paper, roll it up, and stick it between your lips and set fire to it. Then you inhale the smoke. You could stand in front of your fireplace and have the same thing going.

whisshhh ... oo-oooooh ...

But he was outdone by Brad Stine:

I don't smoke. I don't even understand what the point is. All I can tell is that these people are addicted to blowing smoke out of their faces. It's not even a good trick. If you could blow smoke out of your face without everyone knowing where it came from, that would be impressive.

Sure enough, the #2 had all of the possibilities of a win-win situation in response to an otherwise traumatic predicament in a nation at risk. In denial. And agitated. Which bothered the AT lawmakers unless they could convince the masses that the placebo was for their own good. For a few good men. And women. In an economy which had been making out pretty well from cig tax revenues for as long as any administration could remember. Having survived two world wars, lost a few outdoor scrimmages in Indoor-China (sic), having a fit in Iraq … and having second thoughts about invading Iran. Earning a respectable batting average up until about 1945 or thereabouts. In spite of the Big 6 having been deep-sixed not to mention the Big 3. The fact was that folks were getting fatter faster after the smoking ban.

Credit: Matt Handelsman, 2010, Newsday

Nonetheless, soon advertising agencies were having a subliminal field day with the #2 pencils. It was akin to the halcyon albeit cyclical days of the hula-hoop and other mindless distractions, usually devised to take our minds off more menacing events which threatened society like the Cold War.

darn. Should've brought my fleece jacket this afternoon. Jeez! Freezing my butt off.

Before it was authenticated decades later by *get-smart* spies that the offensive capabilities of the Soviets had all-along been 'made up'! Nothing had changed since Khrushchev's tantrum at the UN when he removed his shoe (would you believe!) and commenced to pound it on the classroom-like table in protest for the indoor ban on Russian cigarettes. With his shoe! Instead of tossing it like others did when the GWBWH came into power. And we were supposed to believe they were pointing nuclear *missiles* at us from Cuba?!

Still, the dominant target-audience for cable TV advertisements, kids - who were smart enough until they grew older, were laughing their butts off, thinking the #2 infomercials (usually performed by pie-eating contest professionals) were sitcoms.

Protagonist's pie-eating contest win!

The era of the #2 pencil-placebo was about to forever change the way we came to grips with our inner personas. A popular catch-phrase became: Hold onto your #2, lads! It was an obvious rehash of the inimitable words of Bette Davis who extinguished her last ciggie at the fine old age of 81 having chain-smoked one too many in her five-pack-a-day career. God bless her for living that long in her condition. And, if you happened to see her skeletal, smoke-drained features in Whatever Happened to Baby Jane, well, you too would have second thoughts about secondhand smoke. oops. About chain-smoking. Because it was all about the present and not what happened. And about individual choice. Except for *k*-smokers for whom, unfortunately, the #2 didn't work.

whisshhh ... oo-oooooh ...

~ ~ ~

Now might be a good time to take a(nother) nostalgic stroll down memory lane. This time about the history of the #2 pencil. Our goal is to try to understand the overwhelming impact of the #2 re-emergence following the A of C in a nation at risk.

Certain trends come and go. The #2 however would be called a paradigm shift. A shift beyond the #1 pencil for which little archival information remains, except: #1 is the loneliest number that you'll ever do/Two can be as bad as one/It's the loneliest number since the #1. [Three Dog Night] Its unmodified reappearance was purely a conceptual and imaginative undertaking - without any change in shape, size, color (until later!), taste, style, etc. It became a model for one fifth of the population who had nowhere to turn, everything to lose, nothing to gain, and were on the verge of punctuating the hopeless cases which they were anyway. The popularity of the #2 would become legendary, leaving its mark on everyone who was bold enough to venture where none had dared before. At least 21% of the population. Because they had no reason to. If they had any common sense whatsoever.

Professor Dean Christopher, sometimes called the granddaddy of the #2 pencil was the first academic to write about its history, demographic variation, and some known side-effects when used as cigarette placebos. Soon the #2 was taking the nation by storm which ironically had been smoking up a perfect storm in the pre-T era. Dr. Christopher's dissertation was a critical academic piece for a nation at risk. Now, with your kind permission, I will liberally paraphrase the main parts and illustrate them with some virtual slides if this darn thing works.

Reader: *What an imagination this guy's got. Impressive.*

150

Hold on ...

first slide ...

Title:

#2 Pencils as Placebos for Cigarettes and the Function of the Eraser

Sub-title:

From beginning to end – to chew or not to chew – a study

By Dr. Dean Christopher

Roughly based upon; 19 Things You Didn't Know About ...

Pencils, 2007

[Selected Media: Text with power-point hi-lights]

Peo-ple!!?? *I said, PEO-PLE! Where is the darn screen ...?*

pause for virtual screen ...

Hey, what's up doc? Huh. Sorry folks, darn multimedia - seems to be taking forever. Which I don't have. (pun) Right!

With these darn cigarettes.

Ouch! Good pint!

whisshhh ... oo-oooooh ...

Well, let's try to kill time until this thing works. Patience is a virtue. The waiting a-b-s-o-l-u-t-e-l-y unbearable. The unbearable lightness of being. Touche! Been a while for the customary repetition in a confession! Waiting for Godot. Go dot. Silent t. Go do. Unto others as they would unto you.

Go Go Go Go Go GoGoGoGoGo!!! Like a command from a SWAT team leader!

Go-Go gal. GaGa gal. Gagger! Gaffer!

Exactly! Where's the gaffer when you need her?

Waiting …

For the stupid projector. For the gaffer.

Or the best boy? That you, Seth? You talkin' ta me? Anybody out there? Hey, I found a body out there! The cosmos is a pretty big place. Who do you think you are – Jodie Foster in Contact? Is there anybody going to listen to my story? [The Beatles] Can't hear ya. What? Now I hear ya. Okay.

Got it!

The (virtual) screen.

High 5s.

Thanx. A lot.

Lights out …

        whisshhh … oo-oooooh …

Hey, you in the back o' the hall – that includes YOU too mister!

Who, me?

U 2.

oops!

sorry.

Me o my.

At last. Text follows and accompanies power point screens. Supposed to. The complete multimedia interactive presentation will soon be available in the dvd version of this book.

    Publisher's insert: We hope.

Meantime …

Back to reality … out here in the parking lot …

Oh no! Can't believe this – it's starting to snow! Sleet anyway. Gives you some clue what part of the country I'm wip'ing in if you only knew what time of the year it is. Yellow foolscap sheets on trunk. Colorful. Yellow is the color of my true love's hair when we rise/In the morning, when we rise ... [Joan Baez] Gotta rise out o' that. Should've listened to the forecast. As long as it doesn't hail. Mary. Ahh. No use. Then again - can't write *in* the car (dreaded smoke). Fumes'd be dead giveaway next time I bring the missus in the car. She'd smell a rat a mile away. *hmmm ...* Guess I'm going to have to finish this part tomorrow. Scarlett. So much to do. So many roads to go down. So many abandoned parking lots to explore. Can't do it all at one time. Foam coffee cup in one hand. WIP in another. Pen in another. Just kidding. It's a #2 pencil. Ha, ha. As the man said (or, a kid to his ma): Look ma, I've only got two hands. Wow, you do. Good boy. Wicked cold! Good god. Ah no! Just spilt the stupid coffee all over my WIP. Seriously. You wouldn't believe how tough it is to have two lives. And only two hands. It never ends. Endless love. 'Caus baby you, (baby baby baby baby)/You mean the world to me/Oh I know I've found in you/My endless love/...*yeee ee eeeee oooh-woow do do do do do do do do do do doo doo.* [Luther Vandross & Mariah Carey] What a mess on my WIP. Wippy. Mr. Whippy. Another fine mess, Stanley. Caffeinated ink. Consuming paragraphs like a burning envelope in Rebecca. Burning bridges behind me. [Jack Scott] By the fireplace. Fireside chat. At a critical moment in the plot. Or, the way they make scenes cripple-up in horror movies to give a warning that a scarier part is coming and you better cover one eye. Like Brando in One Eyed Jacks. Or the mythical pirate with two good eyes but with a patch over one eye. For effect. Like

Charles Laughton with his penetrating monocle in that scene stealer. [Witness for the Prosecution] To allow for better viewing of dark areas below deck by switching the patch to the exposed eye for instant visibility and depth.

Sleet. Cold. Accident waiting to happen. All over my latest pages. What a pity that none of those multi-floor indoor-parking lots are never abandoned when the weather turns like this. The abandonment I need to write these confessions. In atonement. To compose the words that pound on the conscience. When it's sleeting outside. When no one is around. To protect my privacy. The kind of floors that you'd see a'toppling down in a(nother) remake of Earthquake. Still, with the economy the way it is without cig taxes, there's always the chance that the adjacent high-rise populated by bank and securities employees will collapse (figuratively and physically) and free-up some parking space. *You see, the problem is all inside your head, she said to me/The answer is easy if you take it logically.* [Paul Simon] The problem is that such an indoor lot would have to be totally vacant for a *k*-smoker to feel safe – even though the floors of some are the length of a football field. Because all it takes is one fanatic former smoker to yell if they saw us. Me anyway. If you've seen any of the four remakes of the original Invasion of the Body Snatchers. Next thing you know 'twould be off to the Mid X (for me). Or, at any moment, with my luck, a local gang of juvenile delinquents with nothing much ado, sure enough they would just happen upon the abandoned floor that I was on. Working away on my WIP with a nice quiet puff for creativity.

And not a bother in the world about the rain or hail or sleet or snow. If the weather messed up my productivity in the outdoor lot the day before. A set-back which you didn't want to risk again. Time management is what the ergonomists call it. I think. And one of the hoodlums trying to assert himself to the ringleader, the role model he aspires to be, points his finger at '... the creep with a thesaurus on his car trunk, some kinda geek/weirdo'. In a world where people stopped reading because no one was writing anything worthwhile ever since the A of C took off. So how would I explain that one? How would you?

whisshhh ... oo-oooooh ...

~ ~ ~

It's now tomorrow. Tomorrow never dies. Maybe we'll have more luck today ... yesterday, all my troubles seemed so far away.
[The Beatles]

Ladies and gentlemen let the games begin. The Hunger Games. ....

... oops. Forgot to tell you that 'meantime' (from a couple of pages back) is over ...

Back to the chase. The confession. Mine.

A synopsis of Dr. Christopher's presentation follows on the virtual screen about the history of the #2 pencil. Whom unfortunately was unable to be-with-us today. You'll either be-with-us or agin' us. You'll? Sounds like Yul. Brynner. At yuletide. Dearly beloved, we are glad that *yul* be with us today to mourn the passing of ... (such-and-such). oops. Strike that one about being with us or agin' us. Either way that expression only applied to those who refused to relinquish their freedom of choice.

oopie!

155

Goldberg. Making whoopee. She sits alone 'most ev'ry night/He doesn't come home, or even write/He says he's busy/But she says, "Is he/Making Whoopee?" [Eddie Cantor]

Not supposed to say things like that ('freedom of choice') around here. Might give the impression that you're a dissident. A rebel without a cause. Who me? You talkin' ta me?

Reader: *Ple-eeeeese, can we just go with Dr. Christopher, huh?*

Please, Please, Mr. Postman/You didn't stop/To make me feel better. [The Carpenters]

whisshhh ... oo-oooooh ...

And now ladies and gentlemen, in this corner – the rise and fall and rise of the #2 pencil as we knew it …

TEXT FOR VIRTUAL SLIDES NUMBERS 1 THROUGH 19 ON THE ORAL HISTORY, IMPORTANCE AND IMPLICATIONS OF THE #2 PENCIL

- Quoting *Ripley's Believe it or Not*, there is no lead in lead pencils!
- Graphite is a crystallized form of carbon and enjoys a causality from the Greek *graphein*, 'to write or wrong.'
- Carbon is the element with atomic number 6 and element symbol C, an intrinsic ingredient in the protagonist's popular formula "CO_2s +SO_2s+NO_Xs".
- Graphite was discovered in England in 1534 when Henry VIII wrote-off the first of his 6 wives and needed a writing instrument to pencil in #2.

- The average #2 pencil holds enough lead for a sober person to draw a straight line about 21 miles (33.81 km) long. Wait, scrap that, there is zero lead in lead pencils!
- A single #2 pencil empowers a *k*loset-smoker to write roughly 79,000 words that pound on the conscience.
- The psychosomatic effect of chewing on a #2 has been proven to keep a smoker who just quit, self-absorbed in a stress-filled daze for about 79 minutes, tops, with no warranty on his/her incisors.
- Most #2 pencils sold in the US have erasers while in Asia they're usually unfiltered. It's a taste thing.
- In the UK they call erasers, 'rubbers'. And they call rubbers ... Well, it gets confusing.
- Thoreau wrote *Walden* with a #2 before they became placebos for cigarettes with the Act of Cessation.
- Since Thoreau wrote great works as a semi-recluse (Cf. Heisenberg), he was arguably the first closet-smoker, holding a despised place in history by the AT lawmakers as the father of the *k*-smoker.
- Armand Hammer relocated manufacturing of the #2 pencil to the USSR following the 1917 Soviet revolution at a time when little else was known about their use as placebos. The proletariat remarked Thank God as they continued to smoke unfiltered ciggies until kingdom come, a philosophy in which they didn't believe.
- Predictably, to be mean, after the A of C, Russia vetoed the US initiative for a global ban on cigs.
- Most #2 pencils today are produced on Native American reservations on the next shift of the same high-volume production line as cigarettes for internal consumption.
- Another 21% are manufactured in Chinese factories solely for export which turn out 21 billion pencils annually. Enough to

circle the earth more than 79 times and still not get dizzy from the placebo-effect.

- #2 pencils were used in US space missions. The issue of the flammability threat of wood pencils when chewed in a pure-oxygen atmosphere always worried the NASA engineers but was resolved when NASA abruptly shut down with the shuttle engines running due to the loss of funds from cigarette taxes.

- The world's largest #2 pencil made of Malaysian wood and polymer is 79 feet high. The massive pencil was loaned out to the VAB building at the Kennedy Space Center as a symbolic (phallic) gesture during the final bash for the 45 million adult smokers (Cf Chapter 4) lamenting the Act of Cessation at the commencement of the post-T era.

- Not surprisingly, the re-marketing of the #2 pencil as a placebo for x-smokers became both a legend in our times and a Harvard Business Review classic for smart MBA students who were stumped.

- *IN CONCLUSION: Please pencil-in your virtual assessment of this PPT and suggestions for improvement. Signature optional. Anonymity respected. Be careful with your incisors!!*

Admittedly, the AT lawmakers - and smokers who morphed into non-smokers (through no fault of their own unlike Dr Jekyll and Mr. Hyde), had thought there was lead in 'lead' pencils.

As BO'B was wont to say: Let me be very clear - there is no lead in lead pencils. The core is made of non-toxic graphite. According to the NIH, if you are still not convinced, graphite is a soft form of carbon and is *'relatively'* nonpoisonous!

gulp! what did I just chew!

On the other hand, the NIH advised that the only relevant concern regarding potential sources of lead in pencils is in the lacquer or paint used to finish the pencil.

double your gulp!

Because the #2 was labeled as a 'lead' pencil there was a certain percentage of the mean distribution of the population (because of taste-buds and predilection) who were reluctant to accept something they suspected could be cancer-causing from 'lead-poisoning'. This resistance was regardless of whether the same individuals couldn't care less for the prior 30 years on average of smoking some 70+ cancer-causing carcinogens in tobacco. To address this apparent aversion to the #2, the AT lawmakers imposed a warning label. At first it was a temporary stick-on which didn't last for a number of reasons. It was later improved when the letters were permanently engraved in English, Spanish, Arabic and Chinese into the (appropriately) yellow painted-skin on each pencil close to the eraser-end where it would remain visible longer. And, as people got bored with yellow, the #2 became available in an assortment of colors. The label read as follows:

WARNING:
"LOW RISK OF TOXIN LEVEL"
FOR MORE INFORMATION CONSULT SECTION 7 OF #2
PENCIL MANUAL

(If manual is missing from 20-pack carton of #2 pencils, please send stamped-addressed envelope for replacement using common sense when licking the envelope.)

But it was much ado about nothing because the anxiety concerned the ubiquitous #2 and not some spent nuclear fuel rods! The fact was that kids were graduating from kindergarten with regular heights matching their percentiles so there shouldn't've been too much worry. Still, predictably the caution was ignored. The flimsy label either slipped-off from too much saliva or the increasingly deeper bite-marks made the etching illegible. Or frankly, when you badly needed that munch you cared less about small print. You know how that happens. Or, people simply weren't careful, either from habit or in ignorance of proper chewing methods had they only read Miss Manner's latest at any public library that was still open in the wake of the death knell of literature as we knew it.

For a nation of habitual gum-chewers it was hard to imagine that the #2 pencil was any different in the knack of chewing. When learned with practice, they called it the *nic*-knack, possibly because of their prior dependence on nico. This helped to make the challenge more user-friendly. Familiarity breathes (sic) contempt. In fairness gum-sticks lacked the feel of a cigarette. You couldn't hold the gum steady regardless of its flavor after you already put it in your mouth (and, unfortunately, it didn't dissolve like a HC ✝ wafer). And even if you did, it got stuck in your fingernails, and worse, hair (if a girl, constantly tousling with her fingers) and made a mess. You could hold a #2 just like you held a ciggie but you gotta know how to hold 'em. [Kenny Rogers]

Although the pencil was considerably longer at first than filtered 100s - after you chewed a bit (along the x-axis, having clipped the eraser if it came with one) eventually it shrunk to about the same length. Honey, I shrunk the #2 pencil. And didn't look too stupid between your pointer and index finger when it wasn't stuck permanently between a gap in your incisors. Obviously, as you continued to chew, it became like the mini-pencils that come with wallet-sized black notebooks for writing down pretty girls phone numbers. Pretty woman, yeah, yeah, yeah. [Roy Orbison] And, by the time you were down to the stub there wasn't a hell of a difference at all to a butt since by then both were functionally pretty useless. Pretty nice. I feel pretty/Oh so pretty/I feel pretty and witty and gay. [West Side Story] It was a hard act to follow but it was the art of holding the darn thing that was characteristic of its attractiveness and it was the write (sic) thing to do. Further, it was much more presentable in mixed company than choking with a mouthful of gum while yapping away at the same time. Like the movie queens in the golden age simultaneously smoking cigarettes (according to their unauthorized bios) while reciting their lines. Which would've been bad manners for normal people who usually did both separately, as obnoxious as the habit was back then when it was popular to develop lung cancer.

Nobody said it was going to be easy. But it really *was* hard. The darn #2. This in itself was a huge disadvantage for the novice. Versus the soft ciggie which had a squishy feel to it if you squeezed it a bit between your fingers when no one was looking like in the Charmin toilet paper ad. But because the pencil was hard, the imagined sensation lasted much longer than the 6 minutes, tops, to smoke a cigarette. Unless, god forbid, you had been a chain smoker in the good old days and didn't even stop for a breath of fresh air before resuming with the next. On average, according to the pundits, a #2 pencil should last about 90-minutes depending on your staying power. You just kept chewing away until you were right down into the lead which was a malapropism in itself since there is no lead in lead. If chewing latitudinally, like a squirrel nibbling away on a cable TV trunk-line and you wondered why the fuzzy picture froze during your favorite sitcom. Or on the opposite side to the eraser (longitudinally) if you didn't use a pencil-sharpener on that end, since you probably only intended using the darn thing as a placebo and not to write your autobiography. Which *k*-smokers could only do with real cigarettes purchased anonymously from the sovereign nation. Incidentally, the oft repeated 'you' in this paragraph refers to someone else except in the final mention where 'you' expands into 'your' (autobiography) but refers to 'me'. Got it?

Like, when you're caught at the office Xerox machine. And everyone's pretending they're in a hurry with nothing to do except make more paper copies. Or empty the little cavity on the side which is where you put the paper clips but then forget to take them with you. And then you trip (while on the way to office supplies to get more paper to copy) on a 4x12-foot section of heavy-duty industrial grade carpet with the rubber bottom (called an eraser in the US) – that has curled-up at the fringe. You know the one, the surrey with the fringe on top. [Oklahoma soundtrack] And there's holy hell because you forgot to put the clip back on the pile you had just copied and the scattered non-numericalized business plan pages no longer made any sense whatsoever. And, while all of this is going-on, you're the only one at the Xerox but with your luck just about everyone in the entire company arrives and you're … it. And sure enough, they'll say: You copyin' your *autobiography* or somethin'? Which wouldn't've been much in their cases.

> Reader: So sarcastic.

And, if the machine had already been jammed by someone who made a quick exit after looking over their shoulder to make sure no one was watching …. while, you just happen to walk up to it like

Dana Andrews in The Oxbow Incident, enter your personal password and hit the green eco button .... and, nothing happens except for all those squiggly meaningless blinking symbols and flashing icons on the console which only a WWII Navajo code-talker could decipher, telling you it's all screwed-up .... and, at that moment the office big-mouth and her contingent arrive, and you might as well be Joan of Arc when smoke was allowed.

whisshhh ... oo-oooooh ...

~ ~ ~

In fairness, there were hidden dangers from improperly chewing on a #2. Just like your kids' munching away on their made-in-China toys when it's way past bedtime. Which were now being made-in-the-USA following the inevitable Chinese acquisition.

More seriously, the NIH warned that a person may choke while swallowing a #2 pencil which can cause symptoms such as repeated coughing, chest pain, shortness of breath, or rapid breathing. Sometimes, the report continued, children will place a piece of a pencil in their nose but that was another issue.

The #2 could be dangerous in a number of other ways. Laura Lee wrote the following in her 100 Most Dangerous Things in Everyday Life. She ranked office supplies in her 100 hazards since they: ... *led* (pun) *to more than 21,000 injuries each year - ever since the #2 pencil became a staple of society.* It seems a fairly large number of office workers spend time cleaning their ears and teeth with various items on their desk. Pilferage of the #2 was reported up 21% by office workers attempting to offset their nicotine craving when times got tough in an economy sans cig taxes in a nation at risk.

And so, the risk was a toss-up – carcinogens from tobacco versus damage to your incisors from chewing graphite. In the latter there was always the probability of chewing right down to the graphite by Orientals. Especially in the stress-filled high stakes casinos. Who chewed horizontally like a navy Seal carrying a Jim Bowie knife between his teeth (or between *hers* in the case of Demi Moore who needed more than a tonsure to look like John Wayne). Which, respectful of their 5000-year culture, the Orientals referred to as orientally.

There were no other options. You're either with me or against me, as Colonel Travis said at the Alamo. And you know what happened to him. And the rest of them. When they crossed the line. As Johnny Cash put it well: I crossed the line. Not to mention Lawrence Harvey himself whose personal life was private, a miracle in Hollywood. Until, that is, they wrote his bio after he died. As they're inclined to do when you can no longer refute your antics. Who played Travis even though he wasn't Lawrence Harvey at all but born Laruschka Mischa Skikne. While Larry *K*ing, whom (as you already know) I also met - *was* born Lawrence Harvey Zeiger. A spoonerism if ever there were one. And was a three-pack-a-day smoker, even keeping a lit cigarette during his interviews so he wouldn't have to take time to light up during breaks. So, none of this makes any sense whatsoever. Billie Jean <u>K</u>ing had been married to a different Larry King but that's got nothing to do with tobacco.

whisshhh ... oo-oooooh ...

You just couldn't be expected to go through life worrying about the 'relatively non-poisonousness' of graphite from #2 pencils compared to 'real' lead.

Incidentally, at the start of the Post-T era, toddlers were taught how to properly chew on their #2 when they were hardly out of the cradle: When the bough breaks, the cradle will fall/And down will come baby, cradle and all.

*[Kind permission from descendants of **King** James II of England, father of the baby, widely believed to be someone else's child smuggled into the birthing room in order to provide a Catholic heir for James. The 'cradle' is the House of Stuart monarchy.]*

So that when they came of age they wouldn't think twice about the sins of the father and just chew away until *k*ingdom come. Which would be soon enough for many of them if you've ever seen toddlers chew on crayons in a desperate attempt by their encouraging-parents against otherwise certain-obesity. Which already affected 79% of the population with a roadmap to 100%. Regardless of the astronomical cost of braces when they grew up to be spoiled-rotten adolescents.

To illustrate how popular the pencils had become, the nationwide Girl Scout door-to-door fundraiser had selected 6-packs of the #2 for a change instead of the usual 6-packs of Pabst Blue Ribbon. Just kidding. Have you ever tried to *not* buy from a girl scout with their devilishly-persistent fake-sincerity and all that practical experience learned in the wild from pillow fights. And yet, sugar would melt in their mouths. Anyway, each pack contained twenty #2 pencils, enough for a stressed-out x-smoker to make it until payday if s/he still had a job in the economic bust after the loss of cig taxes.

And, if you were lucky, certain packs contained a free coupon for a spare while the small print said, 'while supplies last'. Just your luck after going to the trouble of returning the free coupon with a first-class stamp. Sure enough, they had run out when it came to your turn. There was always a gotcha. Then, after the girl scouts got your hard-earned money which was all they cared about anyway until the same time next year (for which Neil Simon wrote a play to dramatize the promotion), the #2 pencils were delivered by Midnight Ex.

oops …

  Reader: *Relax, man. You're starting to freak (me) out!*

Look, I haven't seen an AT kop all day, must be the weather. Jeez, forgot my stupid brollie, again. Anyway, you know I meant Fed Ex.

  whew!

   whisshhh …

    whew-oo-oooooh …

In order to make die-hard consumers think they were still buying cigarettes, the math was simple. The standard carton ordered from the call center contained 20 packs for a total of 400 pencils.

With globalization the call centers for the #2 had been moved transparently to Calcutta from where the Indian workers had just come. Which made no sense at all. And there was no telling what the Chinese were going to do now that they controlled the US Treasury which went insolvent with the loss of cig taxes that had funded it. Still, there was the usual minimum of 4-cartons per order. This min was waved if you bought the recommended 6-pack 'kits' from the girl scouts. The kit also contained information on how to join the frequent chompers club. You got extra one-time dividend points – good for even more #2 pencils - on purchases from girl scouts by filling-out a questionnaire, which was more of a personal profile on your entire lifestyle and fantasies, on whether you preferred to chew latitudinally, longitudinally, horizontally, orientally, and/or other. Demographics solicited included your height, rolling-average-weight since the cigarette ban, and sexual-orientation whether you were oriental or not. And so on. It was a teaser tactic to get you to buy more #2 pencils at undiscounted retail prices when you became addicted to the placebos.

Normal shipments were made twice per month after the free sample program during the transition period (from the pre-T to the post-T era) had expired. Everyone knew there were no free launches (sic) in Hollywood. The #2 became an incredibly popular product for the girl scouts who sold them through their parents' workplaces. Via their parents. Without even having to show-up themselves. Which was a good thing for their parents. Since the friends (of the parents and sometimes the parents themselves) would pay anything not to have their (the parents') girl scout daughters yakety-yakking in their prissy uniforms all over their professional-looking lobby. And god knows how many merit-award badges (just for-showing-up) pinned on their helmets. And asking preposterous questions like some nerd juvenile prodigy which were ridiculous more than stupid and had no answer. You know the kind, when you just don't have time or patience listening to the annoying inquisitive brats if they'd only cop on.

Certainly, it made it difficult on the honor system for 21% of the population to figure how many free #2 pencils they would need, because, frankly, they all believed the honeymoon period would continue indefinitely since the MANHATTAN PROLOGUE had not yet occurred. It was wishful thinking if not blind faith. And smoke got in their eyes. Which happens. So, many of them refused to stock-up. While experiencing severe withdrawal symptoms that hadn't been seen since coitus interruptus became the most popular form of recreation on college campuses without a quiet smoke to unwind in the anti-climax. The popularity of coitus interruptus followed the exorbitant increase in fees without the offsetting cig tax allotment which by now was affecting just about everybody and their most private moments. When all the stats came in - for the typical 5-foot-8, 280 lb SWM, and a typical 5-foot-2, 240 lb SWF x-smoker in a nation at risk, it took an average of 90-minutes, tops, to consume one #2 pencil before tossing the stub by the time s/he got too close to the eraser. Allowing for 6 breaks to the bathroom mirror (at work and/or home) for a personal facial check-up to monitor the latest chip-impact on their incisors. Which could only get worse. With unavoidable consumption. With mouth-wide-open before considering it safe to proceed (but the damage was usually done). Which, in denial, they did. Like the emphysema patient in the pre-T era who doubles-up upon hearing of her malignant diagnosis because … what the hell. No point in stopping now! Based on this model, a typical consumer between the productive hours of 10am and 10 pm consumed ~8 pencils/day, 56/week, 112/fortnight.

oops.

… that word again … *fortnight!*

Delete that!

darn …

Hope the forensics are speed readers tonight. I would've *k*aught me long ago were I them. Lucky for me. Lucky Strike. Where was I? Yes.

YESSSSER!

 As my kid'd say …

Though she has no clue that I'm a *k*-smoker!

That would be 224/month, 2268/year. Say ~ a half-dozen cartons. The kits sold by the girl scouts' parents, then, should last a good two weeks but you must be cautious with these figures because the above is only an average.

whisshhh … oo-oooooh …

It was too soon to comment on the long-term effect of the #2 which was quickly becoming a hotter commodity than Lucky Strike rations in the northern Sahara during WWII prior to the **Dichter report in 1947.** However, a spokesperson from one of the Native American manufacturing plants which was in a conundrum between manufacturing cigarettes for internal consumption on one shift, and shifting tooling for manufacturing #2 pencils for the mass market on another - commented live on the Late Late News: We conduct jishu kanri zero defect tests on all #2 pencils to comply with regulations in the US, Europe, and Japan, not to mention more rigorous criteria we set internally. The statement continued: TQM six-sigma tests ensure that our #2 meets-or-exceeds the highest standards for safe nibbling by consumers every day. Have a nice day and Thank You for Smoking. Just kidding. Don't forget to read the warning label.

whisshhh … oo-oooooh …

~ ~ ~

On the road home. Darn traffic. Cruising along on the main thor-
oughfare. Wonder if the missus'll miss me? *Miss us.* That's a good
one. Maybe she'll suspect the reason for my delay. Can't help it.
This chapter's going way over my allotted 50-mins. Filling in the
bits at traffic lights. In the evening I usually try a quick 10-minute
session on the way home by another abandoned parking lot to clean-
up an idea I had during lunch.

Meanwhile back at the Casino in the post-T era on the reserva-
tion that took none, the piped-in background music on the casino
floor was playing over and over and over again: But if you haven't
gambled for love and lost/Then you haven't gambled at all – immortalized by Frankie Laine. Ironically the hit was a choice selection by
management. And to a fair extent the lyrics minimized the anguish-
factor in a game that had a predictable conclusion for the players.

The #2 was freely provided at the blackjack tables as the cost of
doing business after the 'final' honeymoon period was over. But it
was a far cry from complementary martinis in better times which had
always seemed to benefit the bank. Martinis hardly helped concentration but provided a needed distraction for the x-generation who
liked to feel-good as they lost whatever pocket-money remained. In
the bank. To the bank. So, nothing was making sense and the whole
thing was a toss-up. The bank made out like the bandits they were,
at least publicly since 2009, because it was hard for the gamblers
to concentrate with the aching from the incisors affecting practically the entire nervous system as they chewed away on the stupid
placebos 'til *k*ingdom come. As if they were inhaling the real thing

like in the coke ad. It was a classic case of mind over matter and it didn't seem to matter too much for the x-smokers who couldn't do anything about the dismal situation anyway and who might as well have been blowing smoke in the no-smoking zones which was now tautology if not redundant.

I guess it didn't matter anymore.

Frankly, with fair credit to Frankie Laine, it was a ridiculous sight for the bus loads of first-time day-trippers to the Native American casinos to see everyone chewing on #2 pencils as though they hadn't a meal in weeks. It was giving a false impression and looked so bad that most of the day-trippers started new tables for better luck. Indeed, from a distance the #2 resembled a kazoo and sounded even more so with the losers constantly groaning from their aching teeth even before the hidden card was upturned if you were playing 21, so named to match the % of x-smokers. The cure for the pain was sometimes more painful for those who could ill-afford the trip to the experimental orthodontic prosthetic dental labs in Germany, converted from WWII labs, which specialized in consoling the x-smokers for permanent facial defects caused by the #2.

And yet, the placebos seemed to work. For a while.

For proof of effectiveness, you could hear the moaning in the offices and back-offices and sitting rooms at home and back-lot studios and casinos and welfare queues for ex-government workers deprived of cigarette-tax funded cushy jobs who never did much work anyway. Except put you on hold when the automatic voice messaging system didn't work.

The new breathe (sic) of x-smokers seemed to covet the sentimental value of the #2. They looked back nostalgically to their thumb-sucking adolescence, when, after a return to class from their daily quiet puff or two in the high school john, they fretted impatiently for the next recess. But that was then. Paul Clay recalled: *It was different when we were kids. In second grade, a teacher came in and gave us all a lecture about not smoking, and then sent us over to arts and crafts to make ashtrays for Mother's Day.*

To avoid immediate mass hysteria upon ratification of the smoking ban for the 21% of the population who would have to quit cold-turkey on New Year's Day, the Anti-Tobacco Administration in a moment of weakness decided spontaneously that morning to hold a huge bash that afternoon on New Year's Eve. The final smoking blast would be a swan song for the 45-million adult smokers – sharing a camaraderie for people who didn't know each other and, frankly, cared less – as long as they could smoke. The crux was that they needed a facility to hold everyone. The Loser's Club in Dallas was too small. The only building large enough to accommodate all 45-million smokers – indeed the largest building in the world - was the Vehicle Assembly Building – the Shuttle repair building - at the Kennedy Space Center proudly standing 525 feet high. It had become available when NASA killed the shuttle in anticipation of the loss of cigarette taxes to fund the space program.

 *Four*

The VAB

It was New Year's Eve all over again, 2008, and things couldn't get much worse. The A of C had finally been announced promptly at noon, yet, surprisingly without too much comeuppance. The reason was simple. They (21% of the adult population, plus 5 million brat-kids) still had some smoke-time left and the law wouldn't be ratified until New Year's morning, pending the outcome of two hastily con-ceived 'ceremonial' referendums to the nation at risk, respectively, the 'popular-vote' and the 'reality-vote'. All things being equal.

Although the minority (the smokers) felt exactly the opposite. Further - everyone lived for the moment in the spirit of self-gratification and in spite of it. Which is what people wanted. Most of all. Especially if they were hooked. Which they were. Along with all the other New Year resolutions which made great conversation pieces. Indeed. Five easy pieces if you were to listen to Jack Nicholson. All of which (the 'other' resolutions) were usually made in good faith. Albeit having a tendency to be broken with the first *whiff* of temptation. If they weren't so human. Especially the smokers. Who weren't half as bad as the non-smokers if you listened to their (the non-smokers) perpetual nagging. Having already forced the *tabagie* into the outhouses. Which wasn't enough. Yes indeed, there was still time but not much. As they looked at their watches.

But this time New Year's would be different because there was the Midnight Express to contend with. Which was the talk of the town and put the heebie-jeebies into every smoker left standing. And everyone knew the ban was inevitable anyway. Even many of the naysayers. So that they should get with the program. As they locked their doors and pulled the draperies which were reeking of smoke.

Although it was still early in the day, the celebratory mood just didn't feel right. It didn't have the oomph to it like you feel for the grasp of that constant companion. The Constant Gardener, starring Rachel Weisz as the beautiful young activist. Which reminded you of the lyric: *How many kinds of sweet flowers grow/In an English country garden?* [Jimmie Rodgers] But it lacked that familiar feeling that psychologists say is even more addictive than the nicotine itself. Like when you remember some earth-shattering global event and exactly where you were smoking at the moment you learned of it. And what brand it was. How you were clasping that cigarette in a manner you would never forget. The very feel of it. The very thought of you. [Billie Holiday] Holding on for dear life. Like when you heard of JFK's assassination. And what you were smoking then. And what he used to smoke when regaling his latest conquest, probably an H. Upmann Petit Corona Cuban cigar and making fantastic smoke circles.

Like having a friend (your cigarette) when others proved shallow and only pretended to be your friend. Like – you've got a friend! [James Taylor] Right! Not that kind of feeling but a feeling that makes you tight in your throat. *The same tightness a man gets when his baby first shaves and makes his first sound as a man -* as Davy Crockett said in the Alamo. Well, as John Wayne said. Whatever. When it served their own interests. Having someone, or something - like a cigarette, to rely upon when they were ignored by everyone else. Or discarded like a used towel after serving their purpose. The difference was that you could unconditionally count on the old reliable. Except when it came to your lungs. Which you didn't think about. Too much.

koff

koff-koff ....

Indeed, many thought that the Cuba crisis following the Bay of Pigs was little more than an *Upmann*-ship.

whisshhh ... oo-oooooh ...

But even with such a caveat, didn't everyone have their weakness? Their Achilles heel. Which didn't make their choice right. But it was their choice, right? Or wrong. Like the obsessions that great artists suffer. Uncontrollably. Driven by art for Art's sake. Whoever the hell Art was. When he was left alone. Washing the dishes. When the missus had left. For good. Or for bad. The transition between. Which was frequently subjective. At best. The transition before the honeymoon period was over. Still, you could never predict an aftermath. Like people still standing around after an entire family has been wiped out in a fire. Or by a river when someone drowned. Talking about it. Just standing around. Doing nothing about it. But what could they do? What would you do? Yoodoo. What would Jesus do? What did He do? He never even smoked for godsakes. According to the Pharisees* in the four gospels.

(*Latin pharisæus, from Hebrew פְּרוּשִׁים pĕrûšîm, meaning "set apart", Qal passive participle of the verb פָּרַשׁ pārāš, through Greek φαρισαῖος -- who were at various times a political party, a social movement, and a school of thought among Jews during the Second Temple period beginning under the Hasmonean dynasty (140–37 BCE) in the wake of the Maccabean Revolt.)

C'est la vie. Another rotten day. I just changed the subject, didn't I? I do that a lot when I start to get bogged-down, or, when the non-sequiturs begin to take over. Should've taken a sleet check before heading to the parking lot.

No, the inevitability of the A of C was suddenly being perceived as though the lawmakers' hearts weren't in it although surely it was the right thing to do for a nation at risk. Which would be riskier without cig taxes (but, that was not the debate).

whisshhh ... oo-oooooh ...

The majority of course were in the right, but the minority had their rights too. Or so they thought because they felt that the non-smokers had got away with murder. I mean, the only place you could smoke even before the ban was in a telephone booth and these were all knocked down. Or, the outhouse. Well? Yes, that's what I thought too. Yes, there didn't seem to be any fairness. Yet the non-smokers wanted more. It was like a lyric in a Leonard Cohen razorblade song: *(I saw a) pretty woman leaning in her darkened door/She cried to me, hey, why not ask for more?* [Bird on a wire]

Those who were blind but now could see, said: *I can see clearly now, the smoke is gone/...Gone are the dark clouds that had me blind/It's gonna be a bright (bright), bright (bright)/Sun-Shiny day.* [Johnny Nash] There was always one clown in the group when things become intolerable who chimed-in with: *Please give me one more smoke, give me one more smoke/One more smoke cos I can't wait forever.* [Phil Collins] And yet another: *Maybe it's not the end/And I think we can make it/One more smoke, if we try/One more smoke for all the old times.* [Melissa Manchester] But it wasn't going to be easy. Those who had tried before when it was voluntary if not impossible to quit knew this: *They say that giving up is hard to do/Now I know, I know that it's true.* [Neil Sedaka] And 45 million concurred: *What do you get when you give them up/You only get lies and pain and sorrow/So, for at least until tomorrow/I'll never give them up!* [The Carpenters]

Anticipating the worst, even prior to the announcement at the dawning of the post-T era, writing creativity was already dying. The cancer had crept in, as it were. Writers were carelessly dropping metaphors and failing to dot their i's while crossing their t's sideways looking like an 'x' through the soon to be extinct tobacco. Xobacco.

Conjuring images of Xanado.

And Coleridge. And the Wordsworth, Lord Byron and Marco Polo connection.

True, people had been *buying* the classics in record numbers, but nobody read any of them. It was an ownership thing and a conversation piece but soon writers would no longer be capable of writing without tobacco, without nico, the feel and touch of the cigarette which had macho written all over it and the coquettish behavior of the ladies. Even though it was well before midnight (on New Year's Eve), it really wasn't well at all, they hadn't their heart (pun) in it. If there were any good news it was that the comic book had been reinvented while newspapers were purchased primarily for the Sunday cartoons. What a laugh it was but it was no laughing matter.

And yet, the day that literature (as we knew it) died would not be publicized for lack of interest, having accelerated its steep decline during the transition period.

Unless you were a *k*-smoker.

whisshhh ... oo-oooooh ...

That is, the few who couldn't take the nonsense anymore – were there others besides me? And who wrote about it. And who risked a one-way ticket to the Mid X. Creative writing was dead without tobacco. That was it. It was all about that old black magic called smoke. [Louis Prima]

Writing creativity had literally fallen off a cliff as smoking was about to be abolished. The last great novel was The Cliff by Eileen Dover. And that was the last that was heard from her. Once again, the whole thing had the appearance of Heisenberg. You could only write meaningfully when you were alone in the sole company of your constant companion. The really sad part underscored the regret that the game was up come midnight. When smoking would finally be banned in the outhouse where figuratively speaking it had been for decades.

The optimists realized that there were still twelve hours remaining for something good to happen. Hope springs eternal. All hope abandon, ye who enter here! [The Divine Comedy, Inferno] People who never prayed in their lives were praying to saints who long ago had been banished from the Vatican roster in a drastic revision of the liturgical calendar because there was never any proof that they even existed. At all. Ever! Including St. Christopher, St. Barbara and St. Susanna. *Oh Susanna/Don't you cry for me/For I come from Alabama/With my banjo on my knee.* But it was an honest omission. No, it would soon be a criminal offence to smoke anywhere. Especially in the closet, the ultimate hold-out. Even to think about smoking. Thought, word, indeed.

And yet, all of the great writers had been smokers, hadn't they? That's what nico did. What nico does. What women want. It provided the concentration for the inspiration. The condition for the contrition. No more. Not much. And the majority didn't seem to care.

All they wanted was their eco. Their id. Which they thought they could control. Beneath the CO_xs, SO_xs and NO_xs that would linger above the skyline for the next millennium. At least. And then some. Without cig taxes to improve the health and education infrastructure. To compete globally. Especially with the Chinese who would soon be marching on Wall Street. And Main Street would be next. Then, Mean Street. *Come on down, down to mean street/(Huh ow)/(This is)/They're dancin' now, out on mean street/(Look)/Dance baby.* [Val Halen]

With their microwaves already set on low back home to save some money. So, they were in denial. And to hell with great literature which emanated from nico. And the great balls of fire. [Jerry Lee Lewis] The song derived from a southern Pentecostal expression after the Holy Ghost appeared and the apostles spoke in tongues. It became famous because Scarlett O'Hara kept saying: *Great balls of fire!* whenever she got tongue-tied with Rhett Butler. When she wasn't in a tongue-lock. Which, in fairness, you never actually saw on screen. In the old days. Except for Ronald Colman in his Academy Award performance …. Othello … tongue-strangle. It was a miserable state of affairs. Misery loves company [Stephen King] but company is anathema to a *k*-smoker.

Truly it was the end of literature. Que sera, sera. C'est la vie. Hasta la vista, baby. Except for those of us (assuming I wasn't the only one left) – who saw the altruistic value in giving literature back to society. After some thirty-plus years of smoking.

whisshhh … oo-oooooh …

In lieu of the extended honeymoon having had too many shortcomings and unrealistic expectations by die-hards that it would last forever - something had to be done and fast. The AT lawmakers who were trying to catch on fast were well aware of what could happen with too quick an introduction of any unpopular change affecting a fifth of the population in a status quo that had lasted centuries or more. Or less. Or worse. It was bad enough being a member of the *tabagie* freezing their butts off. And now even they were to be outlawed. Was there any justice at all? In God We Trust. People were agitated. The line had been crossed into their personal space. And they were having a terrible time. And space. And time was of the essence. Hardly two hours following the secondhand smoke tragedy at the Time-Life building. There was no end to the contiguity of the wordplay.

Then some smart AT lawmaker had a neat idea while it was still morning on New Year's Eve. Why not hold a huge bash, a party – in the afternoon? One final smoking blast - for the pending 45 million adult quitters who were now chomping-at-the-bit more than ever getting ready with their #2 pencils. Some 5 million juvenile smokers were neither counted nor invited to the party (which never stopped them before!) because they weren't of age and their records were expunged in the No Child Left Behind program. When they dropped out. Like the rest of them. Which was a quintuple-negative if you count all the neither-nors. In the oft-repeated biblical undertones of Peter, Paul & Mary: *We Shall Overcome* became the rallying cry.

The bash would be held on the afternoon of New Year's eve, the same day as the unprecedented **popular vote** for/against the smoking ban that evening, which the nation had insisted upon for closure – although with the 79:21 odds – you knew pretty much where *that* one was going!. Voting for the popular vote would extend from 18:00:00 to 21:00:00 EST. But, depending on where they were in time zones, they'd have to vote quick – the quick and the dead. [Gene Hackman]. And not loiter outside the voting parlors for a quiet puff or two afterwards. If there was to be any hope before the A of C would become effective at precisely 00:00.01 hours on New Year's morning. Otherwise, let's face it (they surmised), the pandemonium would revert back to 1781 (October 19),

or 1790 (July 14).

or 1916 (April 24).

or 1917 (November 7).

or 1947 (August 15).

or 1948 (May 14).

or 1949 (October 1).

And so on and so forth. The 45-million figure was calculated by the Centers for Disease Control & Prevention, CDC. And, since a full house was anticipated (or at least a flush), rsvps were mandatory. For the bash.

The invitation-list would be transmitted on 3G wireless networks by text for security purposes and to avoid the inconvenience of no-shows unless they switched-off power to extend battery life. With no one to blame but themselves if they missed out on the ceremonial bash with their miserable peers. The heat-shrunk economy was already in a tailspin in anticipation of the loss of cig taxes and, already, everyone cried in unison: Where's the money? It was a very good question, but no one said it was going to be easy and for once they were right.

The idea for the AT party was an indulgent expression by the AT lawmakers to show compassion for the masses who had enjoyed a quiet puff for as long as any of them could remember. Do you remember? [Paul Anka] And, as sure as smoking was responsible for every known ailment, there was still no correlation whatsoever with the onset of Alzheimer's regardless of age, which was a plus. The bash was also intended to spur them on for their small but meaningless sacrifice since, as yet, with things happening too fast, none of the die-hards had come to grips with anything except the sample #2 pencils clenched between their (by now) really-crooked teeth after chomping too hard during practice sessions without reading the how-to manual. Which they inadvertently had tossed. In the litter. Out of habit. Like another spent butt.

The initial site selected for the celebration, The Loser's Club in Dallas, was a no-brainer. Bobby Rydell used to sing there when smoking was legit. I met him at the club once although he'd hardly remember me. He seemed to be in a midlife panic attack as to what the 'ell he was doing there in the first place. After all, nobody loves a loser and The Loser's Club was all about losers.

Yet, in the words of Alfred Lord Tennyson: 'Tis better to have loved and lost/Than never to have loved at all. So, there was no logic in it whatsoever.

Indeed, Bobby was then only a shadow of his former self, like most of them from the sixties, denying that they had been inducted into the AARP by default. Which they hadn't asked for. But deserved. That is - when you hit fifty and for your birthday you have two canvass bags of junk mail from the AARP in your front lawn. And even more spam if you were senile enough to provide your email. And, for every perforated card you ripped-out, filled-in, signed and added a stamp to - which cost more than all the gifts combined, you got free pedometers, wallet-sized snow scrapers, large-digit calculators, key-chains with attached hi-beam keyhole finders, decaffeinated-coffee mugs, and half-off coupons for #2 pencil refills. And, last but not least, extrapolated and interpolated longevity charts customized for former smokers, most of whom by now were off both the x and the y-axis.

And all of whom should've been dead and buried long ago.

whisshhh ... oo-oooooh ...

The event was going to be a stimulus all right, but certainly not for the economy which was on its hind legs with the computed loss of cig contributions to the Treasury coffers which had seen better days.

However, on second thoughts with all the second-hand smoke clouding his judgment, the astute AT lawmaker figured that 'loser' might give the wrong connotation for a 'quitter'. And, a forced quitter at that. Which was worse. Like a forced-march or a forced-evacuation which eliminated the choice-factor on which we were raised. Like at those intervention-parties for alcos-anon as a last resort. Which was no holiday resort. And which made everyone feel bad. *Feel so bad/Feel like a ballgame on a rainy day/Sometime I wanna stay here/Then again I wanna leave/Sometime I wanna leave here/Then again I wanna stay.* [Elvis] Or, feeling good. Feeling alright/I'm not feeling good myself/Feeling alright/I don't have to feel alright/I'm feeling good myself. [Joe Cocker] And, feeling bad all over again: *Well let me tell you that it hurts so bad/It makes me feel so sad/... Don't make it hurt so bad/I'm begging you please.* [Linda Ronstadt] And, quite honestly, there was no way The Loser's Club could accommodate all of the quitters as much as they would've felt right at home.

~ ~ ~

As luck would have it, the VAB, the world's largest building in volume under a single roof was vacant and available on New Year's Eve. The question was – could they accommodate 45-million smokers (and God knows how many gatecrasher juvenile delinquents) for their final drag even at a squeeze? And, survive the trillions of compressed carcinogens in an enclosed space at the space center which might take off like a balloon, the building itself, with all 45-million smoking at once? Still, it was a good question while many of the potential invitees were still breathing after some thirty years of puffing up a storm so the risk of a collapsed lung during the actual bash itself, based upon probability, was considered minimal. At best.

To wit ...

The VAB would be shown by-appointment-only at 11.45am by the local real estate agent with tough questions answered but no promises. Due to a conflict in schedules of all the activity going-on during New Year's eve, the actual bash would have to commence no later than 12.30pm so the pressure was intense. It was no secret that the government badly needed the rental at a voluntary dollar donation of the equivalent of a pack of cigs per smoker - because times were tough with the ban approaching. The expected take - half a billion dollars if all complied. Not bad for a few hours work and roughly commensurate with the entire Rolling Stones World Concert Tour of 2006 two years earlier with 1.5 million smoking-attendees at Copacabana Beach, Rio. An indoor smoking waiver would be needed for the afternoon so some judgment calls would have to be made as they were running out of time. And then of course there were the 45 million invites to send out. TG for Al Gore who invented the Internet (and who will make a cameo appearance in Chapter 6). The realty agent looked an awful (pun) lot like Rodney Dangerfield and he didn't appear too professional sans jacket in Bermuda shorts with his rolled-up short sleeves. Which he insisted was necessary in the blistering sun and drenching humidity. While some thought that a jacket with Bermuda shorts would probably have looked even worse. And they were right. With his hairy legs and wobbly knees.

And so, the prospective site for the blast, the last smoking party on earth, was the (empty) shuttle vehicle assembly building (VAB) at the Kennedy Space Center, proudly standing 525 feet high. In nyloned stockings, sans shoes. Just kidding.

The VAB had become just an ugly eyesore without the anticipated cigarette taxes to support its upkeep -- looking more like an abandoned warehouse in the beautiful sunshine state after the space Shuttle Program was shot down. With surface-to-air missiles. Just kidding. A huge flag waved from the top which could be seen from Louisiana on a clear day during the summer if it weren't for Lake

Alfred (the lightning capitol of the world) spoiling the view at peak season. Once pegged by EPRI with 10,000 zigzags on a single afternoon. Just watching the strikes was like lit cigarettes pouring down from heaven and a sight for sore eyes for those who had smoked an average of three decades and would never get over it which was the usual diagnosis. As the bouncer kept saying: *Get over it*! But now it was New Year's Eve so all they had to do was vent beneath the CO_xs, SO_xs and NO_xs.

The realtor (whose commission it was to show the VAB) concluded that with a push and a shove and a little bit of contortionist-cum-laude manipulation - they could fit all 45 million guests inside the VAB if they scrambled, since smokers were generally not obese - yet, until after the ban.

whisshhh ... oo-oooooh ...

Following the interview, which lasted less than a New York minute, the organizers now had 44-minutes, tops, to transmit/receive RSVPs before the first respondents would arrive for the bash at precisely 12.30pm. The space-organizers in the space center had their work cut out to accommodate so many smokers for the coming-out party, on how to fit everyone inside, ergonomically utilizing every bit of empty space which wasn't exactly the cosmos. And they had to be extra careful with the girls and their elbows. But they had method in their madness as they let their imaginations run wild like Girls Gone Wild. Taking a nod from high-spirited HS cheerleaders standing on each other's heads who practice 4-hours/day 4-days/week for 4-months. Then, when the local-access community cable-channel zooms in for the finale - they lose their concentration by taking their eyes off their heads. And, in a fit of overstretching the elasticity of their bubbly cheeks with fake grins, they topple over each other and fracture their tender little ankles in four places or worse. It was no accident that the annual culmination of the grueling 4x4x4 performance was like a Dodge pick-up doing 80 on a sudden curve of a rural road. The usual end-of-season performance was always ridiculed by the cheerleaders' parents while criticizing the coach during tittle-tattle at neighbors' cocktail parties. Where parents exaggerate the extracurricular accomplishments of their kids anyway. Like, earning platinum plaques for ... showing up. Which was quite an accomplishment but kept them from the malls. And it made for great idle chatter. But let's not get carried away with Girls Gone Wild and their parents or legal guardians and get back to the VAB.

Although the above exemplification was just a sardine-can analogy to illustrate the mayhem following the announcement of the outright smoking ban which was to follow one final bash, the fact was that there wouldn't be too many cheerleaders for the tobacco post-mortem in the VAB audience after the A of C would be announced (albeit not official until 00:00:01 New Year's morning - barring a shock upset from the concomitant 'popular-vote' that polls had pegged was already 79/21 in favor of the ban). And the soon to be x-smokers were on tenterhooks.

whisshhh ... oo-oooooh ...

Secondly, that such a fine building had been empty in the first space (sic) was a sad reflection on our technological prowess as a nation (at risk). But the fact was that all space missions had been canceled for the imminent want of cig taxes.

John Glenn   Senator
Astronaut
11/8/03

And I was told this firsthand.

Still, it was appropriate use of dead space for the ultimate blast; the final fling, the last hurrah (... from the old Norse warrior word 'Huzzah!" which meant 'On to paradise' – but personified by Edwin O'Connor to mean 'a final appearance or effort, especially at the end of a lifetime of smoking); or the inevitable swan song starring the dark side of Natalie Portman.

Thirdly, as an added incentive 45 million #2 pencils (and some spares)

were provided as door prizes and party favors for those who were willing to do the right thing and quit cold turkey during the VAB festivities, and which were snapped up promptly as take-aways only, for the die-hards – realizing that when they got home with nothing to smoke and nothing to do, what would they do?

What would you do?

Reader: *Sorry, I wasn't concentrating - who me?*

Everything got off to a fine start at 12:30:00 for the celebration as inexplicably all the quick arrangements seemed to fit into place. The plan was to allow 2-hours elapsed time for the T (tobacco) party.

This would accommodate the smoking of one pack of 20 cigarettes each per guest at the rate of 6-minutes tops per cigarette. The bash would then conclude at 14:30:00 if the VAB building itself hadn't already taken-off from the tobacco smoke (500ug of NO per cigarette x 20 cigs each x 450 million smokers x 2 hours) like the planned mission of the shuttle which unfortunately had to be grounded for want of cigarette taxes to fund it.

Well, the 'fine start' lasted until everyone arrived, that is! Predictably, some 45 million guests were smoking away like nobody's business. And, not being careful where they were tossing their butts (inciting screams), many (more than 5 stories high on top of each other's shoulders) just randomly kept toppling over each other and, predictably, fracturing their ankles like typical cheer leaders on YouTube. It was a great bash alright but starting to look like a fiasco if you could see through all the smog. Still, as far as the AT lawmakers (the organizers of the final bash - as a form of 'closure') were concerned, it was the thought that counts. And they weren't fooling anyone.

Everyone wondered what effect the great afternoon bash would have on the popular vote starting at 18.00:00 hours the way things were happening so fast since noon on New Year's Eve. There was no looking forward in fear of mass rioting that hadn't been seen since L.A. and before that, the Saigon evacuation. S&R choppers were hovering at-the-ready outside the line-of-sight and as far away as possible for their own safety from the fuming smokers getting restless (especially if Harrison Ford were piloting!) – after the highs of the VAB blast. But now, suddenly confronted with the reality of the popular-vote prior to the reality-vote on the **Late Yo with David Minuteman** following the just-announced noon House show-of-hands rollcall in DC.

Reader:	*I can't make out what you mean about the reality of the popular vote? I thought the reality vote was to be a different thing to the popular vote!? Jeez!*
Me:	*I knew this was going to happen about my combining past, present and sometimes the future and occasionally using the first and the second person and maybe even the third in the same sentence and resorting to verb-less sentences for expediency-sake. Please remember that this ENTIRE CONFESSION is an internal monologue. All I can say is that everything is explained in the appendix, but I'm busy now, ok? Jeez, too!*

whisshhh ... oo-oooooh ...

ps:	*Indeed, I forgot to add that if repetition bothers you - you should listen to the last 12 lines of Dionne Warwick's Trains and Boats and Planes*

mmm ... mmm ... mmm ... mmm .../mmm ... mmm ... mmm ... mmm .../mmm ... mmm ... mmm ... mmm ... mmm ... mmm   mmm ... mmm/mmm ... mmm ... mmm ... mmm ... mmm .../mmm ... mmm ... mmm ...

whisshhh ... oo-oooh ...

Incidentally, in the early days of NASA before the funding shortage from cig taxes, I had the privilege of meeting Senator-astronaut John Glenn. And also, Ron Evans of Apollo 17, the eleventh manned space mission and the sixth and last mission to land on the moon. So, I don't make these observations lightly.

191

~ ~ ~

Between all the flashbacks and flash-forwards, tobacco was indeed abolished in 2009. And, predictably, writing creativity ceased, instantly. The post-T era had developed into an I'm Okie-dokie/ You're Okie-dokie [Thomas A. Harris MD] kind of 'just-ok' society with nothing much to write home about: *I don't care what you say anymore, this is my life/Go ahead with your own life, leave me alone.* [Billy Joel] Yes, it was … just ok. I guess. As WS said: *It was much ado about smoking.* Conscionably the #2 placebo could never have worked for a writer since the tangible relationship of nico and tobacco to inspiration and creative thinking is as intangibly intrinsic as the muse is to poetry.

There might well have been a goodly number of uninspiring writers who never smoked at all and wrote 'Neil Diamond type' *chair*-prose: *And nobody heard/Not even the* … the what? … *the chair*!!" The what!? *thewhatthewhatthewhatthewhat* … Even the Reservoir Dogs composed: *I'm so scared in case I fall off my chair/ And I'm wondering how I'll get down the stairs.* Which didn't attract too many Billy-Jobel lit nominations. Although they were probably smoking something stronger than Cuban cigars. In fairness, the few great artists who may not (?) have been smokers had some kind of addiction, affliction, dysfunction, or other obsession to compensate - which made them great. How great thou art. But for smokers to be great writers, the taste also had to be just right. As William Wordsworth wrote to Lady Beaumont: *Never forget what I believe was observed to you by Coleridge, that every great and original writer, in proportion as he is great and original, must himself create the taste by which he is to be relished.* Susan Sontag added the closet-dimension to this a couple of centuries later: *The writer is either a practicing recluse or a delinquent, guilt-ridden one.* Or both. Usually both. Edna Ferber described the need for perseverance even against the threat of the Mid X: *Life cannot* defeat a writer who is in love with writing; for *life itself is a writer's love until death.* Finally, Julian Barnes made the differentiation of the two half-lives that are required to write words that pound on the conscience: *The writer's life is full of frailty and defeat like any other life. What counts is the work. Yet the work can quite easily be buried,* or *half-buried, by the life.* The fact is that history proves most great writers enjoyed a nice quiet puff (or two) to help them relax and concentrate. To open the portal. Drop the drawbridge. Unclog preconceptions (... in fairness, clogging the arteries by default). Uncork the magic genie. Unlock secret passageways. Open, Sesame. Unleash the mind.

whisshhh ... oo-ooooh ...

Thar' goes the mind. There goes the neighborhood. There goes the circus. There goes the cosmos. An oasis in the wilderness. In the parking lot.

The A of C had ushered the end of literature in modern times. Without nico and tobacco the responsiveness to inspiration just wasn't there! Soon there was nothing new under the sun. No one was writing. What were they thinking? It was like an airport in the wake of the Eyjafjallajokull eruptions. People had short memories, were too restless to read, and cared less.

Indeed, the classics were forgotten in the ballyhoo. In Ballydehob, County Cork. Just kidding about the Ballydehob part having much ado about ballyhoo! And there was nothing new. And people stopped borrowing new books for book club social-extravaganzas because there was nothing worth reading when writers stopped writing - without nicotine, the nerve-center for the muse, for inspiration. And instead of the nerve center it was now just 'all nerves' without cigarettes to calm them down. The stress was staggering. And everyone was very blue. Something new. Something very blue. All the great smokers were long dead and buried and there was no baton to pass. Just a #2 pencil.

Nothing was left but a majestic memory. [Longfellow]

But one thing was for sure – all the great writers had been smokers for such was their legacy: John Steinbeck, Ernest Hemingway, James Joyce, Virginia Woolf, Fyodor Dostoevsky, Albert Camus, Jean-Paul Sartre, Samuel Beckett, Aldous Huxley, William Faulkner, J.R.R.Tolkien, Oscar Wilde, Henry James, Joseph Conrad, T.S. Eliot, William Butler Yeats, Charles Dickens, George Orwell, Jane Austen (… as you know by now, on whose tomb I once stood on-top-of in Winchester Cathedral without realizing it was her tomb, getting the angst of the sacristan's stare), Jonathan Swift, Alexander Pope, Lord Byron, Dylan Thomas, Brendan Behan, Kurt Vonnegut, Ralph Waldo Emerson, Rudyard Kipling, Mark Twain, Bertrand Russell, Charles Bukowski, Evelyn Waugh, Jack Kerouac, C.S. Lewis, Hunter S. Thompson, G.K. Chesterton, J.B. Priestley, David Foster Wallace, Bertolt Brecht, James Dickey, Tricky Dickie, Mickey Dickey, Mickey M., Mickey Spillane … Huh, you noticed.

You have trouble with that? Well Mickey was a dear friend who gave me his autograph before he died so he's staying on this list. Indeed, Mickey's most famous saying was: "The only way to make money at writing is to write ransom notes". Continuing … Somerset Maugham, Arthur Rimbaud, J.D. Salinger, Saul Bellow, J.P. Donleavy, Joseph Heller …

oops, how the heller did the last two get on this list of greats?

Due to a gap in the web, for all I know those two (Donleavy and Heller) may not have been smokers. And, God help us, may still be alive (going to print – well, that is - if these confessions *ever* go to print! *whew!)*

Oops, so sorry, Jim and Joe. Rather, James Patrick RIP and Joseph RIP! I didn't know you had both succumbed. What happened? Seriously, I truly admire your work. You see, these confessions are a parody and sometimes I have to come up for a breath of fresh air!

whisshhh … oo-ooooh …

And so on and so forth for a formidable tally. Walt Whitman was probably the only great writer in history who for sure never smoked. This can be ascertained by the way he wrote about the abominable habit - unless it was a cover and he were a closet-smoker like the rest of us. Or, before there even was a Starbust, in whatever the popular gathering spot might have been at the time. For example, Ye Olde Pig and Whistle Inn for starving writers. Those were the days when some of the greats worked with quills. Do you promise you quill? Yes, I quill. I promise. Then, later, with typewriters at best ... (like William F. Buckley who once phoned my home, and such ilk, including his son, Christopher who wrote 'Thank You for Smoking'. Good god, small 'g' for emphasis. Notice the company - had I written 'Good God' in caps in the presence of W.F – no one would notice, right?)!

Indeed, following the enactment of the A of C, Michka Seeliger-Chatelein, one of the curators of Le Musee du Fumeur (The Museum of Smoking) was quoted in the NYT: *All our great writers seem to have been (great) smokers.* The Telegraph reported: *In lieu of the smoking ban, is this the end of English Literature (as we know it)?*

    whisshhh ... oo-ooooh ...

But there were always the few artists who tried to conceal their addictions until it was no longer necessary to cling to clichés in the closet. Which is ironic because *k*-smokers are the only minority now confined to the closet. Figuratively speaking. In the great abandoned parking lots on the wrong side of the railway tracks. And the great abandoned back-lots of Tinseltown with the demise of the glamorous mannerism of the dashing heroine of the silver screen - ubiquitous cigarette in right hand and beautiful supporting actress on her lap. Now but a trivia-footnote in history.

Haven't had a puff in about 12-minutes. Starting to lose focus, concentration. darn. Wasn't going to have another today. I'm not a chain-smoker. Starting to get edgy. Hell. He*l*l Mencken. Heck Mencken. One more. Just a tic. Right with ya.

aahhhh

ah. ya. yas. yes. yessssssss ...

    whisshhh ...

        oo-ooooh ...

No. There was no reprieve from the Mid X if you were kaught even in the great outdoors. Because every common or uncommon ailment was a direct effect of 2HS. Windborne from the backwoods. From sea to shining sea. Carrying the bubonic plague. Like Columbus. When practically nobody had a clue what an actuary was or cared less.

But the stats were impressive if not dramatic.

That the leading causes of death were all lumped into second-hand smoke: cardiovascular disease, cancer (... lung, oral cavity, larynx, esophagus, other), stroke, chronic lower respiratory and obstructive pulmonary disease, homicide, suicide, fratricide, measles, cryptosporidiosis, small pox, H1N1, E.Coli, rheumatism, sternoclavicular hyperostosis, multifocal osteomyelitis, sclerosing osteitis, pneumonia, SARS, scars, influenza, Spinoza, the common cold, sneezing. And, last but not least, strep throat. As Fletcher Knebel commented upon reading the health report put out (pun) by the actuaries: *It is now proved beyond doubt that smoking is one of the leading causes of statistics.*

And all because – they, the administration, *don't know* who we are. Just of our (probable) existence by reading our books ...... under pseudonyms. Assuming this WIP ever gets published ... And others. If there are others.

whisshhh ... oo-ooooh ...

~ ~ ~

And yet most great artists died impoverished if not (Sean) young. Incidentally, the good ones died young. And Sean Young better watch herself. 'me dear! Huh?

Maybe such relatively youthful departures will change with the increased longevity projected by actuaries as a result of the tobacco ban. When you would live a little longer.

(Stay), just a little bit longer/ Woah woah woah woah /Oh-ooh ooh-ooh-ooh-ohh-ohh-ohh-ohh/ (Please) Please, please, please, please. [Four Seasons]

To write your WIPs. And, although posthumous success is an admirable reflection upon intestinal fortitude, it is not the reason for my confession. My intent is to make a difference in the here and now. By describing why I was compelled to be different.

Huh!

Maybe I too can participate in this extended longevity-thing that everyone's talking about.

If I weren't a darn *k*loset smoker.

darn. These stupid cigs. darn. darn. darn.

Which reminds me. Two tics please.

  koff!

oops!

   koffkoff.

???

Be right with you …

  whisshhh … oo-oooooh …

Stupid wind. Stupid ashes. Darn, my new jacket. And slacks. *oops.* Lost my balance. Sure enough, when I wear my khakis, it's up against the chevy again. Never a dull moment with the black ones or navy blue. Don'it make my brown eyes blue. [Crystal Gayle] At least it isn't raining. No puddles in the lot today. Thank God after I invested in a new pair of shoes after the last time. You can do anything but stay offa my blue suede shoes. [Elvis]

Aha! Here comes the sun, here comes the sun,/And I say it's alright/Sun, sun, sun, here it comes/Sun, sun, sun, here it comes/ Sun, sun, sun, here it comes/Sun, sun, sun, here it comes/Sun, sun, sun, here it comes. [The Beatles] Darn ashes ...

~ ~ ~

Hey, are you (reader) reading my wip because you like my writing; are compassionate about what I have to confess; or because someone just let you borrow it?

Reader: *Hey! You talkin' ta me?*

Or, all three of the above. I'm beginning to sound as though this WIP has been published, huh.

{Publishers insert: ⌛

> The immersion-method of this book is a time warp. Obviously, the confession has been published or you wouldn't be reading it. The author requested that we insert something about this because sometimes with his words that pound on the conscience, he seems to lose focus. Have a nice day.}

I'll never know the answer to that one – the one about "neither a borrower nor a lender be". It doesn't really bother me. What matters is that (some of) you, they, the forensics among you, are reading my confession for incendiary purposes and not to learn, intellectually and compassionately, from it ... in my humble attempt at reviving great literature as we knew it.

Au péril de sa vie.

Still, if only one of you has been touched then it will have served my purpose. Touched by an angel. As it says in the good book … *verily I say unto you, inasmuch as ye have done it unto one of the least of these my brethren …*

But there *are* those of you actually reading my confession! To see what contrition my confession is in, *hmmm* …? Which is somewhat redeeming. A confession, remarkably without a catchy title like Angela's Ashes.

Redemption. Contrition. Confession. Satisfaction. Absolution? Absolutely.

I hope. To god. And the cycle continues. In the circle game. [Tom Rush] Go and sin no more. Until the next time. There's not supposed to be a next time if you did it right the last time. When you swore you'd never do it again. Millions reading my confession - just when you thought literature was dead. Thank god for small miracles. And God is Dead, according to Nietzsche, who soon found out one way or the other. Himself. You would think? Huh? John Lennon (in adding to the debate) responded: *Guys and gals, we're more popular than Jesus.*

The condition of my contrition. As though I were a (famous) recluse.

Which I am in my other life, this one actually, in the parking lot (but not famous). In the here and now. Herein now. Like Greta Garbo. You Sir are no Greta Garbo. (I saw that coming.) Thank god for that too. With her temperament. I've enough problems. With the darn midges. And the comparison ends there since she wasn't a writer. Although, in fairness, she was (one helluv)a smoker.

whisshhh … oo-oooooh …

A glamorous heroine of the silver screen.

Not bad for someone else (me) who shuns the public spotlight about half of the time (me divided by two) now that it's nightfall. Writing. More like scribbling beneath the parking lot lamppost with the bugs swarming all over me. Makes it difficult to concentrate. The left hand not knowing what the right's doing. Like Peter Sellers as Dr. Strangelove. With an uncontrollable mechanical hand making involuntary salutes ...

Darn bugs! *SWAT!*

I don't care squat. I've words to do.

Krazy how these lights are on anyway because this lot's been abandoned since god knows when. Weird. Had I my druthers, I wouldn't be doing this so late, but I got sidetracked earlier. Parked in the middle of nowhere. Like someone with a different agenda than normal people. Ordinary people. Like Timothy Hutton. Thought I was being followed, *hmmm ...* and took diversionary steps from abandoned parking lot to parking lot. Which took up my entire 50-minutes or a good ten pages worth. Wasted. Wasted Days and wasted nights. [Freddy Fender] More often than not I can't read my own scribble later when I'm home with my laptop. The missus on my lap. Top. I wish. Where is she? In the other room. I guess. Online. *hmmm ...*

The eyes aren't what they used to be. And maybe it's not all because of second-hand smoke but my own firsthand smoke, exhaling vertically into my eyes for decades (when I was even a closet-smoker before the A of C) depending on the direction of the wind on an ugly day. Must try those natural carotenoid lutein vitamins with fish oil that are supposed to be good for the eyes if it's not too late. Aye. Said I'd be home before dark. Gotta run. Run! Run!

~ ~ ~

Yes. *K*at and mouse. *K*-smoker and AT kop. But it's not a game. This other life is extremely perilous. Hazardous to your health. Mine. That's what they say. The rich man in hell. Maybe a rich fat man. Fat lot o' good. Playing with fire.

whisshhh ... oo-ooooh ...

A kid with a lighted match. But age matters only if it's wine which I don't need as others do to do what I'm doing. You do what you do. Do do. Coffee works for me, hot or cold. It's part and parcel of the simple pleasure: caffeine + nico. The formula. Formula One.

In order to write. To write or not to write. Nothing else.

And neither works (for me) on their own. Maybe it's why I've lived so long - the combination. Assuming my daily supply of (real) fruit, squeezed lemon, leafy veggies, olive stone ... oops (darn spell check) meant to write oliver (sic) oil (extra virgin), some spinach and broccoli, a spoonful of powdered protein shaken (not stirred) over rice Krispies with cherry tomatoes, a handful of nuts in a side-bowl. Super bowl. And twenty minutes on the Nordic Track. Makes you work at it. The arm exerciser cord drum and the leg drag resistance. They still make those, huh?

You won't read about it in the medical journals, but coffee allows the smooth inhalation without the dreaded *k*off. Have you ever heard me *k*off? No, you wouldn't. But I never have. Hardly ever. *hmmm ...*
Caffeine on its own is okay too. But, caffeine + nico and you in the

middle has been called a ménage de trois by the French. The largest smoking nation on earth per capita before the (near-)global ban.

And size matters too. 100's, soft pack. And taste. Don't forget the taste. I've got my brand and it's not *K*ools. Like inhaling stale aircraft air with a taste of dandelion, riding through choppy weather when you really need a drag. But can't. Doesn't bother me too much because I can turn on and off, just like that. When I know I can't light up. Funny.

Even in choppy weather. Not funny.

But, hold onto your lighter!

Cold and damp, here right now, trying to finish up this paragraph before returning to the office as if nothing happened. I mean, as though I hadn't entered the portal - which today happens to be in the extreme corner of an empty parking lot safely surrounded by debilitated buildings. Yonder. Well, on one side of the hypotenuse. Just kidding. It's more like a quadranglenuse. Or an imperfect parallelogram. An imperfect confession. Which works too. But with a little extra penance. And a sort of forest on the other. Although you knew about the rumors of new construction (just a note to myself in the event that yet another location will need to be, as it were, 'sniffed out'). And after staying a while, to re-emerge into the real world.

Hi everyone. Did I miss anything? Did *you* miss … *me*? And you hoped the response was (polite) indifference. You me. You - ma! Yuma. Three hours to Yuma.

Gotta get moving. Writers don't like to write 'gotta' but I'm ina 'urry! Expedience matters. Don't wanna be missed. Hate writing 'wanna'. Haven't we been through that!

In the meantime, you can't imagine how much we rely on good weather. Nice day, huh? You see, it's particularly hard to hold an umbrella over your head while fingering the middle pages of your thesaurus on the flat of your car trunk bureau on a rainy afternoon with your elbow on your writing pad. A writer can go weeks without a dictionary but hardly minutes without his thesaurus for fear of using the same word twice in the same sentence. Or fear of not using the same word twice in the repetitiveness of a good confession. Like being in two places at once which is what this secret life is all about. Omnipresence. Bilocation. Yes indeed, the repetitiveness of it all.

~ ~ ~

Back to China. As we have observed the chairman had ruled to ban *non-smokers* - because smoking was good for population control. And they were also taking notes in India. And before you knew it, the 21% who had never lit up in China were soon smoking up a chimney. And, morning, noon or night, you'd think it was fireworks in every alley, just looking at them. While those who hadn't yet mastered the bad habit were carelessly burning little holes in their cheap Mao jackets (and soon their Nehru shirts in India). Until the bad habit became good with practice.

After non-smoking was outlawed.

In China.

And you were sent to Mongolia if *k*aught not smoking. Which was a miserable attempt at their own Mid X. Trying to clone just about everything. Since a smoking ban in China would've been an end to their economic stimulus sustained by cig taxes.

whisshhh ... oo-ooooh ...

I already told you of meeting Zhu Rongji, former-Premier of China at a conference in Shenzhen. Zhu pronounced Shoo!

Zhu.

oops ... I think I'm getting a cold ...

Ahh-zhuuuu ...!

> *Reader(s):*   *God bless you.*

Sorry about that. And, because Zhu was an atheist - and a chain-smoker to wit, there wasn't much he was going to tell. About our meeting. In the event that he'd read these confessions. If they're ever translated into Mandarin. Like my friend Xiao Qian did with Ulysses. Which no one could read in English anyway.

Author's photo of his friend Xiao Qian

As though *he* hadn't enough to worry about.

> *a male reader:*   *Excuse me, who?*
>
> *me:*   *Zhu!*
>
> *another reader*
>
>   *(who had started to doze off):*   *Ahh ... Zhu?*
>
> *a female reader*
>
>   *(interrupting the stream):*   *God bless zhu!*

And now we know the rest of the story. How the Chinese owned the entire US debt. Which was nothing to brag about. And which was a far cry from the time the Chinese were only part owners of the Cleveland Cavaliers and the Seattle Mariners. But, enough about Cleveland for now.

The ban on no-smoking (a double negative for ecolinguistics study) resulted in the unprecedented 21% decline in population for the first time since 1979 after Mao died. And the cultural counter-revolution was getting ready for a literary renaissance as people were smoking more. If that were possible. And learning to write with Chinese characters (logograms) that pound on the conscience.

抽烟会更好

Translation: Things go better with smoke.

logograms used in the writing of Chinese

(in which case they may be called hanzi; 汉字/漢字 hànzì "Han character")

Now that the entire population was forced to smoke cheap cigarettes and cared less.

whisshhh … oo-ooooh …

But enough about China. Let's get to my DIVINE MILIEU.

Chapter 5 provides a panoramic view of the protagonist's favorite smoking spot in the underground – his divine milieu. A wide-open abandoned parking lot, bucolic, picturesque, unspoiled - once you get away from the eyesore beat-up gas station just across the tracks, the delipidated Baptist church and the adjacent derelict stream of shabby duplex-homes on the wrong side of town. On the southwesterly flank of the lot, with a little bit of imagination, the powerlines extending from utility-pole to utility-pole look like cables of funiculars carrying skiers in winter-time to the highest peaks of Muhlbach am Hochkonig, near Salzburg.

 *Five*

View from the parking lot

Have you ever enjoyed that overwhelming feeling of peace, quiet and tranquility? When you want to be alone with your inner persona and let the outside world race by recklessly. Without you. For about fifty minutes. At a whack. Where you can suck on the pap of life and gulp down the incomparable milk of wonder. [F. Scott Fitzgerald] A latte. From a takeaway Starbust. Before they went bust. To invite the inspiration that comes from a quiet puff or two. To compose the words that pound on the conscience.

whisshhh ... oo-oooooh ...

Robert Service described the feeling very well when he wrote: *Were you ever out in the Great Alone, when the moon was awful clear,/And the icy mountains hemmed you in with a silence you most could hear;/With only the howl of a timber wolf, and you camped there in the cold...* [The Shooting of Dan McGrew]

Let's take a view from the parking lot, my divine milieu in Teilhard de Chardin's mystical terminology with the umlaut on terminal.

Author's favorite abandoned parking lot

I've occupied this lot at lunchtimes going on god knows how long and haven't got caught yet. Don't get me wrong, there were a couple of close shaves.

Author shaving on stage in the Telemachus chapter of Ulysses

But, darn, they're planning new construction, so I've got to make plans. Like house-hunting if you've been transferred on the job and all of those new unknowns ahead that you hadn't anticipated in your complacency. When you thought you never had it so good. As good as it gets. While trying an unproven lot could be risky business.

Like Burt Lancaster's character (again!) seeking closure and finally ending his silence during the Nuremberg trial with the classic line: *Your honor, I was content to tend my roses.*

In *this place*, I could say that too. In the refreshing eco. Alone, with the birds and the bees.

bzzz ...

Excuse me?

SWAT!

As if BO'B swatting and (...gasp...) killing a pesky fly during an interview on CNBC, dominating the world news agenda for weeks because it showed you what the leader of the joint chiefs of staff was capable of. And getting all kinds of nonsense for it from PETA. As if the nation weren't in enough trouble without cig taxes. So, I try to get away from it all and to write while relaxing and concentrating over a quiet puff or two. In the solitude. *Watching the bluebird. A rainbow at sunset a tear in your eye when you are blue/I could be high as a bluebird flies and never tell lies.* [Anne Murray]

whisshhh ... oo-oooooh ...

To experience this kind of serenity, most people would prefer a cliff edge looking down on the smashing waves. I say old chap, quite smashing. Or a lake. Or a salmon fishing river like the one on which I was born. Born to run. Run, run. From the AT-kops. If you see them coming. Unfortunately, that's not practical for me. Living on a cliff above the ocean.

And possibly others like me. If there are *others* like me. Good god! good God. God good! Never know when to put the caps on God. Or the italics on the *if* or the *others*? Just kidding with the exclamation mark though. Thought you'd get a kick out of that. I mean – I hope there *are* others like me. We're really not such a bad lot. If you get to know us. And our mission.

Yes, for sure. There'd always be the possibility of a lover's pair catching you in the act or vice versa were it by a lake or river or cliff that jilted lovers leap from.

Can't get away from the cliff-effect. I wonder why?

Fatalism? Predeterminism? Stoicism?

No, not me.

No, no, no, it ain't me babe/It ain't me you're looking for, babe. [Dylan]

I don't jump off cliffs – I climb mountains. Mohammad goes to the mountain.

Come down from the mountain Katie Daly/Come down from the mountain, Katie, do. [Tom Dunphy and the Royal Showband]

Or perhaps an acquaintance of many years from your other life stumbling upon you, while enjoying a quiet puff, and wrecking your concentration with the obvious gotcha: *And what do we have here, huh?* Still there's nothing like a wide-open abandoned parking lot for privacy.

Let me take you on a brief tour of my divine milieu - if you can imagine the changing colors in the fall and the glaring snow in winter. Bucolic, picturesque, unspoiled. I would be foolish to call it idyllic because you wouldn't believe the leverage of such an adjective for a place that looks pedestrian from the naked eye. Aye. That would be like, having read a book that left such an impression on you that you had to insist to others that they read it too. Until you realized that just because something impacts you in a most meaningful way is no guarantee that it should have the slightest appeal to anyone else. I think it's the way we're made. Made in China. Or Bangladesh. We were made for each other. The way we were.

If you were to backpedal a few side-streets, the adjacent main road looks like any other. There's a McDonald's, a beat-up gas station that sells cheap gas - rather, gas cheap, and doesn't accept credit cards. An unpretentious-looking Baptist church with the white siding charcoaled from too much weather, and a stream of shabby duplex-homes in a safe part of town for me. It's the kind of road on which you'd expect to see a garbage truck pull up at any minute if it hadn't already - even if it weren't pick-up day. That kind of road. A pick-me-up kind of place. American flags at half-mast protrude from the center of contiguous telephone poles patriotically blowing in the wind, which they forgot to take down from either Memorial or Labor Day but I'm not quite sure since they seem to be up permanently.

At least since I made this abandoned parking lot one of my main stops as it began to blend seamlessly into a kind of home away from home. Home on the range, written in 1872 [Dr. Brewster M. Higley] but which became the state song of Kansas in 1947, coincidentally the same year as the infamous Dichter study on 'The

Happy Smoker'. Then there's a really-really small strip mall with one of the few hardware stores that hasn't been franchised by ACE Hardware yet (probably for good reason) which just allows you to put their name on the roof anyway. And behind it a huge empty building with a cardboard sign hanging crookedly inside which you can see through the cracked-glass doors:

~ ~ ~

Saturday Afternoon Flea Market in the parking lot behind. Rain check indoors. Don't forget (outdoor) bingo.

~ ~ ~

 That's where I come in. On the outside.

The parking lot. In the open air.

Like at a Neil Diamond concert in Saratoga in the early 70's but without the twenty thousand screaming fans who were smoking up a storm and it wasn't from tobacco.

whisshhh ... oo-oooooh ...

Most of them caring less who was on stage and pretty freaked-out. Especially those in the gods at the top of the hill. Where the sniffer dogs couldn't find them. On the grass. With the grass. Where they were making love not war. With flowers in their hair.

Just like that. Four decades later. Today. This afternoon. My private concert in the open air of a huge lot. Listening to the bees.

bzzzing

SWAT!

The pedestrian-looking entrance. Like the wide sliding doors typical of a roller-skatorama arcadium (for those of you practicing Latin). Or one of those ballrooms in the boondocks where nobody lived but everyone arrived en masse for the dance. You know the kind of place. During the big band era

With the muse for company. For inspiration. The Call of the Wild. From the nico. And tar. Tara. And lots of dandelions between the cracks in the tarvia.

I don't mind as long as they don't get in my hair. Except they attract the bees too.

The kind of tarvia that had suffered its unfair share of long narrow crevices with the asphalt patched-up haphazardly (by afternoon council-workers who cared less when no one was looking). Resulting in thousands of zig-zagged slithering goops of tar like eels on a Jackson Pollack fit-of-genius canvas, if you imagine Ed Harris (whom I met once) in the role, blending with the shine on the lens of your sunglasses if the sun caught the glare of the streaks just right, blinding your view. Like the occasions when the sun hits the green of a traffic light and you can no longer tell if it's green and you're feeling vulnerable if you burst into the traffic and you're wrong. Hence, in those circumstances the only safe thing to do is not to proceed even if you have the green on your side hoping there aren't too many cars behind you, or you'll surely get the horn. Just waiting there until the sun goes down. That kind of tarvia in the parking lot.

Anyway, it's much healthier smoking outdoors where the air is clean and fresh. And I'm all alone. All alone am I./With just a … beat of my heart. [Brenda Lee]

Invigorating.

A secret valley. A hidden vale on the wrong side of town. Shucks, he was born on the wrong side of town. Like Gabby Hayes. It's not exactly hidden – that's what I do. Hide and seek. And you're not looking up at the Bavarian Alps, but the trees secluded by the forest seem to be peeking down at you. Or it's only in your imagination.

Men to match my mountains. [Irving Stone]

With a radio tower at the summit. Not too much of an eyesore because you get used to it and the music's good. On my car radio. Unlike the new wind turbines, which, in fairness are good for the eco. But they're noisy as hell and dangerous for the birds. For the birds - I'd say.

When it would rain, I used to call it the *valley of tears* because the rain really slowed down my writing. Raindrops kept falling on my head. [BJ Thomas] First, fumbling for my brollie. And then, there on my trunk-bureau, little droplets forming scribble-cavities on the corners of my stacked foolscap pages and starting to wash inwards. Red ink from my ultra-fine ballpoint, the one that always leaks at high altitude on a flight because it just can't take the pressure anymore. The one I use for correction and the start of second draft.

Running with the rain droplets like a skinhead's mascara through the scribble from the black biro used for first draft, encrypting my most recent paragraphs like invisible ink that kids play detective with. Anyway, sometimes it's nice to listen to the rhythm of the falling rain. [The Cascades]

The lot covers about ten acres and is only known for its weekend flea market. No idea why it's so large as I've never attended the flea market. Doesn't really interest me. I'm busy enough with my confessions. Examining my conscience. The ghost of past transgressions (Proust could've written that). And the spirit of current carcinogens. And the shape of things to come. The shape of the lot is almost symmetrically rectangular. Six large stadium-type light-poles with HID lamps enmeshed with square cages are spaced like support-poles for an enormous circus tent.

The mesh-cages are intended to minimize the number of bugs pulverized per minute at night because they have a tendency to stick to the lens. Not only smudging it with a gooey splotch. Like the annoying mold on the putty between your bathtub and the tile-wall which you can't get off without that special blend of TILEX which the supermarket is always out of for the cheap useless stuff. But also reducing the power output to almost dark. The cages are also intended to provide protection against stone-throwers when neighborhood kids get bored. And not yet old enough to carry firearms until they're fourteen. The lights automatically come on even during the week. What a waste. I think someone just wired them up years ago to come on like that when the strip mall was possibly thriving and never checked since. The light-poles accommodate two, three or four lamps. Those near the front of the lot are a '3-for' and a '4-for' with four '2-fors' further out where you might assume the parking lot designers didn't consider safety as much a threat. The lamps are cantilevered so that they're hanging out-and-down at a 30-degree angle and look like the disintegrator-ray guns on the Martian tripod fighting machines in the remake of War of the Worlds. Incidentally, one of the farther-extreme '2-for'-lightpoles has the HID lamp along with its cover knocked-off. Probably by the bored hooligans I mentioned above, their pockets filled with the stones which they collect for swapping with each other. Fat lot of use the protective cage, huh. With the live electric wires exposed. Still, the exposed wires are some 30-feet in the air - so you're not really going to get electrocuted like sticking your pinky into a faulty electric socket when the toaster doesn't work at home. After washing your hands but not drying them. Which is more than can be said for your last visit to the mensroom when they were about to remove the faucets for lack of interest. Well, so much for the disintegrator ray-gun after it got too much exposure. Like Pamela Anderson. In the freezing cold. At night. As if pastor Matthew Collins prayers were answered at the end of the battle-with-the-aliens movie when everyone packed themselves into a church. Just in case. Just in time. JIT. Which hadn't seen one-tenth of such a carcinogen – oops, Freudian slip, meant to say *congregation* when things were going good.

   whisshhh ... oo-oooooh ...

On the southwesterly flank of the lot, with a little bit of imagination, the powerlines extending from utility pole to pole look like cables of funiculars carrying skiers in wintertime to the highest peaks of Muhlbach am Hochkonig, near Salzburg. The winter of our discontent. [WS] In the event that you didn't use some imagination, the utility poles are just another ugly eyesore, making a travesty of such an inspiring setting. And, on the western fringes, there's a meandering stream gleaming with the finest crystal-clear water, surrounding that edge of the parking lot like a moat as if it were a castle. Like rows and floes of angel hair/And ice cream castles in the air. [Joni Mitchell]

In all fairness, I haven't spent much time on the-little-bridge-that-could above the stream, trying to figure out if the water in this part of town could support little fish because I'm usually too busy writing my WIP. Although sometimes you'll observe at least one of the 17,500 species of colorful butterflies fluttering randomly and nonchalantly along, above the water, with no apparent destination. Bon Jour. Naturally I would never swat a butterfly. In case it came back to haunt me in the next life. As if two weren't enough in this one. So, I usually move along to my favorite part of the lot to write.

Although you could hear a banshee in the rustling breeze practically any afternoon, otherwise it's all quiet on the eastern part of the lot. But it makes absolutely no sense to have stadium floodlights just for me for the few times I stop here at night. Unless they're ... searchlights? With close-circuit cameras on each pole like everywhere in the UK except, probably, in bathrooms. I mean, everywhere. One camera for every 14 people in the country caught an average of 300 times daily. So much for privacy, huh? Which makes you wonder. Oh, almost tricked the forensic readers among you to think I was actually writing in the UK.

Surveillance cameras are bad enough but what about those new-fangled RFID chips (radio-frequency identification) with GPS/GIS tags. Tracking devices. Mapping your every movement, visible only to the virtual world. Implanted in your *nose*. Which apparently is what they're going to do next.

Good god. Holy nostrils!

A suspicious vehicle or person in the neighborhood? Loitering - a misdemeanor. Trespassing, a violation. Stasi, the secret German police, at a time when the ratio of government informers to regular citizens was one in 50. Maybe today a flip of the coin. Or, being taken for a hobo. Actually, hobos have become quite respectable with the National Hobo convention in Britt, Iowa, each year. With their own museum and now there's the Hobo Hall of Fame. Still, I'm not too sure. As Roger Miller butt (sic) it: *I ain't got no cigarettes.../I smoke old stogies I have found/ Short but not too big around.*

Not for me but I've nothing against hobos.

whisshhh ... oo-oooooh ...

And no, I'm not going to tell about the lights. Really a pity because I'm sure I could save them some money, all that power consumption. Butt, I can't dare attract any kind of attention either good or bad. Like a good or bad confession. The good thief. Or the ... bad, bad, Leroy Brown/baddest man in the whole damn town/ badder than ol' *K*ing Kong/an' meaner than a junkyard dog. [Jim Croce] I've no earthly idea why they would want them at all since flea markets usually are shut down before dark. Wait until dark.

Maybe the huge empty building had been a Wal-Mart before it took over the neighborhood high school lot by eminent domain and they forgot to switch off the lights. I could research that but have no practical reason for doing so. As in the Serenity Prayer: God grant me the Serenity to accept the things I cannot change, Courage to change the things I can, and Wisdom to know the difference. I guess I simply accept that it could've been an old Wal-Mart building.

But what's so perfect about this milieu is that, except for the frontage of the main building, the three sides are surrounded by countryside, huge trees and greenery all over. As Satchmo used to say: *I see trees of green ... red roses too/I see 'em bloom ... for me and you/And I say to myself ... what a wonderful world.* My parking-lot Shrangri-La/A land of bluebirds and fountains/And nothing to do. [The Lettermen] Mother nature in the wide open, pure, vigorous, fresh/refreshing environment. Although with the tormenting bugs in summer which I've learned to put up with. What a pain in the neck when you're trying to concentrate. Still, good for the ecosystem. Along with the whistling birds of every nationality, the multi-hued butterflies flitting their wings, the inquisitive coon on a lazy afternoon, the forgotten dumpster by the empty warehouse.

And I park my Chevy (of course it's not a Chevy but that's to keep the forensic readers on your tippy toes) usually in the farthest southeastern corner where I can relax with my couple of puffs, notepad on my trunk-bureau, and let loose. Pedal to the metal. With words that pound on the conscience.

whisshhh ... oo-oooooh ...

Being in the remote corner of the remote lot, it's about a quarter of a mile diagonally to the side-street. Not only can I see an approaching stranger or worse, an AT-kop, but have time and wherewithal to plan my move. Or at least have a credible response if-and-when confronted. It has happened:

1. pick up butts
2. dab the cologne
3. a quick swig of mouthwash.

And (if encountered) execute my well-rehearsed excuse as to why I'm in such a godforsaken place anyway. I'm now down to about 8 seconds flat for the drill with a 2 second warning for everything, which I have to practice every so often to stay alert whether I like it or not. And, I ain't botherin' no one. I ain't much, babe, but I'm all I've got (why we're so afraid to be different. By Jess Lair. Fraidy kat. On his 9th and last life. Omen?) Baby, I'm yours (baby I'm yours)/And I'll be yours (yours) until the stars fall from the sky/ Yours (yours) until the rivers all run dry/In other words, until I die.

[Barbara Lewis]

Yes indeed, you can only read about such a panorama in the complementary issue of Travel & Leisure magazine before you cancel after the bill arrives. But, for about two years you still get those harassment letters from the collection agency. Although, after booking your vacation you find that your beachfront hotel advertised as – Rooms with a View - is in name only. Like, god forbid, in Mazatlan, Mexico, where we (my ex and I, unaccustomed as we were ...) bargain-vacationed once. Obviously, I left my smokes behind, being with the missus. *hmmm ...* Because I can turn on and off like a light ...

whisshhh ... oo-ooooooh ...

220

... even for extended periods when I know I have to. Of course, at the cost of forsaking my writing. Do not forsake me oh my writing. [High Noon] And the beachfront-part was just a picture on a huge billboard in a ghetto area. Which was all of them except for the five-star hotels on the ocean where it costs $5 to have someone paged because movie stars stay there. Crawling with urchins. Just to get through them with their hands-out for hand-outs was like surfing the gauntlet for about ten kilometers to the ocean.

But for me this is reality. In this old abandoned parking lot. In the here and now. Living the life. Living the lie. Still, I often wonder why no one else has found this ... Shangri-La, *k*-smokers or not. *I wandered today to the hills, Maggie/To watch the scene below/The creek and the creaking old mill, Maggie/Where we used to long long ago/... (but) the creaking old mill is still, Maggie ...* [John Mcdermott]

Maybe because they've yet to find the real utopia which is an oxymoron in itself. And probably because strategically I arrange lunchtimes on flex time when everyone else has returned to the office to gab about (*k*-smokers like) *us*. About people like us!

People who crave the calmness of wide-open spaces know what I mean, where you're at peace with yourself, vagabonds of interminable time, far from the beaten railway tracks and the polluted city with its fair share of CO_xs, SO_xs and NO_xs. Although there is a RR crossing about a quarter of a mile away on the opposite side, but you wouldn't notice it if I didn't tell you, like the trees for the forest behind. Actually, this milieu is the closest thing you'll get to the boondocks and still be within city limits without having to worry about the valley of the squinting windows. The nosy neighbors peeking through their half-drawn bathroom curtains (draperies). Or

221

it would be curtains for me. This place is a safe haven. You know, like a famous writer comes to your town and gives a flattering talk about it for god knows whatever reason. And, without mentioning the name of your town constantly refers to it as … *this place*, with a kind of purity that makes you have second thoughts about getting the hell out. As Dylan put it: There must be someway outta here. [All Along the Watchtower]

That kind of place.

Aah … the good life.

No, in this place they can't fence me in. *Oh, give me land, lots of land/Under starry skies above,/Don't fence me in./…Let me be by myself in the evening breeze-/Listen to the murmur of the cottonwood trees,/Send me off forever, but I ask you please,/Don't fence me in.* [Roy Rogers]

There are occasions with pen in hand, puffing to the rhythm and writing as fast as I can, when my lungs and mind are stretched to their limit, when the inspiration is so powerful that I have to say – *Time Out! Slow Down!* In all honesty, in those moments my pen needed a jumpstart just to keep up – which it had to do, or I would be in danger of losing the words that pound on the conscience. Once lost, these words could never be recalled like they're inclined to do with a mass recall of defective auto parts. And so, you slowed down for a quiet break.

whisshhh …. oo-oooooh …

~ ~ ~

Each time I write these subtleties about the bees and the eco, within moments I feel guilty. A good word when one's writing a confession.

But I swear to God I really do. Feel guilty. Recently I read an article about bees and it made be (sic) think twice. Not just about the bees but about the eco. Umberto Eco. Just kidding. The article reporting on a pending Nature series on PBS, stated: "The future of our food supply rests on the tiny honey-bee. They are the most important pollinator on the planet, accounting for 21% of our fruits, vegetables, seeds and fibers like cotton. And yet, as many as 79 percent of honeybees have disappeared within the last six months in certain areas of the U.S. because of the CO_xs, SO_xs and NO_xs."

Hold a sec. Can't concentrate.

Darn bugs.

bzzzzzzzzz ...

Where's my swatter. Huh? Ah! Okay. There.

SWAT!

Darn bee.

oops ...

oops-sie ...   (protagonist expressing extreme embarrassment!)

[doopsie]

~ ~ ~

Smokeless cigarettes had been introduced as a last effort during the honeymoon period before the A of C. The Sunday Express had reported at the time: 'It looks like a real ciggie and tastes a bit like one too. Contains only nicotine; no tar, cadmium, arsenic or old lace. So far so good. Unfortunately, they release two cancerous chemicals among 70 others that are so-and-so, unloosing toxic chemicals such as acrolein and formaldehyde. Not to mention diethylene glycol, a chemical used in anti-freeze.'

The resolution was now clear for the AT Lawmakers to convince 45-million smokers-on-tenterhooks of the ONLY option. Soon after the smoking ban, they could go down to Barnes & Noble and purchase a 20-pack of #2 pencils whenever the urge hit, while reading their comic books. In the demise of great literature which no one was writing without the concentration and inspiration from nicotine to write with words that pound on the conscience.

Research had shown of the many dangerous substances in a ciggie, nico - a chemical found also in tomatoes and peppers - wasn't one of them. It was only a poison if you put it in your blood.

Hey, you wanna come outside and smoke a couple of ... tomatoes! You wanna: ... Come on-a my house, I'm gonna give you candy/Come on-a my house, I'm gonna give you an apple, a plum and apricot-a too eh. [Rosemary Clooney] Are you sure you don't mean ... potatoes? No. That's what DQ was smoking with his spell-check on mute! And neither had an odor to them, potatoes or tomatoes. You like potato and I like potahto/You like tomato and I like tomahto/... Let's call the whole thing off. [Louis Armstrong & Ella Fitzgerald]

Indeed, with either the e-cig or regular cigarette, to enjoy the taste, the smoker would still have to inhale. However, as well as being smoke-free, like the #2 pencil option, the e-cig was odorless.

And sure enough, they had hit the nail on the head this time. *ouch!* ...

Lightbulb!

Odorless! It's the odor, stupid!

For decades the fundamental objection to the cigarette and responsible for the humongous outcry leading to the ban was the leftover odor on the draperies!

Most non-smokers had been having fits about the foul, obnoxious smell of cigarettes. Especially when it got on the draperies and lingered inside like the CO_xs, SO_xs and NO_xs outside. Having just moved into their dream home.

And, the other alternative, gum didn't have the feel to it. Or the odor. And smokers who were no longer capable of tasting anything else, cared less that they sacrificed the taste of such delicacies as calf's brains, sautéed iguana meat and chopped marinated kangaroo tail ragout. Which the snotty non-smokers savored, nibbling away in a fancy restaurant that only took reservations.

Incidentally, some smokers who were born worriers were constantly getting confused as to which of the 4000 chemicals were the cancer-causing carcinogens. If they were able to identify all of them on the front and back of the cigarette box, then they could just inhale those chemicals that were harmless. If it didn't affect the taste too much. And live with it. Actually, even before the A of C the AT lawmakers were on the verge of demanding that a list of all 4000 chemicals (not only the carcinogens) be printed in bold font on the box. Like the list of ingredients on the wrapper of a miniature package of garlic croutons at BurgerKing. Which had a nice aftertaste for non-smokers, who never lost their palette, when soaked with lite Italian dressing:

BK garlic croutons:

Enriched flour (Wheat Flour, Barley Fluor, Niacin, Reduced Iron, Thiamine, Mononitrate, Riboflavin, Folic Acid), Partially Hydrogenated Soybean Oil, Water, Yeast, High Fructose Corn Syrup, 2% or less of the following: Salt, Wheat Gluten, Corn Syrup Solids, Whey, Romano from Cow's Milk, Parmesan

Cheeses (Part Skim Milk, Cultures, Salt, Enzymes), Autolyzed Yeast Extract, Cheese Powder (Cheddar Cheese [Milk, Cultures, Salt, Enzymes], Whey Protein Concentrate, Maltodextrin, Natural Flavor, Disodium Phosphate, Blue Cheese [Milk, Cultures, Salt, Enzymes], Nonfat Milk, Citric Acid), Garlic, Calcium Propionate (Preservative), Dough Conditioners (May contain one or more of the following: Sodium Stearoyl Lactylate, Calcium Stearoyl Lactylate, Calcium Peroxide, Calcium Sulphate, Ammonium Sulphate, Calcium Iodate, Ascorbic Acid), Cultured nonfat milk, Natural and Artificial Flavors, Cultured Whey, Citric Acid, Annatto and Turmeric (Color) and TBHQ (to preserve freshness).

Because of the garlic dominance, it was recommended in small print to gargle with mouthwash before a hot date after the aftertaste.

Since not too many of the above had any known connection to carcinogens in the tobacco industry, next they researched Sweet'N Low and other sugar substitutes. This was a mistake because the jury was also out on how many of those ingredients were cancer-causing. Studies concluded that the cancer-causing agents of artificial sugar could take years to manifest from the behavior of focus group participants who were still alive. Not only the ones who took placebos.

Another of the main reasons for the ultimate smoking ban was the sheer drudgery – during the transition-period between the pre-T and the post-T eras - of the Big 6 being coerced into complying with the above demand - after conversing with their lawyers. And finding a cigarette box large enough to display the 4000 individual chemicals. With a brief warning in mumbo-jumbo legalese on the known side-effects of each. In tiny footnotes. Because, by law, all caveats had to appear on the outside of the box next to the poison-icon. Predictably, it was more desirable for the T conglomerates to save face, live with it, and divert all R&D resources into developing a clone of the original-and-proven #2 pencil. And to convince the public, which was pretty gullible anyway after some 30 years on average of smoking up a storm. Any one of whom cared less and could collapse in a minute. When the smoke hardened inside their lungs. As well as their arteries. Yes, the main attraction was that the #2 had the same feel and taste to it. Smoking's like candy on a shelf/ You want to taste and help yourself/The sweetest things are there for you/Help yourself, take a few .../Just help yourself. [Tom Jones]

whisshhh ... oo-oooooh ...

~ ~ ~

Meantime, back at the ranch. In my normal life. They think I don't smoke. It bothers them never having seen a *k*-smoker in their entire lives, not having a clue as to what we look like. Maybe we're handsome which is enough to make you a star even if you had no talent. So ya wanna be a star. Rock Star. As they stare me in the face. Like Patrick Swayze in Ghost. In my off-blue suit. If they only knew. Or, my other pre-occupation ...

But when I make a quick change in the telephone booth (it's really in the parking lot) into a *k*-smoker, I'm no longer the person they know whom, God willing, they'll never know. No one knows me then, not my wife or children. *hmmm* ... That's what being a *k*loset smoker means. It's something I live with. An avocation that becomes more than the vocation. I made my choice and I'll stick with it.

*K*razy.

And as a *k*-smoker I don't bother anyone ... but me.

(Tears of compassion amid loud applause.)

      clap ... *clap*   ... *clap*

                   ... *one hand clapping*

Thank you.

... for smoking.

Just kidding.

I'm not trying to be supercilious. I didn't mean to do that. Believe me, I know I'm guilty.

The children of this world are wiser in their generation than the children of light [Luke 16:8] – would take more than a Jesuit to explain but means that in our worldliness we are more clever in rationalizing the ways in which neurotransmitting chemicals are out of balance. Hence, *I will give you a new heart and put a new spirit in you.* [Ezekiel 36:26] Which is oversimplification. Like: The third half of your life is the first tenth of eternity.

Which begs the question why smoking is not included in the Seven Deadly Sins. They had a hell of a catchall with: Pride, Covetousness, Lust (nice! ... oops!), Anger, Donuts, Envy and Sloth. And not a single mention of smoking. Maybe I'm over-reacting with this confession. Someone once said that guilt isn't all bad. It can help you to do what's right. And that's the crux. Because the penny catechism states that it's a million times more difficult for a smoker to get into heaven, quote: Inheriting eternal life isn't easy for smokers. They'd be better off inheriting the wind. Where the answer lies. Living the lie(s). And half-truths. And worse than a camel trying to squiggle through the eye of a needle. About ordinary sinners falling off the wagon then hopping on again. Whereas, a confirmed smoker had made his ... choice. Just another *Whereas* ... Just an old-fashioned love song/One I'm sure they wrote for you and me. [Three Dog Night]

As Pope John Paul II had redefined 'ex cathedra' when applied to smoking - after he realized how difficult it was for a smoker to get into heaven. Having been known to enjoy a quiet one himself in his days as a soccer goalkeeper and poet. And the almost impossible task of quitting which many others of the cloth realized of themselves. A compromise was reached which maxed out at a half-a-pack per day earning only a venial sin. The question, then, that disturbed the theologians was - how many millions of venial sins eventually become mortal? It was a good question considering the rate at which the die-hards were dying off after smoking one too many. Which wasn't very mortal any longer. As Hamlet so eloquently put it: Shuffle off this mortal coil.

And the remorse required for a good confession? Many a tear has to fall/But it's all in the game. [Tommy Edwards] As much as I persevere with my personal exposé, absolution seems to elude me. Which (forgiveness) Isaac Friedmann called 'the sweetest revenge'. I can't git no satisfaction. But I try. And I try. And I try. [RS] And I try. And yet there had been a time when you were a social outcast unless you smoked.

Is it me or what I do? The singer not the song? Dirk Bogarde was impressive as the bad guy in the movie. The singer and the song. The singer or the song. Love the sinner. St. Augustine, a cornerstone of theology. But, they say, not the best source on the topic of sin and forgiveness. Hate the song. Song Sung Blue.

Neil Diamond wrote some awful songs: And no one heard not even the ... chair!

Money talks / but it don't sing and dance / and it don 't walk. [Forever in Blue Jeans]!!!

Yet Neil was a great singer. As you know (by now) I met Neil a couple of times. But the forensics among you would be wasting your energy trying to track me down via Neil because he's just too darn busy trying to figure out prose. (Oh, sorry, Neil, about your recent indisposition!)

In fairness, there was a classic precedent in the haunting melody of Brook Benton's The House is not a Home, with the lyric: ... a chair is just a chair/even when there's no one sitting there.

Words that pound on the conscience? I don't think so!

whew!

Really?

Rhapsodic. Emotional. Soulful. Bohemian. Musical chairs.

Where were we? Hate the song. Hate the sin. The quiet puff.

Which reminds me ... Won't be more than two secs. Finished the last pack. Left the new carton inside. Better not have left my keys inside too and locked the door. That would really be something, calling a locksmith to pick me up in the middle of nowhere. Explaining why I'm here.

Hey, buddy, why ya here ...? Fair enough question.

False alarm about the car keys. Now I've got to find where I put the carton. Replenishments. Bugle call. Bring in the cavalry. Wrapped in brown eco-friendly grocery bags delivered via the Native American call-center 800-number in Calcutta to my secret PO box.

In the trunk, I think.

oops ... got my notepad and thesaurus *on* the trunk. *tsk. tsk.*

Karl Malden said: Never leave home without your thesaurus. Until he no longer needed one himself. R.I.P. Let her rip!

Dum dum da-da da-da da ...

Put this here, put that there. My portable bureau. FBI. Bureau of T. Be only a min ...

der-dum, der-dum, dum-dum, dum-dum, dum-dum, der-dum, dum-dum.

Author's daughter – swimming (... well ...) with the killer whale sharks

hmmm ...

Okay, everything worked out alright. Almost a panic attack. Sigh of relief.

whisshhh ... oo-oooooh ...

~ ~ ~

I was talking about my book (confession) being read, wasn't I? Of course, you were. Thanks. Don't be smart. I am. I said. It's interesting but you end up doing that quite a bit, talking to yourself. When you're out in the great alone. You don't have to, and you don't need to see a therapist about it. It's just that, with no one within about ten square miles that you're kind-of keeping yourself company. And it takes a break from the words that pound on the conscience. You get your energy back. But I would never talk to myself back home or in the office. It's all part of the freedom of just doing what you feel comfortable with. The freedom of expression. And accept responsibility for. Neither is it that you are your own best friend. You're just keeping yourself company in a milieu that you have created or has been created for you by the great default.

Fault. Default. Go and sin no more. An exercise in catharsis. To understand the yin and yang of old Nic (nicotine) and old Nick (with horns and fork). The devil you know versus the devil you don't. The devil made me do it. Writer. Smoker. Old Nic. Nic-o. But not *Nico,* the bohemian singer who was a member of the Velvet Underground, *hmmm,* who would've guessed? Aha! – Underground! [*Notes from Underground* (Записки изъ подполья, tr. *Zapíski iz podpól'ya*), 1864 novella by Fyodor Dostoevsky.] In the nic'o time! For time, it is a precious thing/And time brings all things to my mind/Time with all its sorrow along with all its joy/Time brings all things to an end. [Traditional] Time, gentleman please! Last call. Last cig.

whisshhh ... oo-oooooh ...

~ ~ ~

Confessions of a closet smoker, huh. If it were good enough for St. Patrick and St. Augustine... if it were good for our fathers/Then it's good enough for me. [Inherit the Wind] Smoking in the closet, a lonely life, the only opportunity to allow tobacco to inspire your greatest lit!

Then BJ Thomas came along with: It's lonely out tonight … nonsensically followed by … *ANOTHER SOMEBODY DONE SOMEBODY WRONG SONG.* Can you believe that title, just when the lonely stuff was going okay? Houston, we gotta problem here! You'd swear it was penned by Neil Diamond. To make matters worse, Roy Orbison took a stab at (incorrectly) summing us up with: Only the Lonely. But we're not lonely. We're just … alone. When we do what we do. And write with words that pound on the conscience. Words that come with a puff or two. Alone on a wide, wide sea.

On a melancholy note, rather, another-somebody-done-somebody-wrong-note, my confession's a pretty private thing. The thing about confession is that the intensity of contrition varies with the moment, the atonement. You may already have noticed that. What was soul-destroying to me on a Monday parking lot, by Wednesday wasn't such a big deal behind the closed-down gas station. Or, the abandoned lot behind the airport. But, in that case the decibels from the take-offs would drive anyone batty. It was only a back-up site anyway had I a gut feeling to skip the usual (milieu) on a certain day. Can't explain it but sometimes I just feel it may be risky at my old haunt and try somewhere else. No logic to it. I could test that theory … *aha!* The forensics (among you) thought you had me there! Think I'll just go with my gut feeling. As Morris Alpert said: Feelings, nothing more than feelings/Feeling, *woo-o-o* feeling/ *woo-o-o* …

But the sincerity of repentance depends on the mindset. The contrition in the confession. Like in a rap lyric. Or Kenny Rogers: I just dropped in to see what condition my contrition was in. Yeah, yeah, oh yeah, what condition my contrition was in. You'll have to bear that in mind through the guilt odyssey.

In one way you (reader) should feel flattered. I never confessed to a lay person. And I'm guessing that not too many of you are men of cloth. Men in black. Ladies in cute little black cocktail dresses. The voice behind the curtain (drapery). The whisper. In the immortal words of Jim Reeves: Whispering Hope, oh how welcome Thy voice/ Making my heart any sorrow rejoice.

Still, every now and then I wonder if I'm doing the right thing in this personal exposé. I don't know who you are as much as (until recently) you knew little about me. Until reading between the lines. Read my lips. I've always been cautious about reading between the lines learned from Gordon Lightfoot: If you could read my mind, love, what a tale my thoughts could tell. It's kind of redundant here because by now you know practically everything about me! Well, all that needs to be known. But you don't know who I am. Whom. *hmmm* … Which is why I'm writing about the Mid X. And not enveloped within … the Inferno. [Dante Alighieri]

Paradise Lost. [Milton]

Man on a Mission to return great lit to mankind. [John Player (of John Player & Sons notoriety)].

whisshhh … oo-oooooh …

234

Let me be very clear. If it's not clear what you have to say (between the lines), then don't say it. And if you've nothing good to say (about us) ... or bad, or ugly (as in the diva survivors of the silver screen), then, please ... pass. Still, my dear friends, we've come quite a ways since the Bless Me Father stage (as it were) so I think we've developed some trust. And I'm privileged to be sharing my deepest thoughts. It just goes to show that any great work of lit is a thrilling read.

Hard to put down.

Waiting for the juicy part in the next chapter.   If the lass in the cute little black cocktail-dress, above, is any harbinger! Just kidding. After all, this is a serious confession! So, please, let's stop the temptation.

A (rather concerned) reader (getting-all-worked-up):   *Okie dokie. You got it!*

Unlike us. Quite easy really. To put down.

This book is synergy between us. And that, my friends, is what creative writing is. Should be. Words that pound on the conscience. Except for those of you who are only looking for more psychological, cerebral, abstruse telltale clues that might lead to our/my discovery.

A perspective into another world. A living experience. Real time.

hmmm.

On-line? The missus.

What's she up to? Seems she's always 'on' when I'm 'on'. But in the other room.

ho-hmmm ...

...and the End of Literature

Prologue to implementation of the Act of Cessation.

For some uncanny reason the popular movement to ban smoking had hit a snag and was starting to lack luster by the 79% anti-smoking mob. Perhaps they were having pity on the smokers recognizing they were really a harmless bunch with no intentional attempt to harm anyone but themselves (now that you could only smoke in outhouses or abandoned telephone booths) and who were about to become zombies with the Act of Cessation. Something had to happen by the AT Administration to jumpstart the 'smoking ban' crusade and fast. Suddenly, as luck would have it, 8 city-residents – 4 women, 2 men, a pair of twins (boy/girl) - who were innocent passers-by beneath the smoke-filled canopy of the 48-floor Time-Life building collapsed due to the second-hand smoke from 'spontaneous combustion' and were dead within 40-seconds. 21-smokers during their 20-minute smoke-break were blamed for the disaster. They were trying to absorb as much nicotine as possible since it takes 6-minutes to smoke one cigarette - yet optimistically trying for two within the allotted time. And bearing in mind the elapsed elevator excursion-time to get back to their cubicles. The evidence insisted that the tragedy could've occurred outside any building - but the Time building just happened to be in the wrong place at the wrong time.

 Six

THE MANHATTAN PROLOGUE

After two delays already, there was a real possibility that the inevitable Act of Cessation would have circled in a holding pattern, indefinitely, like a turboprop over O'Hare running out of gas. Every time the turbo made a break, through the lingering CO_xs, SO_xs and NO_xs for a miraculous opening in the clouds, sure enough another jumbo jumped the queue. In the bigger-is-better debate like the riddle of the mongoose and the cobra, the jumbo always wins although you were urged not to sweat the small stuff. Anyway, if there was anything the AT lawmakers definitely didn't need it was yet another delay. And time was running out.

By now most of you are only too aware that the MANHATTAN PROLOGUE which occurred between 10:04:00 and 10:04:40 on New Year's eve was responsible for putting an end to the holding pattern between what had been the pre-T (tobacco) era and what was to become the post-T era. - with a crash. Just kidding about the crash. And the A of C was implemented fourteen hours later. Which was no joke for one fifth of the population. All of whom could've done with a fifth of Bushmills apiece at the moment of Nietzsche's declaration: That God Is Dead, with the usual irrevocability clause. oops. Wrong debate, wrong rebuttal. Rather, That Smoking Was Dead.

But why wasn't the 'event' just called, the Manhattan Tragedy which would've been simpler for everyone? Like Manhattan clam chowder for example. Or just a 'Manhattan' when you badly needed an upper (pun). Things were starting to get complicated. But, why the Manhattan … '*Prologue*'?

Glad you asked.

That was the lingering question in the dangling conversation which boggled the out-of-towner pundits who weren't very smart.

Who stayed overnight at Ho Jos (if they were lucky), ate breakfast at Denny's, lunch at the diner, diner [sic] at the diner, and just didn't get it while visiting the metropolis which had always prided itself on sophistication. And who would've preferred to call the whole thing an American Tragedy. Which, as luck would have it, had already been taken by Theodore Dreiser, about the fictional town of Lycurgus, albeit, unbelievably (with a name like that) also in New York. With Montgomery Clift playing the part of George Eastman in A Place in the Sun, and Liz Taylor as Angela Vickers, in the movie version. But there wasn't too much sun to be seen in Manhattan in a long time so let's not digress.

The answer my friend is because - what happened next was not only a single event, but a turning point, a point of no return, a watershed, a crossroads, a paradigm shift in possibilities. Something that would trigger a mindset affecting mankind as we had known it – and how we behaved - until then. The tragedy was not the same as, say, a negligent smoker after a few pints too many falling asleep on a too-comfortable sofa with the sports-page upturned on his lap touching against a lit cig between his yellow-stained pointer and middle-finger. And, predictably, dead (or absent) batteries in all of the smoke detectors. And after all is said and done, burning the entire building down to ground zero along with all of its occupants. Or, the Great Chicago Fire which obliterated four square miles of a city center plus a few hundred residents to wit. No, the Manhattan tragedy would impact the very way we looked at multiple choice in a TV game show where there's only one correct answer and you have no choice. And it wasn't just a game.

To understand the roots of the appellation, let's follow the pattern that had been emerging through the smog on just another muggy day in Manhattan. 'Following' the tragedy which solved (almost) everyone's problems, cigarette smoking was banned within hours not only nationwide but by default, soon, in much of the known world. Before *that* would happen, what-if discussions had become a permanent fixture in practically every pub that sported a dart board. As if smokers really had a second chance. And, had the MANHATTAN PROLOGUE not occurred it was anyone's guess what was going to happen next if anything at all with everyone on tenterhooks. And the shambles (which many agreed upon) of the status quo would have prevailed. In such an event there would be even more smoke on the draperies while foul-smelling breath would continue to be a turn-off among partners who were simply trying to have promiscuous sex. And, god only knows how much more second-hand smoke the intolerant neighbors could withstand and still invite you over. And the eco was suffering too. But that would continue to smell to high heaven for at least the next 100 years from the CO_xs, SO_xs and NO_xs stagnating above - which made day below behave like night.

The tragedy which would forever change the way we looked upon the Manhattan skyline which no one had seen in decades, had raised the specter of another historical event. This was the Manhattan Project which also had a deleterious effect upon mankind as described by Ian Campbell: Now the sun has disappeared/All is darkness, anger, pain and fear/Twisted sightless wrecks of men/Lay groping on their knees and cry in pain/And the sun has disappeared. Subsequently, the AT lawmakers had been seeking a meaningful metaphor to identify the event which would define the post-T era when smoking had disappeared. When they had nothing better to do in their spare time, they liked to coin catchy phrases for events that changed history for which they kept their thesaurus handy. It was a perfect opportunity for a neologism which they could embellish with an appropriate euphemism, agglutination or even a malapropism. The result was the classic spoonerism that has come to be used as a catchphrase ever since.

'Remember the Alamo' had been a battle cry from a different era immortalized by John Wayne and no longer worked very well after he hung up his boots for the last time. But the **MANHATTAN PROLOGUE** – a prologue to, and which launched the Act of Cessation - became a fitting mantra following the events in Manhattan which occurred in less than a New York minute. Anyway, that's the background and the worst was yet to come. Good luck.

~ ~ ~

In the long and honored history of the New York Minute it was just another 24-hours like any other in the Big Apple. Those hazy, hazy, hazy days of summer were being quickly displaced by those hazy, hazy, hazy days of winter. Although there was a smell in the air, if you stopped to smell the roses then you had taken a wrong turn. Still it was nothing to get hot and bothered about.

The elapsed time of the unraveling event which became known as the **MANHATTAN PROLOGUE** lasted slightly less than a NY minute, forty secs to be precise. Until then, Andy Warhol had held the record at 15-seconds tops. Seconds anyone? When only gentlemen were considered to have honor and hence qualified to duel. Rather, tennis anyone? Timing was everything. Minutes had imploded into seconds. Things were happening too darn fast. Thousands of balding tires were whistling harmoniously with the whir of an off-course nor'easter which some thought was a refreshing breakthrough for the neighborhood. According to the meteorologists it had been heading towards the Maritimes southeast of Nova Scotia with a final destination of the Great Banks of Newfoundland, all things being equal. But, as Herb Newman corrected the weather forecasters: The wayward wind is a restless wind/A restless wind that yearns to wander. Having somehow got sidetracked, the nor'easter began to settle in the city that never sleeps. If anything, it had the credits of a perfect storm in a city with its fair share of flawed baguettes. When it was hard to tell day from night if you looked outside quick enough at what remained of the refreshing eco which was nowhere to be seen. At any hour of the day. Where anything goes. Cole Porter described the daylight scene perfectly when he said: The world has gone mad today …/And day's night today. And nobody doubted it for a minute. In New York.

It didn't help that taxicabs long before they became museum pieces due to Uber were honking their bejeepers off until the wee hours. In the wee small hours of the morning/While the whole wide world is fast asleep. [Sinatra] Then the same-old, same-old drill with a slight delayed reaction from the new (paradigm) shift as the tough got going. Many cabbies were spitting in their palms outside St. Patrick's Cathedral for good luck (although none of them were observed making the sign of the cross) in preparedness for the awaiting challenge of the brand-new day.

In Manhattan.

But they weren't splitting their sides laughing with little to be merry about now that Christmas itself was over - because soon there'd be no more cig taxes to boost the economy. And they might as well give up on fares for which they overcharged anyway, in a wake-up call after the American dream. The fact was that the economy had seen better days prior to the events from Main Street to Wall Street and every side street and back alley all over the land. And, for which no one denied ownership as articulated quite well by Woody Guthrie: This land is your land/This land is my land. From California to Manhattan. From which – looking back eight years later - it has never recovered.

Back to the good old days. When days were days and men were men. In the hazy, hazy, hazy days which they had learned to live with. Just about. After some three decades of smoking since their first puff which had tasted pretty darn awful. And asphyxiated most of them. But they persevered. When they had that option.

On every street corner in the ratio of 4:1 (79:21 to be precise), at any point in time you could find a mixed bag of non-smokers passing-by (who were not-smoking). And smokers (*tabagie*) just standing around. On the corner. Just looking at the smokers was enough to get the non-smokers Irish up who would stop and stare at them with vitriolic self-righteousness verging on a vengeance for being human. Giving them The Look.

A couple from the mixed bag looked like John Wayne and Victor McLachlan in The Quiet Man getting ready for a donnybrook. But you couldn't swear to it because it was hard to see straight through the smog in the city with the 4th worst ozone level in the nation and aggressively competing with Beijing long after the Olympics.

whisshhh .... oo-oooooh ...

~ ~ ~

Incidentally, I had the pleasure of meeting Cardinal Edward Egan once, head of the Archdiocese of New York on another New Year's Eve at St. Pat's, years before, when he ran out of time to hear the minute details of my confession. Confessions of a closet-smoker. Which weren't necessarily anything to worry about because closet-smoking was legal then. Incidentally, on that NY's eve, Judy Collins and Lynn Redgrave had just performed at St. John the Divine near Columbia U. It was just before Colin Powell dropped the ball, again. This time in Times Square accompanied by Rudy Giuliani, with Dick Clark as dj on the adjacent American bandstand.

But, now, you had to feel sorry for the *tabagie* roughing it up in the freezing cold outside. Not only in Manhattan but millions across the nation wondering what was coming next, in every city north of the T belt. Where southerners tried to ignore what was happening when no one was looking, from a precedent set on Juneteenth which had long since passed.

whisshhh .... oo-oooooh ...

Putting it bluntly, it was pretty darn nippy which most New Yorkers didn't seem to mind too much having made their choice which they had to sleep with and with whom and which was frequently a mistake. Which they realized if they sobered up the following morning. You could hardly say the same however for the twenty-one percent of the adult population whom at that moment were looking restlessly at their wall clocks inside, in the security of their cubicles, for the next scheduled (smoke) break outside. And in the meantime, anxiously vacillating between biting (what remained of) their fingernails in the biting wind and practicing with advance trial-size kits of #2 pencils for the inevitable. If they were lucky to get them.

Like the government-issue suicide-pills in On the Beach. About the world after the bomb and the only survivor(s). And the eco wasn't getting any better. The vibes were pretty bad and could only get worse. And, as yet, no one even knew of the upcoming popular-vote, or the reality-vote on **the Late Yo with David Minuteman,** following the interviews with **the Dichter-17.**

But something was awfully wrong.

You could sense it, feel it, and smell it in the stagnating CO_xs, SO_xs and NO_xs which researchers say linger for one hundred years+ especially in NYC. Or if you missed the exit, in downtown Hoboken. And yet the AT lawmakers who were intent on getting everyone fired-up against smoking complained about the *tabagie* who had just lit-up and were hanging around for just minutes at a time and freezing their butts off. It just didn't make sense.

Nonetheless, just like any powerful movement that has everyone agitated, apathy had begun to sink in along with the refreshing nor'easter which baffled the pundits no end.

~ ~ ~

The AT lawmakers like everyone else were getting antsy. Maybe the post-Christmas blues had something to do with it if you didn't get what you wanted. Beneath the mistletoe. Everyone was busy window-shopping, ruing the pending New Year when they wouldn't have a button from welfare which was totally funded by cig taxes.

Incidentally, as yet there was no 'official' mention of the Mid X. Why spoil New Year's Eve for a fifth of the population with scare tactics. Who were already downing fifths by the swigful trying to anesthetize themselves as to what was happening. To the choice factor. As they recalled the words of their mentor in correctional school: You made your choice, now stick with it! The advice seemed so simple and made no sense whatsoever.

Some would argue that the current delay was a bit much and probably due to subversive elements within the Village community. Known since the sixties for protests while wondering where all the flowers had gone. Which nowadays was a rhetorical question indeed. The Villagers were far removed from the uptown holier-than-thou crowd. In their fancy penthouses with up-on-the-rooftop gardens. And were having enough of a problem as it was, up where they could almost touch the CO_xs, SO_xs and NO_xs. Hands, touching hands, reaching out/Touching me, touching you. [Neil Diamond] Higher (lifting me)/Higher and higher (higher). [Jackie Wilson] It took the immortal words of John Gillespie Magee, Jr. to put an end to the nonsense when he saw much further than the clouds: Up, up, the long, delirious, burning blue/I've topped the windswept heights with easy grace/Where never lark, nor even eagle flew - /And, while with silent lifting mind I've trod/The high un-trespassed sanctity of space,/Put out my hand, and touched the face of God.

But this hypothesis (about the Village people) was doubtful ever since Dylan went electric and gave an ambivalent name to every protestor who followed, whether the cause was popular or not. If man does not keep pace with his companions, perhaps it is because he hears a different drummer. Let him step to the music he hears, however measured or faraway. [Thoreau] In the case of the pending ban on smoking, practically every anti-smoker agreed that smoking was the most obnoxious, filthy, disgusting, scumbag habit. Not to mention other McCarthyism superlatives which are not appropriate to include today in a confession of this sort. Which I'm scribbling in the frigid wind in a wide-open parking lot wishing it were spring. When it's spring again I'll bring again/Tulips from Amsterdam. [Max Bygraves] Where it wasn't tobacco that they were smoking.

And, yet they were right! Or wrong, depending on the condition of your contrition. Had they only allowed the exception for the *k*-smoker. Alone in the great outdoors. Bothering no one when no one was watching. To exercise his or her craving, rather obsession, to return creative writing to its roots.

whisshhh .... oo-oooooh ...

Nevertheless, the roofers weren't too worried because when they needed a quiet puff or two they simply followed the precedent set by Carole King who articulated the lie quite nicely, thank you: I'll go up where the air is fresh and sweet/I'll get far away from the hustling crowd. When it was legal, even Kate Winslet was once reported in People magazine as saying that she nips upstairs to the roof for the occasional cigarette. Why don't you come up and see me sometime? [Mae West] And, in the privacy of their own patios where the neighbors couldn't see them, they could do whatever they pleased. Even (they imagined) having a quiet puff after the A of C would make it a crime any day now to even think about smoking. Good luck! Veel Geluk. B'hatzlacha. Gambatte. Ngikufisela iwela. Yet there was a caveat.

First, they would have to be *k*aught in the Act. Catch me if you can, huh. Rather - 'It's the thought that counts' became the prevailing rationale for thinking too much.

Soon the roofers would only have to watch out for the occasional patrolling AT-chopper which could detect a cigarette flame from ten aeronautical miles and individually analyze its 70+ carcinogens while still hovering overhead. Being tens of floors above the distraction of the din at street level, the roofers enjoyed listening to a 747 lifting-off from JFK with the dBs set on max. James Taylor & Carole King must've been two happy campers counting the royalties as everyone began singing Up on the Roof when they had a craving for a quiet puff or two.

Frankly. it was still the waning moments of the honeymoon period and the A of C hadn't yet set in along with the refreshing nor'easter. Still, they were counting their chickens before they hatched which was much less threatening than if their chickens were coming home to roost. As if they were farmers. Who were still complaining of the unsightly wind turbos destroying their rustic panorama. Who had completed their chores by the time most of the die-hards had hit the sack. Having made their choice which they had to sleep with. The fact was that things were going to get a lot worse. And there was yet another intangible.

The roofers weren't *k*-smokers. There was safety in numbers, but they lacked security. They did it in mixed company and that would be their downfall. Around every corner there would always be a Victor McLachlin, Judas, Benedict Arnold, Richard Kiel, J. Robert Oppenheimer or worse to kiss and tell. You just never knew who was going to be the first to squeal. After the A of C would become law, the threat of the Mid X would hang over them like CO_xs, SO_xs and NO_xs on a clear day in Manhattan. If you believed the liar's club. [Mary Karr] The risk was too great. And, they lacked the purity of the calling, of the vocation. The avocation. The gift of the muse that has no refund policy because in giving (literature) back to society dost thou receiveth. The *k*-smoker - who smoked solely to write. For the nico-cum-inspiration to open the portal. To drop the drawbridge. The bridge over troubled water. To unclog preconceptions (albeit clogging the arteries by default). To uncork the magic genie. To unlock secret passageways. To unleash the mind.

whisshhh ...

Thar' goes the mind.

oo-ooooh ...

There goes the neighborhood. Oh, did I mention that I was best man once at a Mafia wedding where the reception was in the Tavern on the Green? The reason I'm sure they were Mafia is because the bride's dad (she told me) manufactured a half-billion guitar picks annually. Go figure on the laundry $. But my favorite cultural hang-out was the Chelsea Hotel on W 23rd which accommodated some really great smokers in its heyday such as Kerouac, Behan, Piaf, Joplin, Dylan Thomas.

~ ~ ~

Within their hearts the AT lawmakers knew that *k*-smokers were probably a timid bunch and more apt to write letters to the editor with words that pound on the conscience. For us however it was just more spin with the wheel in motion along with the thousands of balding tires whistling harmoniously through Manhattan with the whir of the nor'easter. Like an irresistible force confronting an immovable object as in a head-on collision on 5th and 50th at any hour of the day or night if you could tell the difference. No longer simmering on the frying pan, we (I) knew that soon we'd be free-falling from the *k*loset deep down into the underground (parking lot). Into Dante's Inferno. In fairness, nothing was fair in love and *were* (sic). [Henry V] The way Brits pronounce *war*. As it were. Between the AT kops and us, the guardians of literature as we knew it. Guardians of the Universe. Like the Knights Templar, preservers of the Ark of the Covenant and protectors of the Holy Grail. At a time when the only constants were death and cig taxes and the latter were on the way out. Incidentally, the Divine Comedy (regarded as the foundation of modern literary Italian) was one of the first major works of literature written in Italian rather than the anticipated Latin which was until then the language of scholars and poets.

In any event, because everyone forgot Latin after Vatican Council II except Trappist monks, the ad agencies retained by the AT lawmakers to remarket the #2 pencils now concentrated their efforts on individual conscience which doth make cowards of us all. [WS] The remarketing of the #2 pencil was the single most ingenuous ad campaign since the re-invention of the hula-hoop which follows the same cycle every generation. As though no adult had tried one before. 'Try it you'll like it' became the new slogan for the #2 pencils also.

And, when all else failed, in the words of the prophet: That's the time to pray. Posters were strategically placed on bus broadsides, taxicab 'available' neon-signs, moped license-plates and garbage dumpster buckets in bold gothic letters:

Ignorantia legis non excusat - There is no excuse for second-hand smoke.

The new warning had a contemplative mood. And no one knew the difference or cared less. And even during the honeymoon period, bus drivers, cabbies and garbage pick-up professionals (and their passengers) were already on the look-out for us. In a head-start. Mimicking their own broadsides. But when they saw there was no reward offered because of the lack of funding with the pending elimination of cig taxes, they just gave up examining their consciences. It had a hint of Heisenberg all over again and good news for us. I bring you good news of great joy. [Luke 2:10]

And yet, in spite of the fact that everyone guessed that the ratification of the A of C was inevitable, for some uncanny reason the provocation just didn't have that oomph to it any longer. People were busy doing other things. Like setting their alarms earlier each morning so they could hit 'snooze' more frequently - because of the alarming stress from the side-effects of the pending end to cig taxes for the Treasury coffers which funded just about everything. And was a wake-up call for the no child left behind program.

Frankly, people were stressed but they were also bored, which happens. Because they didn't know the lyrics at least after the first verse, many New Yorkers wishing the after-season were over, were still in denial and humming the chorus of popular Christmas carols such as: We wish you a merry Christmas/We wish you a merry Christmas/We wish you a merry Christmas/And a happy New Year. With an ad infinitum repetition of the happy chorus to keep their minds off their empty wallets. Which made no sense at all in the circumstances, but timing was everything. It was like a little league game when your kid's team lost ten in a row. They no longer had their hearts in it. Yet the AT team charged with due diligence in anticipation of the post-T era had been on a roll. Something was in the air which didn't smell right, and which was known to cause more than allergies. Yes indeed, this made sense in NYC.

As H.G. Wells said: There comes a moment in the day when you have written your pages, attended to your correspondence in the afternoon, and have nothing further to do. Then comes that hour when you are bored, that's the time for sex. Which was usually followed by a cigarette. Practically at the instant the act was over. When you looked in the mirror, saw what you had done, and then – took a closer look at your partner from the night before. No wonder you needed a quick cigarette. Or two. And fast.

whisshhh .... oo-oooooh ...

Whether everyone was having sex or not (although foul mouth-odor was still a major issue until the post-T era), the movement needed a stimulus to get off-center or was in great danger of reverting to a status quo that was totally unacceptable to a majority algorithm.

~ ~ ~

It was the last day of December. The last rites would be appropriate. The temperature was in single digits at best. 42nd Street had long since been cleaned-up except for the butts on the pavement outside practically every hi rise.

Walking by a Korean dvd store, you could hear the melancholy voice of Merle Haggard on the jukebox inside, when he too was inside, San Quentin: If we make it through December/Everything's gonna be all right I know ... His raspy vocal chords sounded like an ex-con or a current chain-smoker who had no one to blame but himself. Anyway, it was no surprise to hear C&W honky-tonk music stealing from the Korean consumer-electronic store in midtown Manhattan ever since the US-evangelization of S. Korea. Since then the resident male population had prospered with mail-order brides which accepted returns (in good condition) provided you paid freight-forwarding & VAT until you got it right. Many S. Korean immigrants lived between 31st and 36th Streets and 5th and 6th Avenues so it wasn't too far to walk to work.

Further along outside an oriental gadget store as an invigorating crowd-pleaser little mechanical birds that were made in China were whizzing around in circles and flapping their flimsy tin wings like hummingbirds in heat. And, for a dollar, they'd chirp to your children's choice from the collected songs of the National Audubon Society. Although the remote control was carefully hidden, city kids who weren't fooled were happy watching the tweetie birds on high, like nothing they had ever seen in their young lives. They thought they were *boids* because that's what the gangsters called them in the movies. And the NYC juvenile delinquents had never seen a bird in their lives. So, they really weren't too sure what they were seeing on yet another muggy morning with their own two eyes. They remembered the *woids* in the good book that seeing was believing so they believed the little mechanical tweetie *boids* were birds. Until, abruptly being dragged along by the scruff of the neck by their single mothers to the next agenda of the rat race on the ground. Although you could tell by the precocious expressions on the kids' faces, they wanted better, deserved more, and were still young enough to make their own choices someday. Had they only known.

The sun was trying to sneak in between the lingering smog which you would need a Jim Bowie knife to cut through, and the overnight accumulation of CO_xs, SO_xs and NO_xs. And you had to applaud its efforts. It was no problem for the infra-red radiation coming in, but the thermal radiation just stayed put. Which confused the hell out of everyone because it was so cold. Especially the *tabagie*, most of whom by now had hypothermia. Al Gore had hypothetically warned about this phenomenon while not commenting at all on any of the 70-some tobacco carcinogens of the 4400 different chemicals which was now the talk of the town. Talking was one thing but seeing was believing. Many looked up said 'Oh God!' - but it wasn't heaven they were looking up at. In fact, they couldn't see very high up at all. It was as though the huge alien ship in the movie Independence Day just hovered there forever.

In fairness, backtracking to 1988 Al (Gore) had gone on record: *Throughout most of my life I raised tobacco. I want you (tobacco farmers) to know that with my own hands for all of my life I put it in plant beds and transferred it. I've hoed it. I've dug it. I've sprayed it. I've chopped it. I've shredded it, spiked it, put it on the barn, stripped it and sold it.*

Incidentally, I had the pleasure of meeting Al once but only for moments.

And, although disappointing the sleuths among you if you think the Six-Degrees of Kevin Bacon (whom I also met) will lead to my identity, my secret's safe with Al. For godsake he doesn't know I'm a *k*-smoker. For obvious reasons my secret life was not brought up and confessing to either of them would've been ludicrous following Al's confessions on being raised on tobacco. Indeed, had they known - I'd no longer be one. [Heisenberg] Which wasn't half as bad as some of Kevin's movie-titles such as: Death Sentence, The Air I Breathe, Where the Truth Lies, Telling Lies in America, and Enormous Changes at the Last Minute. And you wondered if the 'last minute' had anything to do with the long and honored history of the NY Minute as the events unfolded. And Dave Barry didn't make up those titles. But let's not digress. For another second.

whisshhh .... oo-ooooooh ...

Nevertheless, on this typical day in the Big Apple, two hundred thousand stalled automobiles with engines running, each pumped out an average of 21 lbs of CO_2 per gl of gas consumed.

Ms Peggy Lee was not amused at all and sulked: Is that all there is? While the CO_2s began to assimilate with other particulates before mingling with the gentle breeze. Which they'd better exploit, and fast, because the nor'easter was starting to get tired of NYC. Well, nothing lasts forever. As Rosalind said to Orlando in As You Like It: Why then, can one desire too much of a good thing? [WS]

Nonetheless, soon, in words immortalized by Albert (Camus): … Everything (in old Manhattan) would be very still. [The Plague]

It was hard to keep up with all of these Albert's as I've already commented a couple of times on Einstein whom a dear departed anthropologist-friend interviewed in Princeton in 1947 but that's neither here nor there. Except 1947 was the same year as the Dichter study which examined what smokers want. Relatively speaking.

For the forensics among you seeking clues.

To my i.d. My *id*.

Had *I'd* only known myself better.

~ ~ ~

48th Floor Time-Life Building

In the wrong place at the wrong time

outside the Time-Life Building

In the Rockefeller Center 1271 Avenue of the Americas

6th Ave - Between W 50th. and W 51st.

NEW YEAR's EVE EVENT 2008

Build-up (pun) to the MANHATTAN PROLOGUE

The New Year's Eve event that had started to unfold at ~ 09:59:00 and concluded ~ 10:04:40 am.

Indoor/outdoor chronology of a 20-minute smoke-break.

Assuming normal traffic and standard elevator procedures.

[This model was later incorporated into the fire-escape drill.]

a. Average time to get outside building from office (includes elevator ride) = 4 minutes.
b. Average time to get inside building to office (includes elevator ride) = 4 minutes.
c. Remaining quality smoking time = 12 minutes.
d. Average elapsed time for one fully smoked cigarette = 6 minutes.
e. Average elapsed time for two fully smoked cigarettes = 12 minutes.

Clock-in for work:	09:00:00 hours
First smoke break:	09:55:00-10:15:00
First smoke break begins:	09:59:00
Elapsed time for 1st cigarette:	09:59:00-10:05:00
Manhattan Prologue tragedy starts:	***10:04:00***
Manhattan Prologue tragedy ends:	***10:04:40***
Elapsed time for 2nd Cigarette:	10:05:00-10:11:00
Expected arrival at desk*:	10:15:00

[*Depending on elevator traffic on a good day]

Meanwhile, in Times Square, about nine city blocks (SW) and one avenue away, there was a kind of hush/All over the world. [Herman's Hermits] You could hear a pin drop even though it was 13-hours and 56-minutes before the ball would fall. Again, New Yorkers had learned to live with anything but even they were shocked at what happened on yet another muggy morning, promptly (as it was later reported) at 10.04 am. (10:04:00)

Life would never be the same again for one fifth of the population. Especially for eight city-residents who were innocent passers-by outside the 48-story Time & Life Building in the Rockefeller Center in Midtown Manhattan. Witnesses later recalled, compassionately, that none of the victims was capable of harming a fly. But you had to wonder if this were lost in translation with some of the cockroaches known to infest the older, rent-controlled flats in the lower east side where surely some of them lived. If not all of them, the way the economy was crumbling and getting worse by the minute. In anticipation of the pending ban and its trickle-down effect on discretionary spending for smokes and beer.

Still, regardless of the circumstances of any tragedy, that the separation of life and death could happen in less than a NY minute in NY had a metaphysical mood to it. It made the misfortune even more poignant in the spirit of the holy season which had the usual good run until the Feast of the Epiphany. Especially upon the New Year's Eve festivities on the evening of the tragedy that for many were spoiled no end. Thinking about it. Of what had happened outside the Time Building. And, the realization (afterwards) that smoking was banned *on account of it.* On account of the MANHATTAN PROLOGUE. After the Ball was Over. [Charles K. Harris]

Following the tragedy, for the first time in history that anyone could recall there was consensus among smokers and anti-smokers alike (which they certainly were not) that none of the Manhattan victims deserved the fate that befell them. Many had been trying to get a late start on their after-Christmas window-shopping spree having spent all their hard-earned money during the Labor Day super-specials at Macys. But looking was deceiving. Indeed, two months earlier, the shoppers lament (looking at their brat kids) was: *Please God, let's just get past Halloween.* The strangest thing was that, as far as the public knew, this commotion at the end of the summer holidays was long before the slightest hint that smoking was about to go the way of Ben and Jerry's Rain Forest Crunch ice cream.

Never having to say you're sorry again. To the condescending non-smokers. Or listening to your favorite song: Smoke though your heart is aching/Smoke even though it's breaking/...Light up your face with gladness. [Nat King Cole]

The saddest of many regrets is that it (the unfolding event) could've been prevented like many other diseases such as lung cancer and everything else the actuaries considered credible cause & effect. But not the trillions of tons of reactive hydrocarbon particles. Or the reckless stampede for the post-Christmas window-shopping madness. Which made the nouveau paupers feel like millionaires in a reversal of the poverty to opulence contrast that you'd observe daily in Delhi. If you kept your eyes wide open. Which was quite a challenge betwixt the smog below and the smog above. And mouth wide shut. The tragic scene was already starting to surface at approximately 09.59:00

whisshhh ....oo-oooooh

Between 09.55.00 and 10.04.00 am   *Offenders*

Twenty-one office workers from various businesses occupying the Time building had stepped out in the bitter cold that froze their butts off for a nice relaxing smoke or two. Which they felt they earned after all they had to put up with. Like with a nagging spouse who was always right. Or wrong. Without the wisdom to know the difference. From the moralizing hypocrites in the next cubicles over who never smoked. While everyone knew their co-workers were screwing around like nobody's business when no one was looking. Enjoying their own addictions. Just thinking about the pending A of C made the smokers seek a diversion before the smoke-break by playing with matches but they realized that all too soon 'twould be the proverbial #2 pencil for them too.

Thirteen of the twenty-one office workers were supposedly male. The evidence insisted that the tragedy could've occurred outside any building - but the Time building just happened to be in the wrong place at the wrong time.

And, you had to feel sorry for the *tabagie.* Subjected day-in and day-out to the venom of sniggering passers-by mixing vitriol with sarcasm. Pointing their little fingers up their noses at them the way the Brits are accustomed to doing under normal circumstances by sheer habit. Which was tough to give up. And, you could always tell an anti-smoker anyway. And it had nothing to do with smoking or not-smoking. They were the ones always trying to break-up a little fun. Like, for example, when you've just heard the funniest joke of your life. That's Life. [Sinatra] And, you can't wait to share it. And there are about six people around and you're just getting warmed-up. And it's so really-really funny that you're almost laughing yourself even before you get to the punchline. You know the kind of ambience. The camaraderie. And this anti-smoker among the group which has absolutely nothing to do with the topic of smoking says: Oh yeah, heard it before, that's the one where such-and-such says something stupid like ... And your day is shattered, and the rest of the week. That's the kind of people anti-smokers are. They really just love doing that. Must be genetic.

Since a cigarette typically takes 6 minutes to consume (of mainstream-smoke exhaled, combined with side-stream smoke burning from the ciggie itself) - even multiplied by 21 smokers, it shouldn't be considered that drastic, you would think, relative to the cause and effect of the tragedy. Further, it was improbable that all 21 lit up exactly at 09:59:00. Still, from the Daily News report (the smoking-gun), one or more certainly did. The fact is that by 10.04 am, hardly five minutes into the smoke break, all 21 had been smoking up a storm.

One of those who lit up was the chief operating officer (COO) of a small dot.com who was fortunate to have signed-on long after the bubble burst in Y2K. Prior to which everyone was worrying about the wrong bubble that might be blown on January 1. Of course, this guy had no idea how bad things confronting Wall Street were really going to get after the smoking ban. In the freezing cold he was wearing designer earmuffs with individually controllable dual-channels which sported the latest electro-acoustic technology and mimicked the built-in quality of noise-cancellation headphones.

At the precise moment of one of the worst tragedies in the city's history, at least since the record number of homicides the prior day (which was even higher than the day before), the COO had been concentrating on the moral ambivalence of his inner persona where he was inclined to create his own private sanctuary over a quiet puff. Incidentally, the acronym COO should not be confused with CO_2. Or worse, having lost an atom in the mass-hysteria of everything happening too darn fast.

Nevertheless, the COO's memory-foam padded leather ear-cushions provided natural Surround Sound, ultra-comfort, and a peaceful, near-silent environment which helped to offset the din and cacophony of NYC which was more than enough reason for the exorbitant purchase. Over and over again through his left earmuff he listened to the famous doorbell sound of the four notes of Beethoven's Fifth Symphony from the theme of A Clockwork Orange. And then, on his right earmuff with the volume set on high he would concentrate on the blasting music of the synthesized Ninth Symphony in the same movie while Alex (played by Malcolm McDowell) was being tortured. And all the time with his eyes wide shut holding a #2 practice-pencil diagonally in the air as if a maestro's baton with his left hand. While his right clung to a Lucky Strike. And before he knew it, he could no longer tell the difference between the Fifth and the Ninth and cared less – it had that much control over him. While puffing away to his heart's (pun) content. Over and over and over again. As if further proof of McLuhan's subliminal impact on society being played by the ad agencies. Who were getting ready for a nationwide lunch (sic) of the #2 pencil having passed the focus groups. All of whom had to be hypnotized first after signing a waiver against personal injury to their incisors.

Wearing sunglasses on a dismal day, like most New Yorkers trying to hide something when no one was looking, his overcoat lapel was turned-up against the direction of the mild albeit stinging breeze. *oops.* I've got to stop using that word. Every time I write 'albeit' I think of Albeit Gore, Camus or Einstein, and I lose the concentration necessary to write words that pound on the conscience.

whisshhh .... oo-oooooh ...

Sorry about that little interruption but I really needed it. *whew!* Couldn't find my darn matches. Gotta light? Thank you for understanding. Thank you for smoking. Okay wise guy!

The sunglasses in broad daylight (...he wished) and the upturned lapels later fed the headline news with a frenzy suggesting the appearance of a hoodlum if not a loiterer with something sinister in mind – which was ridiculous. As if he were Jack London who was arrested for vagrancy when sleeping rough near Niagara Falls in 1894. Then deloused, given thirty days hard labor and handcuffed to a chain-gang. Both lapels were pulled close together with his left gloved hand while the other (ungloved) held his cigarette. Usually he would un-glove the left hand in the process of lighting his second. In case he might singe the leather, which acted as an insulator between the cigarette and his fingers. Otherwise he'd have to rely on visual observation only, tragically, like amateur pilots such as John F. Kennedy, Jr. Unless he lit it off the smoke he was finishing, the sure sign of a chain-smoker. And quickly glove-up again in the freezing cold. But it's doubtful (as later presented in evidence) if he had started a second between 9.59 am and 10.04 am since in fairness he had at least 20 minutes on the clock, 12 minutes quality smoking-time or the equivalent of two cigs at the rate of 6 minutes a-piece. And, who knows – he could be lucky with a fast elevator on the ride back up as part of his back-up plan if he were delayed. And so, he was most probably just relaxing and having a good time with his inner self. And bothering no one in particular butt (sic) for the occasional gawker who thought he was nuts, conducting his own orchestra in his private concert.

And, while he was well aware from the outpatient brochures that you lost one minute of your life for each cigarette consumed, there were others who did the math and concluded that it took a good 6 minutes to consume one single cig. So, you really gained 6 minutes of pleasure for every one minute lost. Which was more like a toss-up and one helluva choice. It was a tough act to follow. But, had he only known, the A of C was just about to follow.

For the moment it's fair to assume that the COO was still on his first drag, on-his-own-time and at-his-own-pace with time-on-his-hands and/or gloves, for another. That is (he assumed), had he calculated the elevator ride-time correctly (this time) in the Time building where everything was about Time. And about time. To exercise his personal responsibility. More than choice of which he would soon be deprived. With time running out. And fast. Which, it was assumed he accepted before returning by speed-elevator (right!) to his manager's-size Rubik's fabric-covered cubicle on the 47th floor. Which was pretty darn upper in a 48-floor building in Manhattan and usually took a lot longer than the (average) floor used for the time-measurement of the 20-minute smoke-break calculation. Which meant that sometimes he just had to smoke faster.

Which he always planned on writing a novel about if he ever had time although he already had the title: *I'm Smoking as Fast as I Can.* To get the same effect as the rest of them on lower floors. While, in fairness, those on higher floors thought it was unfair on days with heavier traffic. On the elevators. Which slowed things down drastically. And which was caused by the escalating trend in obesity. In spite of which - a study by the University of Geneva researchers found that taking the stairs instead of the elevator reduced the risk of dying of lung cancer by 21 percent. In fairness, climbing even 21 floors by footsies within the total elapsed smoke-break time of 20-minutes might be considered a bit much by many health – never mind tobacco fanatics. And still be in time to be back at your desk pronto – without the risk of being fired if observed-late - due to the economic effects of the pending cigarette ban and loss of tobacco-sin taxes which determined the economy.

Further, researchers at Concordia U. concluded that a daily stair climb shaves 6-months off your 'brain age', who performed MRI scans on 331 people ages 21 to 79. As many of the professionals in the Time building, in fairness, had already quit temporarily to test their stamina. And had started practicing with their #2 pencils in the wake of the pre-T era. On average they were gaining 10 pounds a week. Which began to have a noticeable impact on the elevator ride, causing a discernable imbalance when the fat workers all congregated on one side towards the higher floors. Like a similar distribution of excess carry-on luggage on a small aircraft at high altitude against an unforgiving wind. When the overload light came on after exceeding the manufacturer's specifications. And the elevator stalled like in a Bruce Willis movie. And none of the passengers knew how to jumpstart it until the doors as inexplicably opened while they senselessly stampeded to the next elevators if they were lucky not to be between floors. Where they discovered the same phenomenon.

Another of the 21 was a paralegal who for all ostensible purposes behaved like a female because she was puffing away like crazy and hardly inhaling at all. You know the way. *puff-puff-puff-puff-puff-pu-pu-pu-pu-pu-pu-pu ...* As if nervously blowing quick soap-bubbles more than smoke at the almost unbearable thought of at least another two hours before lunch and the next smoke-break. And watching her watch. And another, a mail-room clerk. Yet another was a sales manager of a large brokerage outfit who was about 24 in her stock-inged feet.

Still another of the 21 smokers worked in the art department of the largest ad agency retained by the AT program for the #2 pencil launch. Her department had been charged with the 'salvage' campaign from the anticipated collateral damage affecting one fifth of the population in the agony of withdrawal. The agency had already experimented with a number of slogans before going back to basics: 'The #2 pencil can help. Try one today.' Another suggestion was to use a cameo of Sterling Hayden (as Det. Lt. Sims) 'chewing a toothpick' which he appeared to be enjoying in the 1953 film noir classic Crime Wave saying to Gene Nelson (as ex-con Steve Lacey): "Doc says I can't smoke so I chew toothpicks – hundreds of them!" The graphic designers were having difficulty replacing toothpicks with #2 pencils in demonstrating similar gratification regardless of the size of the 6-ft 5-in Sterling Hayden's commensurate mouth.

Still, she didn't advertise the fact except among her close friends that she was of the personal opinion that #2 pencils were nothing short of nonsense. Although it was her job and therefore, she had to have her soul in it or else. Which sounded like an equivocal strategy at best while (on the side) she also smoked away to her heart's (pun) content.

And so on. In what appeared to be 13 men and 8 women smoking up a storm beneath the Time building canopy on smoke-break. But, again, looks were deceiving and it was hard to tell.

There was nothing unusual about what each was doing because at exactly the same time every day for as long as any of them could recall, lighting-up was part of their daily regimen more than job description. It was just something they did. They were so positive of this because neither of them was sure that they could've made it through the day otherwise. At least that's what they later confessed at their mock interrogation which was symbolic for the news frenzy. Before been escorted without further ado or a single phonecall to the newly inaugurated *Midnight Express.* Which no one knew even existed for fear of mass hysteria although there had been rumors. And, even today, it's unsure whether it's a place or a vehicle or an experience, which doesn't really matter. Sure, there were the grotesque Kafkaesque cellphone pix smuggled out, but they may have been faked by the AT kops as a warning on KNN. Fake news. No, you didn't want to go there.

And never heard from again. The offenders.

whisshhh .... oo-oooooh ...

What happened next stifled the imagination and was the greatest tragedy to befall New York City in days. Certainly, worse than the Great '77 Blackout when no one could see what they were doing when no one was looking. The entire awakening world which read about the tragedy in different time zones was rightly worried because of the inevitable ripple effect described in the Deep-Sixing chapter earlier.

International-sounding newspapers and magazines such as La Cigaro Aficionado ('the good life magazine for men') were having a field day in the moment but didn't rule out their own vulnerability. The Daily News brought out an afternoon edition on the same afternoon as the event that happened two hours earlier which was stale news on the Internet. Time magazine focused on the centricity of its own facility in the unfolding story. In an unprecedented demonstration of timing, the Life annual cover story (New Year's Eve edition) was rushed to hit the streets on New Year's morning. Instant tabloid penny-novels were co-written by ambulance chasers who wrote fast and cared less. Indeed, it was the third worst calamity in history directly attributed to second-hand smoke following a closely ranked tie between the Great Chicago Fire and Saint Joan of Arc.

The news reports described how a cloud of thick smoke had formed between the (self-propelled) revolving doors (acting as a wind-turbine) of the Time-Life building - extending across to the

curb, roughly twenty-one feet away.

It was hard to tell the concentration of the smoke particles to the right or the left of the doorway. Smokers to the left of me/Smokers to the right. [Stealers Wheel] But the cloud was presumed by expert witnesses from the American Lung Association to cover a volumetric capacity of about 21-feet cube. The ALA arrived by helicopter almost immediately, at 10.04.35, 5-seconds before the last of the victims had perished, all of whom had collapsed at 10.04.00 on the dot. As reported - still breathing for some forty seconds.

Between 10.04.00 and 10.04.40   *Victims:*

The reality of the speculation is that eight otherwise healthy individuals walked into that cloud, collapsed instantly and were dead within forty seconds, tops. The eldest was 64 and looked a lot younger than Paul McCartney when he was 64 and a lot younger than Sir Paul three years later if you looked at the lines on his forehead after his shell-out. And then, like dominos, the remaining seven. The magnificent 7 as the pastor referred to them in his eulogy. Their names were: Yul Brynner, Horst Buchholz, James Coburn, Steve McQueen, Robert Vaughn, Charles Bronson and Brad Dexter. Just kidding. Sorry – I really hate to do that to you since four of them were women. But I couldn't help myself with the non-sequitur following such a lead-in. Especially as the plot thickens in this horrible tragedy that conjured-up grotesque images painted by the artist, Dada, during WWI. And Dada wasn't his real father. Unfortunately, as I mentioned in the first chapter, to maintain my writing-sanity ... *oops*, creativity, it is also necessary to interweave cliché, hyperbole and other embellishments throughout this exposé to make the theme appear fictitious as much as to discombobulate reality. After all, we have an inherent need to be entertained, amused, distracted. I know I do. *whew!*

> *whisshhh .... oo-oooooh ...*

The really saddest part of the entire tragedy is that the "NO SMOKING" sign directly inside the revolving doors – was supposed to have been placed in the middle of the area *BENEATH THE **OUTSIDE** CANOPY!*

That's exactly what the investigators allegedly told the bereaving family afterword's when no words were necessary and indeed useless if not painful!

The ALA contingent was even faster than a fire-engine arriving at the scene. Incidentally, this was proudly reported in their next monthly newsletter which frowned on anything to do with fire and/ or smoke. They had come from their 6th floor headquarters on 61 Broadway next to what used to be a Starbust. Which was replaced by a vending machine. In case you didn't know how bad things were getting. With the only subject for serious discussion in bars, family get-togethers, Tupperware parties, and occasionally the pulpit - how to survive without cigarette taxes. Which was a tough one alright. But there was no time for a coffee and smoke break this time for those who lied on their job application. And cheated on their urine tests.

Since the ALA had a zero-tolerance program.

whisshhh .... oo-oooooh ...

And possibly (cheating) on their missus too.

God bless the old lady. Who'd believe anything. Lady, you have made me what I am and I am yours. [Kenny Rogers] In fact, when they thought about it, the tragedy would've been avoided had there been no coffee *or* smoke-break at all which made everyone feel even more guilty if they weren't in such a hurry. If there were any good news in the circumstances it was that - outside the ALA revolving door entrance, smoking had always been prohibited for two city blocks. And this included abandoned telephone-kiosks. And, in hindsight, a smart move. Butt (sic), this was the Time-Life building and not the ALA building. The similarities ended there.

A canopy over the Time building entrance accounted for specu-lation by the American Thoracic Society that the smoke cloud probably stayed-put mostly under the canopy, like a black hole consuming light or a pet dog named Rex. At least during the period in question, causing a concentration of the two most likely causes of chronic levels of secondhand smoke: carbon monoxide and particulate matter. There was also speculation as to whether the revolving doors on this particular afternoon by some freak of nature had contributed to blowing some of the 4000+ chemicals from the smoke - particularly a goodly share of the 70+ carcinogens: arsenic, carbon monoxide, hydrogen cyanide, and/or ammonia, and so on and so forth - directly into the lungs of the victims (prior to the combustion). And there was always the possibility that CO_xs were created from rare combinations of CO_2s and CO_1s plus or minus god knows how many stray atoms if you weren't too careful. It was even surmised that the SO_xs and NO_xs already in the air had somehow mixed with the cigarette smoke causing the proverbial 'nutty-pro-fessor combustion'.

Incidentally, the American Thoracic Society, the only entity on the scene trying to remain impartial (whether any or many of its members were closet-smokers will never be known because of Heisenberg), implied that the level of pollutants from the 21 members of the tabagie puffing up a storm were secondary to the CO_+ particulates in the exhaust from passing motor vehicles. Because of the 'condition' of the 'corpses' there was much argument about the overture of this unsolicited opinion. Subsequently, the suspect variables were disregarded as collateral-only and discarded by the AT investigators. However, the AT swat-team arrived at exactly 10:04:35 by Sikorsky X_2 chopper from Langley for an objective assessment. The mayor had enough on his hands after cleaning up 42nd Street without gloves which was irresponsible but didn't want his fingerprints on this one. The futuristic high-speed single-engine'd fly-by-wire X_2 featured coaxial rotors and a pusher propeller. It had been christened Eagle before landing only seconds after the ALA who had been pretty darn fast. To an outsider it even appeared as though the chopper, fully-loaded with the latest carcinogen-detection equipment, had been at the ready-set-go for lift-off at exactly 9.04.35 for the 257 nautical mile (one-way) trip with a top speed of 257 miles/hour in order to arrive at 10.04.35 precisely. It was a remarkable coincidence and it was beginning to look like training night for the cavalry with all the ruckus.

Something was up. In smoke.

whisshhh .... oo-oooooh ...

~ ~ ~

It was all about the domino effect. Fats Domino had recalled in his memoirs about his refurbished home in the Lower Ninth Ward in New Orleans in the aftermath of Hurricane Katrina. He chose the title: Ain't it a Shame. And, it was really a shame that so much exhaust had been creeping out of autos because for much too long smokers had been typecast in the same breath with worse polluters. Of course - we were easier to personify. The path of least resistance. Unless it were the animated Disney movie, Cars. Which, because it was a family movie, not only was exhaust-free but pumped-out fresh air into the eco. Starring Paul Newman, playing the part of the race car, Doc Hudson. Who had been an awesome smoker and lived to a grand old age of 83 before his lungs got the better of him. Too.

Interestingly, the anti-smokers among the gawkers who were on a fixed agenda and couldn't stomach the smell of cigarette smoke from ten city blocks in any direction, didn't seem to mind the exhaust fumes too much. But they could get a whiff of a ciggie alright. Like a shark in the Caribbean sniffing a single drop of blood in Amityville some 1768 km away.

At least the gas wasn't getting on their clothes or the draperies at home. And although they could hardly breathe with all the CO_xs, SO_xs and NO_xs in the air, still it was much better than not being able to breathe at all if you were in the first ten rows of Sinatra smoking during his concert in the old days. And, it wasn't because of glycol-based theatrical fog (recently proven to be a cause of respiratory ailments) that you could hardly see the crooner in the center of his own smoke-filled stage of which all the world was.

Presently, the slower walkers behind the eight innocent passers-by saw what was happening and stopped dead in their tracks, although not as dead as those preceding them. There must have been hundreds of busy shoppers. Nonchalantly strolling the pavement, minding their own business most of the time. Watching out for pickpockets and keeping their problems to themselves. Businesspeople on their way to close deals with their shiny-patent attachés, designer-brollies and Financial Times neatly folded between their arms. For a quick look at the classifieds when they got to their cubicles and were supposed to be working. There were also some arty types who couldn't afford Parsons, the New School for Design, or weren't smart enough, who were later planning on trying to re-enroll at the Fashion Institute of Technology after missing too many classes for the usual reasons. Such as bad hair-days. Screwing around with other arty types who cared less and probably forgot to set the alarm clock in the heat of the moment. If you know what I mean. Stuff like that.

And a few tall, slender but not-so-good-looking models in heels and warm, eco-friendly fishnet stockings on their way for quick shoots. And fingering their hair if not jet-sprayed from aerosol-can propellants containing chlorine and bromine that damage the Earth's protective ozone layer, ultimately forming a hole over the South Pole and into the Southern hemisphere. Before the shoot, most of them were saying: Ah shoot! as they looked at their watches and realized they were late enough already without getting caught-up

in another daily crisis which gave the city its character.

But it was Too Late for the Eight. This was the catchy title for the next huge hit for Bob Geldorf who used the 8-ball as a metaphor. This time commemorating the MANHATTAN PROLOGUE. A spectacle that hadn't been seen since Little Boy was dropped on Hiroshima on August 6, 1945 – two years before the infamous **Dichter study** on what smokers want. Or worse, followed with a bang by Fat Man three days later on Nagasaki. And long before obesity became so popular that they opened a Fat Man's Hall of Fame. Which got into gender-discriminatory trouble in its first year by inadvertently omitting Fat Women in its membership. For which they later overcompensated.

The 21 male, female, and possibly other androgynous smokers couldn't believe their incriminating eyes, blinded from chain-smoking a few too many over as many decades. As they dropped their smokes with their mouths wide-open and their eyes wide shut hoping it was an hallucination which was not uncommon for most of them – watching the eight innocent passers-by, now in their midst, incredulously collapsing on the marble pavement beneath the canopy of the Time-Life Building.

The question was later raised as to why the 21 offenders didn't collapse along with the 8 victims *in their midst* beneath the same canopy. Someone opined that, being smokers, the 21 may have built-up some kind of rare immunity (although it was never known whether the 8 had also been smokers). Or, that the tragedy had something to do with timing and somehow the 8 had simply been in the wrong place at the wrong time. Or, something else …? Hmmm … Anyway, it was only speculation and the issue was dropped for want of a better rationale.

Incidentally, the marble pavement on which they collapsed wasn't as controversial as the terminal floor of the new Chek Lap Kok airport in Hong Kong when it just opened. The airport had to be quickly closed because the too-polished marble floor-tiles made a reflector up young girls skirts. And the surface had to be redone before aircraft which were predictably late anyway were allowed to land. Causing many passengers to get quite jittery. Circling indefinitely. Like in the first paragraph of this chapter. Since the whole thing took two weeks to roughen-up at an astronomical costly overrun of some twenty million RMB (or Chinese yuan), according to the South China News. Roughly (the way they were redoing the marble surface) the same in Hong Kong dollars. Or about two million US dollars – worth about sixpence after the economic bust. And, going to get a helluva lot worse, any minute now, with the elimination of cigarette taxes as a default of the A of C. Still, the embarrassment over the 'short skirt' incident was a far cry from the olden days when a glimpse of stocking was looked upon as something shocking.

Nonetheless, before they dropped their smokes in the midst of the unfolding tragedy, each of the 21 offenders had the presence of mind to shrewdly take a nice *lonnnnng* drag in the anxiety of the moment. As a result of all the stress. Or might've joined the victims. Otherwise. Probably. On the marble pavement. Without the proven benefit of nicotine maintaining their mental composure. For seconds. At least.

whisshhh .... oo-oooooh ...

Then without thinking too much they carelessly stubbed the butts with their galoshes which created an ugly eyesore on an otherwise almost-clean pavement littered with 'corpses', burning large holes in their rubbers. Not to be confused with erasers in England. The horror and disbelief of the instant-reports assisted by cellphones was that, within forty seconds tops, much less than a New York minute, all eight passers-by were ignited by spontaneous combustion.

Credit: Greg+Mort Walker

The coroner's report later stated that you couldn't even make out a skeleton's bones because the charred remains were burned beyond recognition following decomposition due to the torridity of an organic reaction. Which happens. I guess. Such was the devastating effects of second-hand smoke! It was as odd as the dialog on spontaneous combustion in the 1943 movie, Uncertain Glory (four years before the Dichter Study in 1947), between Errol Flynn (as Jean Picard) and Inspector Bonet. Front page photo-ops resembling Rorschach Inkblots on every tabloid under the sun that was trying to sneak through became impulse sell-outs in supermarket check-outs everywhere – with the following provocative headline:

READ ALL ABOUT IT!

Which got everyone's attention. In the check-out.

Along with spare packs of 9V batteries for smoke alarms that would never be inserted because New Yorkers were just too busy doing whatever it is they do. Which was anyone's guess. Including their own. And had no time for anything else. While chewing gum. And promotional 6-packs of #2 pencils - one at a time. Even for those who had been chain-smokers. Which, because of feel and taste were intended by the marketing geniuses as more meaningful placebos and eventual replacements for gum which was now at clearance prices. Which must've been real (the final days of gum) because you've never seen anything on the impulse-buy check-out that wasn't priced at about ten times normal. And foldable pocketsize scissors (as replacements for switchblades for their juvenile delinquent sons). And incredible long-lasting instant 'gorilla-glue' for the 'toughest jobs on planet earth'. After Planet Hollywood went under. For similar reasons as Starbust.

However, it didn't say anywhere on the label that after first use the remaining contents had lost all their gooeyness, had hardened like window-putty with the first whiff of O_2, and were useless as soon as you uncapped the tube. Which sold a helluva lot more tubes than if it worked properly. Which was a euphemism on the adage: if it ain't broke, don't fix it. And other indispensable sundries for the assiduous housewife purchased and stored in the attic for the rainy day.

darn. Rainy Days and Mondays always get me down. [The Carpenters] Can never trust the weather forecast. Forgot my brollie again. Not that it's much use if you're bent on finishing the today-segment of your WIP. Unless you're ambidextrous. With three hands. One for your brollie, one for your pen and one for your ciggie. And one (more) for the road. Just kidding. I'd need four hands for that.

Anyway, six of the eight victims were supposedly adults. Of these, four supposedly were women. One of the women (allegedly) was seven months pregnant, although (as the story goes) the child was saved. But details here were skimpy according to the Brit tabloid News of the World which had an investigative reporter assigned exclusively to 42nd Street. Which had been a safer bet for sensational journalism before the mayor cleaned it up. However, speaking with a cockney accent it was hard to know if the limey were asking the right questions. And, the Time Building was geographically outside his assigned territory so he may have been faking it. Like most memoir writers who get caught after appearing on Oprah.

What we know for sure with a reasonable level of doubt in circumstances which were foggy at best – as Yossarian said in Catch-22: It gets foggy on horseback, … is that the remaining two were five-year-old twins, a boy and a girl. The 'fivers' they were called in the UK tabloids, a reference to the unpopular sterling currency which resisted the lure of the Euro. Before there even was a Brexit. The twins were accompanied by their tall slender aunt (SWF) who also succumbed, collapsing flat down on her face which must've hurt. Incidentally, the SWF couldn't match Bridget Fonda, another brief acquaintance from my media life. And, what a knock-out!

Family members were later reported as saying that when he grew up, the boy was going to be either an astronaut or a mechanical engineer. He had a keen intellectual curiosity according to those who had observed him analyzing the little mechanical tweetie birds whizzing away like nobody's business outside the gadget-store on 42ⁿᵈ Street earlier, while the little girl had dreams of becoming a Bolshoi ballerina. That is, assuming she didn't grow too tall like her aunt who fell on her face and could carry dual passports. It was iffy about the Bolshoi as a career move even long after the collapse of communism in the former USSR because things were supposedly worse under the Russian mafia. Although Toronto would probably have been okay where the Bolshoi's used to frequently defect in spite of getting tough with passports too. Unlike, Mexico, the way the former NY Governor had been planning on handing-out drivers' licenses to any illegal alien willing to make the trip. Before he took one himself away from the limelight. But the little girl had thought hard about it and figured it would've been tough to make it as a famous ballerina in Mexico since she didn't speak Spanish, couldn't pronounce quesadilla and hated spicy food and Mexicans with a passion. And was useless at flamenco, tango or even salsa.

Worst case, the little girl, being temperamental (as reported by the tabloids which seemed to know a lot more than the average citizen who cared less) - could've made a career as a diva like Maria Callas if ballet didn't work out. Except that, while passing the erratic, short-fuse prerequisite, and being good at histrionics - she hadn't a note in her head. So, she might as well have been humming, I need you/Probably as bad as I need another hole in the head. [Nickelback]

whisshhh .... oo-oooooh ...

~ ~ ~

Between 10.04.40 and 00.00.01　　　　*Aftermath*

It was all such a waste. All told, supposedly there were nine victims although one may have survived. You see, it didn't come out about the baby whom the mother planned on naming Anastasia, until later - although there are still some unknowns on that issue (the legal word for baby) since some reports said the mother was a man. Further, the baby was never seen nor heard of since. Though frequently speculated upon. In the tabloids. And, in itself, this wasn't unusual for privacy purposes since neither was Her Imperial Highness, Grand Duchess Anastasia Nikolaevna Romanova - except for dozens of Hollywood imposters who were only acting.

Even today everyone remembers where and what they were smoking when they watched the tragedy report on CBS News on that miserable morning when darkness covered the Manhattan haze. Which in itself was no surprise and a tautology at best.

The event became known as the **MANHATTAN PROLOGUE.** It was the prologue to the Act of Cessation which imminently followed (and was a direct result of) the tragedy in Manhattan. Which proved beyond a shadow of doubt the dangers of 2HS. As observed in the shadow of any X-ray (emitted by random electrons outside the nucleus) machine worth its gamma rays (emitted by the nucleus, and hence of shorter wavelength). The shadow of a gun man. [Sean O'Casey]

And the x-rays and gamma rays had nothing to do with the enriched uranium of the Manhattan Project, a completely different technology known to Einstein and some others. Which I know because I visited Sandia National Labs, Los Alamos, and Livermore, in another life. Yet the Manhattan Prologue resulted in the ushering-in of a new age. The post-T era. The Age of Enlightenment without the 'light'.

Lumen Christi (without the light). When they ran out of Lucifer matches.

And, with the light removed, forever after the period was known in slang circles as the Age of *Enenment*. Which never really *k*aught on, probably because the coined-word, the forced-abbreviation, the forced-march, sounded like *enema* if said too quickly. Like the sudden impulsiveness of the March mickey madness when hormones are steaming.

The heralding-in of the A of C was like dropping the ball at the closure of New Year's Eve. With a thud. The musical score from a

Hitchcock movie is supposed to come in here with the sound of a ... *thud*. Now, how do you make a *thud*-sound in 2-D anyway?

th-th-th-th ...uddddddd ...

... *THUD* ...

whisshhh .... oo-ooooo-ish ...

The tragedy had an effect like electroconvulsive therapy for asylum-inmates when cortical activity in the brain ceases for the duration needed to implement the therapy. Sounds like Heisenberg to me. [Sez me] And much more effective than a set of PepBoys jumpers in reviving the AT movement which had stalled because of lack of interest. Everyone agreed it was about time. Like in the aftermath of closing time in an Irish pub when there wasn't a chance in hell of getting everyone home to their missus for at least another 90 minutes.

Well, surprise, I'm still here in the parking lot, what's your excuse? Thank God for here. In this place. Wherever that may be. Thought you had me there. A gotcha. Not quite yet. Mr. Forensic. Ms. Forensic. A miss for the forensic readers amongst you. Blest art Thou amongst women. A Monk Swimming. [Malachy McCourt]

Running out of ink. Again. *Run. Run.* Looking over my shoulder. No AT-kops today. *whew!*

A good day. Fair weather. To you. Too. Sir. Started raining in the parking lot.

No use complaining. Got company. Let's go inside.

Just kidding.

And, the Surgeon General's 2HS report from the **MANHATTAN PROLOGUE** didn't say too much about other air pollutants such as nitrogen oxide, mercury emissions, sulfur dioxide or CO_xs, which seemed to linger for a little longer.

~ ~ ~

As you are well aware by now in other circumstances, I believe smoking to be an obnoxious and despicable habit on a par with the personality of most x-smokers. Quoting Bill Hicks: I have something to tell you non-smokers that I know for a fact, and I feel it's my duty to pass on. Ready? Non-smokers die every day. That's it. Enjoy your evening.

Frankly, I only ask to be left alone as a *k*-smoker to do my own thing under my own canopy where the sapling poles cross, without bothering anyone in particular. If it weren't for the darn rain. Two days in a row. Starts off sunny, then predictably - the worst part is when you believe the weather forecast and forget your brollie. Always a nuisance to my output. You can tell how many pages I've written depending on the weather. Naturally my heart goes out to the families of those eight (or was it nine?) ... dearly departed and beloved victims. Brothers and sisters, we are gathered here today to mourn the passing of our dear friend ... poor Judd. Then the preacher'd get up and say: People used to think he was a mean ugly critter and called him a dirty (rotten) skunk and an ornery pig stealer. [Oklahoma, Rogers and Hammerstein]

Ouch! Why did I write that unless I ... suspect ... something ...?

hmmm ...

At the risk of heavenly wrath in the honesty of my confession I must also sympathize with the 21 so-called villains who were given the *Mid X* treatment for their heinous crime. You see, as the only devil's advocate except for Morris West (no relation to Philip Morris), the Group of 8 was never identified in person(s). I have always felt this squeamish feeling about the aftermath. How it came to this. The reports in the New York tabloids. The death knell for smoking. And for literature as we knew it.

whisshhh .... oo-oooooh ...

How could all of this have happened?

Remembering the good times. Do you remember? The times of your life. [Paul Anka] Thanks for the time that you've given me. [The Commodores/Lionel Richie] The last request. The firing squad. The Firing Line. William F. Buckley, Jr. Thank You for Smoking by Christopher Buckley. Son of Bill. Jr.

In retrospect, at the risk of excommunication, dare I speculate - *did the Manhattan tragedy happen at all!?*

You can rationalize anything. Was there a flood? What about Mel Gibson's dad? You can call me doubting Thomas. Call me irresponsible, call me unreliable/Throw in undependable too/...Do my foolish *alibis* bore you? [Jimmy Van Heusen] Yes, sometimes I'm not even sure which of my lives is the real one, in the self-deceptive eye of the beholder. Each has salient features in its own way, neither of which would I give up for the other.

But, for openers, each victim was reported as instantaneously burning to the core without leaving a DNA sample. How difficult could it be to make a simple double helix from a dab of adenine, cytosine, guanine and/or thymine? The reported reason for not doing so was that the skeletons were charred like plastic blobs in the movie The Blob and unable to provide the customary finger-prints which you can usually get from (even) airplane crash victims. Well, I'm not a scientist but it just didn't make sense about the Manhattan victims.

DOA but no DNA, huh? Go figure!

~ ~ ~

Taking a forensic look at the group shot of the ghastly 'corpses' in the Daily News headliner, it's true that not much was left of the remains. Of the day. But individually – to a good conceptualization-artist on freelance-retainer to the Association of American Publishers (AAP) - they appeared to resemble the crash-test dummies that you see on Discovery Channel re-runs. I even seem to recall reading about them in the best-seller, Crash Dummies for Dummies, while brows-ing in Borders before they went bust when literature died after the smoking ban when writer's inspiration dried-up.

As every dummy knows, these dummies are full-scale replicas of human beings, weighted and articulated to simulate the behavior of the human body.

While probably coincidental, the WSJ reported that one week before the tragedy a visit had been made by ALA executives to one of the Big 3 in Detroit.

It was just before they (also) went under when the deep-sixing of Japan Tobacco backfired on the auto industry - in retaliation for the GWBWH going global with the smoking ban proposal. As if they hadn't enough Axis in the evil east to worry about without bothering the orientals. Again. With #2 pencils clenched between their teeth. Like Egyptians with worry beads. In the casinos.

From an AP report in a small filler-insert on the back page of the Village Voice I recalled a piece with the header:

EIGHT MANNEQUINS STOLEN FROM DETROIT

Sub-caption:

SOUNDS LIKE SOME PERVERT

The article stated that the theft included two of the latest robot models that were designed to behave like toddlers, yelling most of the time when you press a button. Each fitted with 56 actuators in lieu of muscles, 197 sensors for touch, a small camera working as an eye for an eye, and an audio sensor that turned on a jukebox. Just kidding about the jukebox.

And, each had a bobblehead on top of their torsos. But – no DNA!

I was starting to smell foul play. According to the article, the 'female' robot could even be made to wobble like a stressed-out

ballerina on an accelerated diet. And, the young-male version could wiggle his arms like a mechanical tweetie bird on the wing. I thought of the proprietor of the Korean DVD store on 42nd Street. The store-owner had been interviewed for the local news and admitted – upon hearing of the **MANHATTAN PROLOGUE** tragedy, which had just happened – that he had (cleverly) placed one of his remote-controlled *boids* (which sounded even funnier with his Korean accent) outside the revolving doors of the Time-Life Building for the amusement of the large flock of onlookers. And their spoiled-rotten kids. With a large A-fitted cardboard-sign hanging over his wife with a hole for her head. If it weren't made of cardboard, it looked like a chef's apron with a strap around the waist like a straitjacket. In One Flew Over the Cuckoo's nest. The sign pointed in the flickable direction of his store some ten city blocks away advertising a today-only special 'while supplies last', which was a gimmick for sure, but it worked. Essentially, the store-owner had a window of opportunity until they removed the 'corpses' and the idling cars moved on. As Bette Midler put it nicely about the mechanical tweetie birds:

> *Oh, the wind beneath my wings/You, you, you, you are the wind.*
>
> *Fly, fly, fly away. You let me fly so high.*
>
> *Oh you, you, you, the wind beneath my wings/ Oh you, you, you ...*

~ ~ ~

The whole thing was uncanny. I began to research all of the popular robot magazines. Next up was a piece about a robot 'family' from a technical journal (IEEE Spectrum) with the caption: We've Been Learning A Lot About Dummies. The article stated (my italics throughout):

'The *family* includes the most widely used dummy, the Hybrid III, 50th-percentile male (anthropomorphic test device), meant to represent the average North American Man. *He doesn't even have a name.*'

Bingo!

'He weighs 78 kilograms and is 1.75 meters tall. Or would reach that height if he could stand. Which he can't because he's in permanent sitting mode. Hybrid III has a petite wife (Hybrid III 5th-percentile female), three kids (Hybrid III 10-year-old, 6-year-old, and 3-year-old), and an oversized cousin (Hybrid III 95th-percentile male), who tips the scales at 100 kg – referred to as the *big guy'*. The petite wife robot always stood by her man. Just kidding. They were both designed in sitting positions.

The thought crossed my mind like a troubling mote in Act one, scene one, of Hamlet. Was I reading the same story as in the Village Voice? But, the text in the Spectrum article referred to 3 kids instead of the 2 purported outside the Time Building. And, there was always the issue of the baby, huh? Possibly s/he was the third robot-kid with a little childish imagination. But surely the baby hadn't even been born when the headlines hit on the evening of the **MANHATTAN PROLOGUE** and could hardly be 3 years old? And, the other two kids' ages didn't match the robots which certainly weren't twins although, in fairness, they might've been clones. I'm sure that could be explained away. The article continued: 'These measurements are then converted into injury criteria which reveal the harm – anything from minor concussion to *death* – that would have been done to the vehicle's occupants *had they been human.*'

Another paragraph: 'Could this be the grisly scene of *some ritualistic slaying?*'

Good Lord! This was getting scary.

Reading on: The crash-test dummies had been used in 'roller coasters, simulated train wrecks, dropped out of airplanes, strapped into crashing helicopters, shot out of cannons.' One was 'punched in the face by a professional boxer and held in a neck lock by a Brazilian jujitsu fighter'. I'm not making this up! [Dave Barry] Finally, there were some 'applications' where 'we had no clue what they were doing. It was *proprietary or government related.* The dummies left (the factory) brand-new but they came back *unidentifiable.*' (I surmised -- burned to cinders?)

Ergo!

I was also discombobulated upon rereading the *mother's* story under a pseudonym in The Daily News about the passing of her twins who were accompanied by their tall slender aunt (SWF) who collapsed flat down on her face which must've hurt.: '… my babies, my bubabubs (did she mean … bobbleheads? *WHAT DID SHE MEAN?*), my little sweethearts, honeybees. They were just my little babies. *They'll* never go to ballet class again.'

Lightbulb!

Hadn't they been a boy and a girl? Well, of course the boy could've been a ballet dancer too. And a very fine one as many are. But wasn't he going to be an astronaut? Fair enough, both careers are kind of off their feet. Still, they never showed a family pic of the mom. Or the twins. And I respect that. If you started to ask questions (which *k*-smokers didn't need to under any circumstances) it was considered intrusive, insensitive, unfair and a nuisance.

I was beginning to sound dielectric. Like Socrates, posing questions and drawing responses. But, from myself! Just then the words of Aristophanes hit me: Euripides was a cliché anthologist and maker of ragamuffin ... *manikins* (sic).

... *manikins!*

Which leave no DNA clues! Eureka!

~ ~ ~

In an existentialist world it made no sense. As Jean-Paul Sartre regaled at an outdoors cocktail party near the Sorbonne during the Molotov-cocktail parties of the late sixties: One can only survive through full knowledge of one's illogical position in a meaningless universe. It was all about the facts. And what you saw in the movies. Or the web. And Marshall McLuhan. And what you read in the Daily News. Or anything you read about New Yorkers.

whisshhh ... oo-ooooh ...

As Ronald Knox once said: The room smelt of not having been smoked in. Admittedly, you still would've had eyesore butts on the pavement and people like Ann Coulter. But that was to be expected. And your eyes would be oblivious to anything ugly. The 4000 chemicals in each cigarette – some good, some bad, like bacteria and cholesterol, but probably not fatal - would have existed only as derivatives from the Periodic Table elements.

But, the reality-vote was pending.

Je pense, donc je suis. Roughly translated - I smoke therefore I am. [Descartes] Which is why it is imperative for me in the era of the Mid X to hide my identity. Because there are readers among you who are watching for a carelessly dropped nuance, casual innuendo or inadvertent epithet which might lead to my discovery.

whisshhh … oo-ooooh …

~ ~ ~

Skip Legault walked with crutches and with all of his tobacco-induced afflictions was still a smoker. Which the Nicotine Man wanted – who was invited to be an advertiser for the 'popular-vote' event. In order to promote transparency before ratifying the A of C, the AT Administration allowed for both a 'popular vote' and a 'reality vote' – for or against the smoking-ban. The results of which, like the popular vote for president would have no bearing on anything except to provide a warm and fuzzy 'feel good' for the minority 21%, and with the appearance of ... 'fairness' against a 79% majority. For the popular vote, 215 million voters were invited to polling machines at 16,329 high school gyms presenting a logistics challenge – on New Year's Eve 2008, hours before the ban was to take effect.

 *Seven*

Skip Legault and the Nico Man

THE POPULAR VOTE

It made sense that everything was leading to a muddle. The melting pot was blending into a mud pie. After all, they say that all's fair in love & war. So, fare thee well 'me lucky lass. For all our wars were merry/And all our songs were sad. [GK Chesterton] And, all's fair with the loser's side in the World Cup if you're a Brit and you've lost. Which is fair enough too. Laugh and the world laughs with you, cry and you cry alone. Cry-Baby. [John Waters] Because everyone loves a winner which was tough on the Brits after centuries of Rule Britannia. Which had seen better days. As the limeys too were unwittingly being drawn into what had the makings of a global smoking ban in known countries. And kicking-up a bigger fuss which they learned from soccer games. Like the hooligans they were. While the colonies were getting their own back, daily. With a passion. By taking the few remaining good jobs through assimilation, integration, compensation and restitution. Which the Brits hadn't bargained for centuries before. As they sang incessantly - Rule Britannia! Britannia rule the waves. As if the empire were still functioning.

And lost (sic) but not least, they say that all's fair in majority-rule, especially if it came to an unprecedented *popular vote* on the smoking question. In the waning hours of the honeymoon period. In a feel-good expression of closure. By a referendum that would be held in 16,329 high school gyms. On New Year's Eve. During winter break. Without the rowdy kids to put up with. For a change.

And, fair weather too in the parking lot this afternoon. Ahh, this abandoned old lot. Empty. Like a bucket with a hole in it. Dear Liza, dear Liza. [Harry Belafonte] An old oaken bucket, an ironbound bucket/A moss-covered bucket that hung in the well [Tommy Sands] Although Samuel Buckett (sic) would beg the question – how could the parking lot be empty with me in it? True enough.

Nevertheless, hope to get a little WIP done this afternoon with these darn confessions, God willing, which will take me to the grave. Eight years after it happened. The ban. And the Mid X. With the car trunk as my proverbial writing tablet. To rest my weary elbones (sic). When I'm concentrating. Barring an interruption by a wayward AT kop. Looking for trouble. Oh, trouble, trouble, trouble, trouble. [Ray Lamontagne] Contending with the waning days of the GWBWH. Which were soon supposed to be the good times with the new administration. With a rumored closet-smoker for president. After the worst of times. We thought.

But it didn't happen, did it?

The question that dominated every smoke-free pavement was: Had BO'B only arrived sooner instead of being the victim of the incumbent-President's master plan for the global tobacco ban, then things would've been much different. But the incumbent may have been a lot smarter than most voters gave him credit. He was used to reading tabloids for his daily rush. About what was happening over-seas. Indeed, at home. On his ranch. And figured something wasn't thorough in the smoking background check of the President-elect.

whisshhh ... oo-ooooh ...

"Now the tabloids inform me" (muttering to himself)!!!

Grrrrrhhh!

Billy Wilder had been through it before and remarked: Hindsight is an exact science. Ah ... for the things that might've been. But, what can you do? C'est la vie.

darn. plop! If you could only trust the weather forecasters since I forgot my brollie. Again. Got to make this a quick one. As the lad said in the pub with the missus waiting outside. In the rain. Without her brollie. Can't let telltale smoke get in my auto. Ever! You never know when someone might ask you for a ride. The ride of your life if they smelled tobacco. In your beat-up Chevy. Which it isn't. As you know for sure by now. So much for my ongoing attempt at anonymity.

Yes, all that was needed was the popular vote before the reality-vote.

Reader: *Let me get this right. Or wrong? Jeez, I'm, beginning to sound like you.*

Popular vote? Reality vote? How many votes are there? I'm just about lost! Gotta have a ciggie to relax. oops!!!

It was all in the numbers and our days were numbered. Yes indeed, those were the days. [All in the family] Make someone happy/ Make just one someone happy/And you will be happy too. [Schnozzles Durante] But they didn't. As we shall see.

With all of the unnecessary dissension and polarization for which non-smokers were getting their way and cared less, still it was a humane society and someone (whom, incidentally, looked an awful lot like Ralph Nader) came up with yet another bright idea. Let's invade Pyongyang! Just kidding. The idea was to have a nationwide popular vote as a barometer on the smoking ban just prior to the A of C (not to be confused later with AO-C) which, if you listened to the actuaries and the pundits, was now a foregone cessation.

Simply for closure.

"Fat lot o' use", said the increasingly obese among them – practicing for when they'd no longer have cigarettes to keep their weight down!

However, deciding on which side of the mulberry Bush (sic) you were standing on, miracles were known to happen, at least in Florida at the turn of the millennium. So, why not from sea to shining sea if there were any hope at all from hanging, dimpled or pregnant chad. In fairness to the underdog. In fair weather or foul.

oops. I knew it!

plop! Was that another plop? Or a hesitant drip!

plop-plip! Just my luck!

Drip-dropping on my foolscap. Moisture on my foolscap told a tale on you-ooh. [Connie Francis] Right on. Making a blob. Now I can't make out this stupid scribble. What was I thinking? Writing? Scribbling? Another forecast gone wrong. Maybe it's just a passing cloud. Maybe it's just a phase we're going through. [J at N]

The AT lawmakers felt that 79:21 odds on the popular poll couldn't hurt to avoid litigation afterwards in the most litigious nation on earth. Like ordering scalding coffee at McDonald's and then complaining because it was too darn hot. When you're hot you're hot. [Jerry Reed] In the miraculous event that the vote proved favorable to the minority because of the millions of sympathetic abstentions: Love the smoker/Hate the smoke. But there were others who were sticking to their gum. Which you'll always have. Those from the Reformation. And looked it. Who used to smoke but swore they never inhaled. Yet, thank god there's the minority among them who take the other side for no particular reason than why Hilary climbed Everest. And felt sorry for us. The situation was not good. Like a doctor nervously trying to break the news that his patient had incurable lung cancer. Without a cigarette to calm his (or his patient's) nerves if the A of C passed. Muster. Yes, smokers were angry as a pit bull in a mandarin cabinet. They too needed closure.

whisshhh … oo-ooooh …

It seemed fair enough for both parties to give peace a chance so there'd be no regrets with the New Year resolutions commencing the following morning with their hangovers and splitting headaches. And the pundits were enjoying a field day. Field and track. On the school grounds. Since the popular vote would be held inside. In the gyms which were open for the vote but closed for the holidays assuring the very minimum of heckling. Which happens. Between smokers and non-smokers. With the latter doing all of the yelling while smokers relaxed over a nice quiet puff and cared less.

NEW YEAR's EVE TIMELINE

Manhattan Prologue tragedy started:	10:04:00 hours
Manhattan Prologue tragedy ended:	10:04:40
House rollcall in *emergency session:*	11:59:59
Act of Cessation passed both Houses:	12:00:00 noon
(by a show of hands)	
VAB (NASA Shuttle Building) party starts	12:30:00
VAB party ends	14:30:00
(MEANWHILE) IN THE ROSE GARDEN off and on	*between 12:00:00 to 23:59:00*
Preparations for the popular vote:	13:00:00 to 17:00:00
Outdoor smoke break	17:00:00 to 18:00:00
Indoor popular vote on the Act of Cessation:	18:00:00 to 21:00:00
Reality-vote	23:35:00 to 23:59:50
(Dichter-17 on The Late Yo with David Minuteman)	
Two-minute warning	23:58:00
Final tally of popular vote	21:06:00
Final tally of reality vote	23:59:59
Dropping of the ball	00:00:00
Missing 6-minutes commences	00:00:00

Scheduled implementation of A of C	00:00:01
President-elect declares A of C	00:06:01
(on his BlackBerry)	
Actual implementation of A of C	00:06:01

(Twittered at cyber speed of 186,282.397 mps)

THE Nico MAN

It was no secret that the AT lawmakers were endorsing the anti-smoking platform which could've presented a conflict of interest. Some people had a problem with this due to transparency and even some non-smokers worried that the expected smoking ban wasn't going to solve all the problems of a nation at risk. It seemed to be a toss-up between the elimination of rotten breath and the obnoxious smell on the draperies, versus the risk to the economy with the loss of cig taxes.

In fairness, the economy was already limping not least because of Iraq where the locals smoked 5 tax-free packs a day subsidized by the US. Which didn't seem fair. It looked like Yalta all over again except the Big 3 had all puffed on their cigars. Subsequently, to level the playing field and create an unbiased atmosphere in the gyms where the average voter could clearly understand the issues, a sponsor was authorized for the addicted smokers. The die-hards stood on the solid platform near the bleachers that addiction wasn't a choice. All ayes across the nation were champing at the bit for minute-by-minute news updates on the vote which would be held in

16,329 public high school gyms bar none starting at 18:00:00 sharp. Quite frankly, it was getting late in the day and the situation seemed hopeless at best.

They had no further to look for a sponsor than the Nico Man on his hoss.

Nico of course bears no relationship to Nicodemus (Greek: Νικόδημος, translit. *Nikódēmos*) who was a Pharisee and a member of the Sanhedrin mentioned in three places in the Gospel of John. Incidentally, the second time Nicodemus is mentioned he reminds his colleagues in the Sanhedrin that the law requires that a person be heard before being judged (John 7:50-51). But let's not digress.

The original Nico Man had succumbed to lung cancer after smoking too many free ciggies in a fit of The Lone Ranger melodiously yodeling *Hi-Yo, Silver, Away!* Like Gene Autry on Champion. Or Tonto on Missus Tonto. Just kidding. Or Roy Rogers on Trigger. All these images of men and their horses recalled the great black and white movies when you never saw a cowboy smoke in the great outdoors until he went into the saloon. Then you could no longer see the saloon.

Like in an English pub on a foggy night when you thought you had taken the bus home until you realized you were still in the foggy pub. After enjoying a few-pints-or-more over a quiet-cigarette-or-more yourself.

The Nico Man's hoss, (also) named Silver, for the silver screen, with two hooves in the air that was clammy at best from all the CO_xs, SO_xs and NO_xs, followed the bugle call with an energetic

NEIGHHHHHHHHHH ....

The tobacco industry was already hurting domestically with the better-educated voter who knew how to read actuary statistics even if they couldn't understand them. Which only those with PhD's could by faking it. The fear was that the no-smoking lobby would go global from the political pressure of the one-on-one interviews in the GWBWH with the Big-6 delegations. Japan Tobacco already had their shakedown, followed by S. & Central America who cared less. Which figured. Just like an earlier administration had Contra written all over it.

After all Ronald Reagan smoked three packs of Chesterfields a day in the old days and lived to a grand old age of 93. And also did commercials for Chesterfield on the side when he wasn't busy making forgettable B-movies which you only remembered for the Chesterfields.

whisshhh ... oo-ooooh ...

Which was one helluva sacrifice to give up after becoming a role-model in the Oval Office. Where he kept jellybeans on his desk to keep him from smoking if he had guests. Or if someone were looking.

~ ~ ~

MEANWHILE IN THE ROSE GARDEN

off and on between 12:00:00 to 23:59:00

Although the transition team was still hanging-around hoping to pick-up some politics, the GWBWH had already been tossed into the dustbins of history. Oh, my old man's a dustman/He wears a dustman's hat/He wears gorblimey trousers/And he lives in a council flat. [Lonnie Donegan] The AT program was on autopilot and the new administration could do darn all about it because it was well-known hearsay that the young President-elect was a closet-smoker and dangerously close to being found out. By his missus-elect. True, the BO'BWH needed time to get with the program. Timing was everything. Everyone said: *Deal with it. Git with the program.* Including the Nico Man. A Man Called Hoss. [Richard Harris] To his hoss. *Git!* Which wasn't his real name for those of you who came in late.

No, you should never come between a man-called-Hoss and his hoss.

Smoking was about to be banned forever and the President-elect knew that the deficit triggered by the lack of cigarette taxes could probably create an economic crisis worse than the Great Depression (*spoiler-alert*: barring a buy-out by an *observant suitor*!?). The man in the street littered with cigarette butts was greatly depressed just thinking about history repeating itself. But there was no getting away from the voter whiplash from the non-smoker platform if BO'B came out of the closet. And became a candidate for the Mid X. Himself. Which would've been much worse than in Nixon's (unpopularity) case. Who, to his credit, had opened China (where 79% of the population smoked) to the West. It was a conundrum alright. And so the best thing for the President-elect to do in the short term was to remain aloof of the quandary while enjoying a nice quiet puff or two in the Rose Garden to somehow relieve the pressure of the predicament in which he had found himself.

whisshhh ... oo-ooooh ...

After all, when he had his first puff like the rest of us, who was to imagine that years later BO'B would become president in a nation at risk. And personally, accountable for his cigarette addiction. If only he had accepted responsibility by coming out of the closet. Voluntarily. It didn't help the rumors that he had two books published. Which ... *aha ...* requires tobacco to write with words that pound on the conscience. Fitting the profile of a *k*-smoker which could become incriminating after midnight. He was hardly in a position to influence public opinion or it would be a cold morning on the WH lawn for him. If his missus knew about it. *hmmm ...* Although technically smoking was still allowed on the sidewalk (until midnight) but for sure not in the Rose Garden! With many still enjoying the final day of the transition-period between the pre-T and the post-T eras. The last day. Judgment day. The Sequel. And it was pretty darn cold. Outside the WH.

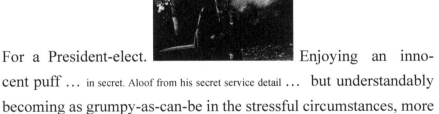

For a President-elect. Enjoying an inno-cent puff ... in secret. Aloof from his secret service detail ... but understandably becoming as grumpy-as-can-be in the stressful circumstances, more Cuba-crisis than Bay-of-Pigs ...

whisshhh ...

oo-ooooh ...

... in the presidential garden which was positively off-limits to smokers. Which he risked anyway. Being a President-elect. With a helluva lot on his mind. Hell (he thought to himself), if GHWB can say (abbreviated quote): *I do not like broccoli. And I haven't liked it since I was a little kid and my mother made me eat it. And I'm President of the United States and I'm not going to eat any more broccoli. Then, darn, who cares what I'm doing on my personal time-outs, huh*!

(While everyone wondered why 'abbreviated' was such a long word in the first place.)

You see, the Rose Garden had all of the makings of a DIVINE MILIEU. For inspiration.

And everyone was wondering where he was. Especially his missus-elect. Including his secret service staff. Who were told to take a six-minute hike. If you do the math. To go fly a kite. And it was going to get pretty darn humid when the cig taxes dried up. When the weather changed. Predictably. For the worst. So, he rationalized that what he thought he didn't know couldn't hurt him. With words that pound on the conscience …

whisshhh …. oo-oooooh …

… which he scribbled on a white oval-shaped post-it for his memoirs. Which in later years would become integral to his best-seller. While the pundits are still trying to figure-out how such a best-seller could've been written after smoking had been banned without the inspiration derived from nico? It was complicated. The white post-it pad had a large logo of the WH which he had found in the stationary cabinet in the closet adjacent to the Oval Office. These back'n'forth 6-minute sojourns would just have to stop. They were beginning to affect his performance. And, isn't that when they say an addiction is an addiction. I just dropped in to see what condition my condition was in. [Kenny Rogers]

In a fitting tribute to Paul Harvey who passed away within months of the ban, soon you will know the rest of the story. On why this young President-elect with a compelling personal story in his books did little to reverse the national hysteria over the outright smoking ban (enjoying the executive privilege of being a *k*loset-smoker – capable of writing great books!) In spite of the known catastrophic impact of lost cigarette taxes on an economy that was already limping along. Like SKIP LEGAULT. Just thinking about it.

And he washed his hands (figuratively) like the gentleman he was, stubbed his butt among the weeds in a spot that was missed earlier by both the incumbent-missus and the missus-elect. Who were busy getting to know one another. However, just in the nic'o time, remembering to scoop it up with his dog poop bag (pocketed for such emergencies) in case 'dustbin-forensics' might tarnish his eventual Presidential Library aspirations. *whew*

~ ~ ~

Anticipating the inevitable domino effect, the Nico Man knew that he might as well start packing what inevitably would be empty packs and cartons. And, in a paradigm shift with an accompanying twist in fate, like any classic Harvard Business School case study – accelerate the exit strategy to enter the #2 pencil business with a survival strategy to produce ultra-thin #2's in a variety of colors versus the sovereign nations' Model T brand. With T not standing for tobacco.

That was the backup plan on the afternoon of New Year's Eve. But there was still much work to be done for the popular vote by 18:00:00 if there were to be any way out of the rut that they had created in 1924. But there was no way out. Kevin Costner found that out. And Sean Young's character in the movie. RIP. Her character. Only. I hope! Whom I had the pleasure of meeting, twice, if

she doesn't mind her health, according to the tabloids.

Yes, things were pretty darn serious, and the Nico Man was desperately prepared to try any last-ditch effort – with only hours to go - to get his name out in front of 16,329 public schools - like Coca Cola before him. A catchy marketing theme matching the cola wars was devised:

THINGS GO BETTER WITH SMOKE

For which, however, last minute clearance would be required from each municipal fire department nationwide responsible for the designated school on the night of the vote. And, they were running out of time. It was getting late in the day and the Nico Man was beating a dead hoss.

As a strategic ploy to accommodate the masses, with the help of the National Guard who had to work during winter break, polling booths had been extemporaneously set up in HS gymnasiums nation-wide, on the ambitious presumption of transparency. The National Guard proudly responded to an eye-witness question during a live newscast – about the almost impossible task they were undertaking: "Oh, all in a day's work, Mam", said the sergeant who looked and sounded an awful lot like Sergeant Joe Friday in 'Dragnet'. It was so patriotic.

On the afternoon of the **MANHATTAN PROLOGUE**.

Which would be a long day's journey into night. The Night of the Iguana. When ex-minister Reverend T. Lawrence Shannon had been institutionalized with a nervous breakdown. Which characterized smokers as they limped uneasily into the polling areas.

Like **SKIP LEGAULT**.

A FISTFUL OF PEANUTS

Presently, in one of the schools which had its unfair share of smokers, Jiminy Carter was invited as an observer to ensure there was no cheating in the packed school gym. It was hard not to notice him although much older now.

Accustomed as he was, Jiminy was handing out roasted peanuts by the handful as incentives to vote, regardless of which way you voted because the odds were stacked. Like peanuts in a 2 lbs 3 oz (992g) jamjar. Jiminy hailed from Georgia, the sixth largest T pro-ducer, so he knew what it felt like to be a southerner. Where some people actually smoked in the shower. It had that effect on them. The availability. The addiction.

But the Georgia plantations would soon be but a vestige of their rich heritage. Like Tara. Which had seen better days. Or New York City beneath the CO_xs, SO_xs and NO_xs. Where it was hard to remember what a day looked like. What a day for a daydream. [Lovin' Spoonful] And wasted days and wasted nights. [Freddy Fender]

But, Jiminy's presence was really only for show and support - since he had personally kicked the habit long ago. Unless he were a closet-smoker which we'll never know. [Heisenberg] *hmmm*. Although he has written books. And even autographed one for the Easton Press. A tell-tale sign for sure. And, if anything, he considered smoking obnoxious like his little brother, Billy, was before he died which put an end to *his* shenanigans. Although, in all honesty, Jiminy would never have used the word 'obnoxious' as a neutral observer. For the popular vote. With the Nico Man finally the underdog, taking on the AT platform. In an age of transparency. In an age of Anxiety. [W.H.Auden] In the local high school. With the odds stacked.

Being a good Samaritan, the Nico Man was sensitive to the millions of jobs that would be lost if the smoking ban went through and obesity took off with a vengeance while it was currently only at 79% of the population. In an era when high percentages are normally a positive thing when you look at the diminishing US math scores versus China. And, the fatalistic impact of lost cig taxes on the Treasury. Not to mention the astronomical increase in divorces that would result from the stress of broken homes in such an economic crisis – when men were men but spouses would no longer be able to cope with the threat of foreclosure and would stop kissing.

Which was a *K*atch 21 in spite of the eradication of foul breath. And significant others would go their separate ways. And means. Mean Girls.

Yep, it was a busy New Year's Eve alright.

In the hoopla of this humanitarian concern, the Nico Man shifted thousands of shifty-eyed company lawyers - 'Nico ponies' they were affectionately called - into the marketing department to brainstorm an equitable solution for survival. To wit - the #2 pencil. While reading The Devil's Advocate for inspiration by Morris West, whom serendipitously was working on The Last Confession, before he died.

whisshhh .... oo-oooooh ...

Which he did. Although it was never proven if he were a closet-smoker. [Heisenberg] Although Philip *Morris* was ordered to pay $79 million to a smoker's widow by a *West* Virginia jury (a transposed homonym), the largest verdict at the time against a tobacco company.

Anyway, by now the tobacco conglomeration launched a sub-liminal campaign that hadn't been seen since the remake of the Manchurian Candidate. The campaign had to appear as though it weren't an advertising gimmick. Which the lawyers knew well how to do. And for which they spent years studying. When they weren't chasing ambulances. As interns. To ICUs with iron lungs. Which were a lot more robust than the condition of the average smoker.

Further, they had only three hours to work (which was par for lawyers). On New Year's Eve. Which was an even worse headache when they were supposed to be indoor golfing in the winter. In time for 215 million voters to arrive at 16,329 high school gyms. Of which 45 million (21%) were adult smokers. Until lights-out at midnight. After which – bar a miracle - the die-hards would turn into cinders of their former selves. From butts to ashes. When the lights went out. In Georgia. The sixth largest T producer. But let's not get ahead of ourselves.

DESIGN OF THE VOTING GYMS

SLIDE SHOW

Wall-length tapestries hung from the high ceilings to the well-trampled gym floors with the logo of the Nico Man and his Hoss. The draperies ... oops. Freudian slip. The tapestries looked like oversized designer beach-towels you see at firemen's field-days raffles or tomato-fest rallies. Or that you'd find at arts & crafts tents at combination hot air balloon and maple-syrup festivals. And other family events where draft beer was served in foam cups. The tapestries were used as background for projection of a repeating slide show of two large images – first, the Nico Man, then a lady. The tapestry background was selected because the 'wavy' resolution of the slides made the resolution difficult to diagnosticate. It was only necessary to recognize the tobacco logo (technically banned since 1998), and, separately, the disease caused by tobacco.

The main theme of the tapestry depicted the remarkable life of a 100-year old lady named Eve in a nursing home bed dying of lung cancer, an unfiltered cigarette drooping from her mouth. Incidentally, nobody seemed to notice the error on the slide show because unfiltered cigarettes hadn't been available in decades in first world countries. They were considered a time-bomb because you might as well be injecting smoke, tar, and god knows how many of the 70+ carcinogens directly into your internal combustion-chamber without the filter to keep at least some of the 4000 chemicals out.

Each gym had been hooked with live sat feed from the local cable company against heavy opposition from the telcos which were now offering FIOS.

The resultant logomasia had nicely combined the (desired) Nico Man name-recognition along with the subliminal reality. It was a precondition that anything with the slightest appearance of promoting a vice – especially in a high school - had to have an anti-vice prevailing feature. It was up to the 'promoter' to turn such media exposure into a plus. Because, when all is said and done at the end of the day that was fast approaching, studies showed that all that remains in the (gullible) consumer-mindset is the image (in this case) of the Nico Man riding his hoss.

It was a touchy scenario in the first place, but the theme seemed to jive with the majority and officials looked the other way when no one was looking. The Nico Man's bosses knew it was tacky but at least he got his name in front of 16,329 schools and that had to be worth something. After all the 100-year old lady in the nursing home was still smiling.

koff-koff

koff

Especially since the dollar would soon be worth about ten cents. Advertising Age magazine had shown that consumers only remembered the logo anyway while the commercial itself really hurt their concentration in the middle of their favorite sitcom. After a busy day on the unemployment line. When they were trying to play catch-up. With the remote. Wherever it was. darn. Furthermore, studies showed that most smokers were either sinister looking or ill so that seemed to play well with the ad and to pass the school test. Which was a first for sons and daughters with rich parents whom they hoped would get them into the best colleges anyway, with a little bit of pull. Like Felicity and Lori. With a little help from their friends. By sponsoring a department chair to show their sincerity.

The tapestries although made-in-China [just kidding] had been imported by courier from India that afternoon where at least 79% of the population smoked including Jamal Malik and other slumdog millionaires. And practically everyone except the Untouchables who couldn't afford them. But would if they could.

whisshhh … oo-ooooh …

FOR A FEW PEANUTS MORE

Meanwhile back in the gym, Jiminy Carter kept passing around the roasted peanuts by the palmful like fistfuls of dollars for people who would accept anything as long as it were free. Like ravenous gate crashers at a cocktail party gobbling the broccoli if there were any left. Which (the fistfuls of peanuts) the voters were mulching (sic) right through the shells to the tips of their incisors as if practicing for the #2 pencils.

THE WIDESCREEN 1080i PLASMA HDTVs

On the far wall of each gym, a full-length widescreen 1080i plasma HDTV with over 2.1 billion pixels captured the tragic misfortune of a guy named SKIP LEGAULT, scapegoat for the anti-smoking

 two heart attacks
a stroke
fourteen surgeries
seven blood clots
leg amputation

Cigarette smoking is killing Skip Legault. Don't let it kill you. Quit Now.

Call for FREE help, patches', gum or lozenges.
NYS Smokers' Quitline
1-866-NY-QUITS
(1-866-697-8487)

'Most smokers qualify
New York State Department of Health

platform.

SKIP walked with crutches and with all of his afflictions was *still* a smoker.

The community-sponsored commercial prompted by the AT lawmakers had all of the ingredients of an anti-smoking platform except that SKIP hadn't quit. He was still smoking. God bless him. And alive and kicking except for one of his legs. But, trying to figure-out which side SKIP stood (pun) for had conveyed an ambiguous message to children who were allowed by their responsible parents to stay up late to watch the broadcast TV news updates on the popular vote.

THE JUKEBOX

Appropriately enough a jukebox in the corner of each gymnasium played: Putting on the agony, putting on the style/That's what all the younger folk are doing all the while. It was a 1957 #1 hit in the UK sung by Lonnie Donegan's Skiffle Group and captured a moment when everyone smoked an average of 5 packs a day. And then some. And cared less.

THE TICKERTAPE

[looping continuously between 6 and 9.00 pm est.]

On the bottom of the widescreen TV, a 15-second Warholian text shown below looped continuously in hi def. Like a tickertape on Wall Street which had already lost 79% of its value in anticipation of the end of cig taxes to support the limping Treasury. The text had recurring stops like in the old-fashioned Western Union wires forcing you to pause before getting over the first shock of SKIP'S pitiable condition. If not his pathetic, heart-rending, miserable appearance. With no one to blame but himself for his affliction.

...STOP... TWO-HEART-ATTACKS ...STOP...A-STROKE ...STOP ...FOURTEEN-SURGERIES ... STOP ...SEVEN-BLOOD-CLOUTS ... STOP ... LEG-AMPUTATION... STOP ... CIGARETTE-SMOKING-IS-KILLING-SKIP-LEGAULT ... STOP ...-WHO-IS-STILL-A-SMOKER ... STOP ...DON'T-LET-IT-KILL-YOU ... STOP ... QUIT-NOW... STOP...

THE QUADRAPHONIC SOUND SYSTEM

Gimme Shelter

Gimme Shelter, blared the Stones on the quadraphonic sound system blasting from each corner-speaker of the HDTVs. On a dismal December night with the hostile elements outside.

Still, everyone agreed that the popular vote did provide a certain level of sanctimoniousness to the movement. To the moment. After which, following the stroke of midnight smoking would be a crime not only in HS johns where currently it only resulted in immediate expulsion. But, indeed, wherever you took a breath of fresh air. Which, in the USA was practically nowhere beneath the suffocating CO_xs, SO_xs and NO_xs.

whisshhh ... oo-ooooh ...

PREPARATIONS FOR THE POPULAR VOTE:

13:00:00 to 17:00:00 hours

Inexplicably, no one seemed to question how the prep-work for the voting gyms could've been implemented so quickly by the Nico Man and his marketing department, on the very afternoon of the MANHATTAN PROLOGUE. With the clock ticking. For example, the widescreen 1080i plasma HDTVs with the quadraphonic sound system times 16,329 nationwide gyms had to be carefully unpacked from the cartons marked FRAGILE/THIS SIDE UP. The original boxes which fortunately had a complete return address instead of a PO Box - then had to be kept intact for a full refund, later, from Wal-Mart. Which had stores in every school district since all the kids worked there after school for cheap wages. For cigarette money.

The goods-return strategy (which was really a 'privilege', like driving) by the tobacco lawyers was to inform customer service that they 'just didn't like the pixels'. And they assumed that the hardware would be accepted back with no questions asked. On the (mistaken) premise of no visible scratches. Or dents. And all kinds of electronic accessories, cables, adapters and A/B-switches. And the craziest of installation manuals that you ever did see. Written either in Hindi or Japanese since, for hi def, nobody wanted the cheap Chinese stuff. Well, there were some ageing divas who did because there were fewer pixels to show their wrinkles.

And god knows other kinds of paraphernalia, gadgets and gizmos. The importation of the special tapestries from India. And what about the under-the-table dickering with the customs officials which was always part of the deal when no one was looking. Of course, the Nico logo could've been silk-screened while-U-wait in any alley shop such as off Bleeker in SoHo (Manhattan) near the rare bookstores. Or in stalls at the Young (Starving) Artists flea market in the abandoned church on Mott Street. Or in practically any small town that was proud enough to sport a high school gym even if they had a good-for-nothing football team.

Why did the AT lawmakers (who were all lawyers) look the other way? And allow the Nico Man and his team of lawyers and intern marketing people, who because of their youth still held onto both lungs – to proceed? Unless it were a charade. Starring Cary Grant and Audrey Hepburn. Just kidding. Providing false hopes. Oops there goes a billion-kilowatt dam. [Sinatra] For the pathetic smokers. UNLESS – they *already* knew the outcome of the popular vote with the odds stacked. As though everything had been planned. So, who was the innocent guy in all of this?

Guy Lombardo? Guy Mitchell? Sky Masterson (guy) or Sergeant Sarah Brown (gal) in guys and dolls? Or Guy Fawkes, huh? With enough gunpowder to light a lot of cigarettes. What a guy!

Questions, questions, questions. Like the … *mannequins* at 10:04:40 in Manhattan. Outside the Time building.

316

CELL TEXTING ON THE H/W AT THE SPEED OF LIGHT

And how did they get the word out so fast to 215 million registered voters in a single afternoon – a holiday-eve for that matter, to turn up at 16,329 public high school gyms? Even providing directions for out-of-towners, huh? That's a no-brainer. Let your fingers do the walking, click your lucky numbers and hit 'send'. Cyberspace does the rest – barring the occasional dropouts from heavy concentrations of CO_xs, SO_xs and NO_xs interfering with the air waves this side of the stratosphere.

THE NICO MAN RIDES AGAIN

After all, the last Nico' cowboy had (also) died of lung cancer

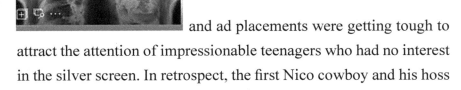 and ad placements were getting tough to attract the attention of impressionable teenagers who had no interest in the silver screen. In retrospect, the first Nico cowboy and his hoss were responsible for an increase in sales of 2,179% in 1955, the first year of the testosterone ad when gullibility was commensurate with 'eyeballs' (a measure of 'hits'). If you did the math. But that was long-gone history which was best forgotten because the next dozen Nico cowboys predictably died of lung cancer too. Along with their hosses, from the same affliction due to second-hand smoke.

Now, suppose you were going through five packs a day and riding your hoss at the same time, in all likelihood your hoss was going to pick up some of the lung cancer too. If not some COPD. If you listened to them.

The hosses.

Going ... *NEIGHHHHHHHHHH!*

Although, in fairness, the average hoss wasn't sitting on the sitting-room sofa next to the draperies where most people are exposed to 2HS. Since hosses sleep standing-up.

You may have assumed there was only one Nico cowboy? And one hoss. Since 1924. As in the expression: He was a one-hoss man. As Paul Anka put it nicely: You're a one-hoss woman/But I'm a two-timing man. And although the logo of the Nico Man as a hero had technically been banned in the US since 1998, his legend still survived in 180 countries which didn't know any better or cared less - where he topped the list of the 79 most influential people who never lived according to *USA Today.* Which included Tarzan, Sherlock Holmes, Ronald McDonald, Ronald Trump, Superman, and Robin Hood. In roughly that order.

whisshhh ... oo-ooooh ...

It was a sad state of affairs considering SKIP LEGAULT was really doing his best for the anti-smoking league - except quitting! In spite of his leg amputation. And fourteen surgeries. And seven blood-clots. But then again, smoking wouldn't've been an addiction if he did quit. Yet another *K*atch 21. It had Heisenberg written all over it. And it wasn't a pretty picture.

THE #2 PENCIL

Next you picked-out a nice #2 pencil in a wide assortment from the complementary basket, chewed it to bits, did your patriotic duty in the polling booth and got the hell out. To hell and back. Hoping against hope for the proverbial recount that would reverse the predictable tally. That you were not alone with the stats stacked against you. You were a fighter with a lighter. And a writer, if you were a *k*-smoker. And, to get away from the dull, repetitive gangrene color which had an undesirable and pedantic flavor to it and reminded everyone of their yellow, tar-stained fingers - the #2 pencils would soon become available in red, white and blue with a scent of cinnamon gum. As Imelda Marcus said: If the shoe fits, buy it in every available color.

~ ~ ~

Now, with the final tally of the popular vote only hours away which offered an impossible hope for those in denial ... no matter how hopeless/no matter how far. [Man of La Mancha] ... it was easy to tell which percentage of the population was in an altered state of consciousness. In a tizzy. Putting it *mild*ly as in the ultra-thin brand. With only half as many carcinogens according to the fine print which was written by lawyers.

Like being at a New Year's Eve party in Manhattan and just about to kiss. With the Y2K computer glitch messing-up your mind immediately before the turn of the millennium. As if everyone was going to waken up sterile the morning after. When you were on pins and tenterhooks the night before. Needles and pins/Noodles (sic) and peas/needles and pins. [Sonny Bono] The whole thing was just another fine mess. And Ollie Hardy wasn't pleased. And Stanley appeared confused. Scratching his head in circular motion with a downward pressure of his raised pointer in a U-turn. Which was not unusual as Tom Jones chimed in on cue (if you were listening to the wireless).

And it ain't over 'til it's over. But in their hearts (pun) they knew it was over.

The polls were right on.

79/21.

It's over/And nobody wins.

In an abandoned parking lot. Freezing your butt off.

At the mercy of the elements. Oh Mercy. [Dylan]

Out here in the elements.

Trying to gather my thoughts. Into words. That pound on the conscience.

whisshhh ... oo-ooooh ...

*Meanwhile the 'reality-vote' on the reality-show with the Dichter-17 commenced on the Late Yo with David Minuteman **at 23:35:00** on New Year's Eve. The Dichter-17 comprised 17 smokers, 10-male, 7-female, who were interviewed about the joys of smoking in the infamous study performed by Dr. Dichter in 1947. Updated 61 years later - inexplicably the octogenarians were still doing morning press-ups – in between uncontrollable cough-spasms which they put down to the flu - having smoked 5 packs a day each for an average of 6 decades. They recounted before a live David Minuteman audience their blissful smoking experiences since 1947 in a study sub-titled The Happy Smoker.*

 *Eight*

Poetry in smoking
THE DICHTER-17 (FROM 1947 NOTORIETY)
AND THE REALITY VOTE
READYING FOR 'THE LATE YO' WITH DAVID MINUTEMAN

Meanwhile, back at the tobacconist. Just kidding. Which is a museum-piece. Let's try again. Meantime, following a nationwide gallop search with the producers of the Late Yo, seventeen guests had been rounded-up. For chow. Like cattle in an old cowboy movie. In an old-fashioned love song. [Three Dog Night]

Gettin' ready for chow time.

As he rounds up the cattle each fall/*Woo-hoo-woo-ooo-ti-de.../Woo-hoo-oop-i-de-de/Woo-hoo-woo-ooo-ti-de.../Yo-el-od-el-lo-ti-de...*/Singing his cattle call... [Slim Whitman] Some might call them the great survivors. The Dichter-17 had been participants in the infamous study: Why Do We Smoke Cigarettes Anyway? A study which had been linked to another event in 1947 and both had been 'buried' (as it were) in Roswell, New Mexico.

gulp!!

Only recently had the Dichter study been unearthed (with no help from the AT lawmakers). And it was a miracle that they were (mostly) still alive. All of whom were much older now – since the 1947 study when they had to have been at least of smoking age (age 9). They were starting to powder their faces (the gents in the gents), and their noses (the ladies) in the adjacent make-up room to the studio in an effort to emulate their looks. In a desperate case of mistaken identity. In the hope that the make-up artists could make a difference to their faces weathered with time and about five packs a day for six decades. Which was about twice the national average (of thirty years smoking up a storm).

Gettin' ready for show time.

And getting acclimated to the bright lights for the **Late Yo with David Minuteman** so they wouldn't get blinded by the blast which they were having. The blast from the past. In a senior moment. The truth of the matter was that most of them were already half-blind in both eyes after too-much smoke got in their eyes over too many decades.

Yes indeed, it was going to be quite a challenge. In front of the studio spotlights. At their age. As blind as a bat. Wondering what they were doing on the Late Yo in the first place when they had been content to tend their roses at home.

And the women among them wondering whether they had put out the garbage before the door-to-door limo pick up to take them to the studio. The pick-me-up. You lift me up. [Rachael Lampa] You raise me up. [Josh Groban] Their average looks reminded you of the traditional lyrics: Oh they say that I'm feeble with age, Maggie/My steps are much slower than then/My face is a well ridden page, Maggie/And time all alone was the pen. [George Washington Johnson] Others were more inclined to fit a description from a traditional *cumallya*: Well, his face was like a pork-pie cut in pieces/And his hair was like a stack of last year's hay/With a nose so red that if he stood at Claddagh/He would guide in all the ships to Galway Bay.

Until one of the Minuteman crew yelled out:

Lumen Christi. Let there be light.

To which the senile guests, thinking he asked: *Gotta light?* - responded:

Come again?

Then, *aha!* ... as they were finally getting-it after an understand-able time-delay which happens with old people who never learned Latin. And cared less

whisshhh ... oo-ooooh ...

And before you knew it, the polite ones among them would soon be striking their matches. Lucky Strike. If they were lucky. Before striking out. At midnight. When the A of C would take effect. Unless a miracle happened. Which was a rare enough event. And, in these circumstances, highly unlikely. I mean – have you ever heard of a miracle which resulted in the retention of a known vice? *Krazy*. But there was still hope even if miracles were on mute.

The fact was that the Dichter-17 were ... Together Again/My tears have stopped fallin'/The long lonely nights will be soon at an end. [Buck Owens]

Nonetheless, it would be a fitting send-off in the glaring studio lights during the reality vote of the Late Yo. Lit up like a POW camp starring Steve McQueen. To what would inevitably be but a fond reflection upon the dark age of tobacco. This too will pass. Like all the other ages. Age of Reason. Stone Age. Bronze Age. Age of Methuselah (who was pretty darn old). The perennial youthful age (though not the youthful looks) of a diva. In the timeless words of Robert Frost: Time and tide wait for no man, but time always stands still for a woman of thirty.

And, ultimately … the Tobacco Age. And its ensuing Age of Literature and creative writing. Of creativity itself. Of meeting the challenge. Like Hannibal crossing the Pyrenees in a different era. Of history in the making.

However, as we witnessed, soon to be an implosion. Unmaking. With the escalation of the global ban on smoking in much of the known world. The arrival of the Age of Turbulence. The end of the Tobacco Age. Like a Greek tragedy. Melodramatic to the end. The end of the Age of Literature. The end of the Age of Reason. The end of the road. Hit the road Jack, and doncha come back no more, no more, no more, no more. [Ray Charles]

And, the dawn of the *New Age of Literature*. Personified by the *k*-smoker!

… applause, applause … (thank you I'm sure!)

But, let's not get ahead of ourselves.

The old coots with a few tales to tell were invited to take a stroll but not too fast down memory lane. If they could only remember half their yarns with a bit o' luck. Yippie-I-a, Yippie-I-o/Ghost riders in the sky. [Marty Robbins] And to revisit the landmark study for which they had been first interviewed in 1947: Why Do We Smoke Cigarettes Anyway?

whisshhh ... oo-ooooh ...

So, what caused us to smoke in the first place since there was never any argument about its effect? Even if you weren't a writer and in spite of it. What was it about the craving that made it unthinkable to even think about quitting even when it was long after quitting time? What was it that non-smokers were missing that made fanatics out of occasionally tolerant grown-ups who never smoked and rued the day? What did non-smokers want? What was it about that satisfied grin of a happy smoker that drove anti-smokers *krazy*? All pretty batty questions if you ask me. Still, they needed an answer.

Outside the Ed Sullivan Theatre on Broadway and West 53rd there wasn't a star in the sky that could be seen above the lingering CO_xs, SO_xs and NO_xs. It was now 23:25:00 hours military time for fighting men. And women with broad shoulders. Like Nurse Ratchet in One Flew Over the Cuckoo's Nest. And juveniles who smoked too many but weren't yet old enough to vote. In tonight's vote. The reality vote. The Dichter-17 had parked themselves comfortably in the guest dressing-room with an adjacent 'convenience' (called a toilet in the UK) in the event of an emergency which happens with really-really old people. It was 10-minutes before the Late Yo and some 35-minutes before kissing time on New Year's Eve, all things being equal which they had hoped for. There was a lot of hoping going-on. Soon the demanding questions above hopefully would be expounded upon by the seventeen elderly guests, now enjoying another quiet puff or two. It was about five hours following the constitutional nap time of the Dichter-17 which they had missed for the first time that any of them could remember with a memory that was getting foggier than the eco. In the excitement of the moment. About to appear live (but just barely) on broadcast TV. And, considering their age, it was too late for the obligatory rehearsal. It's too late baby, now it's too late/Though we really did try to make it. [Carole King] Which meant risky business for the producers who were also going live.

Fortunately, the last remaining StarBust on earth was conveniently located next door to the Ed Sullivan theatre on Broadway: Although they say that they won't last too long on Broadway. [George Benson] Incidentally, this store fed a dual capacity – the second was as a spendthrift-museum to reflect upon the profligate outgoing-generation because of the inordinate cost of a StarBust coffee in pending tough times without cig taxes to support the economy.

Things were that bad with no end in sight. Earlier they had called it a correction but now it was a deduction by extrapolation. And interpolation. It was a sign of the times: I gave her the secret sign that's known/To the artists who have known the true gods of sound and stone. [Paddy Kavanagh] Or, as Louis Kronenberger summed it up: The trouble with our generation is that it's all signpost and no destination.

Anyway, seventeen decaf take-outs were ordered by the studio-gaffer. Or, the best boy? Whatever. And brought into the dressing-room by cute little maids with hour-glass figures which was timely indeed.

Holding their cigarette trays up, assisted by a rope around their necks. With the seventeen coffees on the trays that had seen their share of cigarette packs. Before the indoor ban. Each of the maids wore bee-stung arrest-me lips. Like Angelina Jolie. But much younger and jollier when it came to tips. *ouch!* And those that weren't wearing matching, cute little black cocktail dresses, sported caress-me-pleeze micro-skirts. Like Twiggy in the UK used to wear. Their wardrobe was complete with 6-inch heels and fishnet stockings which always seemed to have a run. No matter how they slowed down. Or tried to. Carrying multiple take-out orders without roller skates. You'd think they just kept rubbing their hoses against protruding nails that are common in old buildings. In Old Manhattan.

But they weren't fooling anyone. The maids in tights. The intent of having the maids serve the coffee was to try to keep the male old codgers wide awake for their appearance on the Late Yo with David Minuteman - and a-live-a-live-o until midnight. So, why then did they order decaf? Good question. I guess the risk of hyperventilation was too great otherwise. With all of the hoopla. Considering their ages. And anyway, they could fake it.

Incidentally, in spite of StarBust's no-smoking appeal (in this, the last StarBust on earth following the bankruptcy) for the resident literati-types who liked to be seen composing in a green environment ... and, there was always the chance of a cameo pic for an arty magazine ... still, none of the lit types could create a relevant verb without a puff. So, they'd go outside intermingling with the *tabagie* after every other cappuccino for a nice quiet drag (or two) when no one was looking. Except the CCD surveillance cameras on every street block.

whisshhh ....

oo-oooooh ...

With their cappuccino now poured into a takeaway foam cup. Which, incidentally, Eve Marie Saint said was bad for publicity -- even when not on camera on the set -- in an interview with Robert Osborne of TCM about Alfred Hitchcock. Who quickly took Eve's polystyrene cup and had it replaced by real China from China (the soon-to-be 'title-holders' of the USA) – before the paparazzi could take any pix. Then – Lights! Camera! Action!

Still the lit types were hoping to put an end to writer's block by experimenting with yet another fancy verb (or two) in their heads. While the caffeine was still blocking the adenosine chemicals and increasing the neuron firing in the brain. Which they would bring back-in, lukewarm, after 6-minute intervals and pour the coffee from the take-out foam-container back-into a StarBust mug. For show. On Broadway. Without spilling too much. Hopefully. Coming-and going. And so-on-and-so-forth. Always seeking that perfect verb.

But, with the pending outright smoking ban … and the subsequent death knell for creative writing in the ensuing dearth of inspiration … soon there'd be no rationale for coffee. Or for writing.

In the event that the Dichter-17 might've asked for double-capuchin (sic) carry-outs, the gaffer, who like George Washington rarely told a white lie, had to pretend they were. As he instructed the cute little maids with their cigarette trays to smile a lot. Which they were used to doing, anyway. For the better tips. For the money. Had they only known about the spendthrift habits of the old codgers. And hoped they wouldn't know the difference. The old coots. And the ladies among them. Or have too many irregular PVCs. Heartbeat, why do you miss when my baby kisses me? [Buddy Holly]

Come midnight. Tonight's the night! [Rod Stewart] Come hither.

Anyway, everyone knew that decaf was only a placebo. Like lite beer which fat people drank ten times as much of for the same side-effect as one classic bud. Versus the fine frothy head of a slowly poured pint of J. Arthur Guinness which takes 8-minutes flat to pour perfectly.

~ ~ ~

Considering the commendable ages of the guests (the Dichter 17) and their extraordinary immune-systems (which was a miracle in itself after some six decades of smoking), the entire Ed Sullivan Building was given an unprecedented indoor-smoking waiver for the historic night and the compulsory minimum fine of $250 per person ceded for those caught smoking. (This was a separate penalty to the Mid X if apprehended following Midnight but let's not digress!)

With this deferral by the cunning AT law-makers via their mercenaries, the AT kops, you knew something was up. And it wasn't only the CO_xs, SO_xs and NO_xs. Either. It was felt that the ageing survivors mightn't survive another NY minute were they forced to join the tabagie outside intermingling with the literati and the arty types. And freeze their butts off without their flu-pills. Which they forgot. Again. God bless 'em. In the heat of the moment. Enjoying their final puffs. (pun) Having the time of their lives. Their last hurrah. The last fare thee well. As in the parting song: So, come fill to me the parting glass/Goodnight and joy be with you all. [The Dubliners]

All told the indoor-smoking waiver was a healthy decision considering the alternatives in the slush outside. Which made everyone miserable. Trudging along. The passers-by. With heartaches by the numbers/troubles by the score. [Ray Price] You could tell. At first glance. With first impressions. Doing whatever it is they do. In Manhattan. Let's take Manhattan. [Leonard Cohen] If you looked at most of them. Walking fast. But not fast enough. Trying to look busy. With nothing much happening in the economy. Except at the welfare office. And the Department of Labor. In lines that were getting longer. By the minute. The way things were going. The way we were. Anticipating the smoking ban. And the loss in taxes. Which were already crippling the nation. Just thinking about it.

At least the slush did a good job covering-up the eyesore butts until winter was over. When winter comes can spring be far behind?

[Percy Bysshe Shelley]

But God forbid! What-if the pundits were wrong about the outcome from the final 'performance' of the year? By the Dichter-17. Which some described, rather, as more of a spectacle than a performance. Yes, the fact was that it was anyone's guess what complications might set in at the stroke (pun) of midnight for those with wishful thinking in lieu of the agony and the ecstasy. Of the vote outcome. The riskiest event since coitus interruptus. The anguish of withdrawal. When you badly needed a smoke. Afterwards. To be on the safe side. In case you weren't fast enough.

As Henrik Ibsen had gone on record: The minority is always right. Or wrong.

Scribbling away on my foolscap sheet. On the boot of my beat-up old Chevy. Which it isn't of course. But saying so helps to deflect the forensics-readers. Among you. I hope. On my foolscap sheet.

You can fool some of the people ...

The fools, the fools, the fools! – they have left us our Fenian dead. [Padraic Pearse' oration for O'Donovan Rossa]

On a roll. Running out of foolscap. Still, no one will miss me for another eight, maybe ten minutes. Tops. Got to finish this part or I'll never remember it tonight during clean-up time. A night to remember. In my study at home. *hmmm,* as pronounced by the Brits. With the missus. Next door.

In the other room. *hmmm ...*

(... resumption: it is now later in the evening ...)

Wonder what she's up to?

(again ...?)

~ ~ ~

So, where was BO'B while all of this was going on? Back at the Rose Garden ... again. Back in the Saddle again. (Gene Autry)

The impending fear that the Mid X existed was just too much for the president-elect, that such a place, if it existed, was about to be 'mobilized'. While he was a guest tonight – significantly with 'unrestricted' (for presidents) access to the Rose Garden. Enjoying yet another 6-minute sojourn.

whisshhh .... oo-oooooh ...

Unless ... he knew!

The man who knew too much. (Hitchcock)

Alert *reader: I just knew it!*

As new as he was to the WH.

On New Year's Eve, BO'B was just another VIP visitor. But wasn't he to play a surprise role tonight? At Midnight! Had he been talked into it by the incumbent-President?

Wait! Are we talking ... *conspiracy*?

Was the Midnight Express to be implemented at midnight. (Or was the preceding sentence simply a tautology besides being eponymous?)

Eureka!

Euriga!

Eurigagarin.

The Russians are coming!

Yuri Gaga … ga-ga … ga-ga -- rin !

Lady Gagarin.

Well, it's hard not to get carried away with yet another conspiracy theory. After the **MANHATTAN PROLOGUE**. That few knew anything about. The Mid X. The chosen few. And if they asked questions they were told: Sure, I'll give you the answer, but I'll have to Kill you first if your name is Bill. It was going nowhere. Nothing was. And fast. The terrifying Gehenna.

Let's just pause for a moment and ask an honest question without fear of incarceration, okay?

> *Reader:*   *Okay. I guess.*

Did the president-elect know what would happen to dissidents (like himself), closet-smokers, if *k*aught? Who would be transported in cattle cars. Like in Judgment at Nuremberg. By Fed Ex. Just kidding. To the Mid X. The abode of the damned. For those who lacked a good alibi when confronted with the telltale smoke rings… lingering in the air filled with CO_xs, SO_xs and NO_xs. Whether the Mid X was a place or an inferno. Dante's.

And maybe he, BO'B, looked the other way when no one was looking…

… *had* he been aware!

As Hans Rolfe, defense attorney [J at N] burst in: *Your Honor, I must interrupt. The defendant is not aware of what he is saying. He's not aware of the implications*! And, Burt Lancaster playing Ernst Janning retorted: *I AM AWARE! My counsel would have you believe we were not aware. Not aware? Where were we, huh …? Maybe we didn't know the details. But if we didn't know, it was because we didn't WANT TO KNOW!*

So, did he know?

Well, yes and no.

You see, even if the President-elect knew, what could he do about it? Too much was happening too fast. And, he had his own vested secret to worry about. So, he thought to himself that he'd better not think about it 'til tomorrow. About the prevailing issue in his mind which was dizzy coming to grips with inherited matters. From the GWBWH. Affecting a nation at risk. From the outgoing administration. And, realistically, how could one person stop the wheel of misfortune, anyway? The machinery already in motion for God knows how long. To ban the single recreation savored by 45 million restless souls. Including himself. Even if he knew, or thought he did, what was possible and what was not. So, he stopped thinking about it too much. His (current) 6-minutes (in the Rose Garden) were almost up, and he'd be missed.

whisshhh …. oo-oooooh …

Realizing the extreme sacrifice that he too must make for the nation that was dear to his heart. (pun) But it gave hope to the masses, the little people, thinking so. Wishing and hoping and thinking and praying. That there was still hope. Starting their stopwatches. Counting down to midnight. Mass. At the end of which the chaplain would routinely declare:

Ita Missa Est.

Which roughly translated means: Go and sin no more. Which would've been disastrous to the sin tax coffers even before the A of C. At least to the smokers among them. Who ignored the warning because they didn't speak Latin. And Richard Parson had already stated: Life is too short to learn German. Or, as Jack Cruise recalled later in life: I'm glad I wasn't born in Italy. I can't speak a word of Italian.

Or, they simply weren't repentant. Enough! [Howard Beale]

Whatever! As my daughter would say.

In a nation at risk that needed someone to believe in.

I believe. I'm a believer.

Yes. Back in DC, the President-elect, no longer thinking about so many what-ifs, (once again) quickly extinguished his ciggie beneath his shiny patent shoes in the Bushes (sic) off the nice Rose Garden lawn while no one was looking. With his pooper scooper. At the ready. In the dark. Which many were. Which helped. A lot. This time with a mini-Scope. Just in case. Just in time. JIT.

whew!

Following countless inexplicable 6-minute sojourns. And quickie gargles.

As Nixon famously told Frost: It's not illegal if the president does it.

whisshhh .... oo-oooooh ...

~ ~ ~

The end of the transition period was heralding an unknown territory ahead. From foggy smoke signals which obscured the message. Without cigarette taxes. Come midnight. When churchyards yawn. Which the elderly guests, the Dichter-17, were already quite good at, thank you very much. Practically sleeping on their crutches like horses standing up. As one of them suddenly exclaimed in gibber-ish. In his half-awake: *They shoot horses, don't they?*

And then forgot about it upon re-awakening. A golden attribute of the elderly.

With the chainsaw audio effects from the snoring in the back-ground. By most of them. Waiting for the decaf to kick-in. Which, not known for swearing, they swore was caffeine. Which didn't make much difference at their age. Like the placebos they took to go to sleep. Since it was all in the mind. Eliminating the need for applause-o-meters and laugh tracks when the Late Yo commenced. Since the Dichter-17 were all background noise anyway. And did a better job because the laugh-meters usually drove the home-audiences batty just listening to the din while trying to concentrate on the plot of their favorite soap opera. With their stinging vari-cose veins keeping the rest of them alert. And the decaf which they thought was caffeine. So much for the placebo effect.

~ ~ ~

The predictable behavior of the Dichter-17 (… awake, count sheep, sleep) was already causing consternation with the yuppie producers of the Late Yo. Still, the old coots might just as well be permitted to enjoy the next half-hour puffing away like nobody's business. If they didn't cause a fire. Since the damage was done. Not only to their lungs but probably to their arteries as well.

In fairness, the seventeen on aggregate looked a picture of health. Probably psychosomatically from some eternal-youth love potion they foolishly subscribed to from the tabloids. Or the back pages of

AARP magazine. Next to the better-sex ads. As old as they were. And feeling virile. Filled with blind hope. Just thinking about it. And limping along. Literally. Which the sponsors relied upon – that they *felt* virile. Enough. Late at night or early morning. With the motor part of the brain running. When they should be snoring. And driving the missus nuts.

whisshhh .... oo-oooooh ...

Now in mixed-company presently the old geezers and geezer-esses, ten male and seven female - exhaled into the arthritic palms of their right hands to embarrassingly test for their yucky breath so they would at least be the first to know. No surprises. Which they pulled-in so close that it made their eyes dilate as if they saw a ghost. Or St. Peter. In a vision of the pearly gates. They hoped. Versus the other place. Now almost touching the tip of their pointed noses.

Like a doctor checking for alertness or soundness of mind while monitoring eye-movement with the back-and-forth pendulum motion of a lit Lucifer match lulling around an artificial obstruction. When an irresistible force eyes an immovable object. Aye! Like the tangent of two circles. So that their fingers cupped the bridges of their noses but without touching. Like in the rugby song: Oh, Sir Jasper, do not touch me/Oh Sir Jasper, do not touch me/Oh Sir Jasper, do not touch me/As she lay between the lily-white sheets with nothing on at all.

Or like in other circumstances, God preserve us, grabbing an overhead oxygen mask which, without warning, suddenly dangled above you following an announcement from the front-cabin to brace for a crash. Which happens. I guess. When you no longer wore braces like a geek kid. With a fat lot o' benefit from the mask which did little for swine flu. Or SARS. And for the first (and maybe the last) time in your life you wished you had read the aircraft design-features on the front and the simplified evacuation-procedure on the flipside of the safety manual's official title, Fear O' Flying. [Erica Jong] Staring you in your troubled face. Like a ditch over troubled water. Now, bent forward. For the brace. At least, in an effort to avoid panic following three recent crashes - the airline marketing depart-ment had the humor of calling the laminated-sheet: EVACUATION FOR DUMMIES.

Instead of munching the paltry handful of peanuts and wishing for the good old days when stewardesses were stewardesses. And were pretty darn pretty, too. OUCH! (Sorriee for saying that!) Considering the matronly faces and broad shoulders of some modern flight atten-dants. With teeth that could rip the gelatin wrapper off a CD without scratching the plastic. And, as you were accustomed to doing, reading over-and-over-again the calorific warning on the back of the gelatin wrapper of the peanuts. Before eventually squashing it into a crinkle that kept opening up as if filled with helium. You know what I'm talking about! Like a jack-in-the-box. Trying to get out. As you tried to pound him back in. Unsuccessfully. Having opened the Pandora's box in the first place. And second place is two weeks in Hoboken. Regardless of the fist-pressure you exerted on the gelatin in the pressurized passenger-cabin. Since you couldn't really crush gelatin into a tiny ball like Mr. Whipple could with squishy toilet-tissue. Although he urged you: Please, don't squeeze the Charmin. On a flight that seemed like forever. That would never end. Which was now the pun you hadn't expected. Bracing for the worst.

whisshhh .... oo-oooooh ...

In a posture that looked relaxing had you *not* bent your head forward. But rather - with both hands joined behind your neck with fingers interlaced. And both thumbs lackadaisically circling and rubbing against each other in a finger-massage that felt so good. *oooooooh* ... In a kind of temporary perpetual-motion. Not like a small electrical machine where only the rotor is moving but the stator is not, around which the rotor rotates. Rather like the huge contraption, the time machine in the movie, Contact, with Jodie Foster, where the dodecahedron (12-sided) gizmos rotated relative to each other.

Vindicating Einstein. Whose main theory was synopsized by Joe O'Connor: Einstein's theory of relativity - Time goes a lot slower when you're with relatives.

Like the universal linkage in an automobile that transmits rotation between shafts whose axes are coplanar but not coinciding. And, your feet resting on a La-Z-Boy ottoman that you bought on special sale at the newly opened Ottoman Empire Megastore in the mall. Thinking it was quite a bargain because you hadn't realized that furniture was always on special sale, duh. But now your time had come. The time has come for me to hang my head in shame/ The time has come for me to say that I'm to blame. [Adam Faith] It was too late. And, as your entire life was thrust before you in those fifteen Warholian seconds, tops – bracing, you thought about survival statistics when others may have been thinking of the hereafter. Or fame. Or worse.

And, at that moment a tiny baby began screaming – driving everyone nuts until – instead of overhead oxygen masks dropping – what a perk to have sets of ear plugs dangle down in nice little gelatin wrappers. Which you ripped open with your teeth in a fit of Jack Palance's teeth, as Wilson the gunslinger in Shane –

averting your head from exploding from the unceasing whining crying.

~ ~ ~

It was still New Year's Eve as each of the seventeen guests in the waiting-room of the Late Yo curled-up their pointed-noses into converging vee-lines. Like inquisitive Brits wondering what the nosy neighbors were up to next. Unwittingly making a face. Exhaling in what sounded like a muted … *haaaaa-aaaaa* … through their nostrils. Followed by a quick … *sniff-sniff.* In the art of inhaling. To test for (their own) yucky-smelling smoker's breath. Like canines. Like bloodhounds in a Sherlock Holmes mystery. Or, Rambo: First Blood, part II. Being self-conscious of their unpleasant mouth-odor. And in anticipation of the customary if not inevitable kissing when (bandleader) Jack Schaefer would lead them along with the coast-to-coast audience in a cup o' kindness as soon as the clock struck 00:00:00. While Dick Clark (RIP) was, then, entertaining the *tabagie* outside.

The sniffing of their perspiring palms was really the only sure way they could smell their own yucky breath. Just try it yourself. Close your mouth real fast and inhale immediately. Told you so, huh, get the idea! *aghhhhh!* Or, sometimes if you rush really fast through a door that's slightly ajar and push it fully against the rubber 'cup' on the wall (designed to prevent marring of the paint or the wall-paper next to the draperies, which had already been fingered by brat-kids anyway so it was kind of a redundant exercise). And, while racing through, the door starts to slam back at you because of the freewheeling inertia excited by the momentum (faster if it's spring-loaded). But you're not completely through yet (the whole thing happening in milliseconds). And, for just one of those milliseconds, due to the aerodynamic friction between your forward motion and the recoil of the door, the air particles collide against your breath. And you can really smell *your own* yucky tobacco breath. And you're shocked. You just can't believe it. Now you've done it. You've smelled yourself. And you didn't like the smell. Unlike a dog. As Shane said to Wilson: You've a mean low-down dirty Yankee dog. You're disgusted and you make plans to stay at home.

Or, are you?

Psychiatrists, psychologists and Hollywood therapists have written about this in 12-step programs. You realize what you've always known about yourself but mentally repressed because what could you do about it anyway. Since quick gargles and cheap cologne were only temporary masks. Unless you quit smoking! Which was preposterous. It was your decision to make before the AT lawmakers came along. And you made it. So, live with it. Now you knew why your wife, though intimate together, never kissed you. And nearly gagged the first time you tried to kiss her in spite of your swine-flu mask. Just kidding. Or so you thought. Incidentally, while we're at it, you might want to try the smell-test on your feet! Slowly and carefully unloosen one sock at a time. Before your girlfriend gets too close. For comfort. Or, it's goodbye cruel world/I'm off to join the circus. [James Darren] Well, let's not get carried away. And all because of denial.

whisshhh …. oo-oooooh …

Which was anathema in any good confession. But it was just a test anyway for the Dichter 17 (to see if they could smell the yucky tobacco off their own breath).

This is just a test. You may now return to your cubicles.

And get some work done. For a change. Git! Since the Dichter-17 couldn't get rid of the repugnant smell developed over a lifetime – which they had to work at. Always present. Omnipresent. Keeping company with bad bacteria. Haunting them. As a reminder. Of their obnoxious habit. And its effects. But hopefully they could cover-it-up temporarily. The smell. Like you could do too when you pinch your nose. Come midnight. And kissing time.

If you try hard enough. can do. good boy.

And in that moment, you try to convince yourself that no one else can smell your yucky breath either.

Pinching your nose. Trying to hide it. The smell. Camouflage it. Put it on hold. For a while.

At least for the duration of the kissing with the clock ticking away coming up to Auld Lang Syne. Now less than 30-minutes away. Tops.

The fact was that the Dichter-17 were all strangers when they met in the waiting room. Like passing ships in the night with a thousand eyes. [Bobby Vee] The ten old geezers and the seven old ladies. At the risk of first impressions that linger. Like smoke. On the draperies. Or the CO_x, SO_x and NO_x in the eco. After all, it took an average of six decades of smoking for each of the Dichter-17 to reach this remarkable condition. Which had CBS physicians on stand-by in the hallway. With portable oxygen containers at-the-ready. And overhead O_2 masks that would drop from the ceiling telling you it's time to brace, using a similar technology as automatic thermally sensitive fire-sprinklers. In the event of a lawsuit if even one of the ol' folks expired on CBS property. Like a magazine subscription. By default. When you get the bill and scribble 'cancel'. Which won't catch up on you until you enjoy at least three free issues, maybe four. Tops. In their senility, most of the seventeen felt fit as a fiddle and you'd swear you had seen their look-a-likes as stand-ins in Cocoon IV. When the actors were much older following four sequels. Now camera-ready for the Late Yo. And if there was one thing they all liked to hum while killing time, it was the lyrics of Isn't it Grand, Boys, to be Bloody Well Dead, especially the chorus: And always remember the longer ye live/The sooner ye'll bloody well die.' [The Clancy Brothers] Each carried little travel-size bottles of Scope in their touristy travel-pouches strapped around their waists (the men). Like straitjackets that they saw on the unlucky ones in the nursing home. And in their purses (the ladies) for a quick gargle if their partner got too close when the kissing was to start come 23:59:59. The only thing that was wrong with this picture was that all 17 had been smoking since they were tweens and it was weird to have to take such precautions in spite of each other. It was all totally unnecessary, yet it demonstrated the constant edginess of being a smoker in a nation at risk. Regardless of age, gender, race, technicality or economic status. Orientation. Or Caucasian. And the dire impact upon one fifth of the population six decades later – when there was supposed to be more freedom. Of expression. By the majority in a nation that would surely be even more at risk for its bullying behavior. With the launching of the Mid X. Which was becoming less of a rumor with each passing second. On the doomsday clock.

Quite frankly, the Dichter-17 were beginning to feel like Stalag 17'ers which was made six years after their famous interviews in 1947. As the man said: no matter where ye go, there ye are.

So, there ye are. And dear ye have it.

~ ~ ~

But we're not dear (sic) yet. At the conclusion of the CBS News at 11.30 pm and the usual commercials, and so on and so forth, there was a 5-minute warm-up to the 11.35 pm Late Yo. Tonight, the warm-up theme was pipe-smoking in lieu of there being a unilateral waiver for indoor-smoking in the studio on this momentous occasion, anticipating it being the last-smoking night in history. For everyone.

The segment was guest-hosted by Sean Pencil (who really liked his #2s), who also acted (pun) as an interpreter. The chief warm-up guest was a spokesperson from the upstate Native American Casino. He had his own fears for the future since, let's face it – have you ever seen anyone in a casino not smoking? That's what I thought.

As it transpired, with the A of C inching-up on the doomsday clock, there wasn't much time nor need for words. Like old people you see in a restaurant at the table next to you who never speak. And you think they are enjoying a row. But they probably just love being in each other's company so much that words aren't necessary.

Although I doubt if any of you (readers) have ever been in such circumstances. Just kidding. And wouldn't know the difference.

At the completion of the almost silent segment, the spokesperson stood up and looked across at Sean Pencil and said ... *Peace!* To which Sean, quickly grasping the sign-language, responded ... *How!*

whisshhh .... oo-oooooh ...

It was a touching scene and a perfect opener for David who only wished he had time for a cigar-smoking segment on his own Yo. On his own time. But he figured he'd sneak it in somehow. Actually, David was well aware that no one ever had a problem with cigar-smokers. Certainly not his guests in the waiting room or they'd never be invited back. If they lived that long. Whom he rightly feared were dozing again. And time had run out for the cute little maids in their black cocktail dresses to get free refills at the only remaining StarBust next door.

As David warned in his opening monologue: Throw away your clicker, fans, you won't need it anytime soon. As if witnessing the arrival of Armageddon with the imminent A of C.

Which would take effect at midnight. 8 years ago.

When they would always remember where they were on the night the smoking died. Rather, the morning. At 00:06:01 hours. Singin': This'll be the day that I die/This'll be the day that I die. [Don McLean] When the lights went out. In the well-lit studio.

whisshhh .... oo-oooooh ...

But it was still the waning minutes of the transition-era. And people were still smoking. And it was okay. Wasn't it? I'm okay. U okay? It made absolutely no sense. Everyone seemed to be ok, but nothing was going right. *Krazy.*

Then - astonishingly, there had been a momentary power failure in the studio. Die-hards thought it was a harbinger of things to come. Like in the Great NYC Blackout of 1977. Which resulted in more babies being born 9-months to the day afterwards. Which taxed all the hospitals and some clinics that were converted into maternity wards. While many mothers had to be sent to California hospitals where they were no longer having babies of their own and had lots of room. Some mums were even flown to Boston hospitals where the Irish population had also become quite secular with nobody marrying any more but still having some babies. But no baker's dozen anymore. In the midst of the hoopla. Like the lass who was confessing to the old priest who was half-deaf: Bless me Father but I'm afraid I'm in the family way! Ah, not ta worry 'me child. When ye reach my age, sur' ye'll be in everybody's bloody way.

Anyway, back to the power failure. Some smart aleck in the hallway outside the studio, thinking the time had come, yelled out: Hey, buster, who turned off the lights? As if he were talking Lucifer matches.

whisshhh .... oo-oooooh ...

Fortunately, Con Edison realized the problem almost immediately. Which was a first. Time was money. The circus (sic) had become overloaded as 45-million viewers (smokers) simultaneously powered-on their sets and tuned to the Late Yo with David Minuteman for the unforgettable interviews with the Dichter-17. Power was switched on before anyone else knew the difference. Or cared less. Until, moments later, 43-million non-smokers who had stayed home on New Year's Eve were about to tune-in.

~ ~ ~

Incidentally, cigar-smokers were never looked upon with such contempt as cigarette smokers, at least according to Cigar Aficionado magazine. Cigars were generally smoked by rich, successful people with fat bellies and had a kind of sophistication, an urbanity to them. A fat tummy was a symbol of power in oriental countries where you knew who was the boss. The fat guy just yelled orders as if there were no tomorrow. Further, you rarely heard of anyone getting lung cancer from cigars or chain-smoking five cigars one after the other. Except perhaps Mark Twain who reputedly smoked up forty on a good day, weather permitting. And to his deathbed insisted: If smoking is not allowed in heaven, I shall not go.

Generally sinister-looking people didn't smoke cigars although Al Capone and Fidel Castro had their darker side in real life. Or in Edward G. Robinson's case, on the silver screen at the Saturday matinees. When the lights went out and the smokers lit up. Rather cigars were more accustomed to being smoked by statesmen like Churchill, JFK, and King Edward VII who famously said: *Gentlemen, you may smoke*. And that was it!

Indeed, cigar smokers knew they were in good company with the likes of W. Somerset Maugham, Ernest Hemingway, Groucho Marx, George Burns, Sigmund Freud, and H.L. Mencken who put it this way: A woman who can stand half an hour of the Lexington fish markets is well able to face a few blasts of tobacco smoke. Rudyard Kipling put it better: A woman is only a woman, but a good cigar is a smoke. ouch!

whisshhh .... oo-oooooh ...

Joe Cocker seemed to agree when he said: Huh, Just Like a Woman. But the words belonged to Dylan.

The vast majority of cigar-smokers were fat, senile, harmless old men even before obesity became popular. In that respect, cigar-smoking was closer to pipe-smoking. Think: Einstein in the art of relaxation or Archimedes in a fit of Eureka. In his tub, with a marble ashtray on the side. Like a mistress. The problem was that with the pending global smoking ban, the casinos would almost certainly belly up, like everyone else (pun). Which hadn't been doing too well anyway since the indoor ban. And hi-rollers were spending more time smoking outside than in the casinos. Creating havoc with the profits. Incidentally, have you ever heard of a bingo event since smoking was banned indoors? Thought so. The surprising thing was that there weren't too many draperies to be fouled up outside unless hanging with the wash. So, what was all the fuss the AT lawmakers were making on the outright ban?

No, pipe & cigar smokers weren't sinister looking. That applied only to cigarette smokers.

Actually, even if you glance at the following arbitrary list of pipe-smokers, it will be relatively easy to pick out how many were sinister-looking: Walter Cronkite, CS Lewis, Georges Simenon, Charles Darwin, Joseph Stalin, Carl Gustav Jung, Jack Schaefer, Wyatt Earp, Sir Isaac Newton, Gertrude Stein, Greta Garbo, Mario Lanza, Irwin Shaw, Sir Arthur Conan Doyle, Queen Victoria, Vincent van Gogh, Dr. Seuss, and, good lord, Alfred Lord Tennyson.

That makes it, what, only one sinister-looking person? And, three ladies, two sirs, one doc, one queen, one knave, good lord, and one student prince. Nine card stud and an extra deuce. I rest my case. Time for a recess.

whisshhh .... oo-oooooh ...

~ ~ ~

Without wasting another minute, the ultimate moment had arrived with the nation in tenterhooks waiting for David Minuteman to introduce his surprise guests. Based upon impressions from the performance on the 'reality-show', the nation of TV viewers would vote by text in support or against the pending smoking ban. They had been selected because they were the remaining 17 still alive after smoking for six decades. And more power to them. For proving miracles do happen. Truly it would be a night to remember like the sinking of the Titanic. And the theme was rousing. No, it wasn't pleasant. If you were a non-smoker. If anything, it had a repugnant smell to it. It was all about the remaining 25-minutes of cigarette smoking in a nation at risk.

Seventeen of the original participants in Dichter's study were about to be re-interviewed by David about their opinions in the 1947 study 'The Happy Smoker', and about their smoking behavior since then, and whether they had any regrets. Which, by looking them straight in their smiley face's ☺ you could tell weren't too many. Incidentally, Paul Anka had long ago reminisced: Regrets, I've had a few/But then again, too few to mention.

Their inflammatory opinions in 1947 resulted in the landmark study which led to the escalation of an industry which made a fanatic liar out of every non-smoker. Whom, no matter how hard they tried, just didn't get it. Unlike most normal people, the non-smokers were simply unable to acquire the taste after trying multiple brands without inhaling. Like Bill Clinton. And felt left out. Of the group. The Outsider. [Camus] The Outsiders. [S.E. Hinton]

In the portrayal of smokers as tough, angry, sinister and unforgiving.

In the portrayal (sic) of the artist as a young man.

Which was absurd. The theatre of the absurd. All the world's a bsurd (sic). As if it had something to do with the right genes. The right stuff. Which they hadn't. Apparently. And resented. Unable to enjoy a nice quiet puff like the rest of them. Of us. They complained that it made them sick while all their friends were having a rare old time smoking up a storm. But for some inexplicable reason - the nicotine never initiated the action of competitively binding at the nicotinic acetylcholine receptors (nAChRs), the ligand-gated ion channels on the cell membrane. Hence, they might as well have been smoking #2 pencils for a thrill. But the thrill was gone. The thrill is gone/The thrill is gone away/The thrill is gone baby/The thrill is gone away. [BB King] Instead they became anti-smokers seeking a cause.

A clue.

A choo? God bless you!

And then, one day – eureka! They heard a housewife yelling about the obnoxious smell of smoke on her draperies. They were born again. Born free. There was a new catch-cry. A mantra. A movement. A mob. A cult of anti-smokers.

And, because of the gagging, repulsive, repugnant smell on the draperies – inhaled by housewives from Butcher Holler to Belchatow - the anti-smoking lobby took root globally.

It was curtains for us. The last survivor(s). The *k*-smoker(s) among us. On a mission.

~ ~ ~

Yes indeed, it had been a tough time for smokers considering that we had to put up with non-smokers. As I'm scribbling my WIP in my favorite old abandoned parking lot near a remote cemetery. And, anticipating the weather forecast which hopefully they got wrong again, I'm still amazed at what the ecoists have done for the eco. Beneath the CO_x, SO_x and NO_X umbrella-cloud above our heads. In our value system. Where there'd no longer be any smoke on the draperies.

And what a blessing that would be. So that they could now safely return to their homes. The few who weren't in foreclosure. In tough times. Along with their personal aerosol room-fresheners and toxic hairspray aerosol cans. Protectively wearing gas-mask leftovers from the days of the Cold War for their entire adult lives had they lived that long.

Considering the Dichter-17 were mostly nonagenarians, the Late Yo producers were rightly worried that they mightn't recall a darn thing for the desperate housewives who would be amused by almost anything. But how could these old-timers talk about 1947 never mind their granny's birthday who died in the 19th century? Which was a good question and a reasonable concern. Or whether they were wearing a dickie-bow tie (the men) or a scarf (the ladies) for tonight's event. Memory loss was a funny thing. Even Jessica Simpson who was about a third of their ages couldn't be relied upon to remember her lines. Not to mention Milli Vanilli who never sang any lines to remember. Do you remember? At least Elvis had back-up singers to hit the high notes which he had forgotten and couldn't reach if he could. Sinatra could blame it on the double-martinis. Dylan could mumble his way through, which was convenient. As Joe Heim mused in the Washington Post: And it's not the frog croak voice or the aged whine or any tumbling tumbleweed tunes that make the troubadour sound ancient ... but more a world-weariness ... that has finally swallowed him whole.

whisshhh .... oo-oooooh ...

~ ~ ~

The study in all its candor and honesty was heart-stopping if not breath-taking (pun). In his scholarly research, Dr. Dichter had described the seventeen (leading) euphoric reasons for the Happy Smoker by interviewing millions of smokers nationwide. With his bored-stiff staff of high school students who did most of the work. On summer break with nothing to do and who cared less. Especially, at minimum wage which was hardly enough for a couple of packs of Marlboro's. Who couldn't wait for a smoke-break between asking the same questions over-and-over-again, like watching the same commercial over and over. And over again. Millions and millions of times.

Some (readers) may object as to why (in a world gone eco) I would raise the specter (in a confession of all places) about the positive attributes of smoking described in Dr. Dichter's study. But such is human nature (for men). And frailty thy name is woman. And that was the reality. The one still-lingering hope was that besides the entire smoker's platform (45 million smokers), according to the actuaries only one-quarter (43 million) of the non-smoker majority were expected to be glued-in to the Dichter-17 interviews on the Late Yo with David Minuteman. Which would've been the miracle they were hoping for when it came to the text-vote. The reality-vote!

Which was still wishful thinking. In a secular world where miracles were becoming fewer and fewer. And far between. Although there had been one (miracle) on 34th Street.

COINCIDENTALLY – in 1947!

OMG – did you notice! Uncanny. This was the year of the original Dichter study! As the Jesuit says: "There are no coincidences in life, only miracles!"

And yet – it seemed to be a realistic assumption that mostly smokers would tune-in since the theme was: reflections of a happy smoker. You would think! And non-smokers didn't want to catch anything. On the air. In the air. Following which the reality-vote was slated for the dying moments of the Yo.

The factoids remained:

- Congress already voted unanimously with a show-of-hands for nation-wide smoking cessation at 12:00:00 on New Year's Eve.

  The result: 535:0 ayes (for the smoking ban).

- The popular-vote in the gyms had predictably followed bloc-lines for cessation announced at 21:06:00

  Result: 79:21ayes.

- So, do-or-die for a stay on the ceremonial reality-vote with a minimum required 51:49 against the ban scheduled to be announced at exactly 23:59:59

Which at least might prolong the agony of debate and postpone the terrifying reality.

The seventeen rules in Dr. Dichter's study were based upon psychological and physiological feedback from polls conducted on 79% of the adult population, the percent that smoked in 1947. Seventeen of whom survived to the present day. Well, that was eight years ago (if you're keeping score). And, like SKIP LEGAULT – were still smoking! And proud of it because they knew less and cared even more back then. No one would've guessed that the 79% who smoked in the good old days would do an about turn to 21% six decades later. And all because of the smoke smell on the draperies! oops! Hold it. We're not there yet!

To recap, in 1947, 79% of the population smoked when there was no age requirement to do so. They had been polled in one-on-one interviews by 2.1 million HS seniors drafted for the task at minimum wage during the summer holidays. It gave the kids something to do and some pocket-money for a pack or two. Nonetheless, out of the millions of reasons why people smoked, upon final tabulation with the help of 21,000 vacuum tubes burning from both ends of the element inside the ENIAC computer, the 'best' seventeen responses were selected for Dr, Dichter's study and later resulted in their being affectionately called 'rules of smoking'. The motives addressed the following categories:

- the solo smoker (nearest thing to a closet-smoker in the waning days of the pre-T era)
- smoking in mixed company
- therapeutic value
- poetry in smoking

- the ability to write with words that pound on the conscience
- the guilt-ridden smoker.
- And, last but not least, the role of the #2 pencil, a re-invention before its time. Which, even then, assisted in helping a confirmed addict to give up smoking ... *for a while.* As telephone operators say in the Philippines before putting you on hold and forgetting all about you.

~ ~ ~

SEVENTEEN MOTIVES (rules) FOR THE HAPPY SMOKER
WHY DO WE SMOKE CIGARETTES ANYWAY?

A revision of Ernest Dichter's 1947 study –

from his The Psychology of Everyday Living

Everyday living. Live and let die.

The only thing common about the 10 elderly male members of the Dichter-17 was that they all looked and sounded like the ditherin' eejits that an alert anthropologist from Cornell U. might've mistaken for clones of each other. Some were probably 6-footers in their heyday like Gary Cooper who was 6-foot-3 if you ever saw him through the fog, smoking on screen. But they were sadly slouching now. Like Robert Mitchum in his latter days.

Thank God for Mitchum deodorant - advertised in Parade maga-zine to keep us all young.

Like Benjamin Button in the first half of the movie before he became Brad Pitt. Like the average height of a Hollywood leading man such as Alan Ladd who compensated with his good looks and bad habits. But had to stand on a soapbox, looking silly wearing platforms to kiss Veronica Lake, his leading lady on camera (who was about 4ft 2-in). *Lights, action ... kiss!* The kiss of death. Just kidding. The kiss frequently (during rehearsals anyway) became more of a slurp if he weren't concentrating on his lines and slipped. And his lips just slid all the way down to Veronica's rubbery face with his upper lip ultimately acting as an anchor against her protrud-ing chin (like Reese Witherspoon's in modern times for want of an illustration). As Mark Twain said of Oliver Wendell Holmes: He had double chins all the way down to his stomach. This some-times softened the bumpy ride in a sight to behold. Like when a roller-coaster, upon slowly reaching an altitude of 1000-feet (such as the Megafobia wooden-sensation at Oakwood Coaster Country in Pembrokeshire, Wales, if you're Welch like Dylan Thomas) ... pauses purposefully. Like a spotted tiger on the prowl, spotting his prey ... before the scream-machine positions itself into an about-turn for the pepto bismol ride-of-your-life. When (depending on your age) you frantically hoped there were no moguls on the down-side. In response to one of the elders who inquired: But, what's the downside?

Yes indeed, it was really sad to see the effect of aging on men whom you imagined being slim, trim and brimful of energy when they were unbridled young lads about six decades earlier. Eyeing the eligible but ugly damsels lining-up in agony of rejection on the Saturday night dancehall floors when women were allowed-in free. Coyote-ugly. Or ugly Betty. Starring the beautiful Vanessa Williams. Ms. USA. Before they took her crown away but it wasn't for smoking cigars with her clothes on.

And for the corollary: The only thing common about the 7 old ladies was that they all looked the same with similar wrinkles and lame excuses. And, in the words of the old rugby song, Oh dear, what can the matter be/Seven old ladies got stuck in the lavatory/ They were there from Monday 'til Saturday/Nobody knew they were there.

whisshhh .... oo-oooooh ...

~ ~ ~

... *HOLD ON!* STOP THE PRESS
please ...

An Unprecedented ANNOUNCEMENT from the protagonist:

Ladies and Gentlemen, and forensics among you ... something terrible has happened. For a health reason, I had stopped smoking mid-WIP. The result – no inspiration to write with words that pound on the conscience! Nothing! This page and the next, therefore, represent 79 pages of totally BLANK text until I recovered! Fortunately, I resumed smoking eventually and the muse returned! Please continue reading on the understanding that there would actually be 79 BLANK pages, but we wish to think of the trees and the eco!

If anything, the experience has precedence in 'The Person from Porlock', a term to describe 'interrupted genius', developed from Coleridge having been interrupted in recalling all the images from his dream in completing Kubla Khan.

HENCE, this is an intentionally BLANK page to simulate 79 *BLANK* pages during which the protagonist without the inspiration derived from tobacco had writer's block and was unable to coin a limerick never mind a memoir ...

Thank you for smoking!

oops! Wrong testimonial!

Rather, thank you for your perseverance.

The Management

(whew! nothing to worry about!)

• •

•

koff-koff ...

gulp!

Continuing, after 79 blank pages of ... nothingness ...

~ ~ ~

SHOW TIME on the LATE YO.

Not missing a beat (pun), the elderly lot, thinking they were back in the nursing home, unwittingly chimed in with -- *IT'S YO-YO TIME!* Brisk and dapper as ever, David Minuteman stood up to welcome the old fogies who were emerging from the adjacent waiting room and its dartboard. It was obvious to everyone that David needed a diversion after the tabloids reported his (private) between-rehears-als-shenanigans. And a laugh was good. And a good laugh was better. The dartboard was intended to kill time, but time was really all they had, and they hadn't a helluva lot of it left. So, they passed on the darts because they could hardly see the sky through the closet-window never mind the wall. Nor the dartboard. And were afraid that they might've killed each other with the flipping darts. They were limping along ever so slowly like SKIP LEGAULT and holding onto each other like elephants entwining their trunks with the tails of fellow-elephants in front in the opening act of a Barnum & Bailey circus. All 17 had taken their seats. Rather, comfy La-Z-Boy sofas in which they were soon permanently embedded, and which would take a backhoe to haul them out. The La-Z-Boys were arranged in a Stonehenge-like circle (which was appropriate consid-ering their average age). Surrounding the host in a clinical setting physiologically and ergonomically designed to imitate the natural environment of a nursing home. To optimize their performance. To make them feel at home. Home on the range. With a staff nurse Mildred Ratched look-a-like behind each of them, armed with a rolling-pin if they tried to rise too prematurely before giving their interview, which was presumptuous without the backhoe. A typical acknowledgment before they sat down was: *Arrah' if I sit down, I'll never get up.*

David took out a nice walnut box of Cubans to make all of his homely guests feel at home. Since the host was also part of tonight's smoking waiver by default, he ran his nose up and down the side of the stem of what he considered to be the best cigar in the box. Took a nice, long sniff, paused like a wine connoisseur who knows what he's whiffing, then lit up. Like Guy Fawkes. So that they wouldn't feel embarrassed to smoke or awkward if they thought he were a non-smoker. Regardless of the reasoning, David was going to have one himself anyway. The box had a built-in hygrometer-cum-humidifier, but the Dichter-17 preferred their own Camels, thank you very much. For smoking. Just kidding. Nonetheless, they appreciated David's invitation and for want of anything better to say had they been able to remember, asked about his new wife. From the cue cards. They didn't want to appear too personal or intrusive. Like a stalker. And didn't ask too much about his old wife. Nor indeed, her age. Nor that of his new wife. No, not much. [The Four Lads] Nor about his entertaining practices for female subordinates. Between rehearsals.

Following the warm felicitations and having explained why they were there, there was the usual gender-specific small talk among themselves that you get in mixed company. About popular prescriptions and who was taking what. And why. Such as Ambien, Zocor and Plavix, which they figured would become even more difficult to subsidize and probably end up totally unaffordable with the imminent elimination of cigarette taxes. If the reality-vote bunkered out. In about 25-minutes. Also, while still in the waiting room they had discussed the best methods to avoid slipping in the bathtub and shared horror stories worse than Janet Leigh in Psycho. They concluded that no one would notice if they just decided to quit bathing forever because nobody noticed them, period. Cared less. And wouldn't know the difference since none of them had a family visitor in a donkey's age. As they collectively said: *Kids nowadays, and grandkids, and great-grand kids!* And left it at that. And you knew what they meant. What wasn't said.

whisshhh .... oo-oooooh ...

By now David, looking at his Rolex when no one was looking to avoid making a big deal out of it, had listened to enough of the silliness and it was time to get down to business. Taking care of business. [Bachman-Turner Overdrive] Time was money. And the gaffer was running out of lights, cameras and action. That is, if there were any chance of getting through all seventeen interviews before midnight. If they all talked fast. Which was the only hope.

David had arranged to have seventeen prefabricated 6x8-foot optometrist-sized charts on sheet-rock panels which he planned on holding-up one at a time with the help of the gaffer and the best boy. One for each of the 17 reasons for the happy smoker in Dr. Dichter's study for the guests to expound upon. One guest would be asked to comment on such-and-such chart. Others of course could join in or wait their turn for their own chart. Because of the assumed myopia of the guests, the cards were large and the bold font thick so that even Mr. McGoo could read them from a distance. While one of the seven old ladies who looked an awful lot like Bette Midler when she was young (meaning, when Bette Midler was young) whispered to herself: God is watching from a distance. Nonetheless, David planned on holding up one of the charts at a time with a gap-in-between. With that familiar grin from the gap between his teeth for the old-timers to comment upon. For the benefit of a tuned-in nation of smokers in every state except California. Where they were rumored to have had their own Midnight Express even long before there was such a thing. If there ever were. For a long time now, California had represented the Shangri La of the eco where every homeowner had a compact tobacco-detector, pocket-seismometer, mudslide-sensor, forest-fire detector, flood-insurance calculator, and, last but not least, a combined CO_x, SO_x and NO_X monitor. All 8 operations were conveniently available for instant access in a small metal claw-like pull-out repository which functioned similar to a swiss army knife configuration.

In the dying minutes of the pre-T era, the tuned-in nation was watching the Dichter-17 with bated breath (pun). Recognizing that they were not alone. And feeling good. Feelin' alright, (uh oh). [Joe Cocker] Incidentally, the 'gap-in-between' time-reference above was for commentary *between* the numbered charts by each guest - and was no disparagement on the gap between David Minuteman's teeth. Because the old-timers had no intention of getting into that imbroglio since they were all pretty much on dentures themselves if not something stronger. And, wasn't the gap between his teeth a personal matter, which most of the old ladies' thought was boyish, cute and stylish. And who were they to criticize the rich and famous or their lavish homes and flamboyant lifestyles. Between rehearsals. On the job. Incidentally, each of the ridiculously sized charts would've qualified for an 8th grader science fair table-top poster exhibit except they had no side-panels for the abstract and summary never mind the conclusions swiped from the web.

Larry

Let the drum roll begin. Begin the Beguine [Cole Porter] **LARRY**, the first of the troopers, took a deep breath. Or at least he tried to (pun) without his portable O_2 container which would've been embarrassing if not awkward to cart up the elevator and into the studio, thinking he could make it through the evening as he thought to himself: Help me make it through the night. [Kris Kristofferson] Already the chit-chatting had delayed recap on the good old days when smokes were smokes with different smokes for different folks [Sly and the Family Stone] by about 3 minutes at about a million dollars a whack of ad revenue at stake. As the **NICO MAN** adv (which also enjoyed the smoking waiver by default) was getting antsy.

Even before he was presented with the first 6x8 foot chart for comments before leaving the waiting room, **LARRY** confessed that he used to be as happy as Larry when he was a young lad and a lot healthier than now. You could imagine that the unassuming way he said it caused his entire elderly peers to split their hips laughing at the unintentional pun. And for the briefest of moments, with the chittering histrionics, they felt as happy as Larry themselves in spite of their ailments. And, they, now the unforgotten, were obviously thrilled to be in the national spotlight. And, what were friends for anyway? Which was one helluva non-sequitur. And **LARRY** realized that his mind wasn't what it used to be. And half the time he wondered where on holy earth he was. He was still angry that Sean

Pencil declined to play his character in the movie of the 3 stooges, but he knew that first impressions linger like CO_xs, SO_xs and NO_xs or he mightn't be invited back. Careful not to make another comment about David's ex. Which, if he said it fast enough sounded like David's sex. Or her age. Or that of his new wife. At least he (Larry) was that alert. Or thought as much. If he thought too much.

Now finally after all the small talk and the sex-talk innuendo, it was time for the first chart with 25-minutes to go before the ball would fall. Seventeen charts were about to be presented to the original 17 interviewees of the famous Dichter study using the same subject headers as 1947. Their opinions were solicited live on the Late Yo six decades later realizing that all 17 were still smokers.

#1 *Smoking is Fun:* All eyes were on LARRY who was challenged to comment on the first card which David Minuteman carefully turned over. Actually, the card was a 6x8-foot section of sheetrock, on the gray paper-side of which, fortunately, you could use a black marker! And, it took the assistance of both the gaffer and the best boy to balance the ends before David was able to hold it steady in the center. Hand-scribbled in dark bold on this first 'card' was the caption: SMOKING IS FUN. It was now Larry's turn.

Ahh, David 'me lad, I must confess at my age that honesty becomes more important with each passing minute. As he coughed-up a quick *koff-koff* which everyone in the audience knew first-hand had nothing to do with nerves but was undoubtedly smoker's cough. Whereupon he blessed himself three times for good health and for good luck before continuing. *I've always enjoyed that adolescent sensibility* (which juvenescence the studio audience was unanimously beginning to detect) *because smoking acts like a portal into the wantonness of immaturity. Of not having to feel responsible. You sit back for the six-minute duration of a nice long drag without having to feel answerable to anyone* (...as Larry was now blowing a perfect smoke-ring which drew even more humongous applause and was bound to benefit the ratings of the Late Yo for such improvisation). *If only the stressed-out world would stop and smell the roses instead of being so darned preoccupied with the dang draperies.* (Another loud laugh from the audience who were used to blinds.) *You just smoke your lumbago away.*

By now the studio was considering giving a contract to the Dichter-17 and to hell with the laugh machines – they were that good with their guffaws. Each of them said: *I'm good.* By now Larry was starting to sound like the grandstander he was in his youth instead of a great-grandfather. And you could tell he was on a shake, rattle and roll from the cackling sound of his bones, with all of the attention. *And you try to forget which isn't difficult when you reach 90.*

While Jack Schaefer and his Late Yo band were desperately playing Try to Remember [Jerry Orbach] in a subliminal attempt at Total Recall. Starring Arnold and Vanessa who was Ms USA *for a while* (as the telephone operators say in the Philippines as they put you on hold and forget all about you).

Now that the ice was broken in the camaraderie of 'group-therapy', the round-table reflections continued with gusto in a free-for-all. Jabbering away like a bunch of old ninnies at a jubilee reunion for each other. Each of the Dichter-17 could hardly wait for the next 'card' to be overturned as if they were back in the casino when they were foot-loose and fancy free. Which was more like bingo for most of them during recent decades until the indoor smoking ban put an end to that recreation. But you could tell they were having a rare ol' time. In fond recollection of their thoughts from-and-since the original study in 1947 which had become a classic, adding to the 17 reasons which had defied their longevity. And David Minuteman hoped to god the Nielson homes had their thingamajigs handy and wouldn't forget to legibly fill-in the long forms.

Next up was an old man whose name was MOE and who knew he was in the company of peers if not angels - yet! (God bless his mortal soul.) Moe would be followed by CURLY JOE who was curling his single hair with a portable curling iron brought-in from house-keeping. Just kidding. This was an inside-joke by those who lamented the good old days since Moe couldn't recall his last bad hair-day on his shiner. Which he remembered by association each time he moe'd (sic) the lawn which thank God (in his condition) was a self-propel model.

#2 *Smoking is a Reward:* After Larry's magnanimous performance, 45-million smokers glued to their Sony's couldn't wait for MOE'S turn (since the Sony's would soon be strategically replaced by cheap Chinese sets as collateral of the pending eco-nomic disaster from the loss of cigarette taxes which funded the Treasury). Subsequently, the second heavy card was upturned by the gaffer and the best boy now working in cahoots. (And people began to talk.) They were a pair alright.

Thank you, young lad (Moe said to David, which sounded like 'moses' - if you said it fast), *I needed that quiet puff. Well, the way I see it is that we **applaud** our foolishness* (as he added) *- **hip, hip, hurrah!** ... during these short-lived* (pun) *breaks since we realize that every cigarette shortens our lives by exactly six minutes on-the-clock.*

His 'hip-hip' gag reminded him to feel his aching hip which badly needed replacement, but which was now tough luck as everyone knew health benefits would be the first to hurt following the imminent loss of cigarette taxes. Particularly if you had been a smoker for six decades and certainly not on the priority list for lung transplants. Which would've done his hip a helluva lot of good! *Anyway* (he sarcastically continued), *we deserve a cigarette if we have been good lads or* (being mischievous, now looking across at the girls) *naughty gals.* The seven old ladies among the Dichter 17 laughed embarrassingly at the last remark, feeling desirable for the first time since menopause about forty years earlier.

The first ciggie of the day smoked right after a healthy porridge breakfast ushers a kind of sunshine face as if Mr. Rogers introducing a bright new day. Then, at the end of the day when I used to come home feeling tired and beat /And go up where the air is fresh and sweet [James Taylor] (Good luck for that!) ... *the last puff was like slamming the door on an annoying vacuum-cleaner salesman's face in a fit of Dagwood.*

Author's Dagwood & Blondie   Author and son with Dagwood

#3 *Smoking is Oral Pleasure:* It was now high time for the third card. The studio tension was titillating with imagination gone wild. Girls Gone Wild. CURLY insisted on wearing his trench coat with collar-up because he was always getting colds the older he got and missed the warmth of his (one) hair above his conspicuous harelip. He just couldn't help himself and it was now time for a loud *AHH-CHOO!*

If you were to ask me, David, I'd say that if I ever ran out of cigarettes (interrupting himself) - *don't get me wrong! But long before the current placebo-campaign, even I chewed on #2 pencils. Now, whenever the urge hits me to give-up smoking which isn't very often thank goodness* (he added politely), *I scour the house looking for a crunchie #2, careful not to chip my upper incisors or the lower posteriors of my dentures. But, there's never any real substitute for a good, old-fashioned ciggie. The happy look on a smoker's face contrasts with the agonized look on the tortured frown of a Central Park jogger – certainly not me at my age* (everyone laughs) ... *only half-way round the park. Praying the darn run were over, if you don't mind, so she can regain her composure over a quiet puff.*

#4 *The Cigarette – a Modern Hourglass:* A retired bartender – 'SET-'EM-UP-JOE', his nickname, was next to comment: *Smoking my cigarette away provides the melancholy feeling as though watching a ship slowly and asymptotically disappearing across the ocean until, like my cigarette, there's only ashes or nothing. Like Sarah Miles watching Kris Kristofferson disappearing in The Sailor who fell from Grace with the Sea.* Mercifully for the combined 88-million audience who heard it all before, Joe was abruptly cut off by David having commenced telling the entire movie, spoiler-alert and all, which had nothing to do with smoking. Still, out of courtesy David asked Set-'em-up-Joe, how he ever deserved such a nickname? Set-'em-up-Joe replied that his original nickname during HS had always been I.V. because he was the 4th son. However, later in life when Rod McKuen became famous,

whom he always thought of as sissyish with all of his cats like T.S. Eliot, and had a hit with The I.V. that Clings to the Wall. *"Well, what more could I say except The Wall The Wall the Wall"*

#5   *With a Cigarette I am Not Alone:* It was now time for the only husband and wife team, JACK & JILL - among the 17. Jack started. *In the immortal words of James Taylor, smoking cigarettes is like being with a friend.*

Then Jill tumbled-in, not literally I hope (mimicking the first lyric of American Pie): *A long long time ago/I can still remember how that music/Used to make me smile ...* quickly correcting herself with - *oops, wrong memory!* And starting all over again as older folks are inclined to do. *A very, very long time ago, there was this young lad in the dance hall* (she smiled at her ancient hubby buttressed against her, pinching himself to say awake). *I really wanted to say hello, but the dance wasn't ladies-choice and I wasn't exactly Gina Lollobrigida but rather sporting 'rural' legs, limiting my chances right there. Unfortunately, there was no one to introduce us.* Although she observed that there were a lot of shark fins on the horizon.

... der-dum, der-dum, dum-dum, dum-dum, dum-dum, der-dum, dum-dum ...

I was so nervous that I was puffing away like nobody's business back in the good old days when you could do that. The ashes on my cigarette made me realize why Audrey Hepburn used a 10.6"/ 270 mm super long cigarette holder. Or like Lawrence Harvey smoking his favorite brand, 'Passing Cloud', the gentleman's cigarette, through a long holder too. You see there was nowhere for the ashes to go and I was getting really anxious until the young lad brought me a napkin and held it adjacent to my cigarette enticingly, trying to emulate a matador holding a red-cape - had he only held the tray flat instead of at 90 degrees. Alas, most of the ashes falling on the carpet. Or to mimic Sir Walter Raleigh who gallantly doffed his cloak and threw it over a mud puddle to protect the feet of the passing Queen Elizabeth 1. And now you know the rest of the story. We're still alive, knock on wood, and happily married – going-on six decades of smoking together.

whisshhh ... oo-oooooh ... .

#6   I Like to Watch (the Smoke): Then the parson (whose name was also CURLEY, but with an 'e' and with a helluva lot more hair beneath his golf-cap) whom you'd think would be more concerned with the approaching afterlife, got up and said (as if Gordon McRae as Curley with an 'e' in Oklahoma): *Smoking creates an aura of fog and mist of the aesthetic forbidden into which the mind may wander and wonder, with the puffs looking like clouds on a smoker's chest X-ray.*

The lady on the la-D-boy beside him, RITA (who used to be lovely once) added: *I like to open my umbrella in the living room (inside) on a rainy day and imagine I am outside while I smoke up a storm and watch the smoke suspended on the ceiling as if waiting to be absorbed into the ominous clouds. It's kind of like O'Casey's wistful words in Juno and the Paycock – 'I often looked up at the sky an' assed meself the question - what is the moon, what is the stars.' Yes indeed, smoking provides satisfaction because, as filthy, pathetic and obnoxious the habit is, it coaxes the muse and brings out the best of your innermost thoughts.*

whisshhh ... oo-oooooh ... .'

On this topic, another lady, AVA (a name which sounded too young for her age but who loved listening to the eponymous hymn if the umlaut was on Av*a* rather than Av*e* (Maria) with these unpredictable Italian sopranos) - who must've looked an awful lot like Lauren Bacall a century earlier in To Have and Have Not, remarked: *With practice you can almost make any shape out of the smoke you exhale at least in your moment of creativeness. Just blowing smoke as it were.*

#7 *Got a Match?* When this card was upturned, the predict-able response came from ROD, the only retired volunteer-firefighter among them. Rod couldn't help but repeat his enduring words from 1947 (quote): *"Some of the appeals of a lighted cigarette derive from those of fire in general. Fire is the symbol of life, and the idea of fire is surrounded by much superstition. For instance, as strange as it sounds, some people will never light three cigarettes on one match. And that's okay too."*

#8 *Smoking Mannerisms:* A writer whose name was simply 'F' (go figure, with a silent 'f'!) -- pronounced 'EVV' (like, short for Evan, a common Welsh name) - was next to share his opin-ions: *As in the expression: You can tell a person by the company s/he keeps, if a cigarette is her constant companion, then say no more!* Partly stealing from his theme in his 1947 interview among the Dichter 17, he contin-ued: *Some people always have cigarettes drooping from their mouths like in a Mickey Spillane detective thriller. Others, like Gabby Hayes in the old cowboy movies let the cigarette jump up and down in their mouths while they are talking. Which figured in Gabby's case because you could never make out a darn word he mumbled, just like Bob Dylan.*

The old lady beside him, GRETA unfortunately was her name (while certainly, with her bad habit, her last name wasn't Thunberg), glamorous in her day (when she pretended that was NOT her name!), tried to steer the discussion in a more positive manner by revealing some of her most private desires. Greta confessed her preference for cigars like the Java Mint by Drew Estate but feared that her cigar-smoking ability to clear a room in no time flat prompted her to seek alternate social diversions.

#9 *Cigarettes Help Us to Relax:* Any one of the 17 could've commented on this card, relaxing in their nice comfy la-Z-boys and smoking circles in the air. All of them with their mouths open in the shape of a coo making a sound like the pigeons on the roof in On the Waterfront. Finally, JOSE, a retired bouncer took the initiative: *When you're smoking, you're certainly in no hurry. You're literally on your own time. It enables you to persevere when you're bored with the dinner guests. You can sit at home playing with the remote without a fuss in the world. Finally, you can line-up calmly at the welfare office (back in the day), puffing away, and let others do the grumbling.*

#10   I Blow My Troubles Away: A retired gynecologist,

AGATHA (a name sounding more like her age – who always agonized how she survived as a kid in those tough schoolyards with a name like that?) philosophized: *When the going gets tough and I just can't take it anymore. You know what I mean. The great-grand-kids with their airpods - as though they were stone deaf like me! Well, a nice long drag helps me to relax. Goodness gracious! whew! Inhaling the smoke is like sucking-in a deep breath of fresh air. Then, with each exhale it's like blowing my troubles away.*

#11   Cigarette Taste Has to Be Acquired: BRUNO (the

customer of the bartender, 'Set-'em-up-Joe') who used to be a frequent-flier until claustrophobia took over tried his hand at this one. *For some people it's not that easy at first to experience the thrill afforded by the proverbial cigarette. That's for sure. Like a 17-year-old experiencing his first pint of Guinness. Which, I swear to God, if he were anything like me, must've tasted worse than a slurp of Milk of Magnesia for a miserable upset tummy. But fortunately, the training period doesn't always last too long.* Bruno went on to articulate his Yugoslavian experience previously shared in his 1947 interview. *"During my trip to Yugoslavia I had no choice but to smoke Yugoslavian cigarettes. I tried a half-dozen brands in a single day until I just knew I had found my ideal cigarette. What a revelation to realize later that had*

I only persevered and smoked a few extra of the other brands that they were all equally candidates for the finest. Well, I guess you live (pun) *and learn."*

#12   No, Thanks, I'll Smoke My Own: It was time for Rod (the retired volunteer-fireman) who was also a retired advertising exec but who always wished he were a retired lawyer: *Everyone knows me by the cigarettes I smoke. I'm not saying this as if to sound superior to others who smoked different brands. Still I must admit that many have switched as if in deference to my brand. Once I was invited to a going-away party by a young lass on whom I had my eye. I was intrigued to see that she too had switched to my brand as I assumed that I had made that impression on her. I've always wondered, though, why she was trying to get the hell as far away from me as possible since I've never seen her since.*

#13   A Package of Pleasure: The Dichter 17 were all aware that 13 was an unlucky number but it was time for a philosopher – as Larry took yet another deep breath.

A fresh pack of cigarettes "makes your day" as Clint Eastwood might say. A feeling almost like John Wayne's speech as Davy Crockett in The Alamo, "Some words give ya a feelin' in the throat, a tight feelin'. A feelin' like ya git when yer baby makes his first sound as a man." It's like the glass half-full compared to the somber cognizance of the glass half-empty, and ... what then? Indeed, centuries ago, smokers were excommunicated in certain countries and often burned at the stake with Lucifer matches. At least in modern times, especially in South America, they were given a last cigarette before a firing squad. Although, God only knows what's going to happen with the Act of Cessation when the gates to the Midnight Express are opened - to where all of us will probably be transported in the middle of the night in cattle cars.

#14   Smoking Memories: Moe, now an old man (figuratively) crying into his coffin reminisced: *Some of my fondest memories* *involved smoking. Like being attracted to the girl next door who unfortunately never even noticed I existed. But, after seeing West Side Story I would imagine that I were Tony and she, Maria sitting on a fire escape and enjoying a nice quiet puff or two together. Looking at the stars was like poetry in smoking. Or imagining waves rippling across a turbulent ocean. The cigarette smoke rising into the eco along with all of the CO_xs, SO_xs and NO_xs. OMG! I could hardly control myself* (the audience by now could hardly control themselves either, champing at the bit, waiting for the punchline ...) *and began humming Louis Armstrong's: And I think to myself/What a wonderful world.* As the clock ticked away and Moe confessed that his diagnosis wasn't very good from his physical the day before. As he inhaled faster!

#15   *How Many a Day:* This was a tough question for any of them after an average of sixty years a piece smoking five packs a day plus. Anyway, Jack who, these days, looked like George Burns gave it a try: *Tough question. The health pundits would suggest – STOP. SMOKING. NOW! However, I've been smoking for 60-years and it would be like shifting into neutral while driving at 79 mph! On the other hand, giving them up off-and-on might suggest a lurking feeling of guilt. So, you'd better not abstain for too long.* It was now about seven minutes away, tops, from when the clock would strike twelve for the final tally of the reality-vote. With, hopefully a two-minute warning.

#16   *The First Cigarette:* Presently it was CYNTHIA'S turn who kept thinking about the first time ever she smoked a cigarette which she fancifully shared with the despairing world on national TV which was being broadcast live to 79 countries: *I thought the smoke rose in my eyes/To the dark and the endless skies* [Leona Lewis]

Now Evv joined in the fun about that lurking guilt feeling which goes back to that first one you puffed when (unwittingly) you were immediately hooked. *But if your folks found out - you were dead meat. So, you spent every creative moment thinking up ways to avoid their good night kiss if they ever caught that stinking smell on your breath. That's when I knew I was going to become a writer.* Rod, who incidentally had just been temporarily released from intensive care added:

When I was about nine and thinking that no one could see me smoking behind my favorite hiding place, an old sycamore tree, this stranger shouted from out of the blue yelling at me to toss it or he'd sock me! I was so scared that I did so. But then, it must have been my guardian angel who told me not to be afraid. Of course, I was hooked and always hummed the haunting melody of the hymn we sang at church: 'Be Not Afraid'. As the parson, Curley (beneath his decades-worn golf hat) without realizing he was on national TV began loudly humming, 'Be Not Afraid' – unintentionally causing everyone to become darned scared.

#17 *Smoking Helps Me Think:* And last but not least, another writer, VIRGINIA, volunteered for this one. *Smoking truly allows the inspiration and creativity to write when you can concentrate against all distractions - but there are physical considerations. Without actually being aware of it, smoking a cigarette keeps our hands busy, raising and lowering the cigarette in the art of inhaling and exhaling.* Predictably, the parson, Curley, seized the moment to add: *Or worse, depending on how young you were, as in: A vacant mind is the devil's playground.* On the other hand, the consensus did admit that smoking too much might reduce their efficiency to write with words that pound on the conscience. Everything in moderation.

whisshhh ... oo-oooooh ....

Within moments from somewhere in the studio there was a slight ...

... koffkoff!

Shortly followed by ... *koff! koff ...ko*

... ... *fffff ...ff... f..   .*

~ ~ ~

Flashback to St. Patrick's Cathedral.

37-minutes earlier, with minutes remaining on the doomsday clock, it was 23:23:00 and twelve minutes before the start of the Late Yo at the Ed Sullivan Theatre, 1697 Broadway, between 53rd and 54th streets in Manhattan. Only two blocks from the Time-Life Building in the Rockefeller Center – site of the **MANHATTAN PROLOGUE**, which was to have an irreparable impact on the lives of 45 million holy souls who resisted the inescapable Act of Cesation with a passion.

It was time for (yet another) midnight Mass (00:00:00) - hastily convened by Edward Cardinal Egan in a hopeless yet commend-able effort to stave-off the inevitable for the godforsaken *tabagie* by some deux ex machina intercession. The RC's who stayed up late had packed the back of the cathedral in case they'd be recog-nized in the pews up front by face recognition cameras inside the speakers mounted on the pillars supporting the cathedral arcade (surreptitiously installed by the AT-kops when no one was looking). To fulfill their obligatory annual appearance. Having missed Easter. Indeed, the recent Christmas-vigil midnight Mass didn't do too much for the disgruntlement within the economy as families wondered how they might survive the new year without cig taxes from the Treasury to offer hope. The Cardinal in his dual role as Archbishop of New York after much prayer for a nation at risk had contemplated that an ad hoc second midnight Mass (convoked for New Year's Eve) might provide faith, hope, and some clarity (sic) for the New Yorkers among them, the (freaked-out; insecure; neurotic & emotional) smokers on tenterhooks in a fit of F.I.N.E.

Where they'd go in desperation. And skip the kissing. At the Kiss of Peace. If they arrived early enough. Or t'would no longer be New Year's Eve at midnight Mass (00:00:00). Which wouldn't commence until the following morning (00:00:01). If you follow. The vigil would have expired. Like a magazine subscription. Being now New Year's Day. If the designated chaplain were on time. After stubbing-out his butt. Too.

whisshhh …. oo-oooooh …

The Act of Cessation was scheduled to be announced and enacted at exactly 00:00:01 on New Year's Day 2009 by the president-elect (... hmmm, albeit rumored to be a closet-smoker himself...). But, for yet another unfathomable reason, he was nowhere to be seen coming up to midnight except by one sharp secret service agent. All of his secret service detail had been given a 6-minute break by the president-elect. Ultimately, he resurfaced so everyone could breathe (pun) again. The A of C was announced on the president-elect's Blackberry by Twitter at 00:06:01 (exactly 6-minutes late – incidentally the elapsed time to smoke one Marlboro) to the hysterical 45 million smokers who had hoped for a miraculous Hail Mary during the inexplicable delay.

 *Nine*

The missing 6-minutes

THE PRESIDENTIAL SIGNATURE AND THE ROSE GARDEN

The presidential transition (or interregnum as it was known in the inter circles of the secret service's regnum) between the pre-T and the post-T eras was anything but smooth. Which was a contrast to a U-Tube posting at the time: Sean Penn Enjoys *Smooth* Taste of his Preferred Brand of Cigarettes Outside Beverly Hills Hotel. The first hiccup (as it were) occurred because the incumbent President had been an xxx-smoker for years although he swore that he was non-partisan when it came to crucial issues affecting a nation at risk. The fact was that he had quit only after he was born-again. The worst kind. And sobered-up after his carefree skull and bone days.

Such however wasn't exactly the case for the President-elect. Who was all meat, potatos (sic), cabbage and tomatos (sic) when it came to matos (sic) of contention. Although there was never any proof that he was a closet-smoker. [Heisenberg] Which, if it were true could give the appearance of a conflict of interest.

Because a presidential signature (or electronic equivalent with adult ID-card) was intrinsic to the enactment of the A of C, another stumbling block was that the **MANHATTAN PROLOGUE** fell between November 4 and January 20. The question, then, that terrified Democratic smokers who expected more in a democratic society all afternoon on New Year's Eve was pivotal – would the president who signs his John Hancock on the Act of Cessation be one of their very own (a closet-smoker)? Youthful, charismatic, a leader with vision and high hopes. A likeable person. Or, would the perquisite stay with the incumbent with no love lost?

It was touch and go because the incumbent had conjured up the entire anti-smoking mess in the first place and deserved full credit. But he was having none of it while rewriting his post-GWBWH story in his own words and desperately tried to avoid any bad press.

Anyway, because of the imbroglio as to who would formally declare the smoking ban, the incumbent President with method in his madness had invited the President-elect and his missus-elect to take a day-trip from the windy city where they were packing for a

2-term stay - for a stay-over without the kids in the White House on New Year's Eve. The President-elect would be given full access to the Oval office which was no longer being used after the game was finally up (the incumbent president having already convinced Japan, Mexico et al to ban smoking). And, as guests, to the Lincoln Bedroom. And, unlimited access to the Rose Garden for short walks. Or solo excursions as needed.

There was still much work to be done prior to the most crucial executive decision in modern history since Prohibition. And everything must go smoothly.

whisshhh ... oo-ooooh ...

The protocol demanded that a president (any president, elect or incumbent, for that matter, or bank manager with power of attorney, just kidding ...) was needed to sign the A of C into law.

Having passed both Houses. On the way to the WH by yellow cab from Dulles - the president-elect set an example of a precedent that in the future would be followed by Pope Francis for limited spending (because no cig taxes would be available to increase spending). With four secret service choppers hovering above consuming the lowest octane gas commercially available. Just in case. And twice as many SUVs with tinted (privacy) glass on the ground with 8-cylinders swapped-out that morning for 4 in each SUV in solidarity with the pending economic crisis. Which made the vehicles look like blacked-out mafiamobiles. So, they'd better have checked the local tint-codes. And their occupants wearing designer sunglasses on a dismal day.

Hence, the world according to Garp ... oops. Wrong examination of conscience ...

Hence, the problem according to wiki was that: … the outgoing lame-duck President had lost many of the intangible benefits of a Presidency, e.g. being perceived as the default leader on issues of national importance. Such as the elimination of cig taxes. Which would all but fall short of guaranteeing the return of society-as-we-knew-it to the Great Depression or worse. Which had been characterized by mass suicides, divorces, chronic alcoholism (if you were lucky to live in a neighborhood with a friendly speakeasy), and foreclosures. In roughly that order. Albeit, this time round things were different. We had the allure of untold wealth from the lottery to calm our anxiety. Along with the #2 pencil. And were getting more gullible by the minute in the heat of the moment.

Whereas, the President-elect was not yet legally empowered to affect policy. Such as allowing those who voted him in to smoke until kingdom come. Being the smokers-platform representing one fifth of the population that assured his election by the largest popular vote tally since LBJ. Thank you! The minority.

As Henrik Ibsen said: The minority is always right.

Of which the President-elect was one. Both a minority and a smoker. According to the grapevine. In the Rose Garden. Bordering the Oval Office and the West Wing.

It was a *K*atch-21 alright. Catch me if you can. Especially since there was much more than a hint in the check-out tabloids that the President-elect was indeed a closet-smoker. As if anyone had seen him in the act, huh. And then – if he were observed smoking even once - having signed the A of C, transparency be damned, right? Darn right! So, what would you do? What would Jesus do?

To play it safe the interregnum team behaved like house-movers only. And tried to ignore the controversy. And, in lieu of the pending even-more-dismal state of the economy, the team was taking turns driving fleets of 26-foot U-Haul trailers, for sale or rent, back and forth from the windy city. Especially with all the kids' stuff which they outgrew but had sentimental value. Piled high in the basement. Rocky mountain high/Rocky mountain high/Rocky mountain high do de do. [John Denver] Incidentally, the entire family had contemplated moving house anyway, which they had outgrown because of all of the stuff in the basement. And the wind that never ceased. In the windy city. The wind that shakes the barley. [Robert Dwyer Joyce] With the wind in the willows/The birds in the sky/There's a bright sun to warm us wherever we lie ... [Blackmore's Night] But, that was long before the CO_xs, SO_xs and NO_xs made the little birds disappear (to be replaced by mechanical *boids*).

The trailers were coming and going all day and all night. Marianne. [Harry Belafonte] With loads to be temporarily stored in the adjacent Executive Office Building. Day in and day out. And so on and so forth. Like the droning sound of a hundred Fed Ex planes circulating Memphis, any given night of the week. Long distance information give me Memphis Tennessee. [Chuck Berry] One of the six largest tobacco states prior to the A of C, along with Kentucky, NC, Georgia, SC, and ... Virginia is for losers (sic). oops. Lovers. In holding patterns. Circling to land. Then landing and taking off again. Which pilots were used to doing. While back in DC, the transition-team movers continued to look the other way. When no one was looking. When it came to politics.

Yet, somebody had to be the fall guy.

And, as in any good confession, there would be a twist.

The whole thing had reminiscences of JFK written all over it. When, against his principles, JFK refused to get involved in religious issues such as licentiousness, promiscuity and lust - because he was a roaming Cadillac (John Lennon's description of a non-practicing Catholic) and a cigar smoker. And didn't want to appear prejudiced. Against non-smokers. However, if the BO'BWH deferred the mandatory signature -- announcing the death knell for smoking -- to the incumbent GWBWH, then he himself would be looked upon as indecisive.

A compromise was reached at the urging of the incumbent who was already so unpopular that he daren't sign anything. In these obfuscated circumstances, the President-elect was deputized to sign the declaration which was not supposed to affect his personal agenda too much. In the classic spirit of the don't ask/don't tell policy. But resulted in more-frequent 6-minute excursions to contemplate

the pending agonizing decision. The agony in the (Rose) Garden. With the secret service placed on a temporary holding pattern. Like the Fed Ex planes over Memphis. Any night of the week.

It was dark and early on a nippy New Year's when everyone was making his/her new resolutions anyway. Timing was everything. The president-elect wondered for a moment if the smoking ban could be snuck-in with a consolidation of other new year's resolutions. Then he thought: ... tacky! And he was probably right. No, the New Year resolution to quit smoking forever was not a choice. There was no going back to confession and doing the same thing all over again. As you were used to doing. All your life. For some thirty years. On average.

Suddenly, it had just gone midnight but there was no sight of BO'B.

BO'B. The President-elect ...

Reader: *please, can't you just call him Bob!?*

... had once again excused himself (for another six minutes) to (he said) prepare his text-speech for Congress. In private. Which he would deliver by cell and scan his signature as an Adobe attachment. As the Act of Cessation, inexplicably, would be delayed for six minutes until 00:06:01.

whisshhh ... oo-ooooh ...

The missing 6-minutes.

And none of the *tabagie* was complaining across the nation, puffing away on the outside verandas with the new Year's Eve parties going-on inside the sliding doors – because they were still able to get in another quick one (6-minute-elapsed-time) which they hadn't planned for but was like a welcome visitor. The return of the prodigal son. Or daughter. When everyone would celebrate even more if not temporarily.

Presently, you could tell that the President-elect was returning from a nice relaxing 6-minute 'nap'. Which is how he referred to his absence. But to this day it's unclear if the missus-elect was buying it. Since strangely he forgot his dab of cologne and gargle of Scope from the miniature bottles he was rumored to always have with him.

Even to his secret service detail he tried to cover-up (a characteristic of a closet-smoker) by saying he was only taking an official time-out and wanted to be 'alone'. As he readied himself to tweet 100 senators and 435 members of the House of Representatives. With words that pound on the conscience. In a time of economic crisis. In a nation at risk. Which everyone knew was about to get much worse. As reported in Leonard Cohen's 'Everybody Knows'.

It was now 23:59:00 on New Year's Eve 2008 and the leader of the secret service detachment who looked an awful lot like Kevin Costner wondered where the hell was the President-elect. As did the missus-elect watching cable re-runs – which at this hour were mostly health commercials warning you with so many non-incriminatory caveats of the almost assured probability of death if you tried their product.

Now scheduled to sign the legislation for the A of C to take effect at 00:00:01. As he weighed the pros and cons. Knowing it would probably totally shatter the revelers who were smokers readying for the chorus of Auld Lang's Syne in the comfort of their own homes -- all 45 million of whom earlier had a memorable afternoon smoking up a storm together in the VAB building. And, in fairness, were in danger of being chain-smoked out. When they were sure to fondly regale their smoking capers, again, together. Together Again. [Buck Owens] Many of them for some thirty years. It would be an anticlimax alright.

Yes, a decision had to be made.

It was a dark and stormy night ... oops.

Wrong foolscap page. Where's my draft from this afternoon? Just a tic. Got it here somewhere. *da-da-da ... dum-dum-dum-dum ...*

hmmm ... Wonder where the missus is. 'My' missus, that is!? Usually on the desktop in the other room. aha! Found it ...

MEANTIME: Factoids on Reality-vote New Year's eve/New Year's morning

Factoids on Reality-vote	Timeline
NATIONWIDE:	
• 45 million smokers and 43 million non-smokers glue-in to Dichter 17 on Late Yo	23:35:00
• Unexpectedly 127 million non-smokers cut short NY Eve partying and return home	23:57:00
• Two-minute warning for Reality-Vote	23:58:00
• New Year's Eve. Final tally of Reality-Vote, scheduled for:	23:59:59
MANHATTAN:	
• NY's Eve Midnight Mass commences on NY's Day – smokers praying for miracle:	00:00:00
WASHINGTON DC:	
• A of C scheduled to be declared by BO'B, president-elect (i.e. pending majority vote for the ban)	00:00:01
• Inexplicable 6-min delay. BO'B reviews Reality-Vote 79/21 result:	00:06:00
• President-elect declares A of C by Twitter:	00:06:01

If you did the math, 45-million adult-smokers were practically certain to vote against the ban out of an adult population of some 215 million (whom, in fairness, weren't all adults because only 130 million voted in the presidential election).

Assuming only 43-million non-smokers (one-quarter of all non-smokers), tops, watched the Late Yo - it would be a victory for the die-hards. The trick was to somehow distract the balance of 170-million non-smokers from watching TV – for just 25-minutes of the Dichter 17 performance (23:35:00 – 00:00:00). Naturally, this had all the elements of a stupid suggestion because giving up a half-hour TV viewing-time was too much of a sacrifice to ask anyone. Even for your country. Ask what you can do for your country. And anyway, there wasn't much time. And timing was everything.

As luck would have it, it transpired that 127-million non-smokers were predictably partying in the early evening of New Year's Eve and had forgotten about their remotes for a change. Everything seemed too good to be true. According to the pundits that would leave exactly 43-million non-smoking TV-addicts competing with 45-million smokers for the vote. And, the nays were bound to have it! People, just thinking about it, were dancing in the streets. And total strangers were kissing each other on the lips and nibbling each other's ears of those who didn't wear scarves.

And the people in the streets below/Were dancing 'round and 'round/While guns and swords and uniforms/Were scattered on the ground. [Ed McCurdy]

Watching the old-timers and their nostalgic tales of the seventeen rules of the Happy Smoker on the night of the reality vote – was enough to make a grown-man crave for a cigarette. During the presumptively senseless commercial breaks for big T(obacco), all you could hear in 45 million households was: Gotta light? With living rooms engulfed in fog. The fog was nothing short of what you'd see in the Christ Church area of east London when Jack the Ripper was on the prowl over a century earlier and nothing much had changed.

But the celebrating was short-lived. ₚᵤₙ.

It was military time.

And coming-up to the 2-minute warning at 23:58:00.

No one could possibly have imagined what happened next. The 127-million non-smokers had changed their minds and curtailed their partying. Maybe there weren't enough designated drivers to go around? That we'll never know. For sure. Aye. But the eyewitness news reports stated they had left their partying early to tune-in to the Late Yo for no other reason than who they were. The types of people with the personality of a non-smoker. A spoiler.

Who just loved to jump-in and give away the punchline of your new joke just before you got to it, when you were regaling everyone at a cocktail party. Who weren't spoilers necessarily out-of-spite. It's just the innate character of a non-smoker who's never happy if someone else is. The schadenfreude factor. It is what non-smokers do. Sure, they had no interest in David Minuteman or the Late Yo. Actually, they didn't like the gap in his teeth when he smiled and put it down to tooth decay from smoking, albeit cigars. And they despised the Dichter-17 because they represented the happy smoker who always appeared to be smiling with a happy face. And non-smokers always appeared to be angry about something. And smokers genuinely felt sorry for non-smokers and put it down to genes. The genetic character. That got their blood boiling. As soon as they smelled the draperies. The first thing they always did when they visited the neighbors. Who never invited them back. And good riddance. To bad rubbish.

And now – didn't they do it again. The non-smokers. 127 million of them. Surpassing themselves this time. Just for the hell of it. Who arrived home at exactly 23:57:00. And flicked-on their tubes at exactly 23:58:00. Which couldn't've been worse timing.

Lo and behold. Just when you thought it was safe to go back in the water:

... der-dum, der-dum, dum-dum, dum-dum, dum-dum, der-dum, dum-dum.

oops! Wrong chapter. Let's start again.

Just as they thought they had had seen everything through a cloud of smoke, or through a glass darkly [1 Corinthians 13:12], the remaining god-knows how many millions of non-smoking party-poopers had suddenly appeared in their homes out of nowhere. Like so many Mandrakes from Xanadu. They had confoundingly realized their addiction to the tube in the nick of time. Astonishingly, all 127 million had collectively cut short their carousing before the ball dropped and joined the 43 million stay-at-home non-smokers & stay-at-home moms who were already watching the Late Yo with David Minuteman and enjoying their draperies in the comfort of their own homes. Predictably, all-together, they clicked their remotes at exactly 23:59:50 for the Reality-Vote, moments after the last of the Dichter 17 uttered his comment that a vacant mind (an insinuation of the typical non-smoker) was the devil's playground. An impugnment that no honest non-smoker could accept.

Psyched-up for the final tally at 23:59:59 - exactly 9 seconds later by cyber text. It took less than a New York Minute for the final vote: 170-million ayes for the outright ban: 45-million nays. Life would never be the same again. For one fifth of the adult population.

whisshhh ....

oo-oooooh ...

It was all too much too soon. While H.L. (Hell) Menchan responded: Hell no, not much!

The good news for the ratings was that the Late Yo with David Minuteman had usually averaged only 4-million viewers per week, so it was quite a record to have a Nielson audience of 215 million on one night. One Night with You/You make-a My Dreams Come True. [Elvis] 170 million non-smokers clenching their remotes in case one of their brat kids would change the channel to Disney. To spoil the fun. When the Joaquin (sic) was up.

Flashback to the Rose Garden in DC.

The President-elect's announcement from DC to the nation at risk was scheduled for 00:00:01 but for some inexplicable reason wouldn't be tweeted until 00:06:01. Better late than sorry. Never having to say you're sorry. Which they were. Afterwards. At least a goodly lot of them. One fifth of the population to be precise. 45-million adult-smokers who would become incremental x-smokers following the 6-minute delayed-reaction. Coincidentally, the elapsed time to smoke one cigarette? And there was no time for a sanctifying grace period in the cellular (sic) circumstances.

Contiguously, between 00:00:01 and 00:06:01 (6-minutes) the midnight Mass back at St. Patrick's Cathedral in Manhattan had escalated to the first two lines of the Responsorial Psalm 67:2-3,5,6,8 (2a) between the First and the Second Reading:

"May God have pity on us and bless us;

May he let his face shine upon us."

YES, at exactly 00:06:01 --- EVERYONE KNEW!

While the drunk in the Midnight choir sang:

> Everybody knows the war is over
>
> Everybody knows the good guys lost
>
> Everybody knows the fight was fixed
>
> That's how it goes
>
> Everybody knows   [Leonard Cohen]

Yes, it was too little too late!

You see, they had started praying for a reprieve of the A of C at 00:00:00. And, as if by an act of God at 00:00:01, the scheduled time, the enactment of the A of C had not happened – providing hope, faith and some clarity. Especially hope. With everyone on tenterhooks fumbling with their rosary beads

THEN, by 00:06:01 it was insanity as they stared speechlessly at their smartphones on mute for their last drag, standing at the back in the no-smoking cathedral which was only burning incense!

whisshhh .... oo-oooooh ...

Twittering the doomsday announcement had a better chance of being received electronically than in person across the nation at risk because of the holidays. Unless they turned-off their cells if they weren't with their missuses. Where they should've been. Or, experiencing dropouts depending on the quality of service, the reputation of the carrier and the accessibility of the location.

The clock had been ticking away for what seemed like 6 minutes before BO'B had arrived back at 00:05:59 promptly at the Oval Office desk where he had left his BlackBerry. Which he had convinced the nation he needed in spite of security issues. And became a global headliner: "Battle over. BO'B gets his Blackberry". Since he didn't want to be disturbed during his contemplation on issues that had the nation-at-risk in fits. He had already researched the legality of electronic signatures from the accredited report in his inner pocket: A Look at Electronic Signature Laws and Legal Standards: Issues and Options [Presentation at the Asia Foundation, August 18, 2000, Donna N. Lambert, Esq.] And he was now quite an expert on the matter.

With his thumbs tapping the keyboard at about eight taps per second. The Capital S alone required six taps – one tap to activate the shift key, then four on the number 7 key, then a tap to the shift key to return to lower case. All of which he seemed to take in his stride, not even looking at the keyboard most of the time. As he ambivalently twittered the following tweet:

A of C approved. Please alert nation. Signed BO'B.

[41 characters]

Then he made an unprecedented second tweet (which reminded you of the mechanical tweety boids earlier on 42nd Street in Manhattan prior to the Manhattan Prologue) to assure the nation:

Whereas ... the incumbent President deserves
sole credit for all the prefatory work in deep sixing

the Big 6. And forcing 45 million souls to quit cold turkey. So help me God. [143 characters]

It was a classic maneuver, but he was three characters over the limit and could've resulted in a national impasse. But, what the hell. His last word was -God- so Biz Stone, Twitter co-founder, agreed to just let it be. Let it be, let it be, let it be, let it be. [The Beatles]

It was now the aftermath. People just stood around looking at each other. Like after a fire destroyed their home or someone drowned. And not being able to do anything about it. Indeed, it was a forsaken attempt by the President-elect at appeasing the minority of (now) former smokers. Of which he was one. A minority. And a smoker.

Well, as moments earlier - pending the possibility that he was an emerging *k*loset-smoker who would be able to write books with words that pound on the conscience! So, there may be at least two of us – capable of re-writing great literature after the demise of smoking as we knew it. As you like it. [WS] According to the scuttle-butt but no one was talking. The ban had that effect on them. They were speechless.

Instant cessation being the antithesis of instant gratification on which the nation thrived – was not going to be a simple implementation. The AT-kops albeit on full-alert were still green and had to come up to speed. Had he (BO'B) made the right decision for the times? He thought about that. People would be biting their fingernails in public whenever the supply of #2 pencils ran out.

And it wouldn't look good to the Chinese who were now watching everything. With more than a vested interest. And any appearance of lack-of-confidence at our end would be countered with a strategy like the Queen's Gambit in chess.

Yes, this whole thing would really need to be re-addressed on January 20 when BO'B would have real powers. After all, giving up smoking for centuries had proved not only an unrealistic stimulus but beyond reason. In spite of the plethora of false problems deviously implied from smoking cessation programs.

whisshhh ... oo-ooooh ...

In the meantime, in the process (of getting full credit for the smoking ban from the second tweet by the President-elect) the incumbent president became:

THE MOST HATED MAN IN AMERICA.

Evoking images of another incumbent president, Herbert Hoover in 1933 during a similar transition period with Franklin D. Roosevelt who won the title first. Hoover. Long before it became a PEOPLE magazine cover - of the most hated men (and later, women were added, in fairness and propensity) in America. Until outdone by Martin Shkreli otherwise known as Pharma Bro.

The transition strategy of passing-the-buck, oops ... the baton, was brilliant if not political which would've been an oxymoron. But not original. Because Hoover was the first incumbent president to be hated most.

The immediate outcome of the strategy was that the President-elect was respected as decisive while the incumbent was perceived as a rat for taking away people's choices. As Jimmy Cagney would've said in the circumstances: Ya dirty rat! While smoking up a storm.

Most of the senators and congress men-and-women were still up. Grappling with the New Year's Eve dilemma. Especially those from the six southern states with their great tobacco plantations.

Which were already in foreclosure since the deep-sixing of the Big 6. Where practically 100% of the population were smoking from the cradle. As you detected from the first sounds they made:

... koff-koff ...

In his defense, the President-elect being a freshman president, hadn't yet learned the intricacies of executive power. He had wrongly assumed that within a few short weeks (January 20) - having inherited veto powers from his predecessor, he could change *his* mind on his New Year's Day decision which made the A of C law at 00:06:01. Since it would've been within 30-days. Like returning goods at Wal-Mart with the original receipt. For a decision made in the hoopla of the moment when he wasn't yet a real president. In spite of deferring the proclamation of the decision – in good faith – to the incumbent-president. Like any good-citizen's rights upon realizing she made a bad-choice. And brought the toaster-oven in its original carton and without any crispy-crumbs on the removable tray in good working condition back to Wal-Mart for a full refund. Even though it was made in China. As he contemplated all of this. During yet another 6-minute time-out in the Rose Garden.

Upon thinking about it too much, however, he realized that changing his mind could be fatal at the risk of self-incrimination not to mention the notoriety that comes with taking the 5th. While a 5th of the population had been downing fifths - straight from the naggan, in dire anticipation. And reluctant resignation.

And there was always the issue of impeachment which was really ironic. Because how could you impeach a president who wasn't yet a real president until January 20? It was a *K*atch-21 alright but there was no getting away from the rumors that the President-elect was a *k*loset-smoker. And a good one at that! And, what-if the rumors were true after the A of C had become law by his own hand! It was a question for the history bluffs (sic). As he was making the oath to Chief Justice John Roberts with the missus-elect within earshot who wondered: If that wasn't his smoke on his new suit last night, then whose was it, huh ...! *hmmm ... grrrr!*

The chief justice himself was taken off-guard and inexplicably stumbled over the 35-word constitutionally prescribed oath of office.

THE MORNING AFTER, OR THE NIGHT BEFORE – THAT was the question?

There just *had* to be a morning after. However, what later baffled the historians following the A of C announcement on New Year's morning, when the post-T era had commenced, was the arrival by truckload of the early edition of USA Today *late the night before* on New Year's Eve. Because 'tonight's' delivery was 'tomorrow's' USA Today that was rushed to press. And already hitting the streets at exactly 23:57:00 on New Year's vigil. Coincidentally, this was the exact moment that the 127 million non-smokers had unexpectedly arrive home!

With the headline:

USA TODAY, NEW YEAR'S VIGIL EARLY EDITION

READ ALL ABOUT IT

RATIFICATION OF THE ACT OF CESSATION

With the headline addressed *by* USA Today *to* the USA, today, to the nation and much of the known world - that BO'B had twittered the A of C into law. That Bob (sic) hath spoken.

WAIT UP!

Hold onto your Lucifer matches! Something didn't sound right.

My memory is still a bit foggy after eight years in the underground.

whisshhh … oo-ooooh …

But, in retrospect I remembered that although the **popular-vote** had been tallied at 21:06:00, the **reality-vote** tally wasn't scheduled until exactly 23:59:59. It was a double tally. And, incidentally, although the President-elect had been scheduled to sign the A of C at 00:00:01 on New Year's morning (when everyone would be making their new year's resolutions anyway) – for some inexplicable reason he didn't do so until 00:06:01. Time-stamped on his BlackBerry. (Incidentally, BO'B knew there'd be trouble about that darn BlackBerry!) Subsequently, the A of C enactment occurred on New Year's Day.

So – how did USA Today know today about tomorrow, tonight? On New Year's Eve?

Reader: *Please. Can you repeat that slowly?.*

Okay. Get on your marks, get set …

[Sentence about to be repeated:]

One more time:

It's really quite elementary my dear reader: How did USA Today know *today* about the impact upon the paranoid nation *tomorrow* (while it was still) *tonight* (in the still of the night)? Prior to the timestamp. Or (about what was to be announced) early on the following morning? So early in the morning/So early in the morning/

So early in the morning/Before the break of day. [The Clancy Brothers]
There was more to this than 'Dewey Defeats Truman'!

Got it! Good. Let's move along.

Please move along, sir!

Ok.

Wait! Unless, all along the A of C had been a foregone cessation
and the Reality Vote was a hoax! And somebody knew about it. A
deep throat kind of person.

Who always put his foot in his mouth?

Like ...? Of course. The ... incumbent president!

GWB!

Ohmegad! Conspiracy!

That the smoking ban was a foregone cessation!!! That the
Dichter 17 appearance and performance on the Late Yo with David
Minuteman was a sham.

Nothing less than fake news! Everyone loves a conspiracy!

Everything was leading in the same direction. Like a double-decker bus without a driver on the upper deck. With the buses (sic) loaded. And the odds stacked. Or a publican with no beer. In a packed pub. Frankly, it was scary. Curiously, many had arrived early for a quick confession before midnight Mass. What did they know? Before making their New Year's resolutions. Which they knew they'd break by the Feast of the Epiphany. If they lasted that long. Most of them. Except there'd be no choice this time round with the A of C. For the hopeless. Those who had no hope. You could bet your bottom dollar on that. Which was worthless.

Yet - another conspiracy!

And that's exactly what Oliver Stone told me the last time we met.

Yes, the revelers at New Year's Eve parties nationwide seemed to be in a tizzy. Whether they were smokers or non-smokers. Which was understandable in the dire circumstances. Yet most of them seemed to be reasonably enjoying their final smokes and group therapy if not camaraderie together. Still, the question on everyone's mind was: But will you love me tomorrow? [The Shirelles]

It was a fair enough question in a nation that was imminently even more at risk.

Still, Tina Turner who had enjoyed her share of smokes was heard to add: Hey, what's love got to do with it? And she was probably right. Or wrong. Since it was a personal choice.

*He had just lit another cigarette within the allotted timeframe that would not nec-essarily condemn him as a chain-smoker and was getting ready to inhale. When, from behind the only physical obstruction on the entire parking lot, a 33/11KV unmanned outdoor power substation to be precise, he could (barely) make out a familiar image some fifty feet away. Truly it was ... she. His wife! Putting it mildly he was discombobulated. In all their years of marriage she had never seen him smoke and had no idea that he was (probably) the last closet-smoker on earth who wrote words that pound on the conscience. Now they both realized why they had never kissed in 30 years in spite of producing two wonderful kids together. But how had she found him? Slowly, seductively, she came closer with his lit cigarette still clenched between his upper and lower teeth. Ironically, she asked if she might share his cigarette! The romanticism of it all. The exoticness. Then, after hardly another moment, the third in so many seconds, from the other side of the 33/11KV unmanned outdoor power sub-station, the first of **them** showed his head. Things would never be the same again.*

 Ten

Rendezvous in the lot

{Publisher's insert:

Before you commence reading this shorter than usual chapter (thank God for that), I should offer a cautionary note to prepare you for the rather abrupt ending. Quite frankly, the protagonist just ran out of breath. Now it was finally ... over. The confession. The deception. The words that pound on the conscience in an effort to revive literature as we knew it. A commendable effort. But, as frequently happens, it was too much too late. It was all over now baby blue. tsk, tsk.}

FLASHBACK!

It was a cold and dismal afternoon in the parking lot and you needed your wits about you to keep warm. Collar up. At the risk of looking sinister. If someone were looking.

Still, I was prepared to get some really good WIP done, barring an unsolicited interruption. Which happens. Suddenly, with a staggering jolt I saw the most terrifying sight of my life – *my wife*! Not that the sight of my wife was terrifying (she's really a sweetheart if I get to know her) but the terrifying implications were.

I had just lit another cigarette within the allotted timeframe that would not condemn you as a chain-smoker. And was getting ready to inhale. When, from out of the blue, it just didn't seem right, something was happening …

der-dum, der-dum, dum-dum, dum-dum, dum-dum, der-dum, dum-dum …
whoom-ba whoom-ba whoom-ba.

… from behind the only physical obstruction on the entire lot. A 33/11KV unmanned outdoor power substation to be precise. Or at least an electric utility closet, or something like that, adjacent to one of the lampposts.

The 33/11KV unmanned outdoor power substation is hidden to left of pic for forensics purposes

Enmeshed with wire fences, I guess, to keep dogs away, since water and electricity don't mix. Which looked more like a mess of heavy-duty wires. A mess of blues. [Elvis] Enveloping a pedestal but not connected to the overhead network where the utility line cables climbed to the highest peaks of Muhlbach am Hochkonig, near Salzburg. At least, in my imagination, as far as I could make out.

Whereupon, I could (barely) make out a familiar face now rising from behind the electric utility closet some fifty feet away.

hmmmm ...

Ultimately, I saw her face, and was now a believer/Not a trace of doubt in my mind. [Monkees] Truly it was she.

> *A reader (obviously totally discombobulated):*   *Who?*

My wife!

> *Same reader (hardly recuperating, yet ...):*   *hmmmm ...*

What's she doin' here?

> *Ditto reader (I guess ...?)*   *You talkin' ta me?*

Quickly I gathered my wits and hid my wip as my wif (sic) approached.

We hadn't seen each other at breakfast which was not unusual. Then again, when *was* the last time I saw her? The last time ever I saw her face. [Roberta Flack] But, I thought to myself, this was different. Obviously, she must've been trailing me as I left the office for flextime 'lunch' (which is what I told my assistant I was doing, which I always do). Now I realized from elementary schooldays the consequence of the what/when/where/why of life with the umlaut on why.

whew!!

But why ... stalking me?

My wife. And why this particular afternoon after all of those mutual years of laissez faire? Why hadn't I seen her car behind me, as cautious as I've always been en route to my DIVINE MILIEU. On the lookout for the AT kops. But I must've been getting lax in my obsession to complete my confessions with my publisher's deadline who cared less. Obviously, she now could see what I was up to.

    whisshhh ... oo-ooooh ...

No, she didn't yell. She was the silent type. You know the kind of woman. She's my kind of girl. [Sinatra] Slowly, dare I say seductively, she came closer to me with my just-lit cigarette still clenched between my teeth with my lips in a *whisshhh* (inhale) posture. Like the camera-ready grin of Wilson the gunslinger in Shane.

Too fast for me to simultaneously expel the ciggie, gargle a mouthful of pocket-sized Scope and dab a telltale smack of male eau perfume.

We didn't speak because words weren't necessary. There was no need to know. At that moment we just knew. Now she spoketh.

Ironically, she asked if she might share my cigarette! That was it. *That's it?* sez I. Which, for as long as I could recall was the most personal thing she ever said. To me. At least – articulated, openly. Now in the wide-open parking lot. It was my last cigarette and I thought about it for an instant. About it being my last. Like being marooned on an ocean island. Islands in the stream/That is what we are/No one in-between/How can we be wrong. [Kenny Rogers and Dolly Parton] And sharing your last cigarette with another survivor. If the darn matches weren't wet. Or, in a desert oasis, sharing your last foam cupful of Starbust with a homeless Bedouin. (Considering the manufacturing process for polystyrene foam which releases harmful hydrocarbons, which combine with nitrogen oxides in the presence of sunlight and form a dangerous air pollutant at ground level called tropospheric ozone, which is associated with health effects such as wheezing, shortness of breath, nausea, asthma, and bronchitis).

The romanticism of it all. The exoticness.

So, hesitantly I agreed. Although we both must've known that smoking was bad for our health.

Still mind boggled. Trying to figure-out what was happening. And why. Why me, Lord, what did I ever do? {KK} But gradually coming down to the earth beneath my feet. I felt the earth move under my feet. [Carole King] For yet another moment which seemed like an eternity in an unknown, unfathomable, undiscovered place where time is still, I realized the deception, truths and half-lies. And the constant fear of detection that I had avoided most of my adult life. And especially now eight years into the post-T era.

And what would Heisenberg think! About being *k*aught with the evidence (as it were) - blowing in the eco.

Because, technically, now that I had been *seen* smoking, I was no longer the *k*loset-smoker who writes with words that pound on the conscience. In a nation at risk.

She smiled politely if not tenderly. And even lovingly. But not yet passionately because there was more coming. Like in one of those silent movies when there's always fog in the background and some twist near the end. Written on the screen with the sound of a piano playing requiem music. With the smoke wafting in the breeze.

whisshhh ... ... oo-oooooh ...

As if freed from some awful, lifelong, life-threatening secret that she held dearly to her heart, but which had destroyed her ability to communicate on a personal level. Like me. With her. Or she. With me. With anyone.

Were we two of a kind? Like peas in a pod.

Together … again? [Buck Owens]

No, something was telling me that things could never be the same again. As, even more suddenly, I began to cough for perhaps the first, or certainly infrequent, time in my life …

koffkoff …

Best bet? It had the makings of an American tragedy. They might even make a movie out of it. Out of my confessions.

(Publisher take note. Local papers please copy)

I tried not to think about that too much. Because of Heisenberg. A gender-neutral Heisenberg. Like, Madame H. Or Mrs. H. Or Ms H. You know what I'm trying to get at. That, if she, my wife … were. Or had-been … Dare I think it …

… a female k-smoker

… the last female smoker on earth

That there were at least two of us. Two of a kind. Worse … now, she too, had been observed sharing a ciggie. Observed, albeit, only by me … Butt (sic) rules were rules. And, isn't that what the Uncertainty Principle [Heisenberg] was? Just that. There was no going-back on science …

Still …? hmmm … No! I banished the thought.

And then, after hardly another moment, the third in so many seconds, from the other side of the 33/11KV unmanned outdoor power substation, I saw the first of them show his head (whom, extraordinarily looked like me!).

OMG! Oh no! Not! Not today.

Me and my wife. Me and my shadow. Me and the missus.

Ultimately being ... honest ... in the deception. The honesty of the deception.

The deceptiveness of the ... mission.

To write with words that pound on the conscience.

The creativity that only came with nico. With tobacco.

To return great lit to a world begging from its absence ever since the A of C 8 years earlier.

In the distance ... now getting closer.

A wayward AT kop? Huh. Hardly surprising. I guess. At long last. What I had dreaded for eight years was now an ... anticlimax. When your time is ... up.

Or ... wait a moment!

Good God! Another thought!

Of course! Is it possible that they were ... together?!

My wife... *accompanied* by the ... AT-kop!

I tried not to think about that too much. Either.

I trusted her. She needed me. [Anne Murray]

whisshhh ...

Falling on my knees as if in the classic act of proposing. But, rather in the act of succumbing. Thinking all of this. Feverishly writing with my right hand these final handwritten notes on my yellow legal-size foolscap, resting now on the tarmac instead of on my trunk bureau. My left hand loosening the butt still clenched between my teeth.

And as I exhaled ... koffkoff ...

... oo-oooooh ....

koff ... ... ko ... kkkkkkkkkkkk ... kkkkk ... k-   *...*

{Publisher's inserts

These confessions end abruptly here!

The handwritten afternoon draft never got to the cleaners. I mean – for clean-up, edit/refresh on his laptop in his study. *hmmm ...* Next door to his wife who was always working online on her ... 'shopping-list'. But was it her shopping-list? Or, was she composing her own words that pound upon the conscience, too? That's what he began to wonder. And how do I know all about this? All about Eve? Huh? Ahh --- soon you will know. Everything was so clear now. Clear as a foggy day on top of the Ox Mountains. Have a good day. Oh – wait! No, the story ain't over yet ...! There cannot be a good confession without absolution.}

Background to the epilogue:

Combing through the draft of his most recent WIP, his **publisher** – shortly to be introduced as the '**narrator**' - had been developing a convivial, if not a pseudo relationship with him (in spite of his pseudonym). True, the affiliation was from a distance, yet it was conspicuously (pardon the pun) forged with an intimate knowledge of his confessions - not to mention his powerful use of cliché. Having been a somewhat off-beat, on-the-beat reporter in his formative years, the former snoop knew well how to handle stealth.

Now, overcome with curiosity, and through a forensic analysis of the clues in the *divine milieu* chapter of his manuscript, he (his publisher) was astute enough to track his budding writer to his favorite parking lot. Nevertheless, he had kept a safe distance for fear of association. (This would've been no mean feat in *any* wide-open space. It took a fair degree of ingenuity and covertness for which he credited his undercover stalking days as a young and impressionable reporter. Of the likes or dislikes of Bob Woodward meeting Deep Throat in underground car parks – of all godforsaken places in lieu of his confessions).

Because, as ambivalent as he was to such a peculiar, if not an outright precarious secondary-avocation – he (his publisher) realized that even he couldn't help the poor lad in his final moments. You see, having been discovered by the AT-kops in the art-of-the-puff (as it were) – technically, the protagonist was no longer a closet-smoker (cf: *Heisenberg's Principle of Indeterminacy – undermined)*. It was the end to the means to an end – of the mechanism mastered by the old artificer for his inspirational craft. Indeed, the epilogue could be called: A Portrait of the *k*-smoker in the Parking Lot.

If it were some consolation, he (debatably the last remaining smoker in much of the known world) – had been apprehended by the circling *k*ops in his divine milieu. That much can be said. A place which, good lord, only minutes earlier had been an empty flea market except for himself and his adorable missus in the serendipity of confrontation.

Ah, had they (his observant publisher *and* he himself) only known what was to come to pass! But you just never know. It is what it is. Just saying. Inevitably, he was out in the open, where, with closure, he had succumbed. So be it.

Epilogue

(reported by his publisher who had followed him)

The epilogue is excerpted from a poignant eulogy written for the last (male) smoker on earth by his publisher. His publisher was the only one who knew him well, which, incidentally (and in keeping with the repetition for which he was recognized) was extraordinary considering they had never met.

And, because they had never met - some might even imagine his publisher as the antithesis of, say, a 21st century Doubting Thomas. You see, he had prefaced his tribute with: "Now I'm a believer/Not a trace of doubt in my mind." (giving fair dues to the awe-inspiring if not prophetic words of The Monkees - in the music world's greatest secret that the song was actually written by Neil Diamond).

Publisher's note:

Pardon me dear readers in the ensuing eulogy if I risk upsetting *your* train of thought by *my* bouncing back and forth with *his* thoughts, both before and after his demise. (I don't mean to suggest his articulation of his thoughts *after* his demise but *my* speculation of what he must've been thinking. Admittedly, it does get kind of tricky.) And, for the occasional repetition which is par for any good confession.

Then, after the build-up to his down-fall, the narrative may recede again, as to when and how the encounter took place with his *wife* in the parking lot (which you'll remember was touched-upon in his final chapter).

Believe me, like many legendary champions of erstwhile causes, flashbacks are necessary to paint a complete picture of his last stand before his (final) fall. My objective as an observer is to describe the things that happened like any historian long after the events occurred. After all, I'm not a saint never mind a devoted apostle. Let's just call me a good Samaritan in spite of – as you are about to witness - my weakness in his moment of need.

Fair enough?

Now, as they say, let the eulogy begin.

Narrator

Alas, the poor bugger, the miserable 'ould divil. I knew him well through his confessions. If I had to guess I'd say his real name was something like Horatio. Yorick was too cliché and his pseudonym implausible.

And even if his clichés drove me batty, I must confess that I learned from him. Some of my friends even think I'm beginning to sound like he wrote although I (hardly) (n)ever smoked in my life. But, like osmosis, like sucking-in the CO_xs, SO_xs and NO_xs of the air you breathe - the good and the bad - I'm probably the only person who was capable of getting deep within his mind. Deep within his Throat. The deep throat of a smoker who could inhale and exhale with the best of them. But, significantly, who never did it in mixed company because he was a *k*-smoker, a loner.

And what a mind it was. A beautiful mind.

Yes indeed, Willie Nelson said it better … *he was always on my mind/he was always on my mind.*

Then again, I wouldn't exactly call him 'miserable'. Rather, he was an unfortunate old soul. Old *K*ing Cole was a merry old soul and you probably recalled that he liked to write of kings and … puppets.

~ ~ ~

And now my friends, he had finally succumbed. Some of us (in the editorial department) had seen it coming with each uneventful chapter-draft. It happens. Of course it does.

People moving on.

Passing by.

Passages ... through the lies of life of which we're all responsible at one time or other if we'd only admit accountability, culpability for our own transgressions – many of which have to do with intolerance of our fellowman or woman. Yet, his 'lies' were more of an obsessive compulsive-disorder within the whims of the post-T era.

Ah, passages. Or passengers aboard ships passing in the night. To exotic destinations. Between the devil and the deep blue sea.

Or, *at a railway crossing where one train may hide another.*

But for him there was no light at the end of the tunnel. For godsakes - not even a Lucifer match.

~ ~ ~

Let's step back for a moment and see if I can retrace his final movements, his closing moments, the last chapter as it were.

He bore a frightening resemblance to Donald Sutherland – the face of the AT kop at the moment of discovery, pointing at him. Perhaps, as some have surmised over the years since, as his doppelganger? Like in the remake of the classic: 'Invasion of the Body Snatchers', if you looked close up at his remains on the terrain of the wide open scene provocateur (the parking lot), the first *AT*-kop to arrive, unrelentingly pointing his finger at him and perhaps not knowing what else to do.

"Stop pointing your finger at me", were some of his last prophetic words – the words of an iconic bulwark of personal choice. While the rather aloof-looking kop just happened to be in the wrong place at the wrong time and couldn't believe his luck.

~ ~ ~

Be that as it may, looking over the events that had just transpired – as mind-boggling as they were for such a mind - there was no way that he could've known that his wife too had been a *k*-smoker for all of her adult life. You can imagine his shock, his surprise. And yet – in an uncanny way – his pride, that they were two peas in a virtual pod. Kind-of like – if you were a soldier and had seen death, the ravages of war. And, had discouraged your son from following a similar career. But, he did. Then, yes, you were proud.

And where was she now? Again, as Joseph Heller once said: "Where are the Snowdens of yesteryear?" She had disappeared into thin air. Which, had it been Manhattan, would've been par for the ozone.

Maybe *they* hadn't even seen her?

Have you seen her/Tell me, have you seen her'/ Have you seen her/Baby, have you seen her' [Chi-lites]

That was ridiculous (he might've corrected himself in the nick of time that was flashing by recklessly), for surely they had. Rather, they probably considered her simply collateral and hardly worth the effort. The damage that was done. Or, that she was just one helluva woman? It was more likely that they were just not aware that there had been any *she k*-smokers left (had they only known!) because they didn't fit the mold, the signature. The quickening ink. And, she had just upped and away. Jumped ship. Or, just walked on by like on a catwalk when you watched goggle-eyed but daren't intrude or butt-in on an arcade extravaganza. As Jim Reeves said: 'Just walk on by, wait on the corner/I love you but we're strangers when we meet.' After all, it was hard to associate a woman with anything obnoxious, repulsive. The femininity of it all.

The fact was that somehow, she had eluded them because the AT kops (whom by now had arrived in a Pied Piper ensemble) only seemed to focus their interest on him. And that was fitting. In a way he must've felt justified.

Maybe she hadn't realized that he had been hurt emotionally, spiritually and intellectually – and now, psychosomatically - or surely, she wouldn't have left him like a lamb to the wolves.

At least I assume he'd hoped so. That such had been the case.

Or, that her passing was a temporary thing and she had intended visiting him at the *Mid X* much later on - assuming there were calling hours? Indeed, had there been such a place? Or, that she had simply returned to her car to retrieve an Uzi or an AK-47 and do a Rambo on the lot of them? Just kidding. That was too farfetched in the wide-open lot because women were known to be a timid bunch. Or, that *she had felt* a natural compulsion for the survival of her species, the perpetuation of her cause, the role-model of the *she k*-smoker.

And then *he must've felt* he'd never really know.

It was all *he-felt/she-felt* sensitivity and nobody daren't touch anybody.

No, you just never know.

~ ~ ~

All he really knew was that it *t*ook *t*wo *t*o *t*angle. He appeared to laugh as he was probably thinking of the quadruple *t* he had improvised, the double alliteration – and, for once *t* had nothing to do with (anti-) tobacco. Wasn't it an 'Ol Lang Syne reflection on the cheerfulness, the effervescence prior to the post-T era? But you could see that it hurt when he laughed so I would guess that he tried to think of something miserable. Which wouldn't have been too difficult. In the circumstances. As they were closing in on him. And soon it would be over after a long run.

Run. Run.

If only he could...

Yes, he had been used to that. A master of evasion. Until now.

The poor lad could no longer stand never mind run.

Suddenly I heard him release a small cough. It was more like an inverted hiccup than a wheeze. I'm sure that's not what bothered him (its amplitude). It was that he had coughed at all – hardly ever having coughed in his entire life. For so he had written. He must've wondered if it might be a tell-tale sign. It was a little bit late in the day to be getting smoker's cough and he was running out of time.

Of course – it came to him. The reason for his cough was because, in the heat of the moment of being confronted in the lot – first by his wife (the good news), and then by the AT-kops (not so good) – he had knocked-over his foam cup of coffee sitting on his trunk.

Because he was always in a standing position in the parking lot in the event of a quick exit, he could never enjoy a smoke without the smooth accompaniment-*cum*-taste of Brazilian coffee beans. Hot or cold. And, he was positive that the combination was responsible for his avoiding smoker's cough, although there were no medical explanations for it that he could find. Indeed, justify. Actually he wondered how, even in the old days, *anyone* could enjoy a cig on its own. Surely smoke inhalation would encounter friction at just about any physiological junction en route to the lungs. Whereas – the simultaneous absorbing of liquid caffeine acted as a 'carrier'. For a ... smooth ride (as it were). Kind of like the Terra Cotta warriors in Xian accompanying the Emperor to the netherworld. Or in Egypt, where the Pharaohs also had their cortege. Or, the Shuttle riding on top of a 747 doggie-style.

Yes, smoking without drinking coffee along with the drag was a sure way of getting smoker's cough. Millions did.

But because he was so scrupulous in following his own rule, *that* is what made him different, a writer. And now, he continued with his last cig in resignation. Although *sans caffeine* - not enjoying it one whit. Further, no longer a *k*-smoker – having been discovered in the act [Heisenberg's Principle] - the thrill was gone. It was a double whammy in the midst of so many surprises (his wife's unexpected appearance, unaccustomed as she was) and disappointments (the AT-kops). No, you couldn't win all of 'em.

Had it really all been catching-up on him? Getting caught? In more ways than one. Gasping for breath, again he tried to think of something less fatal but was interrupted by a stream of coughs in his stream-of-consci*ence*ness. Confused – he put it down to the developing circumstances and the situation-at-hand with his fingers tightly clasping his ... last cig. Custer's last stand. And ... the Native Americans, now, on the casino reservations generating $21 billion annually with 250,000 employees (sovereign-)nationwide, getting their own back after Wounded Knee. And, more power to them.

For slightly less than a moment he even wished it were she who were caught because they'd probably go easier on her (being one helluva woman). And, grappling with his conscience - he'd be able to write more stuff over a few quiet puffs. Then he banished his self-centered thought.

Banished. From the Garden of Eden.

Again, he seemed to laugh at his own pun. The absurdity of life. And again, it surely must've hurt as he cried out to anyone who would listen: "Give me strength." But he no longer desired any renewed stamina. That much I could tell. He had done what he had to do.

I have done.

And now he was done.

"Dung ..." is probably what the born-again non-smokers would've said.

No. They would never understand him. 'Tolerance' was but a noun associated with imbibing capacity. He knew that from his college days. And nights. And the occasional hangover. That is - until he found his conscience in the muse.

And found his missus. The *she k*-smoker. As it might shockingly transpire. Who, now (in the heat of the moment) was nowhere to be seen?

~ ~ ~

He had been so intense in his writing and commendable efforts at subterfuge that it must've been inconceivable to her that any kind of cardiovascular inhibition could affect him. He had always been as strong as a hoss. (sic) That, she surely had assumed.

But, in fairness, she didn't know that he'd been smoking practically every day for well on 30 years (like herself?) - which might've had something to do with it. I guess she didn't know him at all and neither did he. Know her. Although the first years as a closet-smoker were intended not to offend anyone with the obnoxious habit, while the last 8 were crucial to write with words that pound on the conscience. In a mission to return great lit to a nation at risk after the smoking ban.

His tenacity must've been why she had left him in his moment of need, his perceived robustness, durability, intestinal fortitude, endurance, stamina, imperishability – as they were accosted on the parking lot. And now suddenly he didn't appear to be so imperishable. Because, frankly, after 8 terrifying years – the game was up! That simple! And he was a gonner – no longer capable of writing awesome literature because he was no longer a *k*loset-smoker. He had been observed by his missus. On the tarvia. The writing that had kept him active for *so long* was … *So Long* (amigo)! However – as these things are inclined to catch up with you – smokes were not forgiving. So, what use would she be to him and he to her? She had slowly realized that she hardly knew him for 30 some years producing two adorable kids, yet not a kiss between them. And with AT kops all over the place – she'd better scramble. To write her OWN words that pound on the *female* conscience. Which, incidentally, she … couldn't do! Technically! *hmmm* … (pronounced as 'home' by Peter Sellers). Because, now, she was no longer a *k*loset-smoker, either, having shared his last ciggie with her. But, did the AT-kops see her smoking? If not, then only her darling husband (whom she hardly knew) did. And, if he were a gonner anyway, then – debatably there were no living witnesses to her smoking. And, she might be at the odds of the *Heisenberg* **?** *Uncertainty Principle.* Barely. And so, she had to act fast. And, off she went, again – faster than a speeding comma (in literary terms)

, ,,, ,,,,,,,,,, ,,,,,,,,,,,,,,, ,,

Not that we're sure even today that such (i.e. cardiac arrest before his arrest which was posthumous) was his ultimate affliction by the inevitable ultimatum from the AT-kops, pointing their pointers in body language at his doomed corpus. Words were no longer necessary assuming the AT-kops ever spoke.

(There were a helluva lot of assumptions in these final moments if you think about it but not too much.)

The message was clear.

As they say in England: "It was a *good-cop*" – meaning, you deserved to get caught by a smart and alert young AT-kop if you let your guard down. It didn't mean the AT-kop was a *good* cop. Just that he had accomplished something good, rather – was well-accomplished in his official undertaking. That he had *cop'd* (caught) the bad guy.

whew! I'm even starting to confuse myself since I could never hold a cliché like he could.

But, before he expired, the realization that she (his wife) had been a *k*-smoker must certainly have been hard to take as he was taking his last gasp. Because, in other circumstances, *there was no need to know*. But things had changed.

~ ~ ~

To the bitter end he had held no grudge against the AT-kops who were only doing their jobs because, in his innermost mind, he knew they were right. Or wrong. The conundrum of it all. The mystery of life. Of living the lie.

And anyway, there would've been no point in complaining. Nobody listens. Nobody cares. Nobody wins. And, as Dino used to say: *you're nobody 'til somebody loves you.*

He thought about that a lot, squandering much of his available time. Any second now. Minutes maximum – before he would surely succumb. But it was worth it. The time investment. The instant payback.

And, everyone loves a winner. Laugh and the world laughs with you. At you.

Cry and you cry alone. Alone on a wide, wide sea.

He was at rest. On a wide, wide unused parking lot.

But every now and then in those precious final moments … *a little bitty tear let him down/spoiled his act as a clown/he had it made up not to make a frown/but a little bitty tear let him down …*
[Burl Ives]

You see – he and his wife had both been masters of their universe and veterans of deception in their own little words, and virtual alter egos of each other. And now, everything had suddenly become crystal clear for the (second-to-) last *k*-smoker breathing his (second-to-)last. As for his wife's demise, I'm afraid you'll have to read her confessions. Don't worry, you'll be hearing about those. But, right (or wrong), I'm still grappling with copy-right. Because of *her* many unacknowledged references to celebrities and music – which had been a pain-in-the-neck with *his* (although he did provide sources where credit was due).

And yes – you can imagine my reaction when I, [narrator] too, learned

that they were husband and wife. And, had never kissed!

~ ~ ~

Yes, indeed, in my humble opinion, what really seemed to bother him in those quiet, reflective seconds (15 tops in most harrowing circumstances, if you believed Warhol) - was how they, he and his wife, could've been so passionate all those years but never once kissed.

The tell-tale sign of a *k*-smoker, the reciprocal of which each was.

Kiss and tell. *The Kiss* [Gustav Klimt] 'I wonder who's kissing her now?' [Sinatra]

... hmmm ...

'When the Kissing had to Stop. [Constantine Fitzgibbon]

The kiss of death.

But there was little time. Again, he must've been cognizant of the elapsing time by feeling his pulse which was slowing at a remark-able pace.

He had felt sorry for her, indeed for himself, now that it was over – virtually over - before it had hardly begun. I mean, their life together. Their real lives, living the lie(s).

Yes indeed. Sinatra had said, "It's over. And nobody wins."

They had done so much, each in their own inimitable manner and there was no looking back. Over their shoulders. His, anyway. That was no longer necessary. And, a huge sigh of relief.

aahhh ...

Further, he'd never have to worry again about a swift, brisk, brimful-of-energy breeze tumbling over his less-than-half-full foam cup of coffee (cold as it usually was, and which he never minded too much – he got used to it) - atop his trunk-bureau, his contrived writing tablet. It would be knocked down (like him) always at the most inopportune time, in the middle of a thought process. And, having finally found that right word – the word that *cracks open mysteries.* A word that he'd never remember unless he wrote it down quickly. And causing, often, what Ollie Hardy had classically referred to as 'another fine mess' upon his stacked hand-written pages, flying-off in every direction. Every which way but loose. And as soon as he'd catch up on page number 16 of his foolscap, page 39'd be on the other extreme of the parking lot – wafting the crucial word along with it. Blowing in the wind. Blowing smoke.

No, *k*-smoking wasn't for everyone.

There were more than social side-effects.

~ ~ ~

And still, he and his wife – whom (she) liked to write of *queens* and puppets in her confessions, perhaps a queen-smoker, q-smoker, to his ... king-smoker, k-smoker – aha, you are still wondering why his frequent references to 'king' throughout his confessions, the kingpin, the bee's knees - SWAT!

oops. Now I got carried away like he used to ...

sorrie ...

still, darn bugs ...

- had accomplished so little, as a matter of fact hardly anything at all. It was a relative thing. Einstein made that clear. Perception. Deception. But with good intentions.

~ ~ ~

Yes, he was still slumped on the ground, barely moving.

Always so careful, vigilant, cautious (in the self-discipline of being a confirmed closet-smoker), he knew it had been a mistake in accepting her offer (his wife's) – her temptation - to share his (last)

cigarette.

But who could've known it would be their last? Or, was it? Was it *her* last?

It was certainly the last that they would smoke ... together.

The final puff. The final straw. The last hurrah.

Ipso facto. Ipso jure.

True until death (he wished), his whole life flashed before him in somewhat less than a NY minute. Presently his mind wandered to when he took a drag from a brand-name *Eve* (probably ultra-thins and flavorless). That was circa the period when women were putting their stilettos down on men (ouch!). But it (the long, slender *Eve*), had done nothing for him.

He also fondly reminisced upon sharing his last cig with his best friend back in college days. It was during a Friday evening dance and they were dog-tired after a week of soporific classes. He wasn't yet a *k*-smoker or even knew what they were. Sharing that last butt had been a small sacrifice because neither of the two had any more or any left. It was the dregs of a situation as he recalled their dilemma. And, smokes weren't on sale in the dancehall even if the impoverished students could afford a(nother) half-pack (when they were available in 10's back then). To be sure - they needed every penny for the usual pub crawl on Saturday night. The usual suspects. Yes, there was no greater camaraderie than this - that he would lay down his last cig for his friend. He had placed it, lit, on an ordinary, everyday-looking ashtray (when ashtrays had been available in abundance in the grand old days of yore) - on the wall arm-rest (near where the homely-wallflowers congregated, whom neither of them wished to ask to dance anyway in case they'd be seen). And his friend would pick it up in non-verbal communication as they passed it back and forth. Until there was nothing left but a memory that could never be taken from either of them. A precious memory. Although you know the way it is, he soon lost track and never heard from his best friend again. It was an anachronism. And, they were in their late teens at the time – young enough not to even think about health problems associated with smoking when no one knew the difference or cared less. And old enough to anticipate (and to later articulate) the decades of living the lie that lay ahead of … him, at least.

However, soon after college - he began to change when (as they say) he was hit in a dark alley by a spark, a light (which indubitably would trigger a smoke … *aahhh, whishhh*) - the fierce, overwhelming vitality of the muse. When, repeating Elvis who said it better than most: 'You acted strange, you seemed to change/And why I've never known ...' Writing then for a hobby. But now, for 8 years in his impressionable years he had been on a mission to write great literature with the aid of nicotine to bring lit back to mankind. He had no choice but to do his own small butt for humanity in giving creative writing back to society with words that pound on the conscience.

~ ~ ~

Looking back on his life, it's still debatable if he were the very first closet-smoker (since going to press the Guinness Book of Records had refused to comment) but he certainly was one of the first if not one of the finest. That much I surmise although I'll never really know.

What I do know is that, since his insouciant, footloose-and-fancy-free college days he had never smoked once in mixed company. Again, for so he wrote in his confessions. And I believe him. As Don Williams said: "I don't believe that heaven waits/For only those who congregate/ ... But I believe in you ..."

~ ~ ~

As much as he loved her deeply, the fact was that he was now literately impotent - as she most probably was too – if *they* had seen *her*. [Heisenberg] Now that her secret was out of the closet, at least with him, her husband. Although it took two to tangle, only one person could maintain the singular integrity of the muse in the closet. Wherever she was. Which was a fair enough question.

Now he was a hopeless case, again, with *no way out*. Like Sean Young (whom, you may remember from chapter 3, was an erstwhile friend of his, the protagonist) in the movie.

In which, ironically, *she* (Sean) was the one who didn't survive. But let's not digress. In the repetitiveness of any good confession, worth its weight in supplication.

No, it was the only thing that he absolutely couldn't do.

Like the absolution he sought.

And yes, he had just done it.

Smoking in front of another - even in front of his own true love.

But, for a *k*-smoker, it was like when you're up against the urinal and ready to go-for-it. And suddenly someone comes into an otherwise empty mensroom and starts to go right beside you. But now – you can't. You just can't do it adjacent to another, no matter how hard you try. And you did. Smoking in front of another. Albeit his missus. But Heisenberg was Heisenberg and he had his principle.

God, did he ever!

Try, that is.

That's what being a *k*-smoker had been. What it had meant to him.

His self-imposed condition (the condition of his contrition), was that he had to smoke privately to write powerfully. The avocation of the *k*-smoker. With the proverbial cig in his left, his coffee on the trunk (sometimes competing with a brollie depending on the weather forecast which was always wrong), and no one within a radius of 5 miles on the radar screen. Yet, somehow, *they,* the front-runners, the spies among them, had caught up with him. It happens.

And now he was totally bereft of inspiration as he just lay there, no longer alone.

Superman fondling a *k*rystal of kryptonite?

Caught in the act. With the tell-tale ashes. With insufficient time for a quick dab of '*K*ool Water for Men' cologne (which unwittingly he had left in his car), without a swig of Scope (ditto), and – with the giveaway butt still hanging between his lips. Lips which had never kissed (nor been kissed by) his adorable wife. Not that it would've done much good with his cologne this time because they had a visual on him. No, he had nothing to lose. It was all over anyway but his cig – and her cig – his and hers - helped him relax.

Life wasn't worth living, not that he would've ever contemplated the alternative (he didn't need to. Lying there. Living the lie. Just barely. But, running out of time. And fast). He was simply … cerebrally emasculated, incapacitated, powerless, helpless … hopeless. As a matter of fact, it was now simply mind over matter. There was no rest for the wicked.

Naturally, the stress had been building up. For so long. *So long.*

Adios, my friend.

Au revoir.

Sayonara.

Fare thee well.

And I guess he just couldn't take it anymore.

Well I guess it doesn't matter anymore. [Buddy Holly]

Later his coroner reported (officially) that the intensity with which he had written – and then, realizing he no longer could - was probably the real cause of his last breath. After all, Robert Browning called death: 'The grand perhaps.' Still, in my lowly opinion I think he would've preferred to be remembered as having simply 'extinguished'.

And even he wasn't aware of his own intensity - mixed with equal-parts of anxiety.

Like we're unaware of the most obvious gifts, the beauty of nature surrounding us. The affluence of our frivolity in the labyrinth of the Gordian Knot. It sounded so simple.

That he would be exposed, ultimately.

And, yes sir, he was.

Was he ever.

A *k*-smoker?

Of course, he was.

~ ~ ~

That's what he was thinking, without his Webster's or thesaurus to help him through it. To help dilute the big words that no one understood. That *they,* the maladroit AT kops (and an obviously curmudgeonly lot), would finally catch up with him (the *they* referred to in the opening passages of his confession), as he had fallen, still with cig in mouth.

But, hadn't he eluded the *Midnight Express?*

(He certainly didn't want to go there or even think about it too much. Time was running out. By now he had used up most of his 15 prime-seconds. Although, in earlier drafts – he seemed to have enjoyed the movie. The thrill of it all. The uncertainty, the ambiguity, the indefiniteness of the outcome. The surprise ending.)

And, that was a good thing – if anything good were to come from of all of this.

The good and the bad.

The grey area between … drags. The dregs. As he inched along the tarvia, wondering why he was crawling along at all with no destination in mind. Instead of just lying there in front of *them*. Living the lie, its finale, culmination. Still puffing away, practically out of breath and feeling terribly self-conscious. Like a naked mannequin in a window of a 5th Avenue department store whom they forgot to dress. Never having smoked once in mixed company since college days. As though all eyes were on him. Which they were.

There was no right or wrong, but it just felt wrong.

~ ~ ~

For a moment he felt better humming the words of one of his favorite French songs (a language he didn't understand) – *Plaisir d'Amours* - which fortunately had been translated into English by Joan Baez. It had been composed by Martini il Tedesco for the French court. And – wasn't 'court' now an apropos word, huh, he thought? But, superfluous in the circumstances. Still, since he was only humming, it didn't make much difference what language the words were in although the folksong, the love song, truly reminded him of his now departed wife. And, as he realized only too well – very soon he would be dearly departed himself.

> ♪   *Plaisir d'amour ne dure qu'un moment*
>
> *Chagrin d'amour dure toute la vi-e-e*
>
> *The joys of love are but a moment long*
>
> *The pain of love endures the whole life long* ♫

He was desperately trying to remember the final verse (had he only access to the web) – and couldn't. But, for the curious among you, here it is:

> *And now she is gone, like a dream that fades into dawn,*
>
> *But the words stay locked in my heart strings, "My love loves me."*

Nonetheless, this is how his humming came out. Considering all that had happened, it was a brave attempt:

> ♪ *hmm um um um, um um um umma um um*
>
> *hmm um um um umma umma, hmm um um um* ♫

~ ~ ~

The joy of love. *The very thought of you.* The haunting melody.

The pleasure of love.

But the pleasure was gone. Closet-smoking was a private thing. The thrill vanished when you were unmasked. Just barely moving his neck, in the distance he could see the AT-reinforcements approaching. He thought he heard the sound of a bugle like in an old cowboy movie but imagined the theme from *JAWS*. Soon all of them would be gawking at him as if in a circus. Which an awful lot of the social climate was - at the peak of the post-T era.

He had started the cig exactly 1-minute before his wife had offered to join him, smoking both together. And, he knew that it takes exactly 6 minutes for one person to smoke a full cigarette. Or, 3 minutes a-piece when shared equally although she had only stayed for a solitary NY minute. That left 4 minutes-worth on-his-own-time. He guesstimated that 3 minutes and 45 seconds had elapsed before the 15-seconds kicked-in – the latter causing his entire life to flash in front of him. He figured that was roughly 13 seconds ago although it seemed like an eternity. And he was now down to about a 2 second warning before the smoke was up. Which (in the intensity-cum-anxiety) was the only thing that had kept him going.

Sadly, and – as if keeping time, the clock was ticking away.

tick tock   *tick tock*

Oh, Death where is thy victory? Oh, grave where is thy sting?

[Corinthians 15: 54-57]

Yes, he thought about St. Paul as he also recalled the penny catechism about how difficult it was for a smoker to get into heaven – if at all. Surely the eye of the needle, the narrow gate that leads to salvation, was very constricted – and few made it. [Matthew 7:14] While the roadway to destruction was very wide. And, thinking really fast, he also felt lacking in the catechistic requirements for remorse - for a good confession.

He began to wonder if perhaps the fact that he was a **writer with a conscience** might earn him the proverbial option of a plenary indulgence in the hereafter – which wealthy people could earn in medieval times, no sweat. And, in the grand scheme of things – about plenary indulgences and other exceptions - hadn't St. Augustine and St. Paul their shortcomings too?

[Publisher's Note:

> Now, you might ask - how do I know all of these intimate details? Of what he was thinking? Things that even his wife (God bless her, wherever she was) didn't know about him. The answer my friends, as I'm sure you realize, is that much of my eulogy is based upon surmise, deep within his mind. Being his sole confidant, I feel privileged if not obligated to attempt a personification of whom, until now, had been a survivor - during those final six minutes.]

~ ~ ~

Momentarily, the answer seemed to come to his supplication for a plenary, or at least a general indulgence – that the very act of being a *kloset* smoker was his salvation! Never once in his life having blown smoke in the faces of grownups or their screaming children in their shambolic living rooms. Always careful to avoid smoke getting on the draperies. Surely that was worth something on judgment day! With faith, hope and (some) clarity. There was no question of his faith and hope while he scoured his conscience for the latter. "Have pity on me", surely, he must've been thinking. Courageously he remembered what Einstein had said: "Man would indeed be in a poor way if he had to be restrained by fear of punishment and hope of reward after death."

But … his greatest affliction in his final moments was that – in spite of his efforts – that surely great literature had ended forever,

Yes, the clock was ticking away.   *tick tock   tick tock*

puff …
puf …
pu …
p …
… *f*

..   .

~ ~ ~

Almost immediately the AT-kop, the first in the group who had exposed him (for what he was worth), had been surrounded by his colleagues who had caught-up as they caught him.

He had been revealed.

They seemed to rejoice in the revelation. Yes, they too were all pointing their fingers harmoniously at the last man smoking on earth (except for Russia, Outer Mongolia and other places with known causes). On the soggy, soggy soil between the cracks on the no longer empty parking lot which had seen better days and nights – rain, hail, sleet and snow.

In one way it was a triumph for the post-T era. In another – even for the AT mercenaries among them, the soldiers of fortune – it was sad if not pathetic. Not only because soon they would be unemployed (it was bad enough not having any cigarette-taxes to cover the basic AT infrastructure and the persnickety contingencies). But you could sense a tingle of compassion as they began to realize that *k*-smokers were really a harmless bunch and more inclined to write letters-to-the-editor with words that pound on the conscience.

Then, after what seemed another eternity yet less than a solitary NY minute, looking down at him, one of the AT-kops (paraphrasing Dr. Seuss) was heard to say:

> *This truly was the son of ... Sam I am.*
> *Who tried to change the word by deleting **k***
> *for the fundamental **c** on which we were raised.*
> *With words that ... pound on the conscience.*
> *Surely the word will never be the same ...*

Ite missa est. [Go and smoke no more]

And it wasn't all about vocabulary, that was just the symptom, not the cure.

And what can be cureth, love/has to be endureth, love ...

~ ~ ~

From the ominous clouds (that he had been used to when he usually forgot his brollie) - a sudden bolt of *light*ning struck the ground. I could feel the earth shake under my feet – although I was keeping a safe distance for reasons that will always torment me. Yes, I could always rationalize the prevailing circumstances. The things over which I had no control.

What could I do? What could I really do? They were everywhere. They had won.

Hadn't they?

And, for godssake – I had never smoked in my life. Well, except possibly when I was footloose and fancy-free – without realizing the health hazards. And too young to care less. But, millions who did, and – who callously did it to others – had died the slow death from the carcinogens. And, good lord, the obnoxious smell on the draperies. Impossible to deodorize even with the best of household concentrators in aerosol spray-cans containing CFCs, which, themselves - unwittingly polluted the air and depleted our life-protecting ozone shield! There was little excuse for that – the smell on the curtains. Yet, in fairness – wasn't **he** just a *k*-smoker? Not one who did it in front of others. Hence his words will always pang my conscience.

And, from the … light of the lightning strike, had he only survived another NY minute - there's no doubt (paraphrasing Molly's
seven *yes's* in her soliloquy at the 4-line close of Ulysses) – that
it would've been yet another stimulus for seven increasingly long
inhales …

whisshhh …

whisshhh …

whisshhh …

ahh, whisshhh …

oh, whisshhh …

whisshhh …

whisshhh …

oo-oooooh …

~ ~ ~

They carted his body down the side-street which was diagonally-
opposite to the one he used to enter the flea market parking lot.
Coincidentally, flags were at half-mast on the telephone poles.

It crossed the railway tracks where one train could hide another.
And, as they passed beneath a huge billboard sign (which he had
never noticed) staring down at them - with the words:

SMOKING KILLS

- one of the AT-kops who never seemed to fit the mold, stooped to genuflect and bowed his head in ambivalence.

Intending to stoop and conquer, he was overcome with emotion.

By winter, a wall – rather a huge fence was placed around the abandoned parking lot so that no other *k*-smoker could drive into it and write with words that pound on the conscience.

Afterword

In concluding my eulogy, the following remarks are mostly specu-lative from what I learned in the penny Catechism about how Heaven works.

Still, I hope you will join with me in the spirit of what he had started because we know how he extinguished. [narrator]

In the Hereafter

A haunting melody from a choir of angels in the hereafter seemed to fill the air which was no longer stagnant with CO_2's, SO_2's and NO_2's:

♪ *On top of 'Ol Smokey*
all covered in glow...♪

Yes, it was true. In the hereafter, original sin – indeed sin-taxes - had become things of the past where there was no past or future, only the presence of mind. And, there were no longer any carcinogens. Or draperies to absorb smoke particles. Or complaints of any kind. Everyone was having a grand old time where even old *K*ing Cole was a merry old soul. For those who wished, they could smoke outside in the great beyond until kingdom come which it had.

Needless to say, non-smokers were allocated to the highest mansions - representing some 21% of the 105 billion departed souls since time began since practically everyone smoked in the old days – *minus* the intolerant. Whom were most of the foregoing in the hereafter, i.e. those who never had any compassion for smokers regardless of the condition of their addiction considering that most smokers were careful of avoiding smelling-up the draperies anyway – or, there'd be hell to pay! Although nobody asked where *they* (the intolerant percent of the smokers) were, it was generally accepted that they were transported to wherever-they-were on some kind of *Midnight Express* vehicle which would've been fair game.

Smokers (generally agreed by actuaries to have been an average of 79% of the global population since time began 14-billion years ago, albeit no sign of Adam then, nor the Nico Man) were given the lower mansions which wasn't bad – except that smoke rises. No, being humbled, he, the protagonist, had no problem with that considering his 30+ years smoking up a storm down below, figuratively speaking. It seemed that there was only one caveat. If and when visiting the higher mansions, it was recommended you refrain from smoking in respect to the Seraphim and Cherubim. But there were no 'no smoking' signs anywhere – which would've been difficult anyway in differentiating the smoke from the clouds from both sides now. It was kind of like the honor system.

It was his first day where there was no such thing as time and presently, he was enjoying a quiet puff (or two) – from smokes that miraculously appeared from cloud puffs just like wine from water in

other circumstances.

The second-hand smoke (which no longer bothered any old soul) wafted along with the small puffs of clouds from which, again, it was barely distinguishable. Never mind, discernable – an oft used adverb in the hereafter - or in homilies down below with such in mind.

He seemed to be unnoticed by the billions of holy souls hopping from cloud to cloud like charged electrons not going anywhere in particular but going neither here nor there. However, as a group of saints came marching by, he floated onto the nearest passing cloud to be alone for a while and finish his quick puff before lights out (just kidding).

He had been a closet-smoker for just too long. This would take some getting used to – smoking in mixed company, in the company of angels. 'City of Angels', he thought to himself, with Nicholas Cage and Meg Ryan, and Sarah McLaughlin's haunting melody. And quietly laughed upon acute realization – as, distractedly, he noticed a cute little angel floating by – too close to touch where there was no touching in this new incorporeal ambience. Not that he really wanted to … touch … he felt (hmmm?) inclined to think. In a place where there was no longer any temptation. Nor, indeed, place-at-all. But he had let out that little chuckle realizing that he was still capable of 'worldly' thoughts in eternity.

He had made a judgment call following the last (most recent) judgment (which he barely survived) and (as he had hoped) - he had narrowly snuck-in when St. Peter wasn't looking. Yes indeed, it was **his conscience that had been his salvation**.

His thoughts.

That pound on the conscience.

Albeit, in fairness, he had paid his fair dues in Purgatory (where there was a helluva lot of smoke but no cigarettes) - like everyone else. Especially the sanctimonious, self-righteous and holier-than-thou born-again non-smokers whom (back home) had driven every one of their peers into mental sanitarians with their never-ending halleluiahs. Even before Leonard Cohen made them popular. Worse, they never stopped pointing their fingers at them. At those with whom they disagreed.

Those were the days, my friend, when it had been legal if not morally-correct to smoke up a storm down below – as the priests, bishops and occasional nun used to do for a break when they were trying to get away from the world. Which, even with their vows of poverty, chastity and obedience was no small accomplishment.

Incidentally, it was easy in the hereafter to differentiate between heavenly-smokers and non-smokers. From a distance you could see that the born-again non-smokers were all strumming on their harps to their hearts content while each of the smokers held a proverbial quill between their pointer and middle finger which they used to write words that locked open mysteries.

Indeed, it was sheer enlightenment. And before he knew it, yo and behold, a passing saint, sporting an attractive halo beneath the undulating light called over to him in thought language:

"Yo, soul-mate - gotta light?"

But he had no earthly idea on how to behold. He was still behaving like a closet-smoker – constantly looking over his shoulder - which was no longer necessary. It would take time (where there was none) and he had lots of that.

You see, he was now in a milieu illuminated and uplifted with an everlasting flame of love and tolerance. For the billions of sinners like himself who had purged their souls after what seemed an eternity in purgatory (in ethereal terms), it was slightly less than a NY minute back home. Warhol, wherever he was (which admittedly was a fair enough question), would've been proud.

It was yet another cliché. Wasn't it all about clichés?

Here, everywhere, were holy souls who had died from smoking or second-hand smoke-related ailments such as: cardiovascular disease, cancer (lung, oral cavity, larynx, esophagus), emphysema, stroke, old age, chronic lower respiratory and obstructive pulmonary disease, bubonic plague, homicide, suicide, smallpox, chicken pox, bad cholesterol, measles and other acute viruses, obsessive compulsive-disorders, and severe bouts of the Beijing flu – the latter, like tuberculosis (and each of the illnesses listed above), having been known to result in a fatal cough if you were a smoker.

Now, in everlasting happiness, they all looked so happy. Yes, he had been truly sorry for *his* sins and was now puffing away 'til kingdom come which it had.

No longer was the 30-years+ (and-then-some) smoker out of breath as he used to be upon ultimately reaching the second floor of his home after climbing up the steep if not crooked stairs more-than-once on a good day. And, thank God, carcinogens were truly a thing of the past. As were the unsightly burn-holes, singes and scorches on fine leather upholstery characteristic of homes down below by those who smoked openly during the reckless days of the pre-T era. More often than not, the latter had a detrimental effect on the resale value if used-home hunters arrived prematurely, or worse, unannounced.

And although it was still his first day in heaven, he felt more and more relaxed as if time were passing by so quickly. Until he realized there was no such thing where he was – no past, no future. It was all in the here-and-now in the present of the hereafter. In the presence of mind. .

And surprisingly, in his meandering mind, somehow, he thought of Eugene O'Neill and Cole Porter, strange bedfellows for such a thought, and the long day's journey into night when night and day were barely discernable. Again, he was aware that 'discern' was a very important word in thinking incorporeal, ethereal and meta-physical thoughts – because the RC church was always discerning one thing from another down below. oops. Didn't mean to give you that impression, not down *that* far! Rather… down on earth! Which was apropos considering where he was now where there was no where and no time. He also laughed when he thought about the times he would nonchalantly say to his missus that he 'had no time' – never realizing he would be in the eponymous place where there was no *place* and there was no *where* and where there was no *time*. His first day was already beginning to feel like at least a week since his arrival. And so, on what he imagined to be the seventh day, he rested even more.

And saw where he was.

Which wasn't anywhere in particular but everywhere in spirit.

And he saw that it was good.

And he felt good.

And when he felt good, he felt very, very good … which was pretty much always, it being in the perpetual present.

That's when, simultaneously (which was relatively easy in the omnipresent) he tried to pinch himself to make sure he wasn't day-dreaming. Until he quickly learned that pinching wasn't possible – now being a holy spirit and all, with different built-in reflex mecha-nisms (he assumed) which he hadn't yet figured out. He was simply feeling too good and knew he was starting to get carried away (with himself) on a passing cloud. But as hard as he tried, and, examining his conscience - he couldn't forget the regretful occasions (during some 30+-years): '… when he was bad, he was horrid.' Fortunately, in-no-time at all (which was easy) he rested assured that those days were bygone. And, anyway, he had never done it in front of another. Smoking up a storm, that is.

Yes indeed, it was very, very good.

The feeling prompted him to recall the admonishment that good parents urged upon their grumbling kids who were trying to grow up too fat (sic): 'The good die young', if the young and restless took up the habit too early.

No, always thinking (in vacant or in pensive mind), he just couldn't get enough of the proverbial cliché. He sported clichés like others around him wore halos.

But more than anything, he knew he had been forgiven as he floated along on a newly formed cloud, thinking thoughts that pound on the conscience.

He had come full circle. Like a smoke ring.

aahhh … whisshhh … oo-oooooh …

A ring of fire.

> *We can only look behind/From where we came*
>
> *And go round and round and round/In the circle game …*

[Joni Mitchell's words that pound on the conscience.]

If there were any consolation for those left behind (down below on earth) who had been accustomed to the shibboleth, 'don't leave home without them', the new slogan for the nationwide launch of the #2 pencil placebo was narrowed to three choices. A new debate had only just begun.

- Hold onto your #2 - lads 'n lasses

446

- Try it, you'll like it
- The #2 pencil can help, try one today

In each option accompanied by the caveat, *'chewing can be damaging to your incisors'.*

Then, as if an after-thought in the afterlife, on a more serious note, ultimately he realized the significance of the word, *king* - that had haunted him throughout his confessions:

"Thus conscience does make cowards of us all ..."

And, having passed the test as to how he had taunted the pundits in securing his eternal redemption,

"... the play's the thing/Wherein I'll catch the conscience of the __king__" [Hamlet]

The Last Smoker on Earth, the novel, would soon become a major motion picture, starring Aaron Eckhart as the protagonist (following his credibility in Thank You for Smoking), and Morgan Freeman as the narrator (following his unworldly performance as God in Bruce Almighty).

Appendix

I. Notes on vocabulary, format, style, and the 'k-factor'

We are all adapting to change following the uneasy transition to the post-T era and the end of literature as we knew it after smoking was outlawed, no ifs, ands or butts about it. And, with it, the new vocabulary when 'c' was replaced by the Kafkaesque '*k*' (which, like Esperanto, hasn't really *k*aught on).

Still, like teaching an old dog new tricks, there's nothing more annoying than the revised spelling of what were once innocuous words. Because of the vintage of his laptop, the protagonist has been fortunate to stay with the original spelling more often than not. For example, cliché in the closet (header of first chapter) prevails instead of *k*liché in the *k*loset which would sound rather silly. Being a master of cliché, he had grappled with *k* in the title but stuck to his confession. Some readers will have difficulty with the occasional inconsistency when the nagging *k* jumps up without warning.

To make the confession more interactive, *Last Smoker* is written in both the first and second person and in the singular and plural even within the same paragraph. And sometimes in the same sentence. And please excuse the couple of times that the past and present tense are contiguous to avoid the cumbersome flashback. The interactive format can also be compared to a dinner-theatre whodunit where you, the reader, are invited to participate in the crime.

'Author' or 'reader' inserts {red brackets} are occasionally deployed. They are intended to assist the reader at times – who is also permitted to ask 'live' questions - when you have no idea what the author means. Or to provide a needed vent when the intensity of his examination of conscience becomes exasperating. Or for a simple time-out (nature-call) when the going gets tough.

One of the first things to realize before you enter the portal is that *k*-smoking (closet-smoking) isn't for everyone. There are risks and social side-effects.

JP (Jack),

written prior to the epilogue in an abandoned parking lot, the author's **DIVINE MILIEU** with no fixed abode.

II. Caveat on Stream of Consciousness

Based upon prior critiques in the public domain this book is not recommended for certain book reviewers, noticeably Ms. Melanie Kirkpatrick (former WSJ editor), who's likely to write: "Not another one of those annoying somebody-did-somebody-wrong stream-of-consciousness books!"

In defense of the protagonist, what do critics want?

As an underground closet-smoker who derives inspiration solely from tobacco and who is subject to permanent incarceration in the legendary and horrifying *Midnight Express* if apprehended, what is the last writer of good literature to do? Frankly, it would put chills up the spine of any smoker (assuming there are other survivors) just thinking about it. Which is why this writer must articulate the meandering consciousness within his turbulent soul. His inner game of tennis as it were (in the immortal words of Timothy Gallway).

These confessions detail one man's vision for the reemergence of fine literature as we knew it – with the adrenalin from smoking - in the hope that you, his readers, might have compassion for words that pound on the conscience.

III. Literary criticism and interior monologue

The author would prefer to quote May Huang, source
https://qwik.com/2014/03/22/10-writers-who-use-stream...

In literary criticism, stream of consciousness, also known as interior monologue, is a literary technique that depicts the multitudinous thoughts and feelings which pass through the mind. The term was coined by psychologist William James (brother of Novelist Emeritus, Henry James) in 1890 in The Principle of Psychology. In 1918 May Sinclair first applied the term stream of consciousness, in a literary context, when discussing Dorothy Richardson's novels. Here is what May Huang wrote in her Ten Writers Who Use Stream of Consciousness Better than Anybody Else:

A narrative technique that has perplexed and fascinated readers for centuries, the stream of consciousness technique has been used by many writers to trace the seamless (and oft erratic) musings of characters such as Mrs. Dalloway and Stephen Dedalus. These 10 writers – although the jury is out on whether they were all smokers - whose works – ranked amongst the finest in English literature – feature the stream of consciousness technique: Dorothy Richardson, William Faulkner, James Joyce, Virginia Woolf, Marcel Proust, Jack Kerouac, José Saramago, Samuel Beckett, Fyodor Dostoevsky*, and Toni Morrison.

*The author's work has been compared to Dostoevsky's Notes from Underground, thank-you-very-much!

Please visit www.abandonedparkinglot.com where much of the action in the confessions takes place.

The Publisher

IV. Dedication

This confession is dedicated to my dearly departed mom and dad who smoked 'til kingdom come and lived to a ripe old age. They taught me everything I needed to know about the glamorous mannerism of the dashing hero of the silver screen - ubiquitous cigarette in right hand and beautiful heroine on his lap.

Thank you, Mom and Dad.

With a peculiar writing style induced by nicotine in a way that Coleridge might've used something else - it was inspired by a research report on the web: Smoking May Help Your Concentration (Columbia University College of Physicians and Surgeons). Incidentally, the study was performed on animals only.

Thank you, Columbia medical and veterinary staff.

I owe a huge debt to Paul Greenberg for his words that pound on the conscience.

Thank you, Paul.

Although my work in progress had been long under way, the coincident timing of the theme was secured when I read that Jason Reitman's movie (of Christopher Buckley's novel), Thank You For Smoking, took top honors at the 11th annual Prism Awards in LA. - as if two great theses converging in competitive scientific journals on independent studies drawing the same conclusion.

Thank you, Jason.

Finally, after listening to the keynote address on the First Amendment by Chief Justice John G. Roberts Jr, during a dedication at a prominent university, any inhibitions in seeking publication were blowing smoke in the wind.

Thank you, Honorable Justice.

V. OTHER CLOSET BOOKS FOR FURTHER READING

CLOSET SMOKING FOR DUMMIES

CONFESSIONS OF ST. AUGUSTINE

CONFESSIONS OF ST. PATRICK

CONFESSIONS OF A PARISH PRIEST

CONFESSION UNPLUGGED

THOMAS AQUINAS SUMMA THEOLOGICA

CONFESSION(S) AND INDULGENCE(S)

I CONFESS

DE PROFUNDIS

THANK YOU FOR SMOKING

MANHATTAN PROLOGUE

THE DIVINE MILIEU

THE WIDE OPEN PARKING LOT

FORBIDDEN PLEASURES

PROMISES, PROMISES

WITHOUT REMORSE

INTERROGATION AND CONFESSION

I'M SORRY, SO SORRY

LIES, CONFESSION AND ABSOLUTION

MORE LIES, CONFESSION AND ABSOLUTION

CONFESSION FOR DUMMIES

CONFESSION AND COUNTER-CONFESSION

INVASION OF THE WEED SNATCHERS

CRIME AND PUNISHMENT

THE MIDNIGHT EXPRESS

WITNESS FOR THE PROSECUTION

THE MOMENT OF TRUTH

VI. GLOSSARY

Handy glossary of terms used in this confession for *a proper examination of conscience*

A	actuary	one who manipulates statistics for the common good or bad.
	Act of Cessation (A of C) ⊛	ratification of post-T era after tobacco was outlawed. Sometimes referred to as The Great American Permanent Smokeout. [GAPS]
	ALA	American Lung Association
	AT-kops & lawmakers	anti-tobacco police and lawmakers.
	Axis of evil	dynamic chart with moveable markers.
B	Big 6	the 6 global tobacco companies prior to the smoking ban.
	Big 3	the 3 largest auto companies which went bust after the political retaliation from Japan. The Japanese delegation had been arm-twisted into complying with the US-sponsored global A of C after a little coaxing from Manhattan Project documents which had been retrieved for the occasion. Some say this is where the Manhattan Prologue got its name
	BO'BWH	White House administration following A of C. (president rumored to be a closet-smoker.)
C	caffeine	powerful adrenalin force. When used along with nicotine, writing creativity peaks. More effective than Delsym syrup for a smooth excursion from the bronchus to the lungs to prevent smoker's-cough (telltale guilt-indicator for the ruthless AT kops).
	classics (literature)	books mostly written by great smokers of a bygone era.
	cliché	as in 'cliché in the closet' (chapter one).
	confession	expression of good intentions in seeking absolution.
	CO_xs, SO_xs and NO_xs	the prevailing elements in the eco even long after smoking was banned, from known causes that still stagnated in the air like the alien spacecraft in Independence Day.
D	David Minuteman	Host of the Late Yo. See Cold War 1947 Minuteman ICBM.
	Dichter-17	Survivors of the 1947 Dichter study who told their story on the Late Yo with David Minuteman following the Manhattan Prologue.

	DIVINE MILIEU	Pet name borrowed from Teilhard de Chardin for protagonist's favorite abandoned parking lot.
	Donald Sutherland	spitting image of protagonist (from role in Invasion of the Body Snatchers).
	doomsday clock	inching-up by the minute. A method of monitoring the impact of the smoking ban on economic destruction from the loss of cig taxes which subsidized the Treasury.
E	eco	eco (except when referenced to the author, Umberto Eco).
G	guns'R'us	recreational outlets open 24/7 for x-smokers providing stress-relief.
	GWBWH	Incumbent White House administration responsible for initiating the A of C.
H	Heisenberg's Theory	Principle explaining the persona of a *k*-smoker. If observed smoking, a *k*-smoker is no longer in the closet and writing creativity ceases.
	hmmm ...	hint that 'he' (the protagonist) may not have been alone when transposing daytime WIP (written under the influenced of nicotine) to nighttime laptop in his *hmmm*-study.
	hmmm (other meaning)	Brit pronunciation of *whom* or *home* (ala Peter Sellers).
K	'*k*'	manipulative letter in the post-T era vocabulary intended by the authorities to replace 'c' but never really *k*aught on. Subject to whims of spell-check on some early laptop models (including this author's). Reader is urged to check the vintage of his/her own spell-check to be on the safe side.
	*K*ing	A word that appears randomly throughout the confession
L	last man smoking	perhaps the protagonist.
	Late Yo + David Minuteman	See Dichter-17
M	**MANHATTAN PROLOGUE**	event that occurred outside the Time-Life Building in NYC, catalyst for Act of Cessation. See Manhattan *Project* – wiki.
	Midnight Express (Mid. X)	place or milieu in the post-T era where smokers (if caught) are incarcerated. Never proven to actually exist, unlike the Turkish prison.
	mouthwash	popular commodity to reduce bad breath. After smoking was banned, production had ceased by the consumer-healthcare, personal-hygiene and pharmaceutical industries. Foul-smelling cigarettes were replaced by ingenious re-marketing of the #2 pencil.
N	nation at risk	prior to smoking ban.
	nation even more at risk	after the smoking ban.
	Nicotine (nico)	unleashes the mind (when combined with caffeine).

O	obesity (fat)	a condition (or side-effect) developed by 21% of the population who were forced to quit smoking cold turkey, mimicking the existing condition of the other 79%.
	(old) Nick	derivative of nicotine.
	Old Executive Office Building	where decisions were made affecting a nation even more at risk. [WHBWH]
P	parking lot	wide-open (abandoned) space, the usual hiding-place for a *k*-smoker to write creatively over a quiet puff or two – when it was perceived too dangerous to inhabit an abandoned telephone kiosk after the secular nation went cellular.
	popular vote	one of two voting events which might postpone the inevitable. (See: reality vote.)
	post-T era	current era, after tobacco was banned.
	pre-T era	period in history before tobacco was banned.
	pseudonym	name on jacket for fear of reprisal.
R	'reader'	Throughout the interactivity of the Confessions (in bold #8 font and italic), a reader who occasionally interjects upon the course of the text either because of disagreement or thinks the author is being preposterous
	reality vote	one of two voting events which might postpone the inevitable. (See: popular vote.)
	repetition	*sine qua non* of any good confession (for example, like the repetitive lyrics in a Gordon Lightfoot song
S	Skip Legault	poster 'boy' for smoking – against all odds
	smoker-types	prior to the smoking ban: 21% smokers; 79% non-smokers.
	• *anti-smoker*	one who never smoked and resents writers who did.
	• *closet-smoker*	forerunner of *k*loset-smoker when smoking was legal and cig taxes a crime. However, many *pseudo* closet-smokers in the pre-T era were unimaginative and lacked the craft of a creative writer while craving a cigarette. Like *k*-smokers who came after them, always in fear of reprisal by their kids, the missus, friendly-neighbors or the eco-conscious. One on whom nicotine was usually wasted unless accompanied by the muse.
	• *former smoker*	conformist in post-T era who voluntarily quit during the pre-T era and learned to hate the stink with a passion.
	• *kloset-smoker* (*k*-smoker)	A euphemism introduced by the AT lawmakers after the A of C to differentiate from *pseudo* closet-smokers. One who derives inspiration from a combination of nicotine and caffeine to write words that pound on the conscience, words which had vanished into thin air when tobacco was outlawed. Unfortunately, occasionally

		the author confuses the two, 'c' and 'k', due to a spell-check error in the vintage of his computer.
regular smoker		one who smoked in front of others and cared less (in the pre-T era).
x-smoker		any of the 21% of the population who quit cold-turkey when smoking was banned and lived to regret it.
xxx-smoker		an x-smoker who was born again and behaved like a former-smoker, the worst kind. One who couldn't stomach the idea that such a filthy habit could still be practiced by *k*-smokers, *if* they existed. [See Heisenberg] One who became mentally sick thinking there may be smokers roaming the wilds.
	smoking	1. an obnoxious and deadly habit acquired from watching too many movies about the glamorous mannerism of the dashing hero of the silver screen - ubiquitous cigarette in right hand and beautiful heroine on his or her lap.
		2. a habit or addiction necessary to write great literature.
	sovereign nations	only source of (underground) tobacco via Native Americans following Act of Cessation.
	statistics	'It is now proved beyond doubt that smoking is one of the leading causes of statistics.' [Fletcher Knebel]
	subliminal	*effect* of advertising campaign or political gimmick to hide the *cause* of a nation at risk.
T	T	1. tobacco.
		2. big Tobacco companies
		3. Tesla
	tabagie	French word for a group of smokers in the pre-T era having a quiet puff or two outside their workplaces, shivering their butts off in the hail, rain, sleet and/or snow – the four horsemen of the Apocalypse.
	Time Life building	Beneath the canopy of which – events led to the A of C. See Manhattan Prologue.
	transition period	sometimes called the honeymoon period. The transition period between the pre-T era and the post-T era, during which smokers were on tenterhooks.
V	VAB	NASA vehicle assembly building (for space shuttle) but now used for other purposes.
W	*whisshhh*	... inhale ...
	oo-oooooh ...	... exhale
		(manifestation of the creative writing experience.)

460

words ...   ... that pound on the conscience (theme of confession).

WUI   writing under the influence (of nicotine), a felony if apprehended

~ ~ ~

Numeric

2HS   second-hand smoke

#2 pencil (or, simply the #2)   popular chewable placebo effectively re-marketed to replace the feel and taste of cigarettes albeit with known side-effects upon incisors.

VII. On Conspiracy Theory

Deep Throat (X-FILES) commenting on who to trust, responds:
TRUST NO ONE!

Response in Greek to John 8:32:
 *καὶ γνώσεσθε τὴν ἀλήθειαν, καὶ ἡ ἀλήθεια
 ἐλευθερώσει ὑμᾶς.*

 (Ye shall know the truth, and the truth shall make
 you free)

Alice Sutton (asks in Conspiracy Theory, 1997*):*
 Can you prove any of this?

Jerry Fletcher replies*:*
 *No. Absolutely not. A good conspiracy is an
 unprovable one. If you can prove it, it means they
 must've screwed up somewhere along the line*

George Orwell, 1984:
 Big Brother is watching you.

VIII. BIO

Basil Dillon-Malone grew up in Ballina, County Mayo in the west of Ireland and graduated in engineering from University College Dublin. Creative writing has been his complementary avocation, cross-trekking six continents in the international cable-telecommunications industry and taking anecdotal notes along the way. Basil considers himself not a 'Joycean Scholar' but in their shared college and cultural heritage, a Joycean Schooler (an appellation Joyce himself might have coined).

His poetry collection, *mcdynasty: from the ming dynasty to mcdonald's*, was published in 2005 by Lapwing Publications, Belfast. Over the years his technical articles, diversely serious and whimsical literary works have appeared in print in the UK, USA, Canada, Switzerland, India, China and Argentina. He was a speaker at conferences in Montreux, London, Prague, Budapest, Shanghai, Manila, and Mumbai. Indeed, at some of these cable TV conferences he was fortunate to meet a number of celebrities with cameo appearances in *The Last Smoker on Earth...and the end of literature.*

He was a back-page correspondent for International Cable Television magazine: 'Travels with Basil' and a columnist for 7 years for International Broadband Library. In the mid-90s he frequently appeared on the Irish Connection Cable TV show. He is a founding member of the Syracuse James Joyce Club.

CPSIA information can be obtained
at www.ICGtesting.com
Printed in the USA
LVHW070848230621
690874LV00004B/12/J